ARMADA

The Novel

ARMADA
The Novel

Charles Gidley

WEIDENFELD AND NICOLSON
LONDON

Published in Great Britain in 1987 by
George Weidenfeld & Nicolson Limited
91 Clapham High Street, London SW4 7TA

ISBN 0 297 79074 9

Photoset by Deltatype, Ellesmere Port
Printed in Great Britain by
Butler & Tanner Co Ltd, Frome and London

Me, all too meane, the sacred Muse areeds
To blazon broad cmongst her learned throng:
Fierce warres and faithfull loves shall moralise my song.

Edmund Spenser

Contents

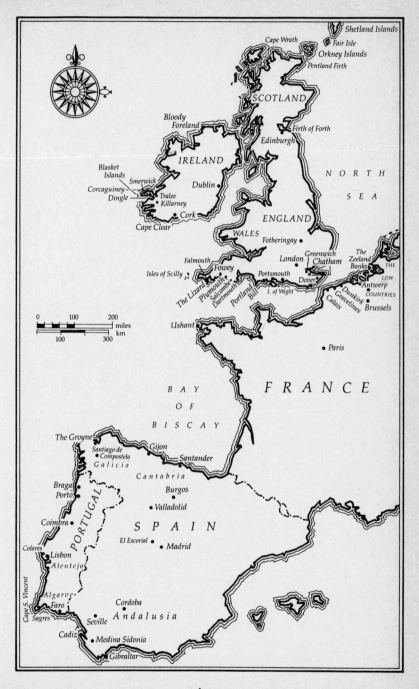

PART I

PROVOCATIONS

The Greater Catch

The castaways were lying together in the bilges of a cockboat when Sam Gristy and Harry Pascoe came alongside. One was a young man of noble birth: he wore a blue cloak of rash with gold lace round the hem, a pair of silk breeches of murrey tinsel, and a buff jerkin laid over with gold lace. The other was much older. He was a priest.

The two boats rubbed and banged at the gunwales, and when Pascoe – a Cornish giant if ever there was one – jumped from one to the other, both craft rocked violently.

The priest's cassock was stained with vomit and blood. He began mumbling in Latin, and attempted to make the sign of the Cross. His companion's tongue had swollen and his mouth was so full of it he could hardly speak. Both were close to death.

The fishermen had sighted the boat close inshore under Gribbin Head, and had hove-to in their ketches in order to row over and investigate. They were within half a cable of the rocks even now: the cliffs, dotted with perching gulls, towered above them, and the roar of breakers made conversation difficult.

The current was taking the two boats down towards the rocks, so Harry Pascoe couldn't afford to waste time. Jerking the nobleman roughly into an upright sitting position, he relieved him of his gold chain and started pulling the rings off his fingers.

'Easy on!' Sam shouted over the noise of the surf.

Harry turned briefly. 'Easy on? Easy off, more like. They're bloody Spaniards!'

Rolling his victim onto his face, he discovered a dagger with an ivory handle and a silver scabbard studded with precious stones. Too weak to resist, the young hidalgo lay quite passive, showing emotion only when Pascoe, on discovering a bronze *agnus dei* on a chain, wrenched it off and flung it overboard. That done, he ripped open the silk breeches and put a hairy hand in to explore the gentleman's privates for hidden belts or purses. Finding none, he turned his attention to the priest.

It was then that the nobleman managed to throw himself over his confessor in a heroic attempt to protect him.

'*Não!*' he croaked. '*Não molesta!*'

There was an audible crack as Harry's fist connected with the cheek bone, and the young man flopped back unconscious.

'Harry!' Sam shouted. 'There be no need – '

But Harry was already pulling the priest's cassock open, revealing flabby white breasts upon which rested a silver Madonna on a chain.

Further down, he found a heavy money belt. It was packed tight along the whole of its length with gold coin.

He swore softly in Cornish. '*Re Dhew a'm ros!* By God who made me! Look at this, Sam! We're bloody rich!'

Taking the belt and feeling the weight of it, Sam was hardly able to believe his own eyes. In the other boat, the priest had started gabbling in Latin – the *Dies Irae*, by the sound of it. And with good reason, too, for Harry had unsheathed the dagger.

It was like a dream that Sam could neither halt nor awake from: the gulls were screaming overhead and the rollers were thundering up against the Gribbin. The blade was going in to its hilt, in, and in again, and the blood was spreading out over the priest's hairless chest. He heard his own voice shout: 'O dear Lord! No! No!'

But it was too late. The priest was dying with a last *Gloria* on his lips, and Harry, carried away upon a tide of hatred for all things Spanish and all things Catholic, had already sunk the blade into the back of the young hidalgo.

A froth of blood and sputum bubbled round the nobleman's mouth; his body gave one last life-jerk and lay still. Harry dipped the blade into the sea to wash it, and dried it on the cuff of his shirt before replacing it in its sheath.

Sam felt sick. 'Give me the Madonna,' he said hoarsely.

'What Madonna?'

He pointed at the priest. 'The one round his neck.'

Harry removed it and handed it across. Sam put the Madonna to his lips and made the sign of the Cross with it before putting the chain about his own neck. Harry rolled the two bodies over the gunwale into the sea, then stabbed twice through the bottom of the boat to sink it.

'You kill a priest,' Sam muttered as they rowed away, 'it's like killing your own father.'

Harry snorted contemptuously. 'They were as good as dead weren't they? We did 'em a favour.' He was sitting in the stern sheets with the money belt in his hands. He began to laugh. His great shoulders shook and his teeth gleamed white against a dark red beard. 'We're made, Sam! I tell 'ee – we're made!'

Astern, a wave caught the bodies of the priest and the nobleman. Carrying them swiftly away on its crest, it hurled them against the black rocks of Gribbin Head.

Harry swore Sam to secrecy, and the two young fishermen told their crews that they had found nothing but an empty boat. So as not to arouse suspicion, they continued fishing as usual, and when one of the bodies was discovered on the beach of Predmouth Bay a week later it had been so battered on the rocks that the Justices at Fowey had no reason to suspect foul play.

But it was a lot of money all the same, and Harry had enough sense not to go throwing it around. He kept the sack hidden behind hay bales in his Uncle Will's barn and passed his evenings in Mother Russell's alehouse figuring out how best to spend it.

Then, on a misty day towards the end of November, a messenger arrived with despatches from London, and the news spread quickly through the village of Polruan that Bloody Mary was dead and her half-sister Elizabeth, the daughter of Anne Boleyn, had been declared Queen of England.

It was as if a great burden had been lifted from the shoulders of the people. In the five years since coming to the throne in 1553, Mary had vented her hatred of Protestantism upon her subjects and had tried – against their will – to force the clock back. She had married the King of Spain; she had restored the Latin Mass; she had required her subjects to acknowledge the authority of the Pope which her own father had so blatantly flouted.

Now all that was over. The new Queen was the child of love, while Mary had been the child of hatred. Mary had been plain, solemn and dogmatic; Elizabeth was intelligent, lighthearted and in love with her country and her people.

Mother Russell's alehouse was full that night – of wood smoke, fishermen and political conversation. Everyone's position was dubious in some respect: no one had been able to stand aloof from the efforts of Philip and Mary to turn England back to popery, and all except the few convinced Romanists in the village hoped that the days of compulsory religion and inquisitions would now be over.

Scurrying about with jugs of ale, the twins – Martha and Ann – took advantage of the new turn-about in political matters by ensuring that the customers' voices were well lubricated.

'They Catholics won't give up without a fight,' old Treffry was saying. 'Mark my words. There be plenty folk still wanting to suck at Rome's tit.'

'Aye, and plenty princes wanting England for a dowry, 'n all,' Frank Polwhele put in. 'Like as not we'll be at war again afore the decade's out.'

'What – with France?' someone asked from the back.

'Spain more likely,' remarked Mr Mayhew, an educated man, who owned land out towards Bodinnick.

'What you reckon, Mr Mayhew? Would they try to invade?'

Mayhew stroked his chin. 'I wouldn't put it past them.'

'Just let 'em try!' Harry Pascoe shouted from the far end of the room, and young Jan Lanyon, who sailed with him, put up his fists and echoed: 'Aye – just let 'em try!'

Harry turned back to Sam, with whom he had been having a private conversation on a quite different subject.

'So it's partners then. Are we agreed?'

'Provided it's fair shares.'

'I'll be master, you'll be mate. One ship, six English guns, and a fortune for the making.'

'Not one ship. Two.'

'Two ships! Two cockleshells, more like. What can we do with a couple of crumsters? That's all we'll end up with if we split the cash.'

'We could build another four ketches and run a fleet, come to that,' Gristy countered. 'There's good steady trade in pilchards. Settle down and marry, that's what I'm going to do. No gallivanting about privateering and getting my head shot off by some greasy Spaniard.'

While this conversation proceeded, both men eyed Martha, who was Harry's first cousin, and who was moving from customer to customer, topping up tankards from an earthenware jug. For a few moments, they admired her dark looks and comely lines.

'And who would you be thinking of marrying?' Harry asked.

'That's my business.'

'Not she, by any chance?'

'Maybe. Maybe not. As I say, it's my business.'

'You keep your hands off her, Mr Gristy, or you'll make it my business, an' all.'

'Why so? I never heard she plighted her troth – to you no more than to anyone else.'

'Just you keep your hands off Maid Martha, that's all I say,' Harry muttered. 'Because Maid Martha belongs to me. She knows it, I knows it – the whole of Polruan knows it. So if you've more than a mite of sense you'll point your base somewheres else. Nothing wrong with her sister, go and make her your wife. But if you start making proposals to Martha Pascoe on the strength of the fortune I been good enough to share with you, you can think again, 'cos you'll have Harry Pascoe to contend with. As for splitting the spoils and building separate, well, you must be off your noddle. Any half-blind booby can see it makes no sense. Come in with me as my lieutenant, and we'll make the biggest fortune ever seen in Cornwall. We'll sail to the Americas and chase the Spaniards from bedtime to sparrow-fart. We'll live in castles, lad. You can have the pick of any woman you want from Polruan to Port of Spain, and a good few more besides. But you'll not have Martha for a wife, not while there's breath left in my body you won't, and you'll not split my fortune, neither, not if you want to live to see your grandchildren.'

'Maybe you'd better do for me too, then,' Sam replied, 'for it was my cockboat we rowed across in, and I'm the only witness to the murder, for that's what it was. And if the Justices get to hear you've got a belt full of golden coins that you've not reported, I think they'll be interested, because whichever way the new Queen jumps, she'll be wanting her fair share.'

'The new Queen can go whistle up her kilter,' muttered Harry, and setting his leather tankard down on the earth floor beside the grate, strode out of the front kitchen and into the foggy night.

He awoke late the following morning, and was immediately aware of the clammy stillness that comes with a Cornish mizzle. After returning home the night before, he had lain awake for hours thinking yet again about the day five weeks before when he and Sam had found the Spanish cockboat. He had recalled the screaming gulls under the cliffs; the staring eyes of the priest, the strange sensation of sinking a blade into his white flesh and seeing the life ebb from him. Then as dawn came up, he had fallen into a deep, dreamless sleep, waking suddenly to find his Aunt Bridget looking down at him.

'All right my dear?' she asked, forever solicitous of his wellbeing.

He sat up and rubbed sleep from his eyes.

'Not sickening, are we, Harry?'

'No, Aunt. I'm well.'

'You'd be a lot better with less ale in your stomach,' she remarked, and left him to get himself out of his bed.

He sat and looked out of the window, which commanded a view of the harbour entrance. He thought again about his conversation with Sam, of his new-found wealth, and of Martha. 'You're a wealthy man, Harry Pascoe,' he muttered to himself. 'A wealthy man.'

He loved the sound of those words almost as much as the weight of the gold coins in the priest's belt.

Sitting there on his bed, he laughed silently to himself. Even with only half those Spanish coins he could buy all he wanted and more. He could have a ship of his own, a house – even a wife.

A wife! The thought of it had been impossible for so long that it took some getting used to. And yet what was there to stop him walking down the hill that very morning and putting the question to Martha?

The thought had no sooner passed through his mind than the decision was taken. He stood up, flexed his powerful shoulders and having pulled on a jerkin and breeches, went through to the kitchen, ate a hunk of fresh-baked bread and walked off down the steep narrow hill that led between stone cottages to Mother Russell's alehouse, where the Pascoe girls earned their living. There he found Ann sweeping dirt out of the front door into the street, and inside, Sam Gristy, who was holding Martha's hand and looking like a cat that's stolen the clotted cream.

'And what the Hell do you think you're up to?' Harry enquired thickly.

Martha tilted her head back, glancing at Sam with some affection. 'Sam here's just been an' asked me to be his wife,' she said.

Harry Pascoe had inherited his ketch from his grandfather, Tristram Pascoe, and at twenty-four he was already one of the leading lights among the fishermen of Polruan. He was tall and broad and muscular; he had a large, square face, a thickly built nose and lips that allowed a glimpse of white teeth when he smiled. His eyes were an astounding blue and his complexion was ruddy from a life spent mostly at sea. Of his voice, it was said that he could make himself heard from the harbour mouth to his Aunt Bridget's kitchen in a full-blown gale; but for all his thunder and lightning, his thigh-slapping guffaws and crude sense of humour, there was in Harry a man who needed the love of a woman, a man who, having been brought up by an uncle with strictly puritan views, longed for the approval and admiration of his elders. This gentler self had been covered by a hard, outer shell. Growing up among the tough men of Cornwall, Harry had come to believe that popularity was all; that it could be bought with success, and that success could be got by a closed fist and a big voice. It was this policy he now resorted to in an attempt to win Martha back.

Ann listened to the argument from the doorway. She knew that Harry regarded her sister as his private possession, and was not surprised to see him stamping up and down and growling like a baited bear.

'Why – Martha, girl – I've always taken it for granted that you and me would – would – '

'That's the trouble with you, Harry Pascoe,' Martha said. (She had a low voice that held every man in Polruan spellbound.) 'You take too much for granted. Sam here's asked me to be his wife, and I don't see why I shouldn't tell him yes.'

Harry looked from one to the other. 'So you've not agreed to it?'

'Almost,' said Sam, and turned to Martha. 'Isn't that right, Mart, love?'

'Don't answer that!' Harry put in, and seizing Sam by the upper arm, dragged him clear of Martha, who was beginning to enjoy being fought over. 'Tell you what we'll do. If Martha here can't make up her mind, I'll make it easier for her. I'll give you a chance to prove your worth, Sam Gristy. I'll take you on at anything you like to name. If you want her, you can fight for her and win her fair and square, and no more sneaking in at doors before honest men are out of their beds. So what'll it be? Wrestling? Singlestaff? Fisting? You name it, I'll take you on, and what's more I'll beat the daylights out of you, into the bargain.'

This wasn't a very fair challenge, Harry being more than a head taller than Sam and built like an ox.

Martha said: 'And what if *I* don't agree?'

'You'll agree, if you know what's good for you.'

'That's typical of you, Harry Pascoe – '

But Sam cut in: 'All right, I'll name a contest. I'll take you on at seine netting. What do you say to that?'

'Seine netting? That's no contest. That's bread and butter that is. Besides, I never said nothing about fishing. I said wrestling or singlestaff or –'

'You said anything I liked to name,' Sam retorted.

'And that's a stramming great lie!' Harry exclaimed, flushing deeply, because he knew very well that it wasn't.

'What I want to know is why there's all this talk of marriage all of a sudden?' Martha put in. 'After all, you've had time enough these past months and years, the two of you. You found a pot of gold under a rainbow, or something?'

The two men glanced quickly at each other.

'Coincidence,' Harry said gruffly, and Sam nodded in agreement.

Martha raised one eyebrow in disbelief. It never failed to amaze her that men should even attempt to tell such transparent lies. But if the two of them had come by a windfall of some sort, she wasn't going to ask questions about it. At the same time she didn't see why she shouldn't benefit from it, and get herself a husband into the bargain. She decided to have a bit of fun therefore – at their expense. 'Then mark this, Master Harry: if you won't take Sam here on at fishing, you'll not have me as a wife. You either win me in fair competition, or you don't have me at all, and there's my last word on't.'

Harry looked at Sam, and Sam looked at Harry. Harry said, 'Conger,' and Sam said, 'No, Pilchard. Three boats and a huer each.'

'Best of three catches.'

'Make it the best of a week's.'

Harry shook his shaggy head. Martha said: 'And don't start making objections, just because you know he's the better fisherman.'

In reply, Pascoe closed up his fist and smote Sam on the chest, sending him staggering back. 'Better fisherman?' he jeered. 'We'll see about that.'

After they'd gone, Ann felt free to talk. 'I don't understand you, Martha Pascoe,' she said. 'You could've had Harry without any competition at all, if you'd so much as bent your little finger. And now, like as not, Sam'll win at the fishing and you'll be trothed to him – a bastard of Sir Gregory's.'

Martha observed that as England was to have a bastard for a queen, there seemed little harm in having Sir Gregory Roscarrock's bastard for a husband. 'Besides,' she added a little tartly, 'most men are bastards, one way or another.'

'Harry's not!' Ann said, flushing deeply. 'He's a fine Cornish boy!'

'If you're as keen on him as that, why don't you marry him yourself then?' Martha replied, and left her twin sister blinking in astonishment at a possibility that hadn't occurred to her before, but which was now enticingly attractive.

There is a sort of agony in loving a man from a distance, especially if you know that your own twin sister is as good as promised to him. You learn to love him through your sister: you learn to enjoy at second hand what she enjoys, and you come to regard yourself as a non-person, an appendage, the other twin, the dull one. But when – suddenly – for no apparent reason your twin rejects the offer of marriage from the man you always believed she loved, and whom you always loved yourself; when she turns round and says you can marry him yourself if you feel that strongly about him . . . suddenly your world is upside down. All you can think of is Harry, Harry, Harry. You watch him going down the street to the harbour. You listen to his gruff voice giving orders to his crew as they row him out to his ketch. You stand on St Saviour's Point to see him going out between the forts, the seabirds flocking after his boat, the ropes screaming in the sheaves as the sails are hoisted. And when he's fishing close inshore, watching the signals from his huer on the cliff path and ordering his boats to cast their nets to enclose the shoals of silvery fish that dart and move just beneath the surface, you look down from two hundred feet and you think to yourself, perhaps, perhaps . . . .

But what an extraordinary perhaps it was! To have him as a husband, she had to hope for his failure. To win him, she must hope for his defeat and long for his humiliation.

The trouble was, Harry was winning the competition. The two men had gone out at dawn each morning, and for five consecutive days their huers had run up and down the cliff paths, whistling and signalling with flags and gorse bushes to guide the two fleets to the shoals; and while everyone in Polruan had confidently expected Sam Gristy to win hands down, it now looked as though Harry had the edge. All he needed – as far as anyone could make out from the hogsheads of salted pilchards that were assembled in two separate groups down at the harbour – was one more good catch and victory, together with Martha's hand, would be his.

Ann walked out of the village and stood on St Saviour's Point. The fleet had gone east to Lantic Bay that day, and the first boats were already returning on the first of the ebb.

Quite suddenly, she was overcome with yearning for Harry, and prayed in a way she had never prayed before. Clenching her fists and raising her face to the grey sky she whispered: 'O Lord, give Sam the greater catch!'

Some folk in the village said it was a public disgrace that a maid like Martha Pascoe should be bartered for with barrels of fish, but most saw the whole affair as a great joke, because when all was said and done, the lass was unlikely to marry Sam or Harry or anyone else against her will, and if she could use their ardour to win a few more stone of pilchards and thereby swell the village purse and give everyone a bit of harmless fun, then more power to her elbow. So when Sam and Harry finally returned to harbour with the last catches of the week, there was a crowd of a hundred or more people present to see the fish landed and the final reckoning made.

First the pilchards had to be gutted and salted, and the red hands and sharp knives of the womenfolk were busy for an hour or more. But this time there was a particular urgency about their work, as if each woman were counting votes for the two competitors.

It was dark by the time they had finished. Fish-oil lamps were casting a yellow light on the damp paving stones of the quay, and a quarter moon was rising above the village. The last fish were tossed into the barrels and the last handfuls of salt; and then the crowd pressed closer as old Jan Treffry started the barrel count.

On the face of it, Harry seemed to have won, and people in the crowd were impatient to hear Treffry announce the result; but the old man kept scratching his chin and shaking his head until the villagers started chanting for a decision.

He called Harry over for a private word, and the two men walked across to Harry's collection of barrels. A lever was sent for, and Harry himself was required to open up one of the barrels filled some days before. People crowded round, and the awful truth came out: the barrel wasn't as full as it should have been. A second barrel was opened, and a third, but some said this wasn't necessary, for it was the accepted custom that if one barrel was found to be wanting, the shortage was assumed to be the same in all the rest.

Harry began shouting, which was not at all surprising, as he was easily provoked and was being made to look a fool. He started accusing everyone from Sam Gristy to Jan Treffry himself of meddling with his fish barrels, and insisted on one of Sam's barrels being opened as well; but when it was found to be brim full Martha told him in plain terms that as far as she was concerned, he had lost the contest.

There was nothing for it but to accept defeat, which he did with an ill grace, stamping off in disgust followed by the jeers of the crowd and several small boys who ran behind him mimicking his rolling gait.

As he reached the end of the quay, where the road ascends steeply from the harbour, he turned for one parting shot: 'You marry him, then!' he shouted. 'You marry him, and see what sort of a husband you get.'

Martha turned to her sister, who had been watching in awe as the miraculous answer to her prayer was provided. 'What are you waiting for, then?' she asked. 'If you want 'un for a husband, now's the time to stake your claim.' And she pushed Ann smartly forward.

A great cheer went up as Ann broke away from the crowd and went after Harry, but she hardly heard it. She didn't mind any more about what people thought. She loved Harry, that was all that mattered, and she wasn't afraid who knew it.

He was striding fast up the hill, and it was all she could do to catch him up. When she did, she told him how much she loved him – how she'd always loved him. 'An' I'll be a good woman to you, too,' she panted. 'I'll look after you as well as your Aunt Bridget, and better. I'll always honour and obey you Harry, and I'll do anything you say or go anywhere you want if you'll only take me for a wife.'

Harry walked on, his face like thunder, his fists still clenched, his self-esteem badly bruised from the catcalls and laughter of the village.

'And what's happened's not just chance, neither,' Ann continued. 'It was sent from God. I prayed – down on my knees on the cliff path out by St Saviour's this very afternoon – I prayed that Sam would have the greater catch, so's you could be my husband.'

He stopped, and looked down at her. She was no great beauty – not a patch on Martha. She had brown, straight hair and Martha's was darker, almost black, and fell in cascades to her shoulders. She had a mild little face, not striking like Martha's, and he could see that she would indeed be totally obedient to him, would cook and mend and wash for him. And bear his children, too, for she was a healthy girl with a good shape to her, and plenty of room round the hips.

'Who told you to come after me?' he asked. It was the first time he had spoken to her since leaving the harbour.

They stood together overlooking the Fowey estuary. The moon, shining through a thin layer of cloud, gave the water a soft, pallid sheen; and Ann's face, white, upturned, was like another moon, staring up at him.

'My sister,' she whispered, looking shame-faced.

He nodded to himself. It was as he thought. Ann would never have taken such a step of her own accord. But if Martha herself had sent her, what hope was there left for him?

He felt suddenly older. He still had the jewelled dagger hidden in a barrel on board his ketch, and he had put the sack with the money belt in an old sea chest left to him by his father. He knew he was wealthy, set up for life, but he was already being made to pay for the taking of those lives: almost every night since, he had been troubled by dreams in which he found himself face to face once more with his victims. Perhaps Sam was right, after all. Perhaps he should abandon thoughts of privateering; perhaps he should settle down and make a home.

He placed his hands gently on her shoulders. Her bosom rose and fell: she was out of breath from keeping up with him.

Looking into her frightened eyes, he couldn't help being reminded of a leveret he had once caught as a boy. It had sat trembling in his hand, its brown eyes full of the same terror he saw now in Ann's. He had tried to keep it as a pet, and had made a cage for it and brought it dandelion leaves to eat; but it never thrived, and had lived only a few days more.

'Very well,' he said quietly. 'If that be so, then I'll take you for a wife. But if it's a lie, then you'll end your days as an old maid, Ann, for I'll not marry a liar, and no other man will have you either, not while I've aught to say about it.'

She surprised him, then. She grasped both his hands and sank to her knees, pressing her lips to his fingers and whispering her thanks – though whether to himself or to God, he could not be sure, and wasn't much interested.

They were good, big bells, the bells of St Saviour's, and when they rang that crisp Saturday morning in December, the echo of their music returned across the harbour to the people of Polruan as they made their way up the hill to see the two couples joined in matrimony.

Martha and Ann were orphans, and were to be given away by the lord of the manor, Sir Gregory Roscarrock. Sir Gregory had been given back much of his estate during Mary's short reign, and his Catholicism, while viewed askance by some of the villagers, was in general tolerated.

Those early days of Elizabeth's reign were a strange time for England, for having lost the kingdom through the death of one wife, Philip of Spain hoped to regain it by marrying another. For the time being therefore, the Pope agreed to stay his hand against the bastard daughter of a renegade heretic. At the same time, most of the gentry – and especially the sea-going west country gentry – were staunchly Protestant, staunchly loyal to Elizabeth, and determined that she should not be lured back to Rome. So while Philip made tentative approaches to Elizabeth, families like the Raleighs, Grenvilles and Drakes put their shoulders to the door and pushed in the opposite direction. Thus, for a short interlude, the religion of the monarch could be said to be neither papist nor Protestant; and while it was safe to admit to either persuasion, it was wise to support neither too vigorously.

Anthony Drew, the vicar of Polruan, was a good example of the effect such conflicts had upon the clergy. He was a big, bald man who had toed the papist line for the past few years under Mary, and was now willing to return to Anglicanism should that be the wish of his Bishop. A physically brave man (he was a noted wrestler and had instructed Harry Pascoe in the art at one time) he was doctrinally circumspect, so he conducted the marriage service in such a way that he could not be labelled as either a papist or a puritan.

Afterwards, when the vows to love, honour and obey had been given by the brides, and the grooms had slipped rings onto their fingers, they sang the *Jubilate Deo*, which was a great favourite:

'O be joyful in the Lord all ye lands: serve the Lord with gladness, and come before His presence with a song.'

Sir Gregory (who was rumoured to be Sam Gristy's father) provided quantities of ale and beef, which were consumed at three sittings in Mother Russell's front kitchen, after which there was dancing to lutes and drums. Aunt Bridget entertained most of the womenfolk of the village to another sit-down feast, and Polruan challenged Polperro to a hurling match 'to the country', the result of which was a draw. The other score – of damage to sons, property and livestock – was never calculated, but the injuries sustained were not considered excessive, and everyone agreed that it was one of the best hurling matches they'd seen in several years.

Harry Pascoe returned from these sporting festivities scratched all over from fighting among the gorse bushes on Pencarrow Head, and found his new wife in her new kitchen.

He had installed her in a cottage on East Street and in the last few days before the wedding she had worked all hours to spicken the place up and turn it into a home for him. The earthen floors were swept and the tables scrubbed; the pots and plans gleamed over the hob, and there was a pleasant smell of baking coming from the wood oven. To complete the welcome, she had – on Aunt Bridget's advice – paid particular attention to her own appearance, making sure that if she smelt at all, it was of dried lavender.

Seeing her all meek and soft and ready for him gave Harry ideas, but he was a good Cornish boy still, and wasn't too sure how to go about it. So he stood with her, and held her; and very soon nature began to teach them both what to do, and before very long the neighbours heard a little shriek come from Pascoe's cottage, and the old wives glanced and nodded to each other, content that the marriage had been consummated, and anxious to share with each other reminiscences of their own experiences in similar circumstances.

Although Harry tried to be tender and attentive at first, Ann sensed from the start that he didn't really love her, and that she would never be able to make him forget the great hurt he had suffered by losing Martha. She heard it in his voice when he spoke to her, saw it in his eyes when he was thinking, felt it in his great muscular body every time she lay in his arms at night.

But his lack of affection for her didn't lessen her love for him, nor did she give up hope that she would one day be able to make him feel genuinely fond of her. She strove daily to be the perfect wife. She cooked his favourite meals, kept the house neat and clean, obeyed him in all things and gave herself to him willingly and frequently. But as the days turned into weeks, she felt even the slight hold she had on him slipping. Gradually, she found herself being turned into something between a useful servant and a source of relief; a person who was little more than a housekeeper and temporary mistress.

She talked about it to her twin, and on Martha's advice tried new ways to please Harry. She tried to smile more, to talk to him about his fishing and his plans for the future. She made believe that they were as happy together as they should be, and was careful to weep only in secret.

Now, four weeks after their wedding day, she lay in bed and watched him peel off his undershirt, revealing a mass of dark ginger curls over his back and chest. She welcomed him into bed, pressing herself tight against him, running her fingers through his great leonine mane and sending him signals to say that she was ready to do her duty as a wife.

He sighed – a little impatiently, she thought.

'What is it? What's troubling you?'

He grunted moodily. 'Nothing.'

She saw that look come into his eyes again – the look that told her so clearly how little she meant to him. Not for the first time, she wished she had her sister's confidence with men, her way of saying just the right thing in the right way to make them laugh, or listen, or love.

She kissed him on the neck. She had made him his favourite bottom pie and onions for supper that evening when he came in from the fishing, and he had gone back down to Mother Russell's after, for a few ales. Now he smelt of sweat, and pork, and onions, and –

'You been drinking Malmsey wine by any chance?' she asked without thinking.

He regarded her balefully and shook his head.

She tried to sound playful, but somehow the words came out the wrong way. 'Yes you have, Harry Pascoe. I can smell it on your breath. I ain't worked at Russell's three year for nothing, you know. I can tell Malmsey a mile off, I can.'

He said nothing. She was suddenly frightened. 'I'm sorry – ' she started, and tried to kiss him again, but he turned his head away.

When he looked back at her, his face was dark with an anger she hadn't seen in him before. He sat up and left the bed upon which she had given herself so frequently since their wedding day.

For a moment, he stood naked with his back to her, his great legs covered with little circles of coarse, red curls, his hair like a mane down the back of his head.

'Mark this well, Ann Pascoe,' he said, and turning, shook a finger over her to drum in his words. 'If you want to be a good wife to me, and only the Lord knows how many times you've said that's what you want, you can stop asking questions and making deductions about where I been or what's passed my lips, see? One thing I'll not abide, and that's a suspicious wife.' Then, turning away to look out of the small, square window he delivered the cruellest cut of all: 'Specially when she's second best.'

At first, it seemed to the village gossips that both couples were happy enough. Ann was her usual quiet self; Harry was a little less wild; Sam was obviously head over heels in love with his new bride, and Martha was clearly content.

What the locals could not fathom out, however, was the reason behind

Pascoe's new-found prosperity. Though he was an adequate mariner, he was by no means an expert fisherman, being the sort of man who makes more conversation than profit from his catches; but after a trip across to Plymouth early in the new year, he returned looking exceedingly pleased with himself, dressed in finer clothes than were often seen on the Polruan side of the Fowey, and full of the news that he intended to commission John Knollys to build him a bark of a hundred tons. Sam Gristy, it was learnt, was to be his partner in the venture, though why that was so no one could make out, as the two men had hardly spoken three words together since the day Gristy won Martha for his wife. Gossip in Mother Russell's had it that they'd made their fortune by some prize, for there were one or two men in Harry Pascoe's crew who thought they had seen strange goings on close inshore under the Gribbin the previous October; but these would not be drawn further, and although it was never put into so many words, people came to accept that the source of Harry Pascoe's wealth was not a safe subject for public discussion.

John Knollys was one of the finest shipbuilders in that part of Cornwall. He was descended (though not through the male line) from the family that had built the ships for the old Fowey Gallants of fourteenth-century fame, those piratical seamen who had dared disobey the Sovereign by plundering Frenchmen and had had their fleet confiscated and sent to Dartmouth for their pains. Now, in these latter sixteenth-century days, Knollys's shipyard had been driven to the building of more modest ships, and confined itself mainly to boats no larger than forty or fifty tons – small merchantmen for the most part, which sailed for their owners to Italy and Spain with cargoes of wool, tin and salt fish.

The yard was situated at the eastern extremity of Polruan, where the forest rises steeply from the water's edge. When working to capacity, it employed upwards of two dozen craftsmen, artisans and apprentices. John Knollys himself was getting on for fifty: a wizened, weatherbeaten man, and a master craftsman and designer. He seldom committed any of his designs to paper, though sometimes, to explain a special feature or new idea, he would use a sharp stone to draw on one of the smooth boulders which surrounded the dock. For the most part however, he kept his curves and measurements in his head, and could measure three feet more accurately between his nose and his thumb than many could with a yard-wand.

It was here, in the first spring of Queen Elizabeth's reign, that the

Russell was laid down. Harry had been all for building a full-blown ship of three hundred tons or more, with four masts, three decks, two castles and ten brass pieces into the bargain, but Sam Gristy had insisted upon a more modest outlay, and a three-masted bark had been agreed upon. As for the name, Sam wanted her to be called the *Martha* and Harry the *Bridget*, and the only way they could resolve the question was to name her after their favourite place of refreshment, instead. In doing so, they unwittingly made a popular decision, for in later years the local men were able to feel easier in their minds about telling their womenfolk that they were 'going down to the *Russell*'.

One afternoon in March when a north-westerly was sending catspaws across the estuary, Harry and Sam took their wives down to see what progress had been made. They were met by John Knollys, who walked with a stick to ease his rheumatism.

'Greenheart oak,' he said, tapping the hardwood underskid that was pinned beneath the kelson. 'That'll take a bashing on a hard shore and never a crack in fifty years. And look at this. Fine English elm, that is, and you won't find a sweeter grain the length or breadth of Powder Hundred.'

'When will it be finished, Uncle?' Martha asked. (Knollys was not a relation, but most of the village called him Uncle out of respect.)

'Michaelmas,' Harry said. 'That's what was agreed.'

Knollys screwed up his eyes and scratched the back of his neck. He was secretly as excited about this new Polruan ship as anyone else. 'Don't want to hurry it, mind.'

They took one last look at the newly laid keel and walked back along East Street together, Harry and Ann arm in arm, but Sam and Martha holding hands, because they were still like lovebirds together and didn't mind the world knowing it.

'So we'll be launching her come St Bartholomew's more'n likely,' Harry remarked.

'Not the only thing we'll be launching, eh Sam, love?' Martha put in.

Sam Gristy went an unusual pink for his dark complexion, and looked proudly at his wife. 'It's true,' he told Harry and Ann when they looked for confirmation. 'We're to be parents.'

Ann was full of congratulations for them, but Harry had an attack of the grumps. When he got Ann indoors to himself, he gave her a basting for getting so excited about it.

'But she is my sister, Harry love,' she said. 'Besides – ' She smiled quickly, uncertainly. 'I'm expecting as well.'

'Well why the bloody Hell didn't you say so out there when we was with them instead of making me look like a bloody fool?'

'I hadn't told you, love. You wouldn't want to hear it in public first, would you?'

'When's it due, then?'

'About the same time. Michaelmas, or a bit before, maybe.' She looked up at him, begging for approval and love. 'Are you pleased, Harry?'

He grunted and turned away. 'Just make sure it's a boy, then I'll tell you if I'm pleased.'

Having been virtually blackmailed into going halves with Sam, Harry deeply resented his partner's share, and was continually seeking ways to score points off him. It was as if he were still competing for Martha: every return to harbour became a race between his ketch and Sam's; every catch had to be compared for weight and quality, and every new little luxury Harry purchased for himself or his wife had to be announced that evening in the Russell alehouse as further proof of his superiority.

Sam, being an even-tempered chap who didn't have the same need to brag as Harry, took it all in good part.

'Tell you what I'll do,' he said goodnaturedly one evening in the presence of Dan Rowe, Peter Trewennick and Tom Jannaway, who were sitting with their tankards resting on their knees, 'I'll lay you a shilling mine'll be a boy and your'n a girl.'

Harry was already convinced that Ann would give him a son. This he had learnt from Ann herself, who had forecast the sex of both babies by means of a golden ring suspended by the longest whisker of a white cat.

'You're on!' Harry shouted, banging his fist on the arm of the settle – and the wager provoked such interest among her customers that Mother Russell (who was grizzle-haired and rather mournful) began taking side bets, with the odds against Harry.

Sam stopped fishing a week before his wife's baby was due. Harry laughed about this, saying that childbirth was like shelling peas to a woman, and that he'd be better off at sea after the mackerel than moping about at home and getting in the way of the womenfolk. But this didn't deter Sam at all, and three days later he was pacing in the kitchen while

Letty Carew and Jane Polwhele assisted his wife in the delivery of a daughter. Sam was so relieved at the news that mother and child were well that the fact that he hadn't won the wager was nothing to him, and when he first laid eyes on the baby all he could do was kneel down and weep for joy.

She was everything he had dared hope for, and more: she had perfect features and limbs, an endearing, screwed-up little face and a trace of dark hair on her pate, just to show she took after her parents.

They had already decided upon a name. Had it been a boy, he would have been Arthur, after that toast of all good Cornishmen, the once and future king; but as she was a girl, she was Jennifer, which was as close as need be to Guinevere.

Having loved Martha from the bottom of his heart, Sam now found that he loved his daughter every bit as much, and could hardly tear himself away from the cradle, where he would spend hours gazing at the fruit and blessing of their union.

The delivery of Ann's child six days later was not nearly so easy. Blue in the face and entangled by his own cord, a baby boy emerged after nine hours of agonizing labour, during which Ann was assisted by Aunt Bridget.

For once, Harry was pleased. Without consulting Ann, he announced that the boy was to be named after his grandfather Tristram Pascoe; and having taken that decision he went off down to the harbour to see if Gristy was back from the fishing and to crow over winning the wager.

Gristy had been trolling for mackerel since dawn, and had had one of his best catches ever. It was late September now, and he had spent the day keeping an eye lifting at the weather, which promised foul. Using the tides to his advantage, he had beaten to windward across St Austell Bay as far as Deadman Point, and to his crew of six who manned the sheets and tended the lines, it had seemed that he had some magic way with him: every time they lost the fish, he would put about and find the shoal again, so that his lads hardly had time to swallow a hunk of bread or a gill of ale from one end of the day to the other.

Now, it was late afternoon. The boat was heavily laden with fish, and a freshening south-wester was sending the ketch surfing down the waves at high speed. This had been Sam's first day out since the birth of Jennifer, and it seemed to all on board that the good Lord was smiling upon them and giving a sign of His blessing upon the marriage.

He stood at the helm, steering on the tower of St Saviour's church, which stood on the hilltop between the village of Polruan and the sea. That was typical of Sam: although he was acknowledged to be one of the finest seamen in the village, he was still young, and reluctant to delegate the steering to members of his crew. So apart from a few minutes to snatch a bite to eat, he was seldom off the helm.

There was good reason for him to remain at the helm now, too: the wind was freshening and veering, so that it was coming closer to dead astern. This meant that steering the boat was made particularly difficult, with the Atlantic swell surging up under the quarter and sending the ketch careering down ever larger mountains of water.

He was just considering whether to shorten sail when the foresheet, which had been under considerable strain and was rubbing back and forth against the port gunwale, parted. Immediately, the foresail went out of control, banging and flapping and whipping back and forth, effectively keeping the crew at bay.

It was not a pleasant situation to deal with in a sea like that, but Sam issued his orders quickly and with complete confidence: the sail was lowered, a new sheet bent on, a reef taken and the sail rehoisted, so that within the space of five minutes they were on their way again, and the Gribbin was drawing abeam.

One and all were pleased with the way the emergency had been handled, and Adam Polwhele summed up their feelings by saying, 'Reckon we did a pretty job there, Sam boy.'

They squatted in the sternsheets, their tough, weathered faces looking to their skipper for approval and reward.

'Free ale all round tonight, lads!' he told them, and they put up a cheer of delight.

Now that the emergency was over, Sam felt the call of nature and he beckoned to Luke Rowe, a promising lad of twenty, to take the helm.

Bracing his knees against the gunwale and steadying himself with one hand on the mizzen backstay, he prepared to relieve himself over the stern. But at the same time, he saw the wave coming. It reared up astern, its crest breaking, the wind turning the surf into a feather of blown spray. And then the stern was lifting higher and higher; the boat was turning broadside on and heeling right over – and Sam Gristy felt himself being catapulted into the sea.

The water was not at all cold, and he was an adequate swimmer. He trod water as the ketch sailed away from him, and raised a hand so that his crew could see him and sail back to pick him up. There was never any doubt in his mind that they would or could do so, and indeed he heard their shouts and as the next wave lifted him was able to look down upon them and see that they were luffing to the wind and preparing to beat back towards him.

It was one of those accidents that took a long time to begin to feel serious. He was amused to find himself surrounded by the dead mackerel of his own catch, and held one aloft, waving and shouting to his crew that if they didn't hoick him out good and quick, there'd be no free ale in Mother Russell's that night. He saw the boat heading back towards him, and at one stage she came to within fifteen yards of him. 'Chuck us a line!' he shouted, and watched in growing rage as Rowe got it caught round his foot, and it fell far short. They made another approach, and missed again, and a third, which took them well clear of him. Suddenly he found himself alone. Where were they? He caught a glimpse of the mast, a cable or two downwind, and it began to dawn on him that they had lost sight of him. He began making calculations as to the strength and the direction of the tide, and faced the stark reality that if they were unable to recover him, he would be carried eastward, past the entrance to the Fowey river, for another four hours or more.

'I'm done for,' he shouted aloud. 'O Lord be merciful, or I'm done for!'

He began to say all the prayers to the Blessed Virgin and the saints which he had been taught at his mother's knee, and all the while, as he prayed, he was aware that under a mile to the west lay Gribbin Head, where murder had been done eleven months before: murder he had been witness to and had profited by; murder he had known full well was mortal sin for which, at the Judgement Seat, he would have to give account to God.

Minutes passed. It became increasingly difficult to keep his head above water.

There was a psalm he wanted to say before he went, but he could only remember the beginning of it, so he repeated the words over and over again: 'Out of the depths have I cried unto Thee, O Lord: Lord hear my voice. . . .'

His last thoughts were of Martha and their new baby. Throwing back his head, he looked for the last time at the cloud-torn sky, and begged the Lord to watch over them and keep them safe; and then he was gone, and all that remained was the surging waves and the cold, white crests of foam.

Nearly all the boats had returned by now. They had come back as a fleet, their sails bellying out under the south-westerly gale, the men shouting to each other across the water to compare catches, and their womenfolk waiting on the beach to help with the unloading and to make a start on the gutting and salting and packing.

Sam's boat was one of the last to sail in between the old forts, and Harry, who was standing at the end of the stone quay in order to crow over the birth of his son and demand payment of his winnings, saw with a twinge of jealousy that Gristy's ketch was well down in the water.

'Trust him to land a good catch on his first day out,' he muttered to himself, and watched as the boat struck her sails and picked up her mooring, which was marked by a pig's bladder float with a feather on it, a stone's throw offshore in the stretch of water known as Polruan Pool.

But as the cockboat went aground on the sandy beach and the six men heaved it above the high-water mark, Harry saw that Sam was not with them, and by the expressions on their faces, he knew that something was wrong. Luke Rowe broke the news to him.

'We lost him,' he said bluntly. 'He went overboard off the Gribbin.'

'Overboard . . . What d'you mean – ?'

'Fell overboard,' Rowe explained, and the other crew members stood around shame-faced, each conscious that he had shared in the incompetence which had prevented the recovery of their skipper.

'But he can swim,' Harry objected. 'Didn't you go back for 'un? Didn't you see him go overboard?'

They hung their heads. Behind them, the women gutting fish had stopped working. A whisper went among them, and when the name of the dead man became known, a moaning wail went up, for Sam Gristy was greatly loved.

Rowe shook his head miserably. 'How're we going to tell his wife?'

Harry Pascoe's eyes narrowed. 'I'll tell her myself,' he said, and the crowd separated as he turned on his heel and strode along the quay and up a flight of steep granite steps into the village.

She knew why he had come before he knocked on her door. Her mother had always said there was gypsy blood in her, and she had often experienced strange insights and premonitions. Seeing Harry coming down the wet, narrow street, she knew straightaway that he was bringing bad news.

'It's Sam, isn't it?' she said immediately he was over the threshold.

'Aye, it's Sam.'

In the corner of the kitchen by the hob, baby Jennifer lay sleeping in her cradle. Harry looked about him at the comfortable disorder of the place, which was not at all like the spick and span home Ann had made for him.

'What, then?' Martha asked. She pushed a dark lock of hair back off her forehead, and looked up at him with a certain defiance.

'Drowned,' he said, and told her what he had heard from Sam's crew. She remained very still. Her silence, her self-control, frightened him. He felt that he was looking into a pool of dark, unfathomable water.

While the silence lengthened, he reflected upon the cruelty of Fate: had he but waited, had he refused to give in to Ann's pleadings, he might even now be in a position to make Martha his own; but as things had turned out he was saddled with a wife he did not love and would never love – however many sons she bore him.

Then he had a happier thought: with Sam gone, Martha would need care and protection. Having been in partnership with Sam in the building of the *Russell*, he would have every reason to keep in close touch with her. Maybe I'll have my cake and eat it after all, he mused.

Aloud, he said: 'Listen, Martha love. I tell you what I'll do. I'll make you a generous proposition, which I think you'll do well to consider. I'll take over his boat for you, sell it and my own, set up as a privateer and give you a quarter share, so's you'll have a bit of income to live on.' He reached out to her, smiling hopefully. In a muddled way, he expected that she might fall into his arms, that he would be able to comfort her and that one thing would lead to another; and so absorbed had he become in the effect Sam's death would have on his own affairs, that he had forgotten that it might have some other effect on Martha's.

For a moment, he thought that his wildest dreams were about to come true: she was staring back at him in a deep, soulful way that he was sure meant love.

'You agree then?' he whispered, and tried to take her hand.

She snatched it away, and her eyes blazed. 'Agree? You come here and tell me my Sam's gone, drowned – ' she broke off and gasped, stifling a sob ' – you come here with – with your propositions and your – your – '

While they had been speaking, Jennifer had woken, and had started to cry. Martha picked her up, soothing her, holding her cheek close to her own.

He went to her and put his arm round her shoulders, dimly aware that he might have hurried her but still convinced that she longed for his comfort and protection. But in that, he was disappointed: she shook him off and moved away.

'I know how you came by your money, Harry Pascoe, and I know that Sam was only in with you because you gave him no alternative. My Sam – he wanted no part of it. So don't come to me offering shares, because I'd rather die a pauper than soil my hands with the blood that's on your money, and there's the truth on't. And I'll tell you another thing into the bargain, so's you won't go harbouring no ideas about me. You lost that contest with my Sam because I decided you had to lose it. Yes, me. I got up in the night and took fish out of your barrels, Harry Pascoe, 'cos I couldn't abide the thought of being wed to you, do you hear me? So get out and don't come back. Don't come back *ever*. . . .'

The full force of her loss came in upon her now, and she gave a shout of anguish. Neighbouring women rushed in to comfort her and mourn with her; and Harry, fuming at her ingratitude and smarting from yet another snub, stamped back to his cottage, where he found Ann weeping bitterly, with Tristram at her breast.

Shadows on the Mountain

'Ireland,' said Gerald Hussey, 'is the fairest country in the whole world, and there is no place in all Ireland more beautiful than the Corcaguiney peninsula. Will you do me the favour of remembering that, Sara?'

They were riding back from Castlegregory, and had stopped at the top of the Connor Pass to rest their horses. The sun was low over Mount Eagle and the western sky was beginning to blaze with its evening glory. Spread out below them were Dingle Harbour and Ventry Bay, and to the west, beyond the sheer cliff of Slea Head, the Blasket Islands poked their treacherous black rocks up through a calm Atlantic.

Sara glanced at her father. He was not given to eloquence about the beauties of the countryside, and she was puzzled that he should come out with this remark.

'It is unlikely that I'll be forgetting it, Father,' she said lightly.

He regarded her with undisguised affection. She was just fifteen: already tall like most of the Husseys, with a serenity of spirit and a proud, obstinate beauty which even now made him fairly ache with fatherly love.

She was his only daughter and the youngest of seven, and he had been at pains to give her a good education. Her mother came from a high-born Portuguese family, so Sara had learnt that language from the cradle; and the devoted services of the family chaplain had provided her with considerable ability in French and Latin as well. She could versify, play the harp, ride horseback, and sing. The only activity Gerald had forbidden her was the embroidery of tapestry, which he had declared too menial an occupation for a young lady of her intelligence, preferring her to accompany him on his visits to neighbouring landlords as she had done that day.

They sat in their saddles, and for a few minutes there was a great peace, as if the world held its breath at the beauty of this Irish evening.

'I have something I must tell you,' he said suddenly.

She was surprised to see that he was struggling for words – something he had not done since the day two years before when her brother Thomas had been murdered by the English. But as they continued down the hill to Dingle and along the road that curved round the harbour to Ballingolin, she was even more bewildered to hear him reciting family history to her – history she had taken in with her mother's milk and knew by heart. He told her of the coming to Ireland of her Norman ancestors, the de la Houssaies, and of their rise to power in Corcaguiney. He spoke of the close links that had been forged through trade with Spain and Portugal, whose wines had been exchanged for skins, wool and fish. He reminded her of the ancient tradition of Christianity in that part of Ireland, one that dated back to the first century after the crucifixion, before Rome was supreme.

Gradually, he led her through the centuries to later years, years that brought about the attempt to overthrow the Faith by the English under Henry, and of the increasingly repressive measures that had been taken by the Lord Deputies under Elizabeth in the last fifteen years.

'Father,' she interrupted eventually, 'why would you be telling me these things when I know them already?'

He sighed deeply: he had insisted upon her accompanying him that day in order to enjoy the last precious hours of her innocence and happiness. Now, he could not delay any further in telling her what had to be told. So as they continued on through the trees to the fort at Ballingolin, with the blackbirds chittering and the smoke from turf fires coming from the farmhouse inside the castle walls, Gerald Hussey broke the news to his daughter that she would be leaving Ireland.

'When your mother was given to me in marriage, my father and hers entered an agreement, Sara. It was this: that as her father had consented to allow her to make her home in Corcaguiney, her family should have the same right of any one of our daughters.'

It was as though she had been hit hard in the stomach.

'But Father – you have only one daughter – '

She looked across at her father and was shocked to see that tears were streaming down into his beard.

As they approached the castle of Ballingolin, a figure on the south tower raised a hand to indicate to them that they had been seen and recognized.

'May I know who is to be my husband?' Sara asked.

'Your mother will tell you this evening,' he said, and the sound of the horses' hooves echoed on flagstones as they went through the arched entrance into the yard.

The kitchen was full of smoke, servants and Sara's brothers, who had recently returned from a day's hunting in the mountains and who were getting in everyone's way by taking their boots off and leaving them to steam before the flames. There was a cheerful, tearaway humour about their chatter, the boys ribbing their sister, and Kate, the old cook, saying 'My soul from the Devil! It is a fine and filthy state you have got yourself into this day, Master Niall!'

In the middle of this pother of boots, brothers, and boisterous behaviour, Leonora Hussey came in from the hall, greeting her daughter and chiding her husband for being so late back.

Gerald was always being chided for something or other: his wife had never entirely lost her Portuguese liking for matriarchal discipline, order and cleanliness – qualities that were not often found among the Husseys.

'And have you told the child what you had to?' she asked.

'Yes, Mother,' Sara said. 'Father has told me.'

Leonora relaxed. 'Then it's no longer a secret.' She turned to her sons. 'Sara is to be married to her cousin, Dom João,' she announced, and her piercing brown eyes scanned their faces to see their reaction. 'Well, could you not find it in you to give her your blessings?'

They came to her one by one: Brendan, Shane, Rhett, Niall and Roger, and she was hugged and kissed by each in turn, so that her cheeks burned from the scrubbing of their coarse beards.

Leonora had had a mutton killed in anticipation of a family celebration, so there was fresh meat for dinner. The kitchen fire was well stoked and the carcass roasted on a spit. The big oak table was laid in the hall, and quantities of Portugal wine brought up from the souterrain. Sara was given a place of honour between her parents, and the beeswax candles gave a gentle, warm light that sent shadows dancing against lime-whitened walls.

Afterwards, when Sara's health and happiness had been toasted, there was music and dancing for the whole household.

While the hall echoed with laughter and stamping feet, Sara saw her mother whispering in her father's ear, and a moment later she was beckoned to their presence. Her mother was holding a small purse of kid leather, which she now untied to reveal a silver chain, upon which hung a medallion of the Blessed Virgin. This she placed round Sara's neck.

'Now you are truly betrothed, Sara, for this is a keepsake from Dom

João, and he has sent it as a token of his promise to make you his wife.'
Leonora admired it for a moment. She was a small, dark woman who had
once been petite. It never ceased to amaze her that she should have given
birth to such tall children. 'You must wear it always, dear,' she added,
'and take good care of it, for there is only one other like it in the world,
and that is at the bottom of the ocean with your sainted Uncle Pedro, God
rest his soul.'

It was a finely worked piece of silver and obviously of great value; but
while she admired it and felt honoured to receive it, Sara could not
honestly say that she enjoyed having its chain about her neck.

That summer was a time of waiting for Sara, and a time when she saw her
home, her family and her native Ireland with new eyes. Conscious that
she must make the most of these last weeks, and grateful for all the
happiness and love which she had enjoyed in childhood, she was
nevertheless eager for the days to pass and for the news to come that João
had arrived from Lisbon to collect his bride.

'You will be married here in Ballingolin,' her mother told her, 'and
when you arrive in Lisbon, you will become the mistress of the Quinta de
Santo António.' She grasped Sara's hands and held them tightly. 'Ah, my
dear! What wouldn't I give to be in your shoes now! To be going to start a
new life in one of the oldest and noblest families of Portugal!' – and she
went into raptures about the climate, the food, the spring flowers, the
language, the culture and the handsome men and women of her mother
country.

From what her mother told her, Sara began to compile her own mental
picture of Lisbon. She imagined imposing castles and cathedrals
decorated with blue tiles and gold leaf; huge argosies and carracks lying
in the harbour, and noblemen everywhere, with stunningly beautiful,
dark-eyed ladies on their arms. Of her future home, she had a picture of a
magnificent pillared entrance round which grew all manner of flowering
creepers and vines; through heavy double doors she could glimpse high-
ceilinged halls, cool from the heat of the sun, tables groaning with sub-
tropical fruits, and everywhere ornaments, paintings and reliquaries of
inestimable value.

It was more difficult – and more intriguing – to conjure up a picture of
her future husband, Dom João. Her mother never tired of speaking of
her own father, Don Humberto, who had been a gentleman adventurer
and a favourite at the court of King John, but she had never met Dom

João and could only assure Sara that if he was at all like his grandfather or his Uncle Pedro (the one who had died at sea) he would be a man of great charm, intelligence and wit.

Usually Sara saw him as a bronzed, athletic man with a steady gaze, manly features and narrow hips. Lying in bed at night, she would remind herself that in only a few months' time she would be his, and would have assumed his name and taken on the position of head of his household. But what was more extraordinary was the knowledge that as Dona Sara Hussey Valdez de Santarém, she would experience with her husband that most intimate of acts, whose mysteries Maria Candida, her mother's Portuguese maid, had already explained in the most amazing and shocking detail.

Lying awake at night and listening to the moaning of the wind and the howling of the dogs, she tried to imagine what it could possibly be like to give herself to her cousin, a man nearly ten years older than herself.

'He will share your bed and possess your body,' Maria Candida had said when asked what it meant for a woman to give herself to her husband. 'He will know your body better than you know it yourself, *Menina*.' (*Menina* was Portuguese for 'Miss', and Candida had called Sara that for as long as she could remember.)

She shivered at the thought of it. 'It is a woman you will be then, Sara Hussey,' she whispered to herself, and lay awake for a long time after, watching a narrow strip of moonlight creep slowly across the wall.

In his letter announcing the betrothal, João had said that he would come to Ireland in the summer in order to take Sara back to Lisbon before the autumn storms, so her expectation of his arrival mounted with each passing day.

Sometimes, waking very early, she would tiptoe to the narrow window and look out across the harbour, half expecting to see a ship at anchor there, newly arrived from Portugal. But although other ships put in – merchantmen from Spain and France and Italy – the weeks turned into months and still João did not arrive.

The effect of all this uncertainty and waiting was that through listening to her mother and Maria Candida, Sara began to convince herself that she already knew and loved her future husband and the country he would take her back to. Having at first pictured João as tall, dark and handsome, she had by now convinced herself that he was unlikely to be any taller than herself, and probably plump and talkative. So vivid was her imagination that she became adept at having conversations with him in which he was always making her laugh, always being to her the sort of person she longed to have as a life companion. Reinforcing this pleasant anticipation of married life were all her mother's memories of a childhood spent in Portugal: of the golden beaches and blue skies, the friendly, gentle people who never went cattle raiding and who were content to live simple faithful lives.

On the other side of the scales was the love she had for her family and Ireland. One morning she rose at dawn and climbed Ballymacadoyle Hill, behind the fort. Here, the cliffs dropped sheer to the sea, and far below her, fishermen were lifting pots close by the rocks. To the south-east, the morning sun was tinting the misted tops of the Macgillycuddy Reeks, and the beauty of it all reminded her again of her father's remarks to her about Ireland and Corcaguiney on that evening when he broke the news of her betrothal. How can I ever leave this behind? she wondered. And how can Portugal possibly be more beautiful than these mountains, and those cloud shadows which sail so majestically on their slopes?

She detected in her father the same apprehension. He was not a man much given to talking, but there were times when she caught him glancing at her in a way that held its own silent eloquence. She found herself being slowly torn apart in her loyalties: on the one hand she felt proud to have been chosen as a wife by the head of one of the noblest families in Portugal, and she longed to start her new life; but on the other, she could not help drawing back instinctively from what lay ahead.

July gave way to August. The mowers went out into the little fields of wheat and oats, and the sheaves stood yellow in the stubble. Stories came in of fresh controversies and skirmishes between the Desmonds and the Ormondes, and Maurice Fitzgerald began making overtures to Spain in the hope that King Philip might agree to support Ireland and throw out the English, once and for all.

At Ballingolin, Gerald Hussey had other things to worry about.

'If he is not arriving soon, he will be too late,' he declared. 'It is the autumn storms we shall be having.'

Leonora defended her nephew stoutly. 'We Portuguese are the finest seafaring nation in the whole of Christendom,' she said, 'and no Valdez de Santarém would break his word. Dom João will be here in his own good time: he has said he will come to Ireland, and come he surely will.'

Another week arrived, but João did not arrive with it. Gradually, the state of anticipation at Ballingolin began to subside like an inflated pig's bladder that has a slow leak. Sara stopped asking questions about Portugal and ceased to look out of her window in the mornings to see if any new ships had anchored in the lee of Beenbeg Point.

'Mother,' she said one day, 'may I put Dom João's medal away until Dom João comes?'

'Faith, you may not!' her mother exclaimed, and smacked the arm of her folding chair with her hand. 'It is betrothed to João you are and that is the sign of your betrothal. He has made his promise and will keep it.'

'But what if he doesn't come?' Sara blurted out. 'Will I be wearing it round my neck like a cow-bell for the rest of my life?' – and she rushed up the spiral steps to her room, to tell herself that she hated João, and Portugal, and even her own mother.

Two days later, when thunderstorms were muttering over the Slieve Mish and the sea crows were circling lazily over the valley, her father and brothers came for her and took her up Ballymacadoyle Hill.

'See,' said her father, and putting his arm round her shoulders pointed to the south-west.

Out towards the Skelligs, a magnificent Portuguese carrack with four masts and lateen sails was heading towards Dingle under a following breeze.

'Will that be him, Father?' she asked.

'Indeed, I think it will,' said Gerald Hussey, and sighed as if he had the cares of the world upon his shoulders.

The ship came round Beenbeg Point under tow and anchored in the harbour when the sun was already down behind Mount Eagle and a seabreeze was sending a grey wraith of smoke from Dingle up the slopes of Ballysitteragh. That night, the glow of her lanterns shimmered on the water like dancing jewels: they seemed to beckon to Sara in a strange, seductive way.

That evening the family ate supper together, but although her brothers made an effort to be cheerful and her mother talked enthusiastically about the wedding arrangements, the clear knowledge that the only daughter was to be taken away caused sighs and long faces among family and servants.

After the meal Gerald asked his daughter to sing for them. The harp was brought to her and she took her customary seat by the huge fireplace in the north wall. The gentle melodies of Ireland filled the place with such tender nostalgia that even her brothers' eyes became moist, and

Maria Candida had to go outside and howl over something she called her '*saudades*'.

Later, in the chapel adjoining the castle, Father Jerome said Benediction and prayed for Sara and the life that lay before her; and then she went up the narrow staircase to her bed and, when Candida had helped her to undress, stood a while longer at her window, looking through the narrow slit at the lights in the harbour and the dark, massive mountains behind.

'Arms up!' Maria Candida ordered the following morning, and when Sara obeyed slipped the kirtle over her head, pulling the skirt down over her waist and making sure the bodice was not twisted on the girl's white shoulders.

'It's too big, look!' Sara said, and flapped the bodice to show how generous the seamstress had been in allowing room for her to grow.

'Hold still then, we'll see what can be done.' Candida set about improving Sara's still boyish figure with a few handkerchieves and pins. While she worked she told Sara how fortunate she was to be going to Portugal and to have been found a husband and how, when she was married, it would be her duty to obey him and remain utterly faithful to him, taking the Blessed Virgin Mary as her model and guide in all things.

'Now let me see myself in a glass,' Sara said eventually, and when one was brought gave a gasp of surprise, because she had not worn the high collar before or had her hair braided, and although these strange garments were a little uncomfortable and restricting she couldn't help admiring the slashed sleeves, the low, square neck and the wonderful wide skirt that swept the stone floor.

'*Ai Menina, Menina!*' whispered Maria Candida, turning the medallion the right way round on its chain and patting the girl's neck. 'If Dom João is not delighted with his bride, he will not deserve her.'

Sara looked in the mirror again.

'I shall be too tall for him, I know it,' she whispered.

'Nobility is not measured with a rule,' said Candida, quoting the dictum Leonora often used to defend her own small stature.

'No, but a husband should not have to look up to his bride.'

Her mother came to inspect her, and after a few minor adjustments declared that she was satisfied with her appearance.

'Now you are to remain here in your room until you are called down Sara, do you understand? And when you come down, remember to do so with dignity, so that Dom João will not be thinking that he is betrothed to a tinker's daughter.'

So she waited, pacing about her room and going to the window every other minute to look across the harbour at the carrack which lay at anchor a cable or so from the town landing stage.

Everything happened agonizingly slowly: it took an age, or seemed to, for the ship's boat to be brought alongside and its passengers to be embarked. The oars dipped unhurriedly in the calm water, and when the boat eventually arrived at the shore there was a further infuriating delay before the procession formed up and began making its way round the harbour to Ballingolin.

But the last few minutes before their arrival fled by. The formal shouts of challenge and reply were made between the guards on the watchtowers and the approaching horsemen, and a moment later there were hooves clattering in the yard.

Sara turned to Candida, her eyes wide with excitement. 'Holy Mother, they've arrived, Dida! He's here!'

They stood listening at the door as Gerald Hussey made a short speech of welcome; then there were further exchanges in low voices which Sara could not make out.

Then it was as if a storm broke. She heard her father exclaim, 'My soul to the Devil, she will not!' which brought forth a gabble of Portuguese from the visitors that was too fast for Sara to understand but which turned Maria Candida as white as a sheet.

'What is it? What are they saying?' Sara whispered, but the servant shook her grizzled head, reluctant to reply.

Sara went to the top of the spiral staircase and crouched, listening to the argument going on on the floor below. She heard her father say, 'Then, by the Holy Sacrament it is his promise he has broken, and cannot expect my daughter to keep hers.'

'I am going down,' she whispered, and before Maria Candida could stop her, had gathered her skirts and was running down to the hall.

There were four Portuguese: a gentleman in a fine lace ruff and blue hose who Sara presumed was Dom João, a weather-hardened man, who she thought might be the ship's master, and two young lieutenants who acted as a ceremonial guard. All four looked distinctly uncomfortable.

Her appearance had an almost magical effect: her father stopped shouting, the Portuguese officers bowed and doffed their caps and the wolfhounds stopped barking and came wagging round her.

Suddenly she thought how ridiculous they all looked dressed up in their best clothes and squabbling like children; and feeling quite calm she drew herself up and turned to the Portuguese gentleman. 'Dom João, I presume? May we be introduced?'

Dom Alfonso Pires da Silva stammered out his compliments and made the speech he had prepared about Dom João being unavoidably detained in Lisbon by pressing affairs of state.

Sara turned to her father. 'So – am I not to be married after all?'

'Not if I have anything to do with it,' Gerald muttered.

'Take no notice of that!' Leonora said. 'Dom João has asked that you travel back to Lisbon to be married there.'

'God between us and evil!' said her husband. 'Dom João promised to come here and he has broken his promise. So it is back to Portugal these Portugals can go, and tell Dom João to find himself a wife elsewhere.'

Leonora had started to weep, and Dom Alfonso was looking sheepish, shifting uneasily from one foot to another. Sara herself felt let down, disappointed, cheated. She was suddenly aware that she had been looking forward to her new life in Portugal far more than she had realized. 'May I be allowed to give my opinion?' she asked.

'Well?' said Gerald.

She tilted her chin upwards and put on her loftiest expression. Apart from her father and her brother Niall who had come down from the watchtower, she was the tallest person present, and her fine clothes lent her a new self-confidence.

'Father,' she said quietly, 'Dom João has asked me to be his wife and I have accepted his keepsake. If I don't go, I'll be breaking my promise. I can't plead affairs of state as he can.'

Gerald looked lovingly and sadly at his daughter, still seeing her as his little girl in spite of her finery. He had never wanted her to be given in marriage to Dom João, and had seen that gentleman's non-arrival as a good way of calling off the match should Sara wish it. But seeing the pleading in her eyes and aware that she was on the very brink of womanhood, he knew that he must give her her head and allow her to marry if that was what she wanted. 'Tell me what you truly wish to do, Sara,' he said gently, 'and if you sincerely desire to sail to Portugal and be married, then I'll not be standing in your way.'

She hesitated, conscious that she was being required to take a decision that must change the whole course of her life. Having spent hours daydreaming about Portugal and Dom João, she had given scarcely a thought to the alternative. Who might she marry? The only suitable families they knew were the Trants, the Rices and the Hoares over at Castlegregory, and the sons of these families were all inextricably involved in the conflicts between the English Lord Deputy and the Irish earls. If she married one of them she could look forward to a life of uncertainty, warfare, shortages, assassinations, massacres and tragedy.

'I have given my word, and I wish to keep it,' she said eventually.

Gerald Hussey saw his wife looking at him in triumph and felt his heart sink. But however much he hated the thought of allowing Sara to commit herself to a man she had never met, he knew her too well and loved her too much to try to keep her at home against her will. So – reluctantly – he gave way. 'Very well,' he said, 'but I will only allow it if you take Maria Candida as a chaperone.'

At this Maria Candida, who had been listening on the stairs, let out a wail of joy at the thought that she would be seeing Portugal again; Leonora went to embrace her daughter and whisper her blessings, while Gerald, who knew when he was beaten and was never any good in emotional situations, announced that he had important business in the castle yard, and would return as soon as he had attended to it.

Captain Duro was anxious to start the return voyage as soon as possible in order to avoid the equinoctial gales, and now that he had given his permission, Gerald saw no reason to delay his daughter's departure further. For a week, while the ship was stored and watered and fresh livestock taken aboard, Sara lived in a strange no-man's-land of emotion in which she alternated between boiling excitement at what lay ahead and abject dolours at the thought of leaving Ireland.

The arrival of the carrack and the news of her betrothal was now well known in the barony, and the valedictory Mass said for her in the church of St James in Dingle was attended by the town Sovereign and the local dignitaries and as many of the working folk of Dingle and the surrounding villages who could find kneeling space in the church. That morning Sara had been up with the dawn to walk for the last time in the castle grounds to say goodbye to her doves, her servants, her horses and her hounds, the last of which seemed to sense what was happening and started howling as soon as she had departed.

She accepted the farewells of her parents and brothers as if in a dream: her real self seemed to hold aloof from the tearful embraces of her mother, the kisses of her brothers, and her father's last loving hug before she stepped into the boat to be rowed out across the harbour.

She was lifted bodily aboard by two sailors and carried down to a panelled cabin where she and Maria Candida were to live during the voyage; and when she had been helped out of her clothes and into simpler garments that were more suited to life on board ship, she insisted upon going on deck to watch from the aftercastle as the mariners sang at the capstan and the anchors were weighed.

Slowly the ship was towed out of the harbour and past Beenbeg Point. The sails were unfurled, and as the carrack emerged from the lee of the cliffs, the first of a westerly breeze came cool onto their faces.

The sailors were up on the yards now, and setting more sails; the huge stretches of canvas bellied outward and upward, and Sara felt the ship come alive under her feet, the bow dipping and the first hiss of white bubbles and foam going along the side.

And then she heard a gunshot and the sound of a horn, and looking back she saw, high on Ballymacadoyle Hill, her own father and brothers and a crowd of others too, and they were waving and shouting – and suddenly she understood exactly what was happening: they were giving her their last farewell; she was leaving Ireland, and might never return.

She resisted all temptations to give in to homesickness: she had been given the choice between staying at home and starting a new life, and having chosen the latter she was determined to enjoy every waking minute to the full. So while Maria Candida retched and wailed and dabbed at her nose in the cabin, Sara spent most of her time up on deck, either with Dom Alfonso, who was acting as Dom João's agent, or – on the calmer days – further for'd, where she could watch the porpoises leaping round the bows and listen to the creak of timber and the wind in the rigging. Never having been aboard a ship before, she found she had a natural liking for the sea life: she suffered no seasickness at all, and as João had sent an excellent chef to cook her meals, she dined well and developed a taste for the green wine of Portugal.

After they had cleared Ushant and started across the Bay of Lyons, the wind veered a point and freshened to a small gale. A long quarter swell built up and for four days and nights the carrack raced along, slipping backwards down each wave as it overtook her, wallowing heavily as the next one came up astern, and making a dazzling white wake that trailed astern like a huge, ragged scar across the aquamarine ocean.

Sara stood on deck for hours, watching the seabirds gliding along beside the ship, listening to the gruff conversations of the men on deck, and wondering – endlessly – what Dom João would be like. Off Corunna, they encountered a huge Levantine merchantman, and exchanged gun salutes with her. On another day they sighted what Captain Duro believed to be an English man o' war. This caused considerable apprehension, for the Queen of England had been excommunicated by the Holy Father only three years before, and her privateers were taking revenge on her behalf by acts of piracy against the friends of Rome.

In the evenings there sometimes singing on deck to the accompaniment of a lute, and sorrowful music it was too, because the songs were nearly always about broken hearts, unrequited love, or dear ones lost at sea. Slowly Sara began to see why it was that her mother was so proud of her nationality, for there was something about these simple Portuguese mariners that inspired confidence and trust, so that she became increasingly sure that her decision to leave home and marry João had been well judged.

One afternoon towards the end of the voyage, when the sun was beating down and a fresh northerly wind was speeding the ship southwards, she leant out over the gunwale to look at the low strip of land that was in sight on the port beam. The captain had told her that they were now off Porto, and that within a few days they would be entering the Tagus.

She stared down at the frothing white surf that slid past the ship's side and fell into a reverie in which imaginings of her future life became mixed with memories of past days at Ballingolin. She wondered what her father and brothers were doing at that moment, and pictured Niall and Roger riding in through the castle gate with more stories of escapades, cattle raids, skirmishes, pranks and hunting expeditions; and so vividly could she imagine them that it seemed that she actually heard their voices, saw their red-cheeked smiles, and smelt the leather of their boots and the steam from their bodies when they came into the big kitchen at the end of a day.

But I must not look back, she reminded herself, otherwise I shall only cause myself unhappiness. And in two or three days' time. . . .

She imagined a gilded barge with João sitting in the stern. She saw him climbing aboard, jumping down to the deck, bowing and kissing her hand.

She was jerked out of her daydream by a shout from the bosun: the crew were sluicing down the deck, and she was in danger of getting her feet wet. She looked up quickly, and as she did so she felt a sharp tug at her neck. She realized what had happened a moment too late: she clutched at the broken chain, missed, and saw her keepsake, the silver Madonna, fall with a plop into the Atlantic.

The carrack was brought to anchor in the Bay of Cascais two evenings later, and after an uncomfortable night rolling about in the confused waters of that harbour, Sara rose early and went on deck to find that a thick mist had descended.

The crew was up early, also. The bosun was directing a mammoth cleaning and scrubbing operation; a new set of scarves and banners were being bent onto halyards ready for hoisting, and every piece of brass in sight was being polished.

'Why are they doing all this work so early in the morning?' she asked Captain Duro when he appeared on deck looking as spruce and polished as he had on the first day she met him.

Captain Duro had become fond of this tall, slightly awkward girl. On arriving at Dingle, he had expected to be given charge of a spoilt, overdressed *menina* who would spend the whole voyage in her cot with her maidservant running about in attendance, so he had been pleasantly surprised to find in Sara an odd mixture of childish enthusiasm and womanly grace. She reminded him of a young colt: there were moments when her legs seemed much too long and her posture quite unladylike – and others when, caught unawares in a reverie, she had all the poise of a marquesa.

'Why? Because we shall be entering harbour on the tide today, and we shall be met by our patron, who expects that everything will be just so.'

'I see,' said Sara. 'And who is your patron?'

He smiled back at her with a look of sad, Portuguese love in his expression.

'You mean – is it Dom João?' she asked, and when he confirmed it added half to herself, 'So he is – quite important.'

'Yes, quite important.'

'Captain Duro – what was the real reason he didn't come to Ireland?' It was the question she had been screwing up her courage to ask him for some time, but Duro pretended he hadn't heard, and turned away to talk to Dom Alfonso.

A few hours later the carrack was proceeding slowly up the narrow entrance to the Tagus between St Julian's Fort and the sandbanks where the long Atlantic swell was making a dazzling white line of roaring surf. There was just enough wind to fill the sails and the sun was breaking through the mist. Around them, other craft were also taking advantage of the flood tide to enter harbour. On shore, dogs barked and asses brayed; Sara could see the people outside their tumbledown houses and could hear the voices of women bargaining with traders. The ship rounded the point and started the last approach to Lisbon, going past the great Tower of Belem and the harbour where a hundred fishing boats made a forest of masts and spars.

And here at last was that great city, Lisbon. This was the city she had dreamt about so often, and although it was not quite as clean and fairy-like as she had imagined, it possessed a quality of age and empire. It was worthy of the great adventurers and explorers who had set out from its quays, and at that magic time of arrival after a long sea voyage, with the mist-filtered rays of the sun touching the cathedral domes and castle towers, the old city of Ulysses fulfilled and exceeded all her expectations.

João did not, after all, come out to the ship in a barge. Instead, Sara was lowered into one and, escorted by Dom Alfonso, was rowed by fourteen oarsmen to the long stone quay which fronted the city. There a reception committee awaited her, at the head of which was a young man who could only be described as beautiful. He had dark, fawn's eyes and wavy black hair; his skin was smooth and the colour of dark gold; he was perfumed, he was coiffed, he was immaculate.

He was Dom João Valdez de Santarém.

She looked into the eyes of this human peacock and found herself at a complete loss for words; and he too seemed surprised by this girl who had agreed to be his bride: he looked up at her (she was half a head taller than he) in a way that she might have interpreted as hostile had she not been in too much of a turmoil herself to notice it.

He turned to an aide – a youth scarcely out of his teens, whose beard was like goose-down on his chin. 'She's like a beanpole!' he remarked, and the young man gave a high-pitched giggle.

Sara knew that she had not been intended to understand this remark, and was hurt by it; but she was determined to show no embarrassment or anger and told herself that Dom João was probably as nervous as herself.

He took her hand, bowed formally and kissed his own thumb. He indicated to her to accompany him along the quay, where a litter awaited.

She was given a parasol against the sun and when she had been shown how to recline in the litter, six dark-faced bearers lifted her up and began trotting barefoot through the city with guards running before and behind.

They went up a long hill and came to an imposing arched entrance. Heavy double doors swung open and Sara was aware of flowering creepers and a statue of the Blessed Virgin over another heavy doorway.

They entered a courtyard. Faces appeared at windows and quickly withdrew. Dogs barked furiously.

A voice at her side said in Portuguese, 'Welcome to the Quinta de Santo António.'

She looked up. Dom João offered her his hand and helped her from the litter. He led her in through yet another heavy door: they entered a wide, tiled hallway that gave onto wide, tiled rooms. Everywhere there were tiles, and all of them were blue. In the hall one of the walls was given over entirely to a tiled picture of Christ displaying His Sacred Heart; another depicted the Blessed Virgin being carried upwards to Heaven by a host of angels, and a third was of St Anthony holding a lily and looking tenderly down at the beholder.

'You admire our *azulejos*?' Dom João asked.

'Yes, they're beautiful,' she replied.

His eyes roamed over her, assessing her. They had been followed into the hall by the young man who had been with Dom João on the quay, and Sara felt that other eyes were watching from half-open doors.

'Come here,' said Dom João, and looked closely at her. 'You're a big girl, aren't you, Menina Sara? You're like a cameleopard!'

'What is that?'

He laughed, and so did his friend.

'A cameleopard is a very unusual animal. Very unusual, and very tall.'

Suddenly he pulled her head down and kissed her on the lips. His breath smelt of the black pickled olives she had first tasted on the voyage from Dingle.

He beckoned her into a high-ceilinged room with a marble floor covered with rush mats. The young man remained in the hall.

'Tell me, *pequena*,' he said in a low, smooth voice. 'Why are you not wearing the medal I sent you as a keepsake?'

She had been dreading the question ever since its loss.

'Dom João – you must forgive me. I – I have lost it.'

His eyes went quickly from side to side. 'Lost it? How?'

'I was standing at the ship's side, and the chain caught on something and broke. It went overboard into the sea.'

He turned away from her and walked to a tall window which overlooked a formal garden with little hedges, statues and fountains. When he turned, she saw that he was trembling.

'Are you sure it went into the sea, Menina?'

'Of course! I felt the chain break – I tried to catch it but . . . I was too late.'

She looked directly into his eyes: the pupils were a dark reddish brown, and the lashes were long and curled outwards.

'And how can I be sure you are not telling me a little *mentirola*? A white lie? How can I be sure you have not given it away to another?'

'No, Excellency,' she said quietly, and made the sign of the Cross. 'I swear by the Blessed Virgin that it fell into the sea.'

He paced about for some time, looking agitated. 'It's not a matter to be taken lightly, Sarainha. That medal is a precious heirloom. It has been in my family for a thousand years. It is the last of its kind remaining. There were only two struck, and the other one was lost when my most beloved uncle was shipwrecked fifteen years ago.' He stopped pacing and pursed his lips, turning the corners right down. 'If it is indeed lost at sea, then I fear for your future. There is a tradition in our family that the Santarém Madonnas will always be reunited with their owners, do you know that? And if it is at the bottom of the ocean – ' He stopped. 'Listen. When you meet Maezinha, she will ask you about it, understand?'

'Maezinha?'

'I thought you spoke Portuguese, Sara. Maezinha means Little Mother, just as Sarainha is Little Sara. As I was saying. When she asks, you must on no account say that it went into the sea, because she will worry that it is a curse on you – or me as well, for it was given to me at my baptism. So when Maezinha asks, tell her it went missing before you set out.'

A bell rang in another part of the house.

'Come.' he said. 'That is the angelus. Let us go to the chapel and give thanks for your safe arrival.'

She met his sisters at supper, after the evening prayers. Maria Iñes was dumpy and talkative; Maria Teresa was dark and very like João, though not quite so good looking, and Maria de Graça was taller, plainer, and so intent upon winning herself a place in Heaven that she had little conversation for anyone apart from Padre Jorge, an oily man with plump little hands and a great anxiety to be first to agree with Dom João in everything he said.

A serving girl took Sara upstairs to a large, sparsely furnished bedroom whose window overlooked gardens where vines grew on trellises and brilliant red geraniums stood in earthenware pots outside an arched cloister.

'I am Ana, most excellent Senhora,' she said. 'Ana is your servant.'

'But I already have Maria Candida as my servant. Where is she?'

The girl – who was no older than Sara – dimpled.

'In the laundry, Senhora.'

'Then go down to the laundry at once and tell her I require her here in my room.'

Maria Candida came in some minutes later, looking hot and flustered. She reported that her supper had been a few broad beans swimming in oil, that the bread was stale and that she had been put under a woman who didn't know starch from steam. 'I tell you, Menina Sara, if that ship was going back to Ireland today, I would be the first on board!'

Sara turned to Ana. 'You may stay as my servant's assistant, Ana, and whatever she tells you, you must do. And the first thing you can do is fetch water so that I may wash off the city dust before I change my dress.'

The girl looked amazed.

'You heard what the lady said!' Maria scolded. 'Water! Go!'

Ana turned and bolted from the room.

Muttering about the appalling decline in standards since she was last in Lisbon, Maria Candida knelt to help Sara off with her shoes, and while she did so, Sara sighed and lay back on the feather bed. The ceiling was decorated with cherubs and angels, and the frieze was inlaid with gold.

She smiled. 'Do you know, Dida – that ceiling is the first part of Portugal I've seen that is just as I imagined it.'

She was summoned to wait upon Dona Marguerita at noon the following day.

The old lady lay in a huge bed, her face caked in paint and powder, her hair an unnatural black, her hands poking out over the coverlet like white, jewelled claws.

'I suppose you want to sit down, do you?' she demanded.

'I am quite content to stand, *Excellentissima Senhora*.'

'In that case you can please yourself.' Dona Marguerita coughed wheezily for a few moments before resuming the interview. 'So. You are to be my daughter-in-law as well as my niece.'

Sara bowed to acknowledge this.

The old lady lifted her chin – or one of them, for the others slid downhill into her neck. 'And my son tells me you have lost the medal of the Blessed Virgin sent to Ireland as a keepsake.'

'I am deeply sorry to admit it, Senhora.'

There was a long silence. Somewhere outside, an oxcart was making its way up the steep hill upon which the Quinta de Santo António stood, and its wheels creaked and groaned abominably.

'Was it stolen?'

Sara felt her heart thumping and the colour rising in her cheeks. 'It was lost, Dona Marguerita. The chain broke.'

The ringed talons clutched at the counterpane. 'In that case we must ask St Anthony to get it back for us. He has found any number of treasured possessions for me. I rely on him entirely. And if we ask St Jude, who is the patron saint of lost causes, to lend his assistance I think between them they should be able to return the lost medal, don't you?'

'Yes, Senhora.'

Dona Marguerita coughed and crossed herself. 'Now – the wedding. The seamstresses will call this afternoon to measure you for your dress, and the Archbishop has agreed to marry you next Tuesday. My son will see to it that you have an allowance to meet your everyday needs, and Padre Jorge will instruct you on the sacrament of holy matrimony and your obligations to your husband.' Dona Marguerita sniffed noisily and spat into a bowl. 'In the meantime, I have directed that my daughters look after you and keep you entertained. You will be going to an auto-da-fé tomorrow, and a tournament on Saturday. So you see, we have your wellbeing at heart.'

'I am truly grateful, *Excellentissima*.'

Dona Marguerita waved a hand in dismissal. Sara curtsied, and backed to the door; and it was only when it had closed behind her and she was standing on the long, tiled landing that she realized that her future mother-in-law had not once asked about her family in Ireland.

The auto-da-fé was held in Rossio Square and was attended by Cardinal Henry and the young King, to whom Sara was to be presented after the ceremony. Solemn Mass was said by the Archbishop of Lisbon, who was assisted by a crew of pink-capped bishops, monsignors and one of the priests of the newly formed Society of Jesus.

The sun beat down upon the crowd and glittered on the richly embroidered vestments. The prisoner, a woman who had refused to confess her adultery to the Inquisitor, was brought out in chains and bound to a post set in the ground. Tinder-dry kindling was placed round her feet: dry straw at first, then twigs, bigger sticks and pine logs oozing with resin.

Seated between Maria Teresa and Maria Iñes, with João in the row in front of them beside his close friend, Fernando, Sara did not understand what was to happen at first, and presumed that the ceremony was some symbolic re-enactment of a past event.

While the preparations went ahead, Maria Teresa chattered about who was there and who wasn't, of the rumours about the King's plans to lead an expedition to Morocco and whether her brother would be chosen to accompany him as a gentleman adventurer.

'There he is,' she whispered excitedly, and pointed out a young man of about João's age, whose lips moved constantly as he said a rosary.

'He looks very devout,' Sara remarked.

Maria de Graça leant across Maria Iñes. 'He is! He is the finest King Portugal has ever seen! We believe him to be a saint, don't we sisters?'

Maria Iñes put her hand on her sister's arm. 'Look! They're bringing the fire!'

The torchbearer crossed the square to the woman at the stake, and the crowd rose to its feet and began reciting the *Dies Irae*.

As the first curl of smoke rose into the air, the full enormity of what was happening came home to Sara. But when she looked away, Maria Iñes tugged at her arm. 'You must watch!' she hissed urgently. 'If you don't watch, it's not a true act of faith!'

Through the leaping smoke and flames, the woman could be seen like a mirage, her bare arms raised heavenward, her burning flesh writhing and twisting in agony, her screams reaching a higher pitch than Sara could have imagined possible from any human being.

João turned back to her, his face strangely animated. 'Don't show you can't watch it!' he shouted. 'They say that if you can't watch an auto-da-fé, you've something to hide!'

Then she fainted.

When she regained consciousness she was lying on a bench with her future sisters-in-law looking down at her. Everyone was talking at once.

Their heads and hands were black silhouettes against a blinding sky.

'It's a touch of the sun, that's what,' Maria Teresa declared. 'She's Irish, don't forget. They don't know what the sun looks like over there.'

She had been carried to the back of the crowd. After a while João came up to see how she was.

'Look at you!' he said. 'I can't possibly present you now, Sara! You realize you've missed a chance of meeting King Sebastian?'

'It doesn't matter,' she mumbled. 'I don't mind.'

'But I mind, I mind very much!' he snapped, and walked with quick, short steps back to Fernando, taking his arm and leading him off into the crowd.

She sat up, holding her head. All around her, people were surging past on their way out of the square.

'I'll try not to do it again,' she said as the sisters helped her up.

'I certainly hope not,' said Maria Teresa. 'We can't have you fainting away every time we go to an auto-da-fé.'

'Do you have them often then?'

'Not very,' said Maria Iñes. 'Only three or four times a year. They have far more in Spain.'

They helped her to the carriage. They crossed the city and began a long, slow climb up through the Alfama district. Children in rags ran along beside them; festoons of washing hung from windows; piles of garbage buzzed with flies, and at every other doorway some blind or leprous beggar held out a hand for alms.

'Why are so many of the women in black?' she asked.

'Oh,' Maria Teresa replied lightly, 'the peasants are perpetually mourning their seventeenth cousin twice removed. I think they enjoy it. Besides, once they've gone into mourning, they find it cheaper to stay that way. Now you see this cathedral? It's the Sé. That's where you're going to be married.' She laughed. 'Do try to look a *little* more pleased about it, Cousin Sara!'

She tried to look pleased about it and tried to feel pleased too, but it was difficult. It was not that the family did not make her comfortable or spare any expense to see that she had the clothes and servants she needed, but rather that she found their way of life, their attitudes, their conversation, humour, tastes and ideas completely alien to everything she was used to. Even their religious faith was subtly different from her own: they seemed hemmed in by a regiment of saints, feasts, rules, indulgences, penances and novenas, and everyone seemed to be permanently on guard against saying or doing anything that might be deemed heretical.

João went off hunting in the Alentejo with his friends for the last three days before the wedding, so Sara had little opportunity to get to know him better. When they were not in chapel, at the dinner table or in their beds, there was nothing at all to do in the house except join the endless gossiping sessions with which João's sisters and cousins filled their idle hours. She was not even able to read: though the family possessed an extensive library, Dona Marguerita had it kept locked and the key lodged with Padre Jorge, who was prepared to issue devotional books only, and that grudgingly.

But everything will change after the wedding, she told herself. We shall go on expeditions to the country, and I shall become the mistress of the house.

She was sitting at the mirror in her room, having excused herself from her cousins' chatter minutes before. That day her bridal gown had been delivered, and the servants had been in a flurry of activity preparing the wedding banquet. In less than twenty-four hours she would be married to João.

What was it Maria Candida had said? She whispered the words aloud: 'He will share your bed and possess your body.'

A donkey was braying on the hill behind the house. She looked very steadily at her reflection, trying to divine from it what sort of person she was, and what sort of woman she might become.

It was a high, sung Mass, composed by Palestrina and performed by the finest musicians in Portugal. A choir of fifty – basses, tenors and falsettist male sopranos – filled the cathedral with such painfully beautiful harmony that some said it was too beautiful and the work of the Devil. The bride and groom knelt before the altar, and behind them the benches were packed with nobility from all over Portugal.

João had been out with Fernando for most of the previous night and looked pale and tired, but Maria Iñes said this was all to the good, because it made him look older and readier to take on the responsibility of a wife. It was noticed, too, that he had taken the precaution of having some shoes with built-up heels made, so that when the ceremony was over and he took his wife's arm to move slowly down the aisle, he appeared to be the same height as her, or very nearly.

For Sara, the ceremony seemed curiously unrelated to herself. Her cousins and servants had been fussing over her since dawn, and the heat in the cathedral was oppressive. There were moments during the Mass when the litanies and prayers, the censers swinging to and fro and the smell of incense made her feel lightheaded, and she was able to believe that she was not really present, not really being married at all, and that at any moment she might open her eyes and awake, to find herself back in Corcaguiney, with the wind ruffling the water across Dingle Harbour and the cloud shadows sailing over the mountain.

But it was not a dream: she heard her own voice making promises to worship João with her body and to be faithful to him unto death; she felt the ring being pushed onto her finger, and found herself looking into her husband's melting eyes. Then the dome was echoing with the last anthem: she was walking out into the September sunshine on João's arm; the crowds were cheering in the streets, gasping at the splendour of her dress and showering her with flowers and petals.

Yes, it was real, it was happening: sitting with her back straight and her head up in the carriage on the way back, she thought how proud her father would have been to see her at the centre of all this pomp and splendour, and found herself mentally comparing his craggy looks and red beard with João's clean-shaven face and small, manicured hands.

Her thoughts were interrupted when, some way ahead of them, a young urchin ran out from one of the side alleys and began chanting, '*Panaleiro, panaleiro, Dom João é panaleiro!*'

'Why is he saying that?' she asked.

'Why is he saying what?'

'That child. Why is he saying you're a pan boy?'

João's expression suddenly froze, and instead of answering her question he raised his forefinger to one of the outriders and pointed. When Sara glanced back a few moments later, she saw that five liverymen had descended upon the urchin and were giving him a beating.

Perhaps my father would not be so proud after all, she reflected, and sat in silence until the wedding carriage went under the high stone archway and into the blue-tiled courtyard of the Quinta de Santo António.

He did not come to her bed that night, nor for many nights after. Having expected that she would become mistress of the household and have much more freedom after her marriage, she was now disappointed on both counts. Her sisters-in-law excluded her from their gossip; the servants behaved towards her with greater formality and at least once a day she was summoned to Dona Marguerita's room to sit with her and listen to her talking about the family's history and her hopes and ambitions for João.

'So are you keeping up your prayers to St Anthony?' she would ask at the end of each interview, to which Sara would dutifully reply, 'Yes, mother-in-law,' while knowing that she was not. This in turn distressed her, because although she had confessed before Padre Jorge to having told a lie of excuse and had been given penance and absolution for her sin, she was being obliged, in effect, to re-tell the same lie over and over again.

But if I tell her the truth and insist upon it, I shall be disobeying my husband and causing his mother unnecessary worry, she reflected, and was forced to accept that having made a cross for her back, she would have to bear it.

The greatest difficulty of all was in having no close confidant, no father or brother to go to for advice or comfort. Candida was all very well, but since returning to Portugal she had found her relations and was settling happily into her new life, and Sara was loth to share any secrets with her because she knew that she was incapable of keeping them to herself. Nor was she anxious to open her heart to Padre Jorge, who seemed on too intimate terms with Dom João and Dona Marguerita for her liking, and who had a habit of making sly jokes to members of the family which barely preserved the secrecy of the confessional.

Of João, she saw little. He had his own rooms in a separate part of the quinta, where he entertained his friends until late at night; at meals he sometimes made a show of conversation with her, but otherwise they were as strangers. She considered approaching him and asking if it might be possible for them to spend more time together, but the difference of nine years in their age put her in awe of him still, and she decided it was not her place to make such suggestions.

When she hinted to Dona Marguerita that she was sometimes bored and would like to get out of the house and see more of the country, the old lady was quick to point out how much had already been done for her. 'I can't imagine how you can be so ungrateful, child,' she said between coughing fits. 'We have done everything possible to make you welcome and comfortable. My daughters have taken you to themselves as a sister; João I know has shown you every courtesy and kindness – and I myself give up valuable time each day to speak to you. As for your complaint that you do not get out enough, I cannot see how you can justify it. You have been to a tournament and an auto-da-fé already, and if you had not embarrassed my son by fainting at the latter event you would have been presented to King Sebastian himself.'

The following afternoon the weather broke. For a week it rained for several hours each day. The water poured off the roofs in torrents, and thunderstorms rent the night skies with brilliant flashes of lightning.

One morning when Sara was trying to concentrate on *The Imitation of Christ*, João came to her door. For once his friends were elsewhere, his sisters were in their rooms, and husband and wife were alone.

He made a little bow and rubbed his hands together. 'Well, Sarainha, how is it with you today?'

Suppressing her annoyance at being called 'Little Sara', she replied that all was well. He came further into the room and stood by her chair. She heard him making little noises with his lips and tongue as if preparing to speak.

'Let me see, how can I say this,' he muttered, 'I have a delicate subject to broach to you, Sara. It concerns our relations as man and wife.'

She waited for him to go on.

'You must be aware – I am sure that you are aware – that you have certain . . . obligations. Towards myself. As my – as your husband. As my wife. You know about all that, yes?'

'Yes I know about it.'

He paced about the room, his heels echoing on the marble. Outside the window a cascade of rainwater was splattering onto the cobbled courtyard.

'In that case – in that case I intend to take advantage of my privileges as a husband with you.' He swallowed. 'Tonight.' He clicked his heels together and bowed. 'I thought you would like to be informed of my intention, so that you could – could make the necessary preparations.'

She stared at him in some amazement, and looking rather confused, João backed out and left her with her *Imitation*.

He appeared at her bedside late that night, an hour or so after she had retired. She could not be sure of it, but just after he entered, she thought she heard footsteps going softly away down the corridor.

'I'm awake,' she told him when he had been standing in silence beside her for some seconds.

He sat down on the bed. The smell of his scent – a sweet, heavy odour – filled her nostrils.

'I'm ready,' she whispered. 'Do you wish to lie with me?'

He made no reply, but his fingers picked at the lace of her nightgown and his hands found their way stealthily in over her breasts. He explored her shamelessly, and his squeezing and probings froze something inside her, so that their effect was the exact opposite of what he intended. She began to tremble, but although he must surely have known that she was not enjoying what he was doing, he said and did nothing to reassure her, nor gave her any sign of love or affection.

She saw his head coming down towards her and prepared to accept his kiss. She disliked the smell of his scent, but was determined to do her duty. Come on then, she shouted silently, let's get it over and done with!

But he drew back, and taking her hand, forced her to caress him in a way that revolted her.

'Dearest,' she whispered, 'this is not the way of it. Come into the bed. Come.'

But he wouldn't, and redoubled his efforts with her hand, using it as his instrument until she hated what he was doing so much that she shook her head on the pillow and whispered, 'No – please – no!'

He stood up with a muttered curse of impatience, and when the lightning flashed a little while later, she caught a glimpse of his hunched back. She couldn't understand what he was doing at first: she thought he was shaking a bottle. Then she guessed what was happening and shut her eyes, feeling disgusted and frightened.

For a while, all she heard was the sound of his panting. Then she felt the coverlet being pulled off the bed and João was on top of her and his sweet breath was in her face and his mouth over her mouth; he was forcing her legs apart until she thought she would split; he was trying to lift them right up over his shoulders, and at the same time trying to enter where she was impossibly small, cursing at his lack of success and finally grunting and gasping, until she felt a little damp fountain on her belly and he rolled off the bed and pattered quickly from the room.

Thunder muttered in the distance. On the other side of the valley a dog was barking and howling. Close under her window a cricket started trilling and ringing insistently.

Ever since coming to Portugal she had stubbornly fought off her feelings of homesickness. But now, as the shock of what João had done to her began to have its effect, the reaction set in and she felt suddenly lonely and afraid.

The tears welled up in her eyes and trickled into her ears and down her neck; she heard her own sobs but made no effort to contain them. All she could think of was home, her brothers and her father; all she longed for was to be back among them, back among the mountains and bays and cliffs that she loved – back in Ballingolin, back in Corcaguiney, back in Ireland.

'Dear God!' she whispered. 'Take me home, please – one day – take me home to Ireland!'

Jennifer

She lived with her mother in the oldest and smallest stone hovel in the village, at the damp and windy end by the fort. The house had four walls, a leaky roof, one window and a low door. When the wind was south-westerly, and it usually was, they made the hearth at the north end of the house so that the smoke could filter out through the stones. When the autumn gales blew you could see the smoke being sucked out through the wall like water out of a leaky bucket. But with anything less than a gale the house filled with smoke and the door had to be opened. Stray dogs and chickens wandered in and had to be shooed out, and in the winter evenings when her mother told stories about saints and piskies and dragon-killers by the light of the fire, the neighbouring children would crowd in at the door to listen, so that after a while her mother became known as the best storyteller in Polruan.

There was a school in the village but she didn't go to it because when she was eight her mother said she had to start earning her keep like everyone else. She had to learn how to gut and salt fish, pour a pint of ale, stack wheat and gather shellfish from the rocks and snails from the hedgerows, and didn't have time to bother with figures or letters. That was for the sons and daughters of richer families like her Pascoe cousins whose father, Uncle Harry, was making his fortune privateering and could afford to pay for Cousin Tristram to go across the water to Fowey every morning and attend Mr Carew's new grammar school. But she didn't envy people who had to go to school. She didn't envy anyone really; but it would have been nice to have had a father, or at least to be able to remember him, and no matter how often her mother spoke about him and told her what he was like, there was a sort of emptiness inside her, and she was beginning to think there always would be.

There was a day in September which her mother kept special to remember her father. On this day, her mother always took an interest in the weather and the direction of the wind, and almost every year she would look out at the white-capped waves and mutter about how the wind and sea looked much the same as it had on the day she lost her Sam. And in the afternoon, at the time he was drowned, her mother would call her inside and bolt the door, and they would kneel together and say the rosary for the soul of the father she had never known; and when all those Hail Marys had been said, and the Glory Be's and the Our Father, and they had made the sign of the Cross together, her mother would pull out the silver Madonna she always kept hidden at her breast and press her lips to it in a way that said everything you needed to know about love and death and being a woman.

They had to be careful about saying anything to anyone about still having a rosary or praying to the Blessed Virgin, because Mr Drew, the vicar of St Saviour's, was pleasing the Bishop of Launceston by being a good Protestant. Her mother said that what he was doing was no better than a husband who runs off with another woman. She said that there could only ever be one true faith, and that must come from the Apostle Peter, the rock upon which the Lord had founded His church and to whom He had given the power to loose and unloose on earth and in Heaven. She said that until England returned to the Old Faith, her people would never be happy but always divided against themselves, always backbiting and fighting with one another. She said she didn't mind Elizabeth being Queen at all, and had no doubt she was a very good one too, but that it was evil and presumptuous of her – the illegitimate daughter of an excommunicated heretic and a beheaded adulteress – to set herself up as defender of the Faith.

'Are we Romanists then?' she asked her mother, and her mother looked impatient and asked her where she had got that idea from. 'Nowhere,' she said, but her mother always knew when she was lying because she hadn't been a bad liar in her time herself, and it took one to know one.

'You don't use grown-up words like that without hearing them first, Miss Gristy,' she said. 'So tell me. What've they been saying?'

It was impossible to hold back when she looked at you like that, half cross and half loving, because they had always been very close, with no secrets at all except the one about Tristram Pascoe, and she was never going to tell anyone that, not even her mother.

'Davy Treffry says my Da was a bastard,' she said. 'He says Sir Gregory got Black Hannah with child, and that we're secret Romanists and should be burnt at the stake!'

55

She hadn't really believed it herself, not all of it anyway; so when her mother started telling her that what Davy Treffry had said was more or less true, she wanted to put her hands over her ears and not listen; she didn't want to know about the argument there had been between her father and her Uncle Harry; she didn't want to hear about how they picked their wives by some silly fishing competition. All she wanted was *not* to know again, so that she could stay a little child and never have to grow up and face the world without her mother to wake her in the mornings and teach her things and tell her stories and pass on all her wisdom about the world and men and how babies came and why the best any woman could hope for in this life was to be able to make one man happy.

She didn't want to hear, but her mother said she ought to know everything so that when Martha was dead and gone and Jennifer had children of her own, she would be able to tell them too. It was true, she said – Sir Gregory Roscarrock was indeed her grandfather, and that was why her father had held fast to the Old Faith. 'So we are Romanists then?' she asked, and her mother said yes, but not to go shouting it around. 'We have to go to Mr Drew's services to keep inside the law, see? But that doesn't mean we can't be true Christians in private and keep the Old Faith alive for the day when the Protestants see the error of their ways.'

So they said their prayers to Mary and all the saints in private; they kept the law of the land by attending the bleak services in St Saviour's (whose walls, even now, were beginning to crumble) while at the same time preserving intact the true Faith. Hurrying under cover of darkness up to Roscarrock Hall when a real priest was visiting from Ireland or Spain, they whispered their confessions to him, received absolution from him and knelt in the Roscarrock family chapel to hear a proper Latin Mass and to receive in their mouths the living sacrifice, the Body of Christ.

It was dangerous, but it was exciting. It made you know you were special, as if you were secret agents in a hostile land.

Discovering she was the granddaughter of a knight was like being turned from a frog into a princess. She understood now why she had always felt extra-special and why her mother had been so strict with her and taught her things about life and men and getting babies. It made up for all the poverty and hardship they had suffered, and planted a new, fierce determination in her to make her way in the world, to marry well and make up for all the injustice they had suffered because of her Uncle Harry.

He was the owner and shipmaster of the *Russell*, and when he wasn't off at sea (which was usually) she sometimes saw him striding through the village with Mr Bryant, a gentleman from Plymouth who went on voyages as navigator with him. He was the biggest man in Polruan was Uncle Harry, a real giant of a man and once she had seen him knock a child over by mistake when all he had meant to do was cuff him playfully on the ear. Only recently he'd bought more land off the Roscarrocks (who were selling to pay their church fines) and built himself a new house made of ship's beams and red brick, with upstairs rooms, a panelled hall, latticed windows and six curly chimneys. His wife, Aunt Ann, was kept heavy with child most of the time, but she lost most of them and they only had the four.

She saw them every week at St Saviour's. They sat up at the front: Uncle Harry at one end (when he wasn't away at sea) and Aunt Ann at the other, with her cousins Tristram, Jill, Nathan and Matthew in between. Matthew was the baby of the family: a big, cheeky-chopped boy with dark red hair who was always throwing tantrums or turning round to make faces at the people behind him. Nathan was a simpleton: fat-faced and cretinous, with a drooly mouth and a silly smile, and when he tried to join in the hymns he made a terrible braying noise because he was turning into a man much too early. Jill was pale and frail and silent and holy. When she prayed, she knelt straight-backed with her hands together under her chin.

It was the eldest, Tristram, who interested her most of all. Her mother said he was the pick of the bunch.

He had left school now, and was apprenticed to Mr Knollys. He wasn't going to be as heavily built as his father, but was lithe and agile, and she loved to watch him going after gulls' eggs out by Blackbottle Rocks, his long legs braced against the cliff face and the muscles in his neck and back standing out like cords as he heaved himself up over a ledge. She wasn't allowed to be friends with him, because long ago she had played with him in the fields while her mother gleaned wheat on Townsend's Farm. They had been caught playing mother and father in the hay rick and Tristram had got into trouble for it and Uncle Harry had said evil things and called her mother a whore. That had been the beginning of the trouble, because her mother had made her swear solemnly, although she was only seven, that she was innocent of all filthiness, and although she had sworn, she knew deep down in her heart that she wasn't. That was the secret she had always had to keep and had never confessed, not even to the Irish priests who stayed secretly at Roscarrock Hall. It was a secret that made her even more different, because now that people were saying that she was turning into the dark beauty her mother had been, she knew much more about why men and women made babies, that it wasn't because it was a duty to God but because they enjoyed it; and seeing him in church every week, noticing that his voice was going deep and that her own body was changing too and that they were becoming man and woman made her think about him and long for him more and more: she wanted to have him completely, entirely for herself. She wanted to do that with him, yes, actually that; she thought about it on and on and waited all week for the moment that might or might not come on Sunday morning in church when, as her cousins went first down the aisle, Tristram glanced in her direction and their eyes met and she was able to send a thought message which said to him yes, I haven't forgotten. But she had been forbidden by her mother to have anything to do with her Pascoe cousins, and she was sure Tristram was under the same veto as far as she was concerned; and for a long time – years – she never even spoke a word to him.

Then, on a sunny day in April, when the bees were visiting the hedgerows and the robins were flying back and forth with their beaks full of moss and feathers, she came down from Roscarrock Hall humming to herself without a serious thought in her head – when suddenly, as she rounded a corner, there was Tristram, his face sun-tanned, his shirt open and his dark brown hair thick and tangled round his face. They nearly collided and stood gaping at each other.

He mumbled 'Hullo, Cousin,' and she returned the greeting. He continued up the hill, and she went on down; but a few paces further on she stopped and looked back, and it was at that precise moment that it happened, because he had turned back as well and for a few moments they looked longingly at each other, each tongue-tied, but each sure, now, of the other's feelings.

Suddenly, all her mother's wisdom and advice about men was forgotten: she was nearly sixteen, it was springtime and she was in love with Tristram Pascoe.

On the way home she made a detour to pick wild flowers for her mother, who was down at the harbour gutting pilchards and would be late back. She went along a path above St Saviour's Point where guillemots soared and gannets plunged, wings folded, into the sea below. Going on down to the house with a posy of cowslips, she was aware of that rare feeling of happiness that comes with youth and the first stirrings of love. I shall make a little surprise for her, she thought. I shall get on with the work and have a sweep out and tidy up, and I'll have the fire lit and the bone broth on before she gets home.

With these good intentions in mind, she entered by the low door, bending to avoid hitting her head on the lintel. It took a moment to accustom herself to the dim light inside, but as she entered a slight noise made her turn.

Her mother was already back: she was lying under a blanket on the bed. Her teeth were chattering, her eyes staring, and her face was deeply flushed.

She had often heard people say how Martha Gristy had been the beauty of Polruan, and she had taken pride in the fact that she was inheriting those looks. But within a few days, all her mother's youth and vigour were gone and the energetic, independent woman whose health and dependability she had taken for granted for so long had turned into a helpless invalid, unable to hold down the thinnest gruel, unable to sleep more than a few minutes at a time, unable even to answer the calls of nature on her own, so that she had to be lifted like a child onto the pot and lifted back into the jumble of stinking bedclothes.

At first she kept insisting she would be right as rain in the morning, but after the blackbird had heralded in three more mornings, it was clear to both mother and daughter that Martha's grip on life was weakening. On the fourth day Jennifer put together every last farthing they possessed and went across to Fowey to visit the apothecary, returning with a malodorous syrup which her mother vomited up within seconds of swallowing. By the end of a week she was little more than a living skeleton: her hand lay all day long in Jennifer's, and from time to time she would open her eyes, staring pathetically up, with a mute pleading in her expression that no words of comfort or whispered prayers could dispel. When neighbours tried to visit, she had Jennifer send them away, and when they said Mr Drew might be coming down to call on her, she became very agitated because the last thing she wanted was a turncoat parson at her deathbed, and she was so afraid that he might confiscate her silver Madonna that she had Jennifer take it from her neck and put it round her own.

The pilchards were in that week, and the wives and daughters of Polruan were busy all day, gutting, salting and packing the fish. They stood among the hogsheads, their wide aprons marked by entrails, their blood-reddened hands dexterously wielding sharp little knives as they slit open the silver bellies and tossed aside the innards – while all the time they chattered endlessly, matching their skill in removing entrails with a similar expertise at gutting other people's private lives.

'You ask me, it's a living scandal,' a toothless old woman was saying. 'There be our Martha lying on 'er bed of sickness while her sister sits up in her fancy house twiddling her thumbs! Mind you – ' She jerked her head in the direction of the *Russell*, which had recently returned from Plymouth and lay at anchor in the Pool, ''E's got a lot to answer for. If it warn't for 'im I reckon our Ann'd've been down to visit ere now. I did hear as how she was expectin' – '

'Have a care, have a care!' warned Nance Rashleigh, and the women looked round to see a boat beaching on the shingle and Harry Pascoe coming ashore.

He was a wealthy man these days, and dressed in doublet and hose with a gold chain round his neck. He was accompanied by his navigator Ralph Bryant, an older man, with greying hair and a stoop. The two of them leapt out of the beached cockboat and strode up past the fishwives, some of whom gave them a 'good day' but most of whom preserved a surly silence.

'I did 'ear she were with child again,' persisted the old hag when Pascoe was out of earshot.

Nance Rashleigh ripped out entrails and flung the gutted fish accurately into a barrel four feet away. ''E don' give her much peace, do 'e? Me, I'd not stand for it.'

'I don't reckon you'd 'ave to, my dear soul,' observed another old woman, who must have been well past seventy. 'I reckon they can afford a good feather tye so's he can 'ave 'er laying down!'

Harry Pascoe heard the laughter following this remark and was in little doubt that it was at his own expense. He was therefore scowling as he bumped into his own wife, who was coming out of the Russell Inn just as he was entering.

'What the Devil are you doing here?' he roared, so that the crowd of young fishermen entering the alehouse would be in no doubt as to who ruled in the Pascoe household.

Sixteen years of marriage and twelve pregnancies had hardened Ann Pascoe. She was no longer the mild, gentle creature who had gone down on her knees to implore him to make her his wife, but a sturdy, tight-lipped puritan of a woman who saw duty before all else and who always took care to drum the same principle into her children. Usually, that duty was clear cut: it meant absolute obedience to her husband, and a rigid negation of her own wishes; but there were occasions when a conflict of loyalty arose between husband and conscience, and the decision to visit her twin sister had been one of them.

'Martha's gone down with a fever,' she explained.

He glanced down at the basket of fresh-baked bread on her arm.

'Fever? What sort of a fever?'

Ann looked up at him. She knew very well that he had always regretted marrying her when he could have had Martha, and secretly longed that the family feud could be ended. But being married to him had taught her that he was not a man who found it easy to forgive or forget – indeed, she was tempted to think that he enjoyed harbouring grudges and taking revenge.

'She's dying, Harry,' she said now. 'And I want to see her before she goes, even if you don't.'

He nodded to himself and stroked the underside of his beard with the back of his hand.

'So you're along to pay her a visit, is that it?'

'Yes,' she said, relieved that he had not forbidden her, and determined to hold her ground.

'In that case I'll accompany you,' he said abruptly, and offered her his arm like the gentleman he wanted to be, so that the women and old men who sat at their doorways in West Street stared in amazement at the unprecedented sight of Harry Pascoe on an errand of mercy with his wife.

By the time they had reached Martha's house, most of the neighbours had come into the narrow street to watch. They exchanged glances and whispered among themselves as Harry put his ear to the door, and crowded behind him as he pushed it open.

But there wasn't much to see. Just Martha dead, and her daughter asleep on her breast, that was all. Staring down at the girl, Pascoe saw in her the Martha he had known as a lad – the Martha he had loved and lost;

and while he stared, she opened her eyes and looked back up at him from the stinking bed of straw, and for a moment he felt a little stirring of fear.

They buried her up at St Saviour's, in the far corner of the graveyard where the ground slopes away from the redstone church. It was the sort of spot Martha would have wanted to be buried, because from her grave you could look out to sea towards the Gribbin, close to where Sam had been drowned.

The funeral service was nothing at all in the way of a ceremony, because Harry refused to allow his family to attend, let alone contribute to the cost, and Martha was as good as a pauper. Old Black Hannah put in an appearance, and one or two other women from the village who remembered Martha as a child, and who, perhaps, shared her liking for the Old Faith; but apart from them, it was just Mr Drew (who galloped through the service as fast as he could), Jennifer and the two grave-diggers, who came in after the blessing and carried the coffin out underhand, dumping it without much reverence into the mortice they had prepared for it.

And then it was over, and Jennifer was left alone to watch as the gravediggers tumbled the pile of earth and stones down onto the coffin, with the wind bending the sea pinks and the guillemots balancing on the upcurrents, and in the distance a farmer's wife calling 'Pru-it!' to her cow.

After a while she wandered away down to St Saviour's Point. There she stood for a long time, gazing out to sea, her heart full of sadness and her eyes full of tears. By evening she had picked her way down the cliff to the rocky ledges at the water's edge, and was the object of interest of two seals, who popped their whiskery noses up from time to time to observe her.

The last gulls and guillemots were returning to their ledges, and a cormorant flew low over the water, hurrying to return home before nightfall. She was cold; she didn't know where she was, and it was getting dark. She sat down on a boulder and put her head in her hands. Nothing seemed to matter any more.

Roscarrock Hall stood at the southern end of the village of Polruan, occupying several acres of terraced fields, outbuildings and woodland. To the south and west a secure boundary was provided by the sheer cliffs and jagged rocks of St Saviour's Point, while running right down to the edge of the cliffs and enclosing the whole of the rest of the property was a high stone wall built two centuries before by Edmund Roscarrock, the founder of the family line.

More recently, in Mary Tudor's reign, the family had come into favour at court because of its reputation for piety and loyalty to the Church, and Sir Gregory had been able to build a new house on the site of the old. But times had changed again. Elizabeth had introduced her system of fines for those who did not conform to the state religion, and the Roscarrocks had been forced to sell off all but this last small bastion of the Old Faith, perched on the edge of Cornwall.

Few people in Polruan knew much about what went on behind the big iron gates that guarded the entrance to Roscarrock Hall, because Sir Gregory had taken the prudent step of making his household almost self-sufficient, and traders were seldom required to call. That the Hall was sometimes used as a refuge for recusants and fugitive priests was the subject of frequent speculation among the fishermen who gathered in Mother Russell's alehouse, but if some knew more than others, they weren't saying: no one could ever be sure, after all, whether Elizabeth might one day be toppled by Queen Mary of Scotland, and England taken back into the arms of Rome all over again.

Thus, a situation had arisen in which the goings on at Roscarrock Hall were ignored or winked at, and the family was left alone by the Justice of the Peace on the understanding that the fines were paid on time.

Sir Gregory took no pleasure in the arrangement, however: although he believed the schism between England and Rome had been a fatal mistake, he was still a Cornishman and loyal to his country, if not greatly enamoured of Elizabeth. Like many of the gentry all over the country, he was convinced that the wound now bleeding Christendom might yet be healed, and the Church, the Body of Christ, made whole; so when he gave sanctuary to young men on their way to train as priests in France, or secret agents from Spain or Ireland, he did so believing that he was acting in the best interests of his country, claiming that if anyone was a traitor it was the ardent puritans like Walsingham and Drake, who by their political manoeuvrings and piratical attacks on Spanish merchantmen were pushing the Queen remorselessly into a confrontation with King Philip of Spain.

Unsurprisingly, it was a subject that frequently cropped up at the dinner table, especially when visitors were present and Sir Gregory was able to pick their brains on the latest news from Rome, Paris or Madrid.

'It would be a war nobody wants, nobody intends, and nobody would win,' he said that night. 'Do you not agree, Father?'

Their visitor, Father Timothy Browne, was a slightly built intellectual from Staffordshire, who was due to take ship that night on his way to join Dr Allen in Rome. He had been trained at the Douai seminary and had been taught the art not only of argument but also of secrecy. So while he could have given this kind old Cornish gentleman an eye-opening insight into the plans being made on the Continent of Europe to bring England back within Rome's jurisdiction, he was content to let his host do most of the talking.

'Certainly it would be a tragedy to see the two most powerful nations on earth destroying each other in such a way,' he agreed, 'and let us pray that such a day never comes.'

'Nevertheless,' put in Sir Gregory's youngest son Amyas, tapping the tips of his slender fingers lightly together, 'there are many who believe that the day will come when the prophecy of Regiomontanus will be fulfilled.'

Lady Roscarrock, who was fascinated by prophecy, joined her hands beneath her chin and leaned earnestly forward in her chair. 'Yes – now what is your opinion of that, Father?' she asked, glancing at her sisters-in-law. 'We should really be most interested to hear it.'

Father Timothy laughed rather condescendingly. 'Ah yes, how does it run? "If then the wretched world be not quite plunged in doom, and fire doth not earth, sea and sky consume – " '

' "At least in tragic tumult shall great kingdoms fall, causing loud outcries and dire miseries withal," ' Amyas chimed in.

His mother looked at her youngest son approvingly. She was not a greatly intelligent woman, being one of those persons who always seem busy without ever achieving anything in particular, and it never failed to amaze her that her son could actually remember what he read when she had difficulty remembering the day of the week.

'No, I don't think we should pay too much attention to Regio-montanus or Johann Müller or whatever it was he called himself,' laughed the priest, 'even if he did manage to forecast a comet or two.'

'Nevertheless, the year is coming rather near,' put in Vera, one of Amyas's several maiden aunts, 'and quite honestly I hope I'm not here to see it.'

'It's only ten years, dear!' Lady Roscarrock told her sister-in-law. 'I'm sure you'll last that long!'

'More than that, surely,' said Amyas. 'It's 1588 isn't it? So you've got another thirteen years to go, Aunt.'

'Thirteen!' exclaimed Vera, and crossed herself.

'Enough of this,' said Sir Gregory, and nodded to Father Timothy, who bowed his head and gave thanks for the meal before his host led the way to the chapel to say the last prayers for a safe voyage and a timely arrival.

Sir Gregory, Amyas and two menservants were to take him down to the landing stage where a boat was waiting. When the last goodbyes and blessings on him had been murmured by the ladies, two dimmed lanterns were provided by Mrs Prynn the housekeeper, and the priest was led down to the kitchens and into the stables, under the floor of which a tunnel led steeply down to the shore.

They went in single file, stooping frequently, clutching a handrope to prevent themselves slipping on the wet stones underfoot, exchanging brief whispers of warning to each other to beware a pothole here or a slimy boulder there.

And then a dim light opened out ahead: their boots crunched on pebbles and they emerged from a small cave whose entrance was uncovered only at the lowest of low tides.

Leaving the lanterns in the passage they dragged the boat down over cloths to muffle the sound, and as soon as it had been launched and the oars shipped, Sir Gregory turned to Father Timothy. 'Godspeed you, Father, we shall pray for you and all your intentions,' he whispered, and with Amyas steadying the boat, the priest stepped aboard, to be rowed out to an awaiting bark.

For a minute longer father and son stood watching as the boat was rowed almost noiselessly out to sea; and they were just about to return and make their way up the passage to the house when the sound of falling stones broke the silence of the night.

They spun round and discovered Jennifer Gristy, who was trying to look invisible against the cliff face not ten yards from where they stood.

She looked from one to the other, clearly terrified. 'Sir –' she began, 'I didn't mean – I wasn't – ' And she began weeping bitterly, her hair coming down over her face and hands, her shoulders shaking pitifully.

Amyas took her by the arm and helped her to her feet. He turned to his father: 'What do we do with her? We can't leave her here!'

Sir Gregory knew that was out of the question, but it was also essential that she should not see the entrance to the tunnel. 'Put your hand over her eyes,' he said, and when he saw his son's head turn in surprise added, 'Do it! Do what I say!'

So with Amyas's long, damp fingers pressed against her eyes, Jennifer was led stumbling into the passage, and on the way up to the house Sir Gregory tried to think how he was going to pacify his wife, who had never been able to forgive him for his infidelity and who had always resented the presence of his bastard's daughter under her roof when she came to hear Mass.

'Now remember what I said,' whispered Mrs Prynn the following morning. 'Go straight in, curtsy to Her Ladyship, then stand up straight with your hands joined and answer all her questions truthfully.' The housekeeper pushed Jennifer in the small of her back, and she found herself walking into a panelled room, in which Lady Roscarrock sat in an ornately carved oak chair.

'Thank you, Mrs Prynn, you may leave us now. And – close the door, if you please.'

'Yes, ma'am.'

The oak door clunked shut, and Jennifer realized that she had forgotten to curtsy, so she managed an awkward one without toppling over.

Lady Roscarrock watched this performance without any sign of amusement or compassion, and after a lengthy silence in which a mutual appraisal took place, gave a great sigh and said, 'Well? And do you know who you are?'

'Jennifer Mary Gristy, your Ladyship.'

Lady Roscarrock seemed to be containing some inner pressure that was about to erupt. 'And do you know who is your grandfather?'

But Jennifer was determined not to be overawed by this thinly severe lady.

'Yes, ma'am, I know,' she replied confidently.

'Who is it, then?'

'I believe it was one Arthur Pascoe, ma'am. Being as he was my mother's father, like. But I never set eyes on him, me.'

'And the other? Your father's father?'

Jennifer's eyes went sideways. 'I'm not so sure of that, ma'am. To be honest with you, that is.' Then she looked straight back into the old lady's pale grey eyes and added, 'Though I did hear tell that it was Sir Gregory himself, ma'am.'

A trace of colour stole into Lady Roscarrock's powder-whitened cheek.

'Then your informant was correct.'

Jennifer said nothing, as nothing seemed called for.

'And tell me, child, would you willingly betray your grandfather?'

'No ma'am!'

The other looked at her searchingly.

'I know what you be thinking, ma'am,' Jennifer ventured, 'but last night – I wasn't there a-purpose, like. I warn't spying nor nothing, honest to God I warn't!'

Lady Roscarrock's hand trembled on the arm of her chair. 'Then swear to me now, swear that you will never speak of what you saw or heard. Swear that you will never speak of it to a living soul!'

'But ma'am! I didn't see nothing!'

'Swear!'

'I swear it, ma'am. I do swear it.'

She stood over a great, three-legged cooking pot, but the stew she was pounding with a pole was not for eating: it was the monthly wash. She held the pole two handed, as if administering the death thrust with Excalibur, plunging it up and down in the soggy mass with a ferocity that had little to do with getting the clothes clean. Her face was red from the steam and her hair had gone into rats' tails. She had been working every day for over a month, and had not received a penny for her labour.

It had been thrilling at first to start work for a real knight and his lady and to live in this tall mansion with its halls and parlours, its tapestries and suits of armour. She had gone to work willingly, seeing no injustice in the fact that she got no pay and slept on a straw pallet in the lower scullery; she felt honoured to be a part of the retinue of servants who made up this little Catholic community. She enjoyed attending in the whitewashed chapel where compulsory prayers were conducted three times a day and did not feel ill-used when Mrs Prynn chastized her with a whip for letting slip a blasphemy or lying abed longer than she ought. But anyone could have too much of a good thing, and now she was hot and tired and angry.

One more basket to go, and then she would be done. She lifted the clothes out of the pot on the end of the pole and transferred them to a fresh-water butt to rinse. In the old days, there would have been two or three servants to do the monthly wash. They would have been finished by noon, and the clothes would have been draped over rocks and bushes to bleach overnight in the moonlight. But – as Mrs Prynn was grimly fond of explaining – those days were past. The law of the land saw to it that gentry who did not conform to the new religion had to pay for the privilege. Not that there were many burnings these days because the Queen was too intent upon popularity for that. No, there were subtler ways of changing people's minds than burning their flesh. The most powerful were imprisoned; traitors were beheaded and Catholic land-owners like the Roscarrocks were fined so heavily that they were forced to sell property and make do with fewer and fewer servants.

She began plunging the pole down into the pot once more but, feeling suddenly rebellious, she stopped work and went outside for a breath of fresh air.

She was just about to go inside again when over to her right, by the high stone wall that marked the boundary of the Roscarrock estate, she heard a single, high-pitched whistle, and looking round she saw a face observing her from the other side.

She gave a little gasp of surprise. It was Tristram Pascoe.

She stared back at him, and when he raised a hand raised hers in reply. He nodded and beckoned to her; she shook her head, as if to say 'It's impossible.' But he nodded more forcibly and beckoned again. She held up her hand to him to say, 'Wait while I see if it's safe,' and darted back through the kitchen and into the house, listening in the big hall where suits of dull metal armour stood mutely by the heavy oak doors. But there was not a sound: it was that time in the afternoon when Mrs Prynn was down in the village, Sir Gregory and Amyas were at their books, and the ladies in their chambers.

She ran back through the kitchen and down the steps into the lower scullery, but when she came out by the back door and looked across to the wall, Tristram was not to be seen. She was just cursing herself for not having had the courage to go straight over to him in the first place when he appeared again, a little further down.

This time she needed no further invitation. She ran along the side of the house, round the back of a stone-stilted granary and down behind the dovecot, and then darted across the last few yards to the wall.

It was a high one, but although she was confident she could climb it, she knew that if she tried to do so she would risk being seen from the house; but beside it was a shallow grassy ditch where she could remain out of sight, so bending double she ran along this ditch, and came to the spot where she had seen Tristram.

The apiary was nearby: half a dozen hives faced south down the slope, and the air was alive with a constant hum. When she looked up she could see the bees shooting up and away over the wall, and by each hive there was a continual coming and going of bees, some of whose pouches were brilliant with golden pollen.

She heard a whispered, 'I'm further along! There's a hole!' Then his hand appeared through the wall a couple of yards down and waved about to attract her attention. She crawled along to it, and a moment later they were face to face through a large chink, Tristram grinning, his teeth white and his face sun-darkened, and the sight of him made her feel safe and loved again, as if she had arrived home.

He reached through the hole and whispered to her to take his hand. She did so willingly: it was the first true gesture of kinship she had received since her mother's death. Their fingers interlocked and tightened, and when he pulled her hand back through the wall, she made no effort to resist him. She felt her hand being placed against his cheek, and then his lips pressing kisses upon it; she pulled his hand back, and casting all caution to the winds pressed his palm to her own lips, fondling it, examining the scratches and chisel scars on his knuckles until he wanted her hand back again – and the manner in which they took it in turns to kiss hands through the wall became a competition between them to see who could demonstrate the greatest fondness, a competition that Jennifer was now desperate to win because all her instincts were telling her that Tristram was the only man she could ever love, and that through him lay her path to freedom and independence.

She knew how to win that competition, too: when he reached through to her the fourth or fifth time, she did what she had often dreamt of doing before: kneeling up against the wall, she guided his hand and put it to her breast.

She found his whispered reaction no less gratifying than his gentle, exploring touch. 'Oh – Jennifer!' he sighed. 'Sweet lovely Jennifer!'

They got away with it – that day and three more days in a row: each afternoon when she heard his whistle she stole out and crouched in the grassy fosse beneath the wall. Linking hands, they whispered their love for one another, and although they were kept physically apart by those old granite stones, they were in another sense brought closer together by them, for it is curiously easier to give your heart away through a hole in the wall than to swear your fidelity between the sheets of a feather bed.

But inevitably, it was not enough to kiss fingers or allow a caress at arm's length: she wanted much, much more. Pressing his hand against her bosom or kissing his fingers softly and reverently, she told him that she knew and had always known that only she could make him happy, that there was already a mystical bond between them and that if she could not soon feel his arms about her and his lips upon her own, she would sink away into despair.

So they risked all, and late one night when she heard a low whistle she rose from her straw pallet in the lower scullery and crept out of the house; and when Tristram had climbed over the wall, she gave herself to him there on the midnight grass with the summer moon blazing down through the trees and the scent of honey wafting up from the silent hives.

They were boy and girl together, as innocent as Adam and Eve. She took him to herself and loved him in the mystical, supreme way she believed her mother had loved her father; she gave him everything – her innocence, her youth, her maidenhead. Gently – and a little inexpertly – he gave her his first love in return, and that joining of soul to soul and body to body convinced her that in love it is indeed better to give than to receive. But it could not go on for ever, both of them knew that. Even four successive nights seemed an almost too generous slice of happiness, and on that fourth night, with the waning moonlight glittering on the sea and the crickets noisy in the hayfield on the other side of the wall, she gazed sadly up at him and asked the question that had been uppermost in their minds for some time.

'What are we going to do, Trist?'

He bent and touched her lips with his own, and drawing away, shook his head.

She traced a pattern with her fingertips on his forehead. 'Can't we run away?'

He smiled and frowned in the way she loved. 'We could try, but we wouldn't get far.'

He was silent after that for some time, and eventually she asked what he was thinking.

'Of Nathan,' he said. 'And of my father.'

She knew from village gossip and her own observation that Harry Pascoe treated his second son cruelly. Her mother had once remarked that it was her opinion that Harry had actually caused Nathan's idiocy in a fit of temper soon after he was born, and through whispered gossip over the years she had guessed that Tristram had become the focus of conflict between his parents and that he had found it increasingly necessary to defend both Nathan and his mother against his father's violent outbursts of temper.

'Are you frightened of what would happen?' she asked now. 'If . . . if people found out about us?'

He rolled onto his back, and she lay in the crook of his arm. When he spoke, it seemed to her that he was listening to his own thoughts as much as conveying them to her.

'I think . . . if my father discovered about us – I think he wouldn't punish me so much as my mother. As for Nathan, I don't know. Sometimes I look at my father and I wonder what's going on in his mind, why it is that there's so much hatred, so much poison inside him. Yes, of course I'm frightened of what might happen. Trouble is, I don't know what he'd do – ' He broke off suddenly and turned his head away, whispering, 'My father, my father, my father. . .' in a way so bitter and desperate that she turned to him and held him; and although they had already stayed far longer than on previous nights, she had a sudden foreboding of events, so that she needed to love him again, now; and a little while later, without thinking of the danger, she cried out with the joy of him: a single shriek in the night that echoed in the trees below the house and was followed by a strange, almost tangible silence.

The moon went behind a cloud, and the wind off the sea was suddenly chill. Nearby, the first blackbird began to sing, and the sky behind the chimneys of Roscarrock Hall was beginning to lighten.

'You must go back,' he whispered at length, and they stood up and prepared to depart.

'Tomorrow night?'

'Yes. Every night.'

'Until we're caught?'

He grinned. 'Probably.'

She reached up, and kissing him fiercely on the lips, whispered a rhyme she had made up years before: 'Tristram Pascoe, Tristram Pascoe, never, never let your lass go!' – and when they had hugged, she watched him climb nimbly over the wall and heard him jump down into the hayfield on the other side.

The dawn was already coming up. Going back along the ditch and down beside the house, she tried to convince herself that no one would have heard her love-shriek, but she was already frightened that they had, and when she tiptoed into the scullery and crossed to her straw pallet in the corner, her fear increased tenfold, for she was immediately certain that the blanket had been moved and that someone had been there in the scullery only minutes before.

That day was the feast of St Peter and St Paul, and it dragged by. Already exhausted from her night's activities, she was also acutely aware that she must give no sign of tiredness for fear of arousing suspicion. At the same time the near certainty that at least one member of the household knew she had been out of her bed before dawn put her in a state of nervous watchfulness.

If anyone did know her secret, that person certainly concealed the fact well. Mrs Prynn left her to get on with her duties without any unusual comments; Lady Roscarrock appeared to be her normal self, and the aunts and sisters dozed in their chairs or whispered their rosaries in much the normal way.

They are setting a trap for me, she decided. They are lulling me into believing that they suspect nothing, so that they can catch us together. And then. . . .

The more she thought about it, the more clearly she saw that she must somehow get a warning to Tristram.

But it was impossible. No traders were likely to come to the Hall that day or any other, and she could hardly risk being seen speaking to them even if they did. Leaving the grounds was equally dangerous: she would either be seen, or missed, or both.

Stifling her yawns and fighting to keep her eyes open during the Litany of the Saints, she wrestled with the problem, terrified that Tristram might be caught trespassing but unable to think of any way to warn him.

After evening prayers something happened to arouse her fears further. All the members of the family, along with Mrs Prynn, the head groom and Sir Gregory's personal manservant, were called to attend at a private meeting in the refectory.

Jennifer already knew that such a meeting nearly always heralded the arrival of a secret visitor – usually a priest. Two such visitors had come and gone since her arrival at Roscarrock Hall, one an Irish priest on his way out to Galicia and the other an Oxford scholar on his way to train as a Jesuit in France. On each occasion, every available manservant had been posted to keep watch for soldiers, and she knew that if ever there was a night Tristram should not come visiting, this was it.

The evening dragged on. She completed the usual task of washing and scouring the pots and dishes after dinner, and when Mrs Prynn had inspected her work and approved it, she lay down on her narrow bed and began the long wait for darkness – and for Tristram.

She awoke with a start. She had dropped off to sleep in spite of herself, and now it was a black night with a wind getting up that was making the beech trees creak and rattling a shutter on one of the upper windows.

She lay listening to these signs of a weather change and wondered whether Tristram had decided not to come after all. If only that could be so! Even now she was undecided what to do should he make his signal. If she made no response, he might well climb over the wall all the same, as he had on the previous night; on the other hand if she went to him and they were caught his offence would be deemed the worse, for being found on Roscarrock property was one thing, but being caught dallying with a servant girl was another.

Time passed – she had no idea how long. Though she listened for sounds in the house, she heard none: Sir Gregory's organization ran smoothly, and all the watchers would have been sent to their posts long before.

And then she heard the low whistle – once, twice, and a third time; and while she lay frozen by terror into indecision, a yet more dreadful possibility occurred: what if Tristram were caught, and were led to believe that she had betrayed him? What if, by her doing nothing, they were able to convince him of her treachery and turn him against her for ever?

She waited no longer. Whatever the risk, she must go to him and tell him to go back.

She got up off the bed and went to the door, her heart thumping wildly. Swiftly and almost silently she ran along in the darker shadows beneath the gable to the granary and from there to the dovecot. The moon was not yet up and a high, thin bank of cloud obscured all but a few stars. Pausing to listen for any sounds of activity before making her dash across to the cover of the fosse, she found herself automatically reciting part of the Litany to the Blessed Virgin: 'Mother most pure, Mother most chaste, Mother inviolate,' she whispered. 'Mother undefiled, Mother most admirable, Mother of good counsel, Mother of our creator, Mother of our Saviour, Virgin most prudent, Virgin most venerable . . . mystical rose, Tower of David, House of Gold, Ark of the Covenant. . . .'

But if the Mother of God heard, she must have decided that the cause was not a worthy one, for as Jennifer moved out from behind the dovecot she felt herself seized from behind. A hand was clapped roughly over her mouth, and she was almost lifted up by the arms and moved at the run back into the house, where Mrs Prynn was waiting in her nightcap and gown, with the trap door into the cellar open and the key in her hand.

They brought her out thirty hours later, though she had no idea how much time had passed. All she knew was that she was cold and hungry and thirsty, that she had not slept for more than a few minutes at a time and that all her thoughts were with Tristram.

The trap door above her head opened suddenly, and she was blinded by the daylight. A ladder was lowered, and Mrs Prynn looked down.

'Look sharp, then! Unless you want to stay down there!'

She went up the ladder, and was immediately grasped by the upper arms and marched unceremoniously into the great hall, where the family had gathered.

Her head was swimming and the floor seemed to be undulating as if she were at sea. She was aware of five pairs of aristocratic eyes glaring at her: Lady Roscarrock, Sir Gregory and Amyas in the centre, flanked by the sisters Vera and Margaret.

It appeared that Lady Roscarrock was going to take the lead. 'What have you to say for yourself, child?' she asked in a dangerously gentle way.

'Answer!' hissed Mrs Prynn, and dug her in the back.

'My Lady – I – don't know what I'm accused of.'

'Where were you going? What were you doing, stealing out in the middle of the night?'

'The truth, child,' Mrs Prynn whispered behind her, and her voice was insidious, like the Devil's tempting. 'Tell the truth.'

'I was hot – I couldn't sleep. I went out – for air – '

Lady Roscarrock gave a sigh of pleasurable anticipation. She had been looking forward to this moment, for it promised a long-sought revenge: a revenge not only against her husband for the bitterness and suffering he had caused her, but also against the harlot, Hannah Gristy, whose lithe body and brazen looks had tempted young Gregory into fornication nearly forty years before, and of whom this insolent little slut was so painful a reminder.

'So you went out for air.'

'Yes, my Lady.'

'Nothing else?'

'Nothing else, my Lady.'

Lady Roscarrock glanced at her husband, whose eyes were directed firmly at the rush matting. Before this interrogation, he had reluctantly agreed to allow his wife to conduct it, being unable to argue against her contention that if he were to perform that duty, his questioning would inevitably be biased in the girl's favour.

'And is that the truth?' she asked. 'Will you swear upon the Cross it is the truth?'

She beckoned to Mrs Prynn, who stepped forward and put a crucifix into Jennifer's hands.

'Kiss the effigy of the Saviour and say, "I swear I have told the truth." '

She stared down at the crucifix, wondering desperately how much they knew, whether they had any knowledge of her liaison with Tristram or whether these questions were merely based upon suspicion.

Looking steadily back at Lady Roscarrock, she raised the crucifix to her lips and kissed it. 'I swear I have told the truth,' she whispered, adding mentally: 'and I have also told a lie.'

In reply, Lady Roscarrock clapped her hands twice.

'Fetch him in!' she ordered, and a few moments later Tristram, gagged and hand-tied, was brought into the great hall.

Lady Roscarrock was quivering with the rage of one who is certain she has God on her side.

'So this is the "air" you went for is it? An "heir" indeed, Miss Gristy, yes, an heir to base lies and fornication, and if I had my way you would be joint heirs to a pile of dry wood too, together with flint, steel and a box of tinder!'

Hill House, the new home which Harry Pascoe had had built for himself and his family a few years before, stood in solitary grandeur on the high ground out towards Townsend's Farm. Standing back from the road in its own grounds, it commanded an extensive view of the sea to the south and the patchwork of stone walls and green fields to the north. But while it was an impressive building, with tall chimneys and fancy brickwork befitting the residence of a man making his way in the world, there was something about Hill House that was not very welcoming. Perhaps it was the lack of trees to soften its outline, or the dark stare of its latticed windows that gave it such an austere look; but whatever it was, uninvited visitors were a rarity, so that when Amyas Roscarrock rode up on that showery day in July, his arrival attracted immediate interest among the family.

With Matthew clutching at her apron, Ann, who was servant as well as mistress in her house, bustled to open the door, while Jill peered cautiously round the kitchen door and Nathan began making those deep crooning noises that indicated he was becoming excited.

Amyas gave a slight bow and handed over a sealed letter. 'For Mr Pascoe,' he said in his nasal voice. 'I shall be obliged for an answer to take back to my father.'

Nathan came out of the kitchen. 'Hollo!' he boomed, and sidling up to the visitor, tried to take his hand. Jill darted forward and pulled him aside, giving his wrist a sharp slap to teach him manners.

Ann wasn't sure whether to ask Amyas in or not, so she left him standing outside and hurried into the large parlour, where Harry was experimenting with tobacco.

He looked up from a cloud of blue smoke. 'Who is it?'

She whispered Amyas's name and handed over the letter. Harry broke the seal and unfolded it, taking his time over the reading of it, for although he could read adequately well, Sir Gregory's handwriting was not easy to decipher and there were a number of peculiarly spelt words.

Ann waited in growing apprehension. There had been an almighty family row a fortnight before: Tristram had remarked that she was overworked and that they could easily afford a servant, and Harry had taken exception to the suggestion. Father and son had become locked in a verbal jousting match which had ended with Tristram stamping out of the house and staying out all night. Since then, he had returned only when his father was down at the harbour overseeing the refitting of the *Russell*, staying out all night and sleeping rough, and for the last three days she had not seen him at all.

She knew better than to ask her husband what this letter was about however, and awaited his reaction in the reserved, watchful way which she had found safest to adopt in her husband's presence and which usually concealed more vehement feelings.

He handed the letter back. 'Tell Master Amyas,' he said, loud enough for Amyas to hear, 'that if his benighted father has anything to say to me, then let him get on his ass and come and say it to me direct, because he won't get me setting foot on his popish property, not while there's breath in my body, he won't.'

76

Ann glanced at the letter. 'But – won't it be about our Tristram, Harry?'

Harry clenched his teeth so hard that the stem of his clay pipe broke, and he had to spit the bits into the hearth.

'You heard what I said, woman. Now go and do as you're told.'

Sir Gregory had a painful discussion with his wife over how they should react to Pascoe's snub, in which Lady Roscarrock gave vent to her outrage saying that they had every right to keep both Tristram and Jennifer in custody indefinitely; but Sir Gregory wanted the whole business settled and finished with, so after a lengthy wrangle he swallowed the family pride and went over to Hill House.

Harry received him in the large parlour, against whose windows a summer gale was hurling heavy drops of rain.

'Clearly, your son is guilty of trespass, and we should be within our rights to hand him over to the Justices,' Sir Gregory said, standing very straight-backed by the table, while Harry glowered at him from the hearth. 'But I have no wish to bring dishonour on you or your family, and am quite prepared to hand him back to you and forget about the whole matter – on one condition.'

'Oh aye, and what's that?'

Sir Gregory's fingers tapped lightly on the oak table. 'On condition that you take the Gristy girl in and give her a home.'

Harry Pascoe chuckled, and stroked the underside of his beard. 'So you want to be rid of her now, is that it? *Why* would that be I wonder?'

Sir Gregory had no intention of admitting that he had given way to his wife's insistence that Jennifer must go, so he refrained from giving Harry any sort of answer.

Pascoe went to the window and stared out at the slanting rain. 'And what if I say no? What if I say you can do what you like with my son? After all, he's old enough to answer for his own actions. He doesn't need his father to bail him out of trouble any more. So if I was to say to you that you can take him to the Justices if that's your pleasure – ' He turned and fixed Sir Gregory with eyes that radiated hatred from beneath fiery brows – 'I don't think you'd like that, would you? Because you'll still have Miss Jennifer on your hands, right? Which means, if I'm not mistaken, that you haven't come here to offer me my son back so much as to ask me to relieve you of Miss Gristy. Now am I right or am I wrong, Sir Gregory?'

He was right, and they both knew it.

'Look here, Pascoe,' Roscarrock said, sounding tired of the whole affair. 'She's my granddaughter – I make no secret of that. I took her in after her mother died, but she hasn't settled down – '

'You mean her Ladyship doesn't want her to settle down!'

They faced each other, Harry standing with his hands on his hips, Sir Gregory forcing back his shoulders as if he were on parade and trying to reassure himself of his own rank and standing.

'You can put whatever interpretation you like on it,' he said quietly. 'All I want is to see her in a place where she'll be cared for. She's your kin as much as mine, Pascoe, don't forget that. You have as much responsibility to see she's not abandoned as I do. You know what might happen to a girl in her position if she's not looked after, I don't need to tell a man of your experience that.'

'And what about my son? Are you not afraid he'll corrupt her?' Harry put his tongue in his cheek and looked sideways at Sir Gregory.

'Clearly there is a fondness between them, but both are innocent – of that I am certain. Their midnight meetings were no more than childish pranks.'

Harry folded his arms, smiled as if he knew better, and strolled about the room. 'I tell you what I'll do,' he said eventually, and paused, weighing up how far Roscarrock could be pushed. 'I'll take her in – yes, why not – I'll take her in for a small consideration. What shall we say, twenty shillings? I think you can run to that, can't you Sir Gregory? Yes, for twenty shillings I'll take her in and give her house-room. Do we have a deal?'

Roscarrock could ill afford it, but short of putting the child out in the street he had little alternative; so they struck hands on it, and that evening, when the money had been paid over and a receipt obtained, Tristram returned home in the company of Jennifer Gristy to be greeted by his father's stinging sarcasm.

'Here he comes, wife, here's your golden boy, your Pyramus!' he sneered. 'And here's little Thisbe, frightened by a papist lioness!'

But he quietened down soon after, because when Jennifer turned her dark eyes in his direction he was put suddenly in mind of Martha and understood very well why Tristram had been unable to keep away from her.

It was past their supper time already, and the first question that arose was whether Jennifer should sit at table with them. Ann whispered the question discreetly to Harry while the new arrival was being led upstairs by her cousins to see the house.

'Sit with us at table?' He replied aloud, so that Jennifer must hear. 'Of course she must sit with us! What do you think she is, a skivvy?'

So an extra place was laid, and Jennifer allowed to sit between Jill and Nathan, with Matthew pulling faces to amuse her from across the table and Tristram in a flame of embarrassment at having her so near and yet so far.

Harry was enjoying himself: he had been drinking, and was in that pleasant state of semi-inebriation that softened his tongue and turned him into a quite amiable human being. He was also very taken with Jennifer.

'And how often did you get good roast beef like this down at Sir Gregory's, Miss Jennifer?' he asked, helping himself to a generous dollop of honey and making patterns with it as it streamed down onto the slab of red meat on his plate.

'I never did, sir,' Jennifer said.

Harry turned to his youngest son, who sat on his left and who was the family favourite. 'When did we last have it, Matt, can you tell us?'

'Yesterday!' cried Matthew and raised his knife at arm's length, as if he were St George and had just slaughtered the dragon.

'*And* most days before, too,' Jill said, anxious for her share of approval.

'Well, it's easily roast and very nourishing,' Ann said almost apologetically to Jennifer.

Harry beamed. 'Aye, and makes good strong Englishmen, too, not puky little weaklings fed on white fish and rabbit flesh like that Amyas, isn't that right, Nathan?'

Nathan boomed and brayed so enthusiastically that his mother had to mop up a dribble of saliva that trickled out of the corner of his mouth.

Harry explored between his back teeth with his tongue and, failing to extract the piece of gristle that had lodged there, used the tip of his knife as a toothpick.

'Right then,' he said, when operations were satisfactorily completed and he had taken a swill of ale, 'let's not back and fill, let's have everything full and by.' He shot a glance down at Tristram, who was keeping his eyes on his plate, and then across to Jennifer, who was doing likewise. 'Here's young Jennifer, come to live with us, right? Aye, and sitting down at our table like she was one of the family. And there's Master Tristram pretending he's not listening to his father, who might've been sitting in the Fowey stocks by now if it wasn't for that same father's efforts.'

79

The atmosphere of bonhomie was suddenly gone, and in the frosty silence that followed, Harry Pascoe swayed deliberately from side to side in his chair, as if he were in his cabin aboard the *Russell* and a gale was blowing. 'Well?' he barked suddenly. 'Do I get a word of thanks or do I not?'

Tristram looked up. 'Thank you, Father.'

Harry's eyes went back and forth under bushy red eyebrows.

'And there's your mother, overworked and underpaid if I'm to believe my ears, and in need of a skivvy. Yes?'

'I never said a skivvy,' Tristram said quietly. 'I said she could do with more help.'

Jennifer looked from son to father and back to son. This was an argument between them of which she had no knowledge, but it was clearly a bitter one that rankled on both sides.

' "More help" then,' Harry was saying. 'Well unless I'm very much mistaken, "more help" has hove up over the horizon as you might say. Would you agree with that, Miss Jennifer?'

'I'm not afraid of hard work, sir,' she said, and turned to Ann. 'I'll help all I can, Aunt.'

'Well there, now, Mrs Pascoe! Did you hear that? So we needn't have any more from you about the twinges in your knees or the tweaks in your hips, or your back giving out, eh? As for you,' he went on, pointing his knife at Tristram, 'if you think you can start playing troll-madam under this roof, you can think again, because this is a good Christian household and that's the way I intend to keep it.'

Sitting on his right, Jill put on an expression of self-contentment born of the knowledge that she was blameless in her father's eyes.

'And let it be said,' Harry went on, 'now we're talking straight, that Miss Jennifer here can forget all the Romish ideas she was fed on down at Roscarrock Hall and start eating Protestant pie, which she'll find suits a Cornish stomach a sight better than all that hocus-pocus-nomminy-dommy rubbish they peddle down at Holy Joe's.'

He sat back and drained his jug of ale. Slamming the tankard back on the oak table, he smacked his wet lips and sucked at his beard. 'Well, Annie-the-Silent, shall we be hearing your dulcet tones at all this night, or isn't it rough enough yet for the storm thrush to sing?'

Ann looked up and forced a smile; and when Jennifer glanced up the table at the master of the house, Harry replied with a wink.

The effect Jennifer had on him was so obvious that Ann was amazed he made no attempt to disguise it. Before Jennifer's arrival he had left Hill House early in the morning and had returned home late; now he sat over his breakfast in order to ogle her when she brought it to him, and came home early – and sober – to mooch about the house and engage her in conversation while she swept the rooms or tended the roast.

But what was going on inside Jennifer's mind? Ann found it very difficult to tell, just as she had found it difficult to fathom out the workings of Martha's mind in the days before she and her twin were married.

Harry had told her very little about his discussion with Sir Gregory: all she knew was that Tristram had been caught trespassing and that Jennifer had been caught going to meet him; but although each had sworn that nothing untoward had happened, and their reserve and good behaviour seemed to confirm their innocence, Ann could not forget the scandal they had caused ten years before, nor could she believe that Tristram would have scaled the Roscarrock wall simply to sit with his cousin and talk.

Perhaps she would learn a little more from them when Harry had gone off to sea again, an event she had learnt, over the years, to look foward to.

He was planning a more ambitious venture this time. Earlier that year he had met a merchant from London who had money to spare and was looking for a likely speculation and Harry, being in the right place at the right time for once, had sold him the idea of investing in a privateering cruise to the Americas. For several weeks the project had been the talk of Polruan: the *Russell* had been put into extended refit, volunteers had been sought by extravagant promises of Spanish prizes and – to prove that this time Harry's adventure was to be more than just talk – two six-pounder sakers and a couple of falconets had been delivered aboard a hoy from Plymouth, and hoisted onto the *Russell*'s deck under Harry's personal supervision.

But the sailing date kept being put back: first for lack of volunteers, then because of uncertainty about the activities of the ubiquitous Francis Drake – who disliked other privateers poaching prizes he regarded as his own – and finally for a wealth of reasons so small that Ann began to suspect that they were nothing more than a smoke screen, to hide her husband's ever-increasing infatuation with Miss Jennifer Gristy.

Jennifer was aware of a strange feeling of expectation during those first weeks after going to live with the Pascoes, as if the months of July and

August were an interlude between two completely different stages in her life. She felt now that her future was settled: her uncle would soon go away to sea; Tristram would be freer to be seen in her company and perhaps, if her prayers were answered, they would be able to persuade Aunt Ann to let them be married. That was how she saw things, and although she tried to foresee other ways in which events might turn out, she could not imagine any future that did not include Tristram. Having given herself to him, she was his.

She shared a bedroom with Jill. It was an awkward relationship from the start: Jill had always considered herself her father's favourite, and was naturally hurt to have her position usurped. But there was more to it than that: as the only daughter and elder sister to Nathan and Matthew, she had become far more involved in the running of the household, and had been witness to her mother's frequent pregnancies, miscarriages and confinements. Such experience had aged her in advance of her years, and Jennifer was sometimes inclined to think that Jill was two or three years older than herself rather than eighteen months younger.

She was also inclined to be bossy.

'Where did you get this?' she asked one evening, lifting Jennifer's silver medallion to take a closer look.

It was nearly two months after Jennifer's arrival. They were sitting on the bed in their night things, their hair long down their backs: Jill's light brown, Jennifer's almost black.

'It belonged to my mother,' she said. 'She gave it me before she died.'

Jill turned it over. The medal was backed by a small oval of wood, polished smooth by centuries of wear. 'Do you pray to it?' she asked, looking closely into Jennifer's face with her pale, protruding eyes.

'No! Of course I don't!'

Jill let the medallion drop back on its chain. 'Then do you pray to *her*?' she asked darkly.

Jennifer shook her head.

Jill went and sat on the windowsill, and swung her bare feet back and forth. 'Mr Drew says that wearing anything like that is idolatry. He says all those trinkets and crucifixes should be melted down.' She stopped swinging her legs and bit her nails instead. 'If he knew you had that, he'd have it off you.'

'Well he doesn't know and you'll not tell him, will you?'

Jill laughed. 'Perhaps I won't, perhaps I will.'

They got into bed and snuffed the candle. Jennifer was ready for sleep, but Jill was in a mood to talk.

'Did my brother ever kiss you?' she asked abruptly.

'I said – I told you before – I'll talk about anything, but I won't talk about that.'

There was a silence, then Jill said. 'I bet he did!'

But Jennifer was determined not to be drawn, and another long silence followed.

'Jen?'

'What?'

Jill propped herself up on her elbow. 'Might you be in need of some darnel seed by any chance?'

Jennifer yawned deliberately. 'No? Why should I be?'

'Well that's what Mother uses. When she's late with her flowers, you know.'

'Her flowers?'

'Her flux, then, but we don't call it that, Mam and me. We think flowers is a much nicer word for it.' Jill paused. 'You have started, I suppose? Me, I was early. I started when I was only twelve! You *have* started, haven't you? I mean – well – you look as though you should've, like. But you haven't had them since you been with us, have you? The flowers, I mean.'

Jennifer was pressing her hands hard against her face, and sobbing silently.

'Did you hear what I said Jen? What is it, what's with you? Why be you a-weeping? You're not – Oh, my Lord and Saviour! You don't mean – you're never with child are you? You're never with child by our Trist?'

It was true, it was true, it was true: secretly, instinctively, she had known it for weeks. She had been giddy in the mornings and tired at night; her breasts felt different, she had been sleeping badly, dreaming dreams, longing all day for Tristram to come and take her in his arms and love her, when instead she had had to be content with no more than a covert glance from him when he came home from Knollys's yard in the evenings, or a touch of his ankle under the table at supper time. If only his father would go away to sea! If only he would stop staring at her and winking at her and getting in her way about the house so that she had to brush past him!

'Please don't tell on me,' she whispered. 'Please!'

Jill was silent for some time. 'What was it like?' she asked eventually.

'I don't want to talk about it.'

'I do, though.'

Jennifer remembered Tristram's face grinning through the wall, and the firm warm clasp of his hand as he reached through to her; she remembered a night when the moonlight was like mercury on the trees – and she remembered her own sudden cry of love and joy, which Mrs Prynn had thought was the deadly shriek of a mandrake and which had caused her to go down to the lower scullery to see if Jennifer was safe.

'If you won't talk about it, then I don't see why I shouldn't tell,' Jill said softly.

Jennifer turned away, despairing. 'All right then, tell them. It won't make no difference. Not now, any road.'

But it did make a difference – she realized that in the long hours she lay awake thinking about it. If she could only keep the secret a week or two more it might be possible, after her uncle had gone away to sea, to persuade her Aunt Ann to let them marry. And having married, they could start their life in the little stone house at the end of the village that had stood empty since her mother's death.

'Cousin,' she said the following morning as soon as Jill was awake. 'Please, for your brother's sake if not for mine, don't tell on me! Let me tell them myself, in my own time. Will you?'

Jill thought a moment then announced her decision, which was that she agreed to keep the secret provided Jennifer riddled out the cinders every morning from then on, instead of taking it in turns.

So she agreed to that bargain, and for a few days more kept the secret to herself, still hopeful that she might be mistaken, and yet at the same time aware of a feeling of inner triumph at the knowledge that she had her very own baby growing inside her womb.

A few evenings later, in Russell's alehouse, Ralph Bryant told Pascoe that as far as he was concerned, there was no reason why they should not sail on the Sunday following.

'And it were better we sailed sooner than later,' he added. 'The autumn gales'll be on us in a few weeks, and the volunteers won't be so easy to come by after that.'

Harry quaffed down his ale and called to Marion Treffry for more. 'Let's hope you're right,' he muttered. 'I could do with another half-dozen ship-boys.' he snorted. 'Tied to their mothers' apron strings, half of them, that's the trouble.'

'We'll have a last-minute rush, more than likely. You know how it is with volunteers, Pascoe. As like as not, we'll have more than we can quarter by Sunday.' Bryant turned to Marion, who had arrived with a full jug of ale. 'Your brother Davy made up his mind yet, has he, my dear?'

The girl dimpled. 'I don't know, sir.'

'Well if he doesn't soon, it'll be too late, and he'll have missed the chance of a lifetime.'

Marion Treffry looked uncomfortable. There had been a lot of talk among the customers about Harry Pascoe's venture to the Americas, and not all of it had been complimentary. 'I'll tell him that, sir,' she said tactfully, and moved away.

Harry looked round the crowded room. It had been all very well announcing that he was going to make a privateering cruise, but the preparations for it and the difficulties in getting a crew together had been enormous. Now, having already risked a considerable outlay on refitting and storing the ship, he was faced with the possibility of having to sail from Polruan with several hands short of a full complement.

Bryant interrupted his thoughts, and by what he said, seemed to have read them as well.

'I tell you one way you'll recruit a few more of the local lads,' he remarked.

'How's that?'

Bryant hesitated a moment: he knew Pascoe well, and was aware that he did not take easily to unsolicited advice.

'Take Tristram along as a younker, and let it be known in the village you're doing so. That'll loosen a few apron strings, I guarantee it.'

Pascoe glanced quickly at his navigator who, over the years, had often been the source of sound advice. Although he didn't like the thought of having his own son sail with him, the idea did present one advantage at least: by doing so, he would put a stop to any further goings on between Tristram and Jennifer.

'I'll think on't,' he said, and having drained his tankard again, pushed his chair back, tossed a few pence to Marion, and elbowed his way to the door.

He thought about it all the way up to Hill House. 'Where is he?' he demanded on entering the kitchen.

Jill and her mother were up to their elbows in flour. 'Out playing games, Father,' Jill replied with a hint of disapproval in her voice. 'With Jennifer and Nathan.'

'Is he indeed,' muttered her father, and went through to the back where there was a newly planted orchard and a herb garden. There he found them playing tig round the apple trees. For a few moments he watched them, and hearing their laughter and seeing the flush of innocent enjoyment in their faces he felt a sudden bitter pang of resentment that they should have their youth still and be free to enjoy it.

'Master Tristram!' he bellowed, and the game was ended.

He came across immediately. 'Yes, Father?'

Looking down into his eyes, Harry Pascoe knew instinctively that there was in Tristram the makings of the sort of man he would have liked to have been himself: a man of honour, a man untroubled by jealousy or a guilty conscience. The knowledge of it caused a strange mixture of pride and jealousy, love and hatred, which troubled him and even now made him stay his hand before announcing his decision. But wasn't it for the best that his son be separated from Jennifer? Could anyone deny that it was unhealthy for a young man to become attached to a girl so early in life? He glanced across at her: she had stopped playing and was watching them, and the resemblance of her to Martha was so strong that all the old bitterness and resentment flooded suddenly back. If I can't have her, he thought, I'm damned if he shall, either.

'What's this, playing infant games still?' he demanded, and was gratified to see the flush of embarrassment in Tristram's cheek. 'Well I've news for you, Master Pascoe. Mr Bryant has suggested to me that it would be no bad thing to have your youngself aboard the *Russell* when we sail Sunday next, and I've agreed. It's time we made a man of you, aye, and time you stopped fooling with girls and halfwits.'

Tristram's face went white. Over by the apple trees Jennifer had covered her mouth with her hands.

Harry chortled. 'Well say something, boy, if it's only goodbye!'

Tristram turned to Jennifer, and she came and stood at his side. Seeing them like that, and the strange fear in their faces, stirred Harry in a way he could not quite understand, and for a moment he almost felt sorry for them.

'Well?' he said.

'Father – is it possible – is it possible that Jennifer and me could be wed before I go with you?'

'Wed?' Harry let out a great snort. '*Wed*?'

Behind him, Ann had come out of the kitchen with Matthew clutching her skirt. Pascoe turned to her. 'What sort of ideas have you been putting into his head, woman?'

'Uncle,' said Jennifer suddenly, 'there's something you should know.' She bowed her head and shook it, as if by doing so she might rid herself of what she had to say. 'I'm with child,' she whispered, and faced them, tears going down her cheeks.

He was taken in for a moment, and believed her. But then he saw that he could not afford to believe her, because if he did he would allow her a tactical advantage, a small victory that would lead to greater ones.

'Oh aye?' he muttered. 'That sounds very convenient to me, that does.' He turned to Ann. 'Did you know about this, Wife?'

Ann shook her head.

'What about you, Jill?' he asked his daughter, who had come out to see what the crisis was about. 'Did you know Miss Jenny was in the family way?'

'No, Father!' Jill replied, looking quite scandalized.

'Yes she did!' blurted out Jennifer. 'She did so! She found out a week back!'

'Jennifer wouldn't lie to you, Father,' Tristram said in a low voice.

Nathan had come up now, and placed a heavy hand on Tristram's shoulder. 'Hollo!' he boomed. 'Hollo, Tistum!'

Harry's eyes narrowed, and he swayed from side to side, shooting malevolent glances back and forth between Tristram and Jennifer. 'I suppose you're thinking I'll be so frightened of scandal I'll say yes, is that it? Well that's where you're in error, both of you, because I've set my course as far as you're concerned, Master Tristram, and now I'll hold to it. You'll be aboard my ship when we sail on the Sunday tide, and I'll warrant you'll thank me for it in the years to come. And if you think I'm to be taken in that easy, Miss Jennifer, then think again!' and muttering to himself that it was as great a pity to see women weep as geese go barefoot, he took Ann by the arm and went back into his house.

After he had gone Tristram and Jennifer went down to the end of the orchard where they could be out of sight of the house. There they stood for a long time by a low stone wall, staring hopelessly out at the yellow fields of stubble, where the wheatsheaves were stooked and ready for gathering into the barn.

'A curse on him!' he whispered suddenly. 'A curse on him!'

She leant against him, her head turned to one side beneath his chin, her arms tight round him. 'No, Trist,' she whispered. 'You mustn't say that. Curses never bring good to those that lay them. Besides – he may change his mind.'

She felt him heave a great sigh, and when she looked up saw tears running freely down his cheeks.

'He won't change his mind,' he muttered bitterly. 'Not my father.'

Ralph Bryant read out the hundred and seventh psalm the following Sunday at the morning service in St Saviour's, and the congregation listened with rapt attention to those words which applied so directly to the men and boys who were to sail in the *Russell* that day:

'They that go down to the sea in ships and occupy their business in great waters; these men see the works of the Lord and his wonders in the deep . . . so when they cry unto the Lord in their trouble He delivereth them out of their distress. For He maketh the storm to cease so that the waves thereof are still. . . .'

Many of the women wept unashamedly, for Tristram was not the only Polruan boy to be going to sea for the first time. There was Davy Treffry and little Nick Polwhele who was only thirteen; and Tom Rowe, whose father had been lost at sea three months before. Their mothers and sisters looked upon them in a new way, because until now they had been sons and brothers, but were from that day to be turned into men by the strictest mistress of all.

So they sang the old hymns with tears in their eyes and an ache of pride in their hearts. Kneeling in the pews they bent their heads to join Mr Drew in the Lord's Prayer and sang that great Lutheran hymn, 'All people that on earth do dwell' in a defiant way that is peculiar to the English, and to the people of the west country in particular.

And then it was over, and they were coming out into the grey, windy day, the mothers trying not to look at the white-capped sea beyond the point, the boys suddenly gruff and silent now that the moment of parting was come.

Ann thought it unseemly to kiss her husband in public, but she had no such reservations as far as her son was concerned, and hugged him tight, choking on her words as she whispered to him to take care of himself. 'And say your prayers regular, Tristram, that the good Lord may bring you back safe to us,' she added before turning quickly away to leave him face to face with Jennifer.

Lost for words, he looked shyly down at her, smiling sadly so that his dark eyebrows puckered into a frown.

She put her hand in her bosom and took out the silver medal. 'Help me off with it,' she whispered. 'I want you to have it. Please, Trist. Put it round your neck and wear it always, and when you come home, you can give it me back on our wedding day.'

She put the chain over his head and tucked the medal under his shirt. She felt that her heart would burst with the ache of love, and searched in her mind for words that would bind him to her and bring him back.

'It's me that's the only one who can make you happy, Trist. You'll not forget that, will you?'

'No,' he whispered. 'I'll not forget.'

He could still not understand what was happening to him, or the far-reaching effects it must have upon his life.

'I suppose it's goodbye, then,' he said; and when she replied 'Yes, I suppose 'tis,' it was as if an invisible wall sprang up between them.

There was nothing more he could say: all that remained was to turn from her, pick up his bundle of clothes and hurry to catch up his father and Mr Bryant, who were already striding away down to the harbour.

Tristram the Navigator

The coxswain of the *Russell*, Jan Lanyon, was waiting with the boat when Pascoe came down to the landing stage with his navigator and his son. Seeing this formal reception, Tristram hung back to allow his elders into the boat first but Lanyon, who had served with Pascoe since before the *Russell* was laid down, put him wise.

'You first, lad,' he said. 'The master's always last into the boat and first out.'

As the oarsmen gave way and the boat started out towards the ship, Tristram sat in the bows and looked back at the little cluster of houses and the narrow street that went steeply up through the village to the church; and with every dip and jerk of the oars, he saw the gap between himself and his past life widening. Lord, he prayed silently, bring us all back safe one day.

Lanyon shouted, 'Way 'nough!' and the boat went alongside. The three passengers went nimbly up a Jacob's ladder, and Tristram jumped down onto the deck.

On board there was a confusion of activity. Fresh provisions had arrived alongside only minutes before, and were being struck down to the storerooms by a gang of swabbers under the charge of the captain of the hold. Up for'd, the forecastlemen were hoisting the fore-course in ties, and half a dozen ship-boys were already aloft to bend the heavy canvas to the yard. Abaft the mainmast the main topmen were taking the anchor hawser to the midships windlass and being cursed at by the bosun for trying to use the wrong-size block; while right out on the bowsprit, Davy Treffry was retrieving the spritsail brail, as a lesson to him for letting the end go.

Tristram followed Mr Bryant and his father up the accommodation ladder to the aftercastle, where the lashings were being taken off the whipstaff and the mizzenmen were making ready to hoist the lateen sail. Although he had been on board his father's ship before, Tristram had never sailed in her, for he had not been intended for a sea life, and it was only now that he began to appreciate how little he knew.

Unsure where to go or what to do, he decided to keep out of the way, and contented himself with learning as much as he could by watching the operation of putting to sea.

His father was a changed man now that he was aboard his own ship. It was as if he had taken off one personality and put on another. All his customary surliness was gone, and in its place was a crisp and decisive manner that Tristram had seldom seen before.

One by one his yeomen reported to him: the purser, the quarter-master, the bosun and the captains of the three parts of the ship. The cockboat was hoisted aboard and the longboat brought close up under the stern for leaving harbour; and then the order was passed down to the men on the capstan to weigh, the windlass clanked round and round and within minutes the great iron anchor was coming dripping up from the water, to be catted under the port bow.

Half a dozen harbour launches had by now passed their lines up to the bows, and the *Russell* was taken in tow, the wind being south-south-west and blowing straight in between Polruan Fort and Fowey Castle. Thus the departure was not at all a brisk business but an agonizingly slow one, with the shore going by at little more than a walking pace.

At the water's edge by the fort, a crowd of women and children had gathered to wave the ship farewell, but the men on board had sterner business to attend to, and few waved back.

As they came out past St Saviour's Point they felt the full force of the wind, and the ship began to move uncomfortably in the short sea, rather as a duck, on entering the water after a spell on the bank, shakes her feathers and waggles her tail before paddling off into the main stream.

'Brace all yards a-port!' bellowed Pascoe. 'Stand-by fore-course, stand-by main, stand-by mizzen!'

Under the roared orders of Bosun Rashleigh (an immense man with a broken nose, a cauliflower ear and a filthy cap that he wore right on the back of his head) the men ran about the decks to obey, and the ship prepared to stand off on the starboard tack.

'Let go all tow lines!' Harry ordered, and up on the forecastle there were further shouts down to the towing launches as the lines were hurled across, snaking down into the boats. Then, having leant over the port side to check that all was clear, Pascoe gave the order, 'Let draw!'

'Let draw! Let draw!' repeated the bosun, and with a thunder and a clap, the great sails opened out and filled; the men sang in rhythm as they hove in the tacks and braces, and the *Russell* was suddenly alive, the wind singing in the stays, the great masts speaking their own language of creaks and groans and the first feather of white spray finding its way up over the beaky prow and onto the heads of the crew, who gave a cheer at this first baptism.

But Tristram did not feel like cheering: looking astern, he had caught sight of Jennifer, who was standing alone on the clifftop of St Saviour's Point, and the sight of her there with the wind blowing out her skirts and her face white against the scudding clouds filled him with a sudden ache – of love, of sadness, and of fear that he might never see her again.

He was still wondering how many days would pass before he would take Jennifer in his arms when a summons from his father jerked him back into the reality of the present.

He ran to obey, tripped over a coaming, and went flat on his face.

'Right, then, marry,' said Pascoe when he had stopped laughing. 'And what are we going to do with you, young sir?'

They were standing by the whipstaff, where Jan Lanyon was steering on the wind, squinting up at the sails and leaning back on the great spar as a gust forced the ship's head up to windward.

'I'd like to learn navigation, sir.'

Harry turned to Bryant, who was taking a transit bearing of Fowey windmill on St Kathern's Point to check the compass error. 'Hear that, Pilot? This son of mine wants to learn navigation!'

'A very creditable aspiration,' replied Bryant in his precise, gentlemanly way, and returned to the business of scribbling bearings on a slate and making mental calculations.

'Maybe so, but it were better he learn seamanship first.' Harry looked back at Tristram. 'Do you hear what I say?'

'Yes, Father.'

Pascoe made a sneering imitation of his son's voice. ' "Yes Father" he says! What do you think I am, some damned papist? No one says "Yes Father" to me in this ship. It'll be "aye, sir" to you the same as every other soul aboard. So let me hear you say it.'

'Aye, sir!' shouted Tristram, and lifted his chin rebelliously to meet his father's stare.

For a moment, father and son were eye to eye with each other, and in that moment it was plain to all that there was no love lost between them; then Pascoe turned, and cupping his hands, bellowed: 'Captain of the forecastle, lay aft!' and a few moments later a wizened-looking ape of a man called Garrett ran up the ladder to the aftercastle and touched his forelock.

'Here's an upper yardman for you, Mr Garrett,' said Pascoe. 'He's green as grass mind, but I don't doubt you'll find use for another hand on the fore-topsail.' He turned and shook a finger at Tristram. 'And when you can name every sheet, halyard, stay and clew line aboard my ship – every mast, spar, block and tackle; when you can steer ship in a gale, box the compass backwards and take over the duty of any soul aboard that I care to name, then maybe I'll consider inviting Mr Bryant to take you on as a younker navigator. Until then, you can live for'd and stand your watches with the rest, and if ever you're not first aloft when the foretopmen are called away, I'll know the reason why.'

That winter of 1575 was a long and bitter one. Soon after sailing for the Americas, the *Russell* was badly beaten in a storm off Ushant, and Harry was forced to put back to Falmouth for repairs. There, several men deserted, and shortage of funds and more bad weather caused further delays to the start of the cruise: first a week, then a month and then until the new year. So instead of sailing west under blue skies as Harry had promised, the ship tramped about the British seas to earn her keep. She carried coals from Swansea to London; French wine, salt and canvas from St Malo to Looe and Portsmouth; English soldiers and arms from Chatham across to the Low Countries, and yet more soldiers and more arms to Ireland, where the Queen's Lord Deputies were bogged down in wars with the Ormondes and the O'Neills; and although the ship must have passed within a few miles of St Saviour's Point a dozen times that winter, Harry Pascoe was in such fear of losing more of his crew by desertions that he never once risked putting into Polruan, and never once allowed his men any shore leave.

He held to his promise about his son's sea training, however: Tristram lived among the ship-boys in the forepeak, sleeping wherever there was a space under a part of the deck that didn't leak, flogged once a week for the good of his soul, awakened at any hour of the night, driven up the ratlines at the end of a lash and learning – like so many before him – that there is no worse place to be in a gale at night than the lee yard of a fore-topsail. So when the ship called in at Plymouth in late February, the crew was weatherbeaten and exhausted, the ballast was stinking and the ship badly in need of rummaging and careening.

But there were other reasons for putting into Plymouth at that time. Two years before, Francis Drake had returned to England with a massive haul of Spanish gold which he had captured from a mule train within shouting distance of Nombre de Dios, and although the expedition had provided the royal purse with a dividend big enough to pay for thirty warships, Queen Elizabeth had felt embarrassed by the success, fearing that it might provoke Philip of Spain to war. As a result Drake had been invited to lie low and withdraw into voluntary exile, and had gone to serve with the army in Ulster for two years to allow time for the wound to Spanish self-esteem to heal. But now 'The Dragon' was back, and rumour had it that he was planning another cruise. Excommunicated by Rome and increasingly threatened by the growing strength of Spain, Elizabeth was now less inclined to appease Philip, and was prepared to finance Drake in private while publicly denying any share in his enterprises. Privateering was therefore gaining more official approval and – as Harry Pascoe was well aware – Plymouth was the best place in the west country to hear the latest news and pick up the fattest commissions.

The *Russell* came up the Sound under spritsail, forecourse and mizzen. Anxious to make a good first impression, Harry had put on his best doublet and cloak, and was standing amidships on the aftercastle, bawling his orders down to the team two decks below, who heaved on the rudder tackles this way and that to keep the ship steady on her course. Steering on Plymouth church tower he ran in towards the Hoe past St Nicholas' Island and close in under the fortifications before bracing the yards a-port and putting the helm down to round the tricky bend into the Cattewater anchorage.

Slowly, the ship drifted on in a great arc, the anchor cable being paid out so that a stern anchor could be dropped and the ship middled between them. And then came that pleasant moment known to every mariner when the ship has got her cables and she's safe in a calm haven – the moment when there's time to pause and look out over the harbour to the roofs and spires of the city and contemplate the thought of a full night's sleep and a taste of fresh provisions in the morning.

Having put the fore-topsail into its harbour-furl, Davy Treffry and Tristram Pascoe (who had become firm friends since sailing from Polruan) were balancing nonchalantly on the yard and savouring such simple pleasures when the voice of Mr Garrett interrupted their conversation.

'Boy Pascoe lay aft!' he roared, and before the echo had come back from the fortifications, Tristram was running along the yard, swinging one-handed over the foretop and dancing nimbly down the ratlines.

Leaping down from the high bulwark to the deck, he ran aft and touched his forelock to his father. 'Boy Pascoe, sir!' he reported, wondering why he had been sent for, as Harry had not spoken to him once since the day they left Polruan nearly six months before.

Harry jerked his thumb. 'Come up,' he ordered, and Tristram scrambled up the ladder and stood barefoot and in rags before him.

Six months before the mast had changed Tristram. In place of the tall, love-struck youth who had looked disconsolately back at Jennifer, there was now a young man with not a pound of puppy fat left on him, whose sinews were like steel ropes in his shoulders and neck and whose narrowed, watchful eyes and salt-whitened face bore witness to the character-building qualities of a life at sea.

Harry noted the change in his son with a grudging approval. He turned to Bryant. 'Can we fit this ragamuffin out with clothes, Pilot?'

The navigator smiled cautiously. 'I have no doubt of it, sir,' he said.

Harry turned back to Tristram. 'In that case you can set about scraping some of the brine off yourself, boy, because I'm taking you on a run ashore.'

The Pelican Inn stood at the top of the Hoe and was a popular meeting place for the sea captains and local worthies whose patronage had all but turned it into an exclusive club. In the summer, customers could hire the terraced bowling green for a small fee or sit with their jugs of ale on the benches outside, and in winter the landlord, Mr Adams, made sure a log fire was kept roaring in the hearth. It was here that the powerful and the brilliant met to take their ease – men like Hawkins, Raleigh and Grenville; and the presence of such men, whose reshaping of the Queen's navy and whose daring exploits abroad were catching the imagination of every patriotic young man in the west country, itself drew other customers to the Pelican, some out of a need to mingle with the mighty, but most because of ambition and the hope of personal gain.

It was for this last reason that Harry Pascoe had insisted on his navigator accompanying him ashore and had dressed his son up to look like his lieutenant, and as he pushed open the door into the public parlour he was optimistic that at least one wealthy gentleman might have witnessed the smart arrival of his ship and would be impressed by his own commanding appearance and the seamanlike look of his two officers. But he was to be disappointed, for the parlour was so jam-packed with merchants, shipmasters and gentlemen adventurers that they could scarcely get in at the door, and their arrival went quite unnoticed.

'Three jugs of best ale, and make it lively!' Harry ordered, elbowing his way through the throng as if he were the Pelican's oldest customer. 'You!' he shouted to one of the serving girls. 'Let's have a bit of service if you please!'

'I'll attend to 'ee by and by, sir,' the girl told him, and hurried off to refill the tankards of a group of gentlemen by the fire.

Tristram saw his father's forehead go pale and two red splodges appear on his temples – a sure sign that he was about to lose his temper.

'God's vengeance!' he roared after waiting less than a minute, and grabbing another girl by the arm demanded, 'When are we going to get some service, eh?'

'I'm sorry, sir – I can't serve you afore they gentlemen. You'll just have to wait your turn, sir.'

'Now see here, woman,' Harry shouted. 'I want service and I want it now, understand?'

The girl went suddenly red in the face and her eyes filled with tears. 'I can't serve 'ee yet, sir. Now if you'll let me pass – '

But Harry gripped her tighter and let out a long stream of abuse.

'Who is this loutish fellow?' a voice enquired at Tristram's elbow. 'Do we have to put up with him? Mr Adams!'

The landlord – a small Devonian with rosy cheeks and a gentle smile – appeared from his back kitchen. 'May I know your name, sir?' he asked.

If Harry had wanted to get himself noticed that day he had certainly achieved his aim, though not in the way he had expected for there was now a sudden silence, and Tristram was so embarrassed that he wanted to sink into the floor.

'Aye, you can know my name,' Harry announced. 'It's Harry Pascoe of Polruan, and if I don't get some service soon I'll know the reason why.'

'Then let me give you the reason why to save Mr Adams the trouble,' another voice said from the back, and the crowd parted to reveal a small, swarthy man in his early thirties with a sharply pointed beard, penetrating eyes and a wart on his nose. 'The reason why you will not be served is because Mr Adams here is not in the habit of serving ruffians, let alone allowing decent serving girls to be browbeaten. So we shall all be much obliged to you, *Mr Pascoe of Polruan*, if you will take yourself off along with your henchmen, and in future choose someone your own size and sex to manhandle.'

Tristram had never before seen his father so completely snubbed. Standing with his fists hanging clenched at his sides, Harry glowered at the assembled company in the way a baited bear glowers at its antagonist before taking a swipe. But he took no swipe, and instead contented himself with a muttered 'Bunch of snivellers!' before turning on his heel and going out into the chill evening.

Bryant and Tristram followed him out. 'Who was it?' Tristram whispered to the navigator. 'Who was that gentleman?'

Bryant glanced at the young man and wondered at the ignorance of youth. 'That was Drake,' he said.

They went down through the Barbican to the Turk's Head after that, and Harry set about searching in the bottom of his tankard for his lost face. He was better known here, and his willingness to spend money won him all the attention he could have wished from the serving girls. He ordered oysters and roast beef for supper and a quantity of Gascon wine, and after the meal they were entertained by a troupe of tumblers who walked on their hands and threw backward somersaults.

Tristram was seeing his father in a new light. At home he had come to know him as an overbearing and sarcastic father who scorned women; at sea he had seen him as a good seaman, if a little weak on matters of navigation. Now, his face flushed with wine and his hands pinching the bottom of every passing serving girl, Harry revealed himself as a lecher and a drunkard, and Tristram found it hard to keep himself from showing his disgust.

He turned to Bryant for conversation. 'May I start learning navigation soon, sir?' he asked. 'That is – if my father allows it?'

Bryant had already been impressed by the way Tristram had taken to the sea life, and was well aware of the embarrassment Harry was causing him. 'We can start now if you like,' he said, and over the din of drunken singing and laughter began talking in general terms about navigation and its history, and the great responsibility that rested upon the pilot of a ship.

'What's this?' Harry interrupted a while later. 'Having a little lesson are we, Master Tristram?'

'We were making a start on the navigation,' Bryant told him.

'Is that so? Navigation is it?' Harry swayed about in his chair, slopping his Malmsey as he raised it to his lips. 'Navigation, eh? Well let me tell you something, boy. *I* can teach you the sort of navigation you'll never learn from Mr Bryant, isn't that right, Pilot?'

Bryant laughed indulgently. 'Oh – I'm sure it is!'

'An' I'm sure it's bloody right, too!' Harry shouted, and thumping his fist on the table, stood up. 'You come with me, Master Tristram, I'll teach you all you'll ever need to know about navigation! I'll teach you more in one night than most learn in a lifetime!' He winked broadly at Bryant. 'What d'you say, Pilot? Shall we point our cross-staffs at Venus tonight?'

'Not for me, sir, I'm for my bed.'

Harry punched his son in the belly. 'Then that leaves you and me, Mister . . . Mister Tristram, and I'll not take no for an answer.'

Rolling about from side to side of the road, he led the way down to a boarding house on the water's edge by Sutton Pool where a large, slatternly woman he called Aunt Nell welcomed them at the door. She bade them make themselves comfortable in her parlour while she fetched ale for them, and when she returned she brought down two sleepy girls who were still in their night things and who dumped themselves without ceremony on the knees of their clients.

Harry wasted no time, and immediately started inspecting his lady friend's topsides, which he proceeded to squeeze and fondle with the expertise of a connoisseur.

Tristram was full of ale and was also very tired; and although it had by now dawned on him that this was a brothel, he didn't care much what his father did any more, but only wanted to sleep; so having offloaded Faith from his knee he put his head back and closed his eyes, and within minutes was out to the world.

Some time later he became dimly aware that the girl was whispering an invitation to 'come up to bed', and the thought of a feather mattress was too enticing to refuse. After all – there was no need to be unfaithful to Jennifer – all he wanted was to sleep. 'There's naught I'd like better,' he mumbled and, kissing him wetly on the cheek, Faith put her arm round his waist and helped him upstairs.

When she pushed a door open however, he held back.

'Come on my lovely,' she coaxed. 'Never mind they two!'

But he did mind, for his father was coupling energetically with the other whore, and the sight of them made his stomach revolt. Turning abruptly away he went back along the landing, down the stairs and out onto the dockside, where he was violently sick.

There were no more boats running to the ships that night, so he wandered until dawn about the empty streets, trying to forget what he had seen, yet repeatedly reminded of it by the rats that humped along in the city gutters.

Bryant sent for him as soon as he arrived on board, and Tristram found him sitting in the great cabin with several charts and almanacs spread out on the table. He looked up and asked kindly, 'Well Tristram, and did you have much sleep last night?'

'No, sir. None to speak of.'

Bryant nodded as if Tristram had given him a detailed account of the previous night's activities. 'Where did he take you – Aunt Nell's?'

'Aye, sir.'

Again Bryant nodded. Then he said quietly, 'Don't judge him too harshly, will you, lad?'

'I don't judge him at all, sir,' Tristram replied, but the words almost stuck in his throat, and he was unable to meet Bryant's gaze.

The navigator changed the subject and became suddenly brisk. 'Now tell me, do you have any Latin?'

'No sir – '

'Then I shall translate for you. Remember this: "It is not necessary to live, but only to navigate." That's why I'm going to teach you. Are you willing to learn?'

Tristram's face broke into a broad smile. 'Sir – it's what I've always wanted – '

'Good. Then listen. First you must learn how to learn. Not by rote as you did in your school at Fowey and not as a drudge or at the end of a lash. You must learn because you want to learn, not with your memory but with your understanding, for once you understand a thing, it needs no memorizing. Now shut your eyes.'

'Sir?'

'Shut your eyes, lad, shut your eyes! Good. Now, imagine you're up in the foretop and we're four leagues south of Fowey. We're on our way home to Polruan, and you're looking northward for the old landmarks on the shore. What do you see first? If we are at four leagues, remember, and Fowey is to the north.'

Smiling at the thought of it and unable to stop thinking of Jennifer, Tristram kept his eyes shut and said, 'Marry, sir – at twelve long miles, I wouldn't see much more than the hump of the Gribbin and the hills of old Cornwall – '

'Very well. Now we're getting closer and you can see the landmarks much more clearly. No, keep your eyes shut and tell me what you can see.'

'Well sir, I can see the beacon on Gribbin Head, and then over a bit I can see St Kathern's, and Fowey Castle, and the old windmill at the top of Fowey Hill, and then hard by on the other side of the entrance there's St Saviour's on the hill above the cliff sir, and further along the Blackbottle Rocks and Lantic Bay – '

Tristram opened his eyes and found Bryant chuckling at him. 'You want me to go on, sir?'

'No, you can tell me something else. We're in the mouth of the Fowey now, and going between the forts. Where's the old windmill now?'

'Why – over to port sir!'

'And what compass direction would we be looking in to view it?'

'West, sir, or a bit north of west, for the sun sets south of the windmill from our house in midsummer, that I do recall.'

'So the direction we looked in first to see the windmill was north, and has now changed to west, is that right Tristram?'

He stroked the beginnings of a beard. 'I suppose 'tis,' he said, 'though I never thought of 'un that way before.' He smiled suddenly. 'Aye – you're right, Mr Bryant! It *was* north, true enough, but now 'e's gone round to west like!'

'So provided we know where we are, we can tell the direction of different landmarks, do you agree?'

'Aye, sir. I'll go along with that.'

'Now then – consider carefully. If we can tell the direction of a landmark when we know where we are, would you agree that by discovering the direction of landmarks with a compass we could find out our position?'

Again Tristram considered, and this time, instead of a grin, a cautious twinkle came into his eye, for he could see what Mr Bryant was driving at and was already captivated by the ingenuity of it; but he was just about to reply when he heard a movement behind him, and looking round saw that his father was back on board.

'Good morning, sir,' Bryant said very civilly, and got to his feet.

Tristram followed suit. Though there was no reason at all for it, he immediately felt guilty.

Harry looked down at the charts, then at Bryant. 'What's this, Pilot?' he enquired eventually. 'Setting ourselves up as a schoolmaster are we?'

'I thought it a good time to make a start on the navigation, sir,' Bryant replied evenly. 'Your son's proving a model student, too.'

'Is that so?' Harry muttered, and Tristram saw in his expression a look he had often seen before but had never properly understood. What was it

– shame? Contempt? Or simply hatred? He didn't understand his father, nor what caused the enmity between them which had existed for as long as he could remember. It was as if that enmity were a living thing, an independent being which was kept in existence by them both, so that whatever one said or did the other automatically detested him for it.

'And I suppose he thinks he can mess aft with us now, does he?' Harry continued. 'Though for the life of me I can't recall telling him so.'

'I sent for him, Mr Pascoe,' Bryant said quietly. 'If that was against your wishes, then I take the responsibility for it.'

Harry had seen Tristram's brief entry into the room the night before and was inwardly ashamed. Even from his earliest years the boy had somehow been able to see right into him, as if he were his own conscience personified, as if he knew his every darkest secret. Even now Harry felt Tristram's disapproval as acutely as Tristram felt his father's. The boy's very presence in the cabin was like the foul taste of bile that lingered in his mouth from the previous night's drinking. To allow him to remain there, to share a table with him and witness his progress in the art of navigation – an art that Harry had never been able to grasp – was unthinkable.

Tristram seemed to have divined his thoughts. 'If you want to land me here, Father, I can easily make my own way home to Polruan.'

Harry felt a sudden whiplash of jealousy: at Tristram's youth, his popularity, his natural ability – but most of all at his love-bond with Jennifer. 'Oh yes!' he sneered. 'You'd like that, wouldn't you? Back to Polruan, back to your little papist whore!'

Tristram went white in the face and his lips curled back off his teeth.

Harry spread his arms wide. 'Come on then,' he taunted. 'Hit me, and see what you get back!'

Shaking visibly, Tristram let his fists drop. 'I wouldn't dirty my hands on you, Father,' he whispered, and went for'd to rejoin Davy Treffry and the other ship-boys in the forepeak.

Tristram was not allowed ashore again, and the *Russell* sailed from Plymouth a fortnight later, having been rummaged, careened and replenished. Though there were many in the crew who hoped that Pascoe would put in for a last visit to Polruan before sailing for foreign parts, this he declined to do, fearing that mass desertions would put paid to his enterprise. So in the middle of March the ship sailed out of Plymouth Sound and, with a brisk north-wester on the starboard beam, made a fast passage diagonally across the Sleeve, past Ushant and out into the Atlantic.

Harry's plan was to head south-west for the West Indies, where he hoped to prey on the traffic of Spanish slavers and treasure ships which provided King Philip with a large proportion of the revenue needed to further his wars and territorial ambitions. In doing so, he would be following in the footsteps of many successful privateers before him and – as he was fond of telling his crew – striking a blow for England against the evil of popery.

Now that the skies were cloudless and the weather fine, morale on board began to lift. Every day at dawn and dusk Mr Bryant's stooped figure was to be seen up on the aftercastle sighting the stars with his cross-staff, and every day hopes of intercepting a prize grew higher. From time to time Bosun Rashleigh (who doubled as the master gunner) took the guns' crews to drill, and the roar of the sakers and the white clouds of smoke that issued from their muzzles gave to all a feeling of heightened confidence and power. Meanwhile in the forepeak, an ever firmer camaraderie grew up between young Treffry, Polwhele, Rowe and Pascoe; and though Tristram was often ribbed for falling out with his father or being in love with Jennifer or wearing her Madonna round his neck, he was also respected and liked by the other ship-boys, who came to look up to him as their spokesman and leader.

As dawn came up on the fifteenth day out of Plymouth there came a cry of 'Sail-ho' from the foretop and a buzz went quickly round the *Russell* that the sloop which had been sighted was a Spaniard.

Harry Pascoe paced up and down slapping his meaty hands together and issuing orders. The bosun's call trilled and Rashleigh bellowed down the hatches: 'For'd part for'd, after part aft! Guns' crews stand to your guns, ship-boys to the magazine!' and within seconds the early-morning quiet was transformed into a flurry of activity. The gunners were shouting '. . .and, heave! . . .and, heave!' as the sakers and falconets were taken from their sea stowages and trundled into position; Nick Polwhele and Tom Rowe were scurrying about with kegs of powder, and Davy Treffry and Tristram Pascoe were staggering under the weight of several roundshot apiece.

'Ease bowlines, ease yard braces, bear away!' Pascoe roared, and took up his position next to Jan Lanyon on the whipstaff to con the ship into a windward position for the attack.

The gap between the two ships narrowed rapidly as the *Russell* bore down, and before they came to within gun range, the sloop struck her topsail and hove-to as a clear sign that she would offer no resistance. But Harry, having made up his mind to give his men a taste of blood, ignored the signal and held on to close the range.

'Sakers port side, with round shot, *load*!' roared Rashleigh, and a cheer went up as the powder and ball were rammed home.

As they closed with the sloop, the captain could be seen gesticulating wildly, and he began shouting across in Spanish, his voice little short of a scream of terror.

'What's the bloody man trying to tell us?' Harry demanded.

'Could be a trick, sir,' Jan Lanyon observed. 'She hasn't struck her colours.'

'Aye, you're right Coxswain, so it could. I think we'll do well to shoot first and talk later. Mr Rashleigh! Engage when at point-blank!'

'Light the matches!'

'Light the matches, sir!'

'Sakers – *fire*!'

There was a hiss followed by a roar and the first ball whizzed out towards the sloop; then another hiss, and a double roar – followed by an astounding explosion aboard the sloop that literally tore her apart and left her in smoke and flames from stem to stern.

'Gunpowder,' Treffry muttered as the sakers crew stared fascinated at their own handiwork. 'She must have been plum-packed with gunpowder. . . .'

In the water a few survivors were struggling and crying out for help, and many on board the *Russell* assumed that Harry would lower a boat and pick them up; but in this they were wrong: Pascoe declared that he had no wish to entertain any Spaniard aboard his ship, and gave orders to make sail again, so that within a few hours the *Russell*'s first prize was little more than a smudge of smoke on the horizon astern.

It was young Nick Polwhele who later expressed the opinion of the forecastlemen most succinctly. 'There warn't no glory in it,' he observed, and the remark was circulated round the ship, for everyone on board except Harry Pascoe himself knew that he was right.

A few days after their encounter with the sloop a rumour started that the navigator was sick. Although he continued to take his evening sights on the pole star he was not seen on deck so often and when he was, it was noticed that his servant supported him as he came up the ladder and helped him to hold the cross-staff as he aimed it at the heavens.

Such maladies were not uncommon at sea: no one had believed that the *Russell* would return to Polruan without suffering some losses, whether through sickness, accident or action; but it was unusual for the pilot himself to be the first to be struck down.

The rumour was confirmed one afternoon a day or two later, when Tristram was sent for by the master. The ship was rolling on under full canvas: the sea was a brilliant blue and white to the horizon and the masts creaking rhythmically as the prow plunged down into each wave. Men paused in their work to glance at the master's son as he ran aft and up the ladder to the aftercastle, and an hour or so later, when he had still not emerged from the after cabin, word went round the ship that young Tristram was being taught navigation by Mr Bryant.

He was required to work at navigation all day and every day from then on. He was excused all duties and relieved of all tricks as lookout and steersman. He carried his bedding aft and began taking his meals with his father, who said as little as possible to him and treated him as a stranger.

Having explained the rudiments of coastal navigation and the art of dead reckoning, Bryant proceeded to introduce Tristram to the mysteries of the heavenly bodies and their movements in the firmament.

'Listen here, lad,' he said one afternoon when Pascoe was snoring in his bunk below decks and the steersman was singing a mournful song at the whipstaff. 'When you're a league off a cliffy coast, the cliffs are no more than a finger height above the horizon, but when you're less than a cable off, why you have to crane your neck up to see the top of them. And it's the same with the pole star. The closer we sail to the top of the globe, the higher we have to crane our necks to see Polaris until, if we were able to reach the pole itself – which we can't, as it's covered over in ice – we should have to look directly up to see the pole star at an angle of ninety degrees; and conversely, the further down towards the equator we go, the lower she slips down to the horizon, until on the equator itself she touches it and the angle is nought.'

They were sitting on the poop deck in the sun, Tristram in nothing but shirt and hose, but Bryant, who had the bloody flix and was hollow-eyed and gaunt, shivering under a cloak in spite of the sun's warmth.

'So what we need first, is to know how high Polaris stands in the sky at a place we know – like Plymouth for instance, or Ushant, or Flores or Nombre de Dios – and then, if we can measure its height above the horizon, we shall be able to compare it with one of these, and so find how far north or south we are of that place.'

'But not east or west, sir,' put in Tristram, who was learning fast.

Ralph Bryant looked kindly upon the boy, and wished that he could have started teaching him weeks before. 'No indeed, and there's the rub, for that's more difficult, and we have to use dead-reckoning most of the time to do that. Now hand me the Mercator.' He paused, summoning his strength, and when Tristram had put the chart in his hands proceeded. 'See – along the side edge here, we have a scale in degrees, and these degrees, each of which represents three score long miles, correspond with the height of Polaris, measured with the cross-staff, from that latitude.'

Tristram had been longing to use the cross-staff for the past week. 'So will you show me how to use it now, sir?' he begged, and added, 'I do understand the principle of it, I promise you, sir.'

Bryant would have liked to go back over what he had taught that day, but he felt it important to impart as much knowledge as he could now, for an instinct was telling him that he had not long to live. So he took up the cross-staff and began to explain.

'See here: we hold this end to one eye, thus, and use the plumb line to find a vertical. Now, keeping the lower end of the crossbar on the horizon, we move it along the staff until the upper end coincides with the heavenly body whose altitude we wish to measure and – ' He broke off, unable to support the weight of the instrument any longer. 'I'm not the man I was, Master Tristram. Here – have a try, see if you can measure the angle between the horizon and the lower limb of that cloud.'

So Tristram took the cross-staff in his hands for the first time, aware as he raised it to his eye and took the angle between the edge of a cloud and the horizon that certain members of the crew were watching him and that as far as they were concerned, the very fact that he was using this instrument turned him into a navigator and gave him a new aura of authority.

'Now let me see,' Bryant said when Tristram had adjusted the crossbar to his satisfaction, and taking the staff showed him how to read the graduated ivory scale. 'There – the altitude of your cloud above the horizon was thirty-seven degrees, so if that had been a sight taken on Polaris, you can see from the chart here that it would give us a latitude equal to that of the Azores. So if that were the case, in what direction should we have to sail to reach Flores?'

'Due east!' replied Tristram without any hesitation, and his father came out on deck in time to hear Bryant congratulate him.

Pascoe peered over his navigator's shoulder at the chart. For a week before sending for his son he had struggled to master the principles of celestial navigation, but had made no progress, and although he was relieved that Tristram seemed to be learning the knack of it, he was also jealous of his ability.

'Due east for the Azores is it?' he remarked.

Bryant looked at Tristram. 'Well lad? Is that right? You were asked a question.'

Tristram got to his feet. 'No, sir,' he explained, feeling embarrassed that he should now be more knowledgeable about the ship's position than his own father. 'We were only saying that if the altitude of Polaris chanced to be the same as that – '

But he was interrupted by a cry of 'Sail-ho!' from the lookout on the foretop and thoughts of navigation were immediately forgotten.

It was not one sail but three, and as the *Russell* closed them it began to look as though the first were being pursued by the other two. From the foretop Davy Treffry sent down a stream of further information: 'She be under full press of sail sir, with her bonnets on and every stitch drawing!' he yelled down excitedly, and several other mariners swarmed up the rigging to get a better look. 'And the other ships – they look to be smaller sir, but lively withal and they be overhauling the carrack bit by bit, sir!'

For the second time in a week Pascoe gave the order for the guns' crews to close up and the boarding party to stand by, but this time the atmosphere on board fairly crackled with excitement, for the carrack was clearly bigger than the *Russell*, and more heavily armed.

As the distance closed however, one of the smaller ships astern of the carrack began hauling into wind to intercept the *Russell*, and when she was less than a mile off a puff of smoke appeared from her bow chaser, and a report was heard a second or two later.

'He's coming between!' cried Treffry from aloft. 'And he looks like an Englishman – '

And then there was another, louder report as the Englishman fired a heavier gun, and a moment later three plumes of spray rose in the air not a hundred yards off the Russell's port bow as the shot skimmed the surface.

Pascoe's reply was a torrent of abuse so foul that Jan Lanyon, who was a good puritan, looked askance at him and muttered that that was no language for a good Christian to use.

Having taken a while to close, the ships were now suddenly almost within hailing distance, and Tristram, watching the proceedings from the poop deck, saw that unless one or the other gave way there was a danger of collision. But what concerned him more was that the two smaller ships were undoubtedly English, and of the new type being built under the royal commission in Plymouth: they had the long, low lines and squat aftercastles, and were heavily armed with the longer-range demi-culverins instead of the short, fat cannon and basilicos favoured by the Spanish. But that was not all: in a flash of insight, he saw that his father had completely misjudged the situation: far from pursuing the carrack to attack her, these two English men o' war were escorting her, having already taken her as their prize. He saw it all: the *Russell* had been spied on the horizon, and this lightly armed galleon had been sent to intercept and ward her off. She had fired two warning shots, to no avail and now –

Now the two ships were bearing dangerously down upon each other; Harry was storming up and down the port gunwale, and every man on board was either cheering or shouting abuse.

Harry began yelling orders so fast that there was no hope of the bosun repeating them. 'Down helm, back the forecourse, let fly main sheets and bowlines, man the lee braces!' he bellowed, but as the *Russell* began to put about the other ship, intending to pass to windward, also altered, and a collision became inevitable.

Seconds before impact every man jack fled from the port side to the starboard. Then there was a grinding, jarring crunch, and the sound of splintering wood; and out of the chaos, as the two aftercastles bumped again and drew apart, an authoritative voice came to them across the water.

'You bloody idiot! Clear off immediately or I'll sink you by gunfire!'

Tristram turned away in shame, reflecting that only *his* father could be fool enough to challenge the Queen's own ships and collide with one of them in mid-Atlantic. He glanced aft, interested to see Mr Bryant's reaction – but on doing so his musings turned suddenly to horror, for the navigator had collapsed on the deck: his head hung backwards over a coil of rope; his mouth was overflowing with yellow bile, and his eyes were staring blindly into the sun.

They sewed him up in a canvas bag with a couple of rounds of saker shot to weight it, and when they had sung a hymn and said the Lord's Prayer, Mr Lanyon tipped him over the side.

Harry put on his cap. 'That's it, then,' he announced abruptly to his assembled crew, and beckoned to Tristram to follow him to the cabin. 'So,' he said, ducking to avoid striking his head on the compass lantern. 'You're the navigator.'

'Aye, sir.'

Harry regarded his son with narrowed eyes, his great frame swinging back and forth as the ship rolled. 'So how far are we distant from the Azores?'

'I reckon five days' run, provided the wind holds,' Tristram told him, being sure to err on the pessimistic side as Bryant had advised him.

Harry stroked the underside of his beard and wondered if he would have to turn back for England. The collision had sprung a couple of strakes on the port side which would leak if they encountered heavy weather. He had no confidence in his son's navigating ability and didn't feel able to rely on him to make a safe landfall in the West Indies. But all was not lost: the island of Flores provided a good anchorage where they could repair the ship and replenish with fresh provisions and water, and he might be able to use it as a base for privateering operations against Spanish shipping bound eastward for Seville.

'And the course is due east,' he said, more as a statement than a question. 'So the wind's fair.'

'Er – not due east, sir.'

Pascoe turned. 'What d'you mean, "not due east"? I heard Bryant say so with my own ears. They were the last words I heard from him.'

On any other occasion Tristram would probably have bowed to his father's pronouncement, preferring to let him find his mistake in his own time; but if he was certain of nothing else it was that the previous evening Mr Bryant had taken the elevation of the pole star and found it to be forty-one degrees, which put the *Russell* in a latitude that was over a hundred miles north of the Azores.

Telling Harry Pascoe he was wrong was dangerous in any circumstances however, so he proceeded with caution. 'Sir – when you came up on deck, we were not speaking of the ship's actual position,' he said uneasily. 'In fact, I had taken the altitude of a cloud which, had it applied to Polaris, would have put us in the latitude of the Azores, and when you came up on deck, Mr Bryant was merely testing me with a question that was – was, as he called it, "hypothetical". You see sir, it was not a real question. That is – the question was not founded on our ship's real position, but rather the imaginary position that would have been deduced had the elevation of Polaris been equal to that of the cloud.'

He stopped, and saw in his father's expression that same old look of surly disdain he had seen so many times before, the look that had made it clear to him from his earliest years that he was good for nothing and would never make his way in the world, the look that had spurred him, year after year, to prove himself – whether by daring to scale the sheerest cliffs or take on the strongest adversary or risk a day in Fowey stocks by swimming in the sea.

'In short, sir,' he concluded, his heart thumping in his rib cage, 'it's my judgement that we should first steer south until we reach the latitude of the Azores, and then proceed east. If we don't do that, I fear there's a danger we might pass clear to the north of Flores.'

Harry spread the chart out on the table. He placed his massive hands on either side of it and stared down at it in silence. 'That's what you think, is it?'

'Aye, sir.'

'Though I heard with my own ears Mr Bryant say the course was east.'

'No, sir. What you heard him say – '

Harry's face mottled suddenly. 'What I heard him say was that the course was east!' he thundered. 'But of course Mister bloody Tristram Pascoe thinks he knows better! The course for the Azores is east, I tell you! East, east, east!' and he smashed his fist down on the table so violently that a pewter mug jumped over the fiddle and rolled on the deck at his feet.

For a few moments they were in direct confrontation all over again, Harry's face working with fury, and a pulse throbbing in Tristram's cheek as he struggled to keep calm.

'If you want me to navigate this ship for you, you'll have to trust my judgement, Father,' he said quietly, but his words were like cold water on red-hot iron.

'Don't "Father" me!' Harry roared. 'Get out of here! Get for'd and stay for'd where you belong!' and following Tristram on deck he went to the top of the ladder to the waist and summoned the captain of the forecastle. 'Mr Garrett! Put a pail in this swabber's hand and tell him to navigate it round the bilges!'

'Talking when you should have been listening, Trist?' Davy Treffry enquired, and winked at the other ship-boys; but for once Tristram was not inclined to take the joke in good part. Instead he went for'd to the eyes of the ship and stayed there until long after sunset, gazing out at the dark, tumbling waves and wondering how to convince his father of his error and persuade him to steer a sensible course.

The trade wind blew steadily, day and night. Looking over the side at the froth of bubbles, Tristram estimated that the ship was making good a speed of five knots, which meant a daily distance run of a hundred and twenty miles. At that rate, he calculated, the ship would pass to the north of the Azores after three days.

Using a sharp knife on the deck of the forepeak, he etched out a map of the eastern Atlantic as he remembered it from Mr Bryant's Mercator chart, and as each day passed and the *Russell* sailed further and further east, he kept a record of notched dead-reckoning positions, so that if ever the time came when his father turned again to him for assistance, he would have some idea of how far west the ship was of the Lusitanian peninsula. Remembering Mr Bryant's account of the earliest means of navigation used for centuries by Phoenician and Arab sailors, he also constructed for himself a crude means of checking the altitude of Polaris: with a weighted length of fishing line attached to the end of a long staff, and with Davy Treffry helping him to hold it steady and Nick Polwhele marking the horizon line with his thumb, he was able to record the elevation with a knot, so that any significant movement north or south could be detected.

At first his primitive efforts at navigation were a subject of derision among the crew and they nicknamed him Vasco da Gama; but when the days turned into a week and no sign of the Azores hove up over the horizon, the first whisperings of unease began spreading between decks, and Tristram found that an increasing interest was being taken in the little notched position mark he placed on his makeshift chart at sunset each day, and that the jokes about moonraking or gathering stardust when he sighted the pole star with his stave were becoming fewer.

Gradually, the weather changed. From blowing steadily north-east for day after day, the wind began dropping away at night and freshening to a small northerly gale every afternoon.

It was damper, too: when the moon rose on the ninth evening following Bryant's death, it was encircled by a pale, misty circle, and by dawn the *Russell* was enveloped in fog.

Harry was in his cabin when Jan Lanyon came aft that evening. He was sitting at his table under the compass lantern, whose inverted card gyrated back and forth with every heave and roll of the ship. Before him lay an old portulan of Africa, whose coast was hedged by a continuous bristle of named ports, landmarks, headlands and river estuaries – but whose interior, unknown to civilization, had been decorated with elephants, dragons, cameleopards and prancing unicorns.

Lanyon's heavy tread came down the six steps of the ladder into the cabin, and he rapped on the doorpost to announce himself.

Harry beckoned him to enter, and the coxswain removed his cap and held it in a roll between his hands.

The two men knew each other well: Lanyon had been coxswain of the *Russell* on her maiden voyage and over the years his way of sensing the smallest changes of morale among the men had proved invaluable.

'Well?' Harry said. 'Have you sounded him out?'

Lanyon glanced at the charts on the table. He had been summoned by Harry earlier that day and ordered to engage Tristram in conversation and try to elicit from him exactly where he calculated the ship to be. Lanyon knew very well that he would not have been given such a task had not Pascoe been reaching the limits of desperation over the ship's navigation, and he was also shrewd enough to see that by acting as a go-between for Pascoe he was performing a face-saving duty as much as one concerned with the safety of the ship.

'Aye, sir, I have,' he replied, 'but without much success. I think he has as little idea of our position as – ' He stopped himself. ' – as ever,' he finished, avoiding Harry's glaring eyes.

Harry tugged thoughtfully at his beard. 'But what of this cross-staff he's been playing with? Has he said nothing more about that?'

Lanyon shook his head. 'My opinion, sir, for what it's worth, is that he has no more idea than the man in the moon where we are. I had it from Frank Garrett today that he heard Master Tristram telling the other ship-boys that if his calculations were right, we'd be up in the mountains of Andalusia by the morning. But that was only a jest like, beggin' your pardon, Mr Pascoe.'

Harry shook his head gloomily and stared at the Mercator. He knew very well that his ship's company were losing faith in him, and was beginning to lose faith in himself. But what alternative did he have? If he climbed down and sent for Tristram, he would have to take his advice; and if Tristram claimed that they had sailed past the Azores, he would then have to decide whether to turn back or go on until they reached Africa . . . or Spain, or France – or even Ireland!

'Will that be all sir?' Lanyon asked.

He had practically forgotten him. 'Aye, that'll be all, Mr Lanyon, I thank 'ee,' he sighed, and when the coxswain had gone back up the ladder, he sat thinking for a long time: first about the ship's position and what course to steer; then about Tristram, and the long history of disagreements and conflicts between them over the past years – and finally about Polruan and little Jennifer, who had held such a fascination for him and who had reminded him so forcibly of Martha.

The ship crept on through the night. Swinging gently back and forth, a lantern cast a yellow light onto the fog bank, upon which the huge, elongated shadows of the masts and sails danced ceaselessly. Leaning on the whipstaff, Tristram stared as if mesmerized into the dimly lit box compass. Down in the waist, some of the crew were waiting for the dawn. Between decks, many of them were unable to sleep. Every man knew that they were lost now: some were already spinning yarns about ships that disappeared mysteriously, claiming that although the earth was a sphere, there might yet be undiscovered ledges and caverns where the sea poured down in mighty waterfalls, plunging poor mariners and their flimsy craft into the white-hot hades of the centre of the globe.

So when the damp, eerie silence was suddenly broken by what sounded like a woman screaming, it was not long before every man on board was awake, and terror-struck by this strange new portent.

Tristram was one of the few who were not afraid. 'It was no more than a great seabird, asleep on the water,' he told the men gathered on the forecastle. 'We nearly ran 'un down, and the poor creature went off in a flap, that's what.'

But the men were not to be reassured. Some fell to their knees and besought the good Lord to save them; others murmured angrily against the master, and many said that whether or not it was a seabird, such an occurrence was a sure sign of evil, and that Harry Pascoe and his ship were accursed by God.

In the morning Pascoe assembled the whole ship's company, and with Lanyon standing at his side, addressed them from the commanding height of the poop deck. It had come to his notice, he told them, that certain voices among them were making mutinous whisperings and croakings against him. 'Let those people know from my own lips, that the first man I or my coxswain here catches making mischief or sowing fear or dissension on this ship, the first man – or boy, come to that – who spins any more yarns of this sort will hang from the neck at my order and for the good of us all, for he'll not be croaking only against Harry Pascoe, but against the Lord God Almighty in whose Holy Name we set sail from Polruan this eight month gone, and whose blessing was given us in the church of St Saviour by Mr Drew himself.'

The men shifted uneasily, glancing covertly at their mates to see the effect of Harry's words.

'Let it be known here and now,' Harry continued. 'We have water and provisions a-plenty and can sail on eastward for another week with no discomfort. And, what's more, this change of weather we've had, this fog, and the finding last night in the morning watch of a seabird sleeping on the water, are all sure signs that we are nearing the coast of Flores, where we shall find a safe anchorage, aye, and dry land to set our feet on.' He paused, swaying back and forth to keep balance as the ship rolled; and standing directly below him, little Nick Polwhele couldn't help thinking that he looked like Cormoran the giant, stories of whom he had listened to at his mother's knee only a year before.

'So – cheer up my lads,' Harry concluded, trying to look a lot happier than he felt, and, having ordered Lanyon to make an issue of the last of the English ale, went back to his cabin to hope fervently for the best.

Another day, another night, another day: the fog persisted. It was damp on the decks and chill on your back in the night watches; it made rows of drips along the slackly hanging feet of the sails. It dampened the hard tack and ship's biscuits, the bedding and the spirits. Having been warned not to grumble on pain of death, some of the crew made a joke of it, and the saying went round that while you'd get hung for complaining about the weather you'd only get keel-hauled for sneezing. But whatever else Harry had said, one thing did make sense: more and more seabirds were being seen, and the occasional piece of flotsam and seaweed too, so that it seemed increasingly probable that the ship was near land.

But what land?

Tristram lay awake thinking about it. Since leaving the trade winds behind, he had not found it nearly so easy to estimate the distance run each day, and had given up trying to mark a position when his notches had over-run where he had believed the coast to be. Ransacking his memory for what the coast of Europe looked like, he tried to work out how it could be that they had travelled east for so long without sight of land. The only possibility he could think of was that they had entered the

Bay of Biscay and might fetch up on the coast of Gascony. But wherever they were he desperately wished that his father would heave-to until the fog cleared in order to effect a less hazardous landfall.

Another forenoon dragged by, the ship creeping along under light airs which sometimes chased all the way round the compass, so that the sails banged and flapped lazily as they were taken aback. Then in the mid afternoon the mist began to thin overhead, until it was little higher than the mainmast, and you could see blue sky above.

No masthead lookouts had been posted since running into fog, as there had seemed no point in doing so; now, Tristram went to Mr Rashleigh and told him he was going up the mainmast.

'Is that so?' Rashleigh drawled sarcastically, and made a joke about putting his head in a cloud; but Tristram ignored him and went shinning up the ratlines, over the maintop and right up to the truck.

There, with one bare foot taking the weight of his body and one arm round the topmast, he turned to look for'd and saw a sight that sent a thrill of terror down his spine.

Rising out of the mist to the east was a mountain whose slopes were yellow with spring flowers, while much closer – barely half a mile distant – was the jagged top of a black, volcanic cliff.

'Land!' he shouted, his voice breaking. 'Land dead ahead at four cables!'

Running down the tarred ratlines, he was already conscious of the danger in which the *Russell* now lay. This was no time to go cap in hand to report what he had seen to his father, who would waste vital seconds by doubting the report and sending another man up the mast to confirm it. For the first time in his life he knew with an absolute certainty what he must do, and that certainty gave him a new, undeniable authority.

As he jumped down to the deck it was as if an invisible cloak had been thrown down upon his shoulders: a cloak of responsibility, a cloak of awareness of his duty not only to the ship, not only to his father and these men who stood staring at him in disbelief, but to himself. Hearing his own voice confidently issuing orders to lower and man all boats, prepare tow lines, strike sails, he was dimly aware that within the space of a few moments he had changed from a boy into a man, a man who had a duty to use his power of command to organize the towing operation and save the ship.

And he saw, too, that these men recognized the leader he had become:

a part of him that was quite detached from the urgency of the moment noted with relief and a little pride that the coxswain, the bosun and the captain of the foretop repeated his orders with as much alacrity as they had ever done for his own father, and that the men and boys of the *Russell* leapt willingly to obey.

Only one man dissented, and that was Harry Pascoe himself. His voice roared out over the pandemonium of shouted orders, of men running hither and thither and of boats being manned and lowered, and the effect of it was almost literally petrifying: men froze where they were and looked aft to the poop where Harry Pascoe stood scowling down at them like a massive monument cast in bronze.

'Mister Rashleigh!' he roared. 'What's the meaning of this?'

'We're on a lee shore!' Tristram yelled back from the forecastle where he was supervising the lowering of a cockboat. 'We must tow off or go ashore on the cliffs!'

For a few moments a silent battle of wills took place between father and son, a battle which was watched by every man on board, a battle that everyone knew must end in one or the other establishing his ascendancy, once and for all.

That battle was won by external forces however, for now, in the silence, came the thunder of Atlantic rollers, and at the same time the dark shape of the cliffs loomed out of the mist, towering higher than the masthead.

Without further thought, Tristram turned his back on his father and shouted, 'Full speed now lads, get these boats into the water!' and Harry was left on his own poop watching powerless as his son took charge with the assurance of one who knows not only what must be done but also how to do it.

They had the cockboat in the water first, and Tristram went with it, shouting up orders to Davy Treffry to throw down a rope, and immediately organizing Tom Rowe and Evan Goodall to start pulling for dear life in order to swing the ship's head round towards the open sea. Within minutes he was joined by the longboat, which added the muscle power of fourteen good men on the oars, and shortly after that the jollyboat was in the water too and another line being thrown down to be made fast to the sternpost.

And now the life or death struggle to tow the *Russell* clear began in earnest: swinging back and forth until their bodies ran with sweat, the oarsmen heaved and heaved on the oars – at first without any apparent result, but later to be rewarded by the sight of the bow swinging slowly round, and the frothy bubbles beginning to move away aft as the ship gathered an infinitesimal headway.

They rowed hard for upwards of half an hour, and that's a long time for any man. Gradually, but agonizingly slowly, they began to win: the prow of the *Russell* rose and dipped over the long, high swell; the coxswain of each boat cajoled his crew to ever greater efforts, and on board, two long sweeps manned by half a dozen men each were used as added propulsion.

Nobody noticed the wave until it was upon them. It was not much bigger than the rest, but just big enough to be breaking at its crest, and it caught the cockboat beam on and hurled it downwards and sideways under the ship's forefoot, capsizing it and throwing the three occupants –Tristram Pascoe, Tom Rowe and Evangelist Goodall – into the sea.

Neither Goodall nor Rowe could swim, and both panicked immediately. They went down the starboard side screaming in terror, their heads going under, coming up again, crying out. Lines were thrown down to them, and Rowe was lucky to catch one. But he was already exhausted, and when the men on board tried to heave him up the ship's side, he had not the strength to support the weight of his body, and fell backwards with a pitiful cry of despair.

Tristram had gone down the port side.

'A line!' he yelled from the water, trying vainly to keep up with the ship, but unable to match her speed through the water. 'For mercy's sake, Father, throw me a line!'

Harry looked down at him from the height of the poop. The ship was still close to the shore, and there was no line readily at hand. He was suddenly conscious that what was happening was the pre-ordained will of God, and that it was no business of his to interfere.

He turned away. 'Keep her going, Mr Rashleigh!' he called. 'Don't let 'em slacken off!'

Later, when they were clear and the boats were being hoisted inboard and stowed, Rashleigh came up to the poop to receive his orders for making sail.

'There was naught we could've done, sir,' he said in a low voice. 'They died like honest Cornishmen, and that's a consolation.'

'Aye, that's a consolation,' echoed Pascoe, who was staring aft at the black, satanic cliffs.

He turned and felt the first breath of a northerly breeze. 'We'll lay off on the starboard tack to make an offing, Bosun, if you please,' he said briskly.

PART II

PREPARATIONS

The Fugitive

Dom João was strolling in his garden with his confessor.

'I have no fear of fighting for my country, Padre,' he was saying, his small, pointed shoes clicking on the paved way between the oleander bushes, 'but rather a sense of responsibility towards Maezinha.'

Padre Jorge interlocked short white fingers across a well-rounded belly. 'She would not be entirely alone,' he pointed out. 'Maria Teresa will be here and I myself – '

'If I go to Africa with Sebastian, Padre, I shall want my confessor to go with me.'

'Ah,' said Padre Jorge. 'Ah.'

They walked down a short flight of steps to a terrace which overlooked the Tagus. Below them, beyond a low stone wall, the clay-tiled roofs of Lisbon made an umber patchwork, and lying at anchor in the harbour were the beginnings of a fleet that was being prepared to take the King's regiments south on a crusade to Morocco.

Dom João's predicament was not at all uncommon among the young men in court circles: having won a place as one of Sebastian's aides, he had now been invited to join the King on an adventure that seemed to many to be doomed to failure. But King Sebastian's love of riding and military exercises, his fanatical piety and his boyish good looks had made him the darling of every woman and girl in Portugal, and one had to think very carefully before declining an invitation to fight alongside him.

'If only I could have a sign. . .' João muttered, stroking his lips with the tips of his fingers. 'If only I could be shown where my duty lies.'

Padre Jorge nodded gravely. He had been João's confessor for nearly twenty years, and had heard every stammering confession of impure thoughts and actions, fleshly desires, lies of excuse and political manoeuvrings the young man had made in that time. He knew that João's marriage had never been consummated, and that its outward appearance was no more than a sham. He also knew that although this smooth, olive-skinned gentleman made a great show of enjoying the good life – of revelling in the company of his fawning friends, of staying up late gambling or listening to the *fadistas* strumming their lutes and wailing out their mournful songs – underneath lay a troubled, unhappy child, a child dominated by his mother and driven by an insatiable need for adulation and approval.

'I begin to think,' João said suddenly, 'that Maezinha may after all be right when she blames the loss of the Santarém Madonna for all the difficulties which beset me at this time.' He turned to the priest with a shiver. 'I can never forget that it lies at the bottom of the sea, Father, and that if the saying is true, I must one day lie with it.'

So that was it! At last the truth had been admitted: this son of a sea captain was terrified of the sea.

But Padre Jorge had not trained at Coimbra for nothing, and knew how to manipulate a situation to advantage. 'My child,' he said softly, falling back into the jargon of the confessional. 'There is a very simple solution. You must inform his Majesty that you have consulted your confessor on the matter and that he has suggested, in view of the ancient traditions attaching to the Santarém Madonna, that we offer special prayers to St Anthony and make a novena to Our Lady for the intention of its recovery, and that as soon as it is found, we shall gladly join the sacred mission to Morocco.'

Dom João blinked rapidly for several seconds.

'But . . . it would be nothing short of a miracle if the medallion were to be found!'

The priest smiled. João had always been slow as a child, and he wasn't much brighter now.

'Exactly,' he murmured. 'Exactly.'

They turned and made their way back to the house; and behind them, hidden below the low wall, Sara let out a long, slow sigh – both of relief at not being discovered and of disgust at the cowardly way out of the dilemma which Padre Jorge had devised.

'Benedicat vos omnipotens Deus. . . .' The voice of the Archbishop echoed under the high, vaulted ceiling of the Santa Sé cathedral, and he raised a frail, blue-veined hand to make the sign of the Cross.

'Pater . . . et Filius . . . et Spiritus Sanctus.'

'Amen!' responded the glittering congregation of courtiers, nobles, admirals, generals and Jesuits, and the building filled immediately with the soaring voices of the choir.

Kneeling before the high altar, a boyishly good-looking man of twenty-four now became the focus of all attention. Clasping his hands before him, he had thrown his head back and was staring up at the crucifix with an expression of rapt devotion, so that many of the women wept openly at the sight of their darling Sebastian dedicating himself to this noble, hopeless cause.

After several minutes of silent prayer the King rose to his feet, bowed to his great-uncle, Cardinal Henry, and, flanked by ceremonial pikemen, proceeded down the long, echoing aisle. He was followed closely by his bishops, his regents, his secretaries and his aides, and when he emerged into the blinding July sun, he was greeted by the hysterical enthusiasm of the awaiting crowds.

This was the long-awaited day that King Sebastian was to take ship for Morocco and fulfil his childhood dream of becoming Christ's captain against the Infidel. This was the day when all the arguments and objections put up by the late Queen Catarina, by Cardinal Henry and even King Philip of Spain were to be finally brushed aside. What did it matter that the country had been made bankrupt to finance the campaign? Who cared that the Spanish had already acknowledged the Infidel's supremacy in North Africa? What if the expedition had been hastily planned, and vital intelligence of enemy forces ignored? All that mattered on that brilliant, blazing afternoon was that King Sebastian was going to lead Portugal back to greatness and empire, that the cause was just and that, having invoked the intercession of St Anthony and the glorious and ever-virgin Mary, the expeditionary force that now lay at anchor in the Tagus must surely overcome.

Perhaps, therefore, the young Sebastian could be excused for swaggering as he made his way in procession across the Palace Square to the landing stage where he was to embark, and perhaps his councillors, aides and secretaries (of whom Dom João was one) could be excused for hanging on his every word.

Further back in the procession that now followed the King to the water's edge were other members of the Santarém family: Dona Marguerita, who reclined in a litter; her two married daughters, Maria de Graça and Maria Iñes, with their Spanish husbands Don Luis de Bertendona and Don Martin de Alvarez, and immediately behind them Dom Fernando Gomes de Carcavellos (João's best friend) and Padre Jorge, who walked on either side of the tall, serene Dona Sara.

Sara had been married to João for nearly five years now, but although she had adopted the style of speech and dress that befitted the wife of a royal secretary, her height and her bearing still marked her out as an *estrangeiro* – a foreigner.

The procession came to a halt: King Sebastian had reached the quay, where a galley magnificently painted in green and red and gold leaf and bedecked with scarves and banners, was berthed stern to the wall; and a delay of several minutes ensued during which Sebastian was seen chatting to his young aides, who clustered round him like drones about a queen bee.

'What are we waiting for now?' muttered Don Luis to Don Martin, and winking to his compatriot added in a low voice: 'Typical Portuguese muddle!'

Dom João came hurriedly down the line of the procession. 'If you would all come forward, and spread out along the quay, Excellencies, so that we can give his Majesty a proper send-off . . . that's the way, move right along the quay. . .' and on he went, repeating his message with a schoolboy self-importance that caused Sara to suck in her cheeks in the way she sometimes did when she had thoughts about her husband which could not be expressed.

The nobility moved up to the quay, from where they had a better view of the assembled fleet. In order to minimize desertions, the army had already been embarked. Four Portuguese regiments of professional soldiers formed the backbone of this army, and it was augmented by several thousand mercenary Germans, Netherlanders, Andalusians (who had ignored King Philip's veto on the expedition) and gentlemen adventurers. These, together with countless slaves, servants, confessors, catamites, whores, washerwomen and quantities of livestock were already cooped up on board the five hundred galleys, caravels, galleasses, foysts and zabras; and it seemed that the whole of Portugal had crowded into Lisbon to see them off.

And now the King was about to embark: he was embracing his great-uncle the Cardinal, and with a last wave to acknowledge a happy deluge of red carnations from the crowd, he turned and went down the brow onto the aftercastle of the galley.

Trumpets brayed and drums rolled; the lines were let go; the two long banks of oars rose in unison and as the blades slipped down into the water the galley moved smoothly away from the quay.

It was then, as the royal galley proceeded out into the main stream and the flagships prepared to follow in its wake, that a splutter of arquebus fire came from another, smaller galley that was anchored a cable or so distant, and for a terrible moment it seemed that the shots were being directed at the King himself.

A confusion of shouts came from one of the ships moored closest to the quay; men were crowding along the gunwales and pointing down into the water.

Sara was able to see what was going on over the heads of those in front of her. Something was splashing in the water between the King's galley and a large Andalusian galleass. She saw soldiers struggling with their long-barrelled weapons, balancing their weight on the ratlines and firing down into the water.

One of the slaves had jumped overboard. The sight of a man defying the laws of nature by swimming was revolting to many of the onlookers, and a great confusion of shouts and screams went up from the crowds on the quayside. Even the nobility pressed forward to get a better view.

Seeing the fugitive splashing in the water, Sara was reminded of the days when she had watched her brothers landing fish from the rivers of her home country. But that thrashing, splashing animal was a man, not a fish, and she was suddenly filled with a fierce hope for his survival. She saw a dark, shaggy head go under and an arm flail. 'God save him!' she prayed suddenly, while all around her were screaming for blood.

The diversion was quickly over. The ebb tide was running fast, and even if the shots had not found their mark, the would-be escaper must by now be out of range and being taken away downstream, where he would meet the watery death he was considered to deserve; and besides, there were other, grander events to catch the attention: the great galley, with the King standing bolt upright on the aftercastle, was turning to starboard and heading for the open sea, and behind it other galleys and galleasses followed, their long banks of oars dipping and dipping, so that they looked like massive waterborne centipedes. Shouts were echoing across the harbour as the caravels made sail; canvas flapped and thundered, and as the fleet went out past the Tower of Belem, a cannonade of gun salutes was exchanged, so that the whole city rocked and rocked again with the noise of it, and flocks of pigeons, disturbed from their shady perches on the palace balconies, flew up in wheeling clouds and swooped low over the fleet.

Now that the spectacle was almost over, João bustled up full of self-importance and reflected glory. Because he was a member of the royal council, his mother and sisters treated him with awe and reverence, as if he were a candidate for beatification. Maria de Graça and Maria Iñes wanted to know exactly what the King had said, and whether João had been able to convey to him their humble duty; and when João let drop that his Majesty had kissed him on the cheek, the ladies demanded to kiss him on exactly the same spot.

Dom João, basking in their adulation, turned to Sara.

'Well, dearest, don't you wish to place your lips where his have been?' he lisped.

'I feel hardly worthy,' she replied, but kissed his cheek with suitable reverence nevertheless, and everyone pretended, as they always did, that husband and wife were the happiest couple in all Lisbon.

As there was such a carnival atmosphere abroad in the city that day, João decided on the spur of the moment to hold a celebration feast. Surrounded by his family, friends, fellow secretaries and bodyguards, he announced in his adenoidal voice that he proposed to walk up through the Bairro Alto to the Quinta de Santo António instead of riding in the carriages, and that all were welcome to walk with him. Two servants were sent ahead to inform the cooks that company was expected, and the party set out, chattering and gesticulating and laughing among themselves, excited by this departure from normal custom.

They were scarcely across the Palace Square however when a shout went up behind them. Stopping to look, they saw a man running naked through the crowd. It must have been the galley slave who had escaped by jumping overboard, for he was still wet from the harbour: his dark hair was flying and scattering drips, his white teeth were bared and his eyes were like those of a hunted beast that is searching desperately for cover.

Perhaps it was his very nakedness that protected him, or the extraordinary animal power of his body – whatever it was, it made women scream and stare in horrified fascination, and paralysed the men into inaction.

Sara watched this extraordinary dash for freedom with as much fascination as anyone else, and was suddenly aware that she was on the side of the fugitive, and willing him to run and run and run for his life; and when two of the city guards tried to stop him by standing in his way with crossed pikes, she wanted to cheer as he made a feint in one direction then sidestepped and vaulted over a handcart, upsetting it in the process (it was full of dried cod) and dashing on, up a narrow alleyway and out of sight.

In the weeks that followed she found her thoughts going back to that tangle-haired savage. One hot night in early August she had a vivid dream in which she walked unclothed into an orchard and found him waiting for her among the trees; but although he reached out to her, and although she longed to surrender herself to him, something prevented it, and she awoke breathless and hot with a feeling of unsated lust so intense it was like a roaring fire whose embers retain a fierce heat for days afterwards.

She was in the chapel when João arrived back with the news of the defeat at Alcacer-Quivir.

A shriek from Maria Teresa announced it, followed by a babble of voices.

'No! No! I won't believe it, I won't believe it!' Maria Teresa wailed, and when Sara came out of the chapel, she found half the servants gathered in the hall looking shocked and white-faced.

João was already on his way upstairs to report to his mother. 'What is it, what's happened?' Sara asked, but he ignored her completely, and a few moments later a dreadful howl of anguish came from Dona Marguerita's room.

Following the example of Maria Teresa, the servants became hysterical. They buried their heads in their aprons; they clutched at each other; they rolled their eyes back into their sockets and pretended to swoon.

'*Ai, Excellentissima!*' Maria Candida sobbed, pushing her fat fists into her eyes. 'What will become of poor Portugal? When shall we ever see his like again?'

Bit by bit the rumours found their way back to Lisbon, and out of these rumours the sombre reality of the Portuguese defeat at the hands of the Infidels emerged. Sebastian and his fleet had made a safe journey to Arzila where the army had bivouacked for nearly a month while the staff officers argued among themselves about how to feed the men and provide them with powder and ball sufficient for the assault. At length, Sebastian's patience had run out. Ignoring intelligence reports of a superior force marching from Sallee to meet him, he had led the army inland, so that by the time it met the Moroccan army at Alcacer-Quiver food and water were short, the men were weakened by the desert heat, and the lines of communication with the fleet were broken.

The battle became a massacre, and was quickly over. Eight thousand Portuguese were hacked to death and fifteen thousand taken prisoner. Afterwards, a hundred and fourteen survivors managed to make their way back to Arzila, and one group, having difficulty in persuading the guards on the city gates to admit them, claimed that the King of Portugal was one of their number, and a rumour started that Sebastian was alive and would return one day like a messiah to lead his country again.

Soon after the defeat Cardinal Henry was proclaimed King, and as he was not expected to live long the court circles began buzzing with speculation about the succession.

Like many members of the court, Dona Marguerita was sure that when the Cardinal died, King Philip's claim to the Portuguese throne would be incontestable. The only remote chance of securing a legitimate Portuguese succession (and most people dismissed the claims of the bastard António, Prior of Crato) was the possibility that Cardinal Henry might obtain papal dispensation to be released from his oath of celibacy, marry the thirteen-year-old daughter of the Duchess of Bragança and get her with child before his death.

Having made successful matches with Spanish gentlemen for her daughters Graça and Iñes, Dona Marguerita saw this possibility as a threat to the family's influence, so when she caught wind of it from Padre Jorge she was careful to inform her son-in-law, Don Luis, who passed the report on to the papal nuncio in Madrid so that Pope Gregory could be warned in advance of Cardinal Henry's intentions.

Thus a bedridden old lady helped to scotch the plan from the start, and played her part in changing the course of Portugal's history.

Although the defeat of the Portuguese army was mourned as a national disaster, there were certain benefits to be gained from it and Dona Marguerita was anxious that her son make the most of them. Now that so many of the nobility had been taken prisoner in Morocco, wealthy families all over the country were bankrupting themselves in order to pay the ransom demands, and several valuable estates were being put up for sale at ridiculously low prices. As one who had been closely involved in raising loans to service the royal debts for the importation of pepper, João was in an excellent position to benefit from this situation, and on his mother's prompting purchased a large quinta a dozen or so miles north of Lisbon at Colares.

Soon after the sale had been agreed, João summoned Sara to an interview. He received her in the library, looking as immaculate as ever in white silk and blue velvet, his stomach protruding fashionably over his codpiece.

'Well, Sarainha, I have some news for you,' he said, pressing the palms of his hands tightly together.

She brightened immediately. 'News? Of Ireland?'

'No, not of Ireland. Of my estate in Colares.' He paced about, glancing sidelong at her and making little squeaking noises between the palms of his hands. 'I have decided to make you mistress of the Quinta de Piedade.'

She was quite taken aback.

'You've said often enough how you miss the country,' João continued, 'and I know you will find your life at the Quinta de Piedade agreeable. Well? Have you nothing to say at all? Am I to have no thanks for keeping your happiness and wellbeing so constantly in mind?'

She knew very well that his only motive in buying the quinta had been to make a profit, and that far from having her wellbeing at heart, the real reason for sending her to live at Colares was simply that he and his mother wanted her out of the Quinta de Santo António. But for once João's wishes exactly coincided with her own, and she was able to speak with complete sincerity.

'My dear husband, you are more than generous,' she murmured. 'I really can't thank you enough.'

Sara was taken to see her new home on a windy day in early October when the leaves were flying from the trees and the road was full of muddy puddles from recent rain.

She travelled on horseback in company with Dom João and Dom Fernando (both of whom were excellent horsemen) together with a small troupe of liverymen and soldiers. The day before, João had informed her that as the mistress of the house at Colares she was to have her own personal bodyguard, a powerful young mulatto known as Pepito, and he now rode alongside her while her husband went ahead, talking nonstop with Fernando.

They went up the long, straight road that links Lisbon with Sintra, and having passed through the narrow streets of the latter town, took a track that led anti-clockwise round the mountain.

After what seemed like an endless succession of hairpin bends and steep hills, they rounded a corner to find a valley opening up to their right and in the centre of this valley, through which the River Colares ran, a white-walled quinta nestled among orchards, vineyards and decorative arbours.

'There it is!' João called over his shoulder to her. 'The Quinta de Piedade.'

They followed the road in a long curve to the right, going through the village of Colares and on down a long avenue of almond trees to a shaded, white-stone square.

The house was built in the shape of an L, with an arched terrace facing south, a small balcony outside each of the upper windows, and a formal garden of evergreen hedges and flowering shrubs on the east side. Beyond that, the river ran swiftly between high, man-made embankments that were decorated with blue tiles, and passed beneath a delicately arched bridge fifty yards downstream.

The hooves clattered on stone cobbles, and the party dismounted. For a moment, all was silent, and Sara was aware of a great sensation of peace.

'So,' said João at her side. 'Do you approve, Sarainha?'

For once, it did not even irritate her to be called 'little Sara'. This will be *my* house, she thought. This will be where I hold undisputed sway. Aloud, she said: 'It is the most beautiful place imaginable.'

'More beautiful than Ireland?'

'As beautiful – but in a different way.'

Dom Fernando accompanied them into the house, which was still furnished, the contents having been sold with the estate.

'See these tiles?' João said, pointing out a wall design of primitive birds and beasts. 'Roman.' He led the way through to a large bathroom and indicated a fine mosaic floor. 'Also Roman,' he said, and the very brevity of his announcements added somehow to the feeling of antiquity and wealth which Sara sensed between these thick stone walls.

She wandered about the house on her own while the two men stood in the main vestibule talking about the purchase. She went out onto the balcony and looked out over the sleepy fields, the vine trellises, the orangery and the river.

Yes – she certainly approved her husband's choice this time, and felt a sudden lift in her heart. Perhaps this new house might bring about a change for the better between herself and João: perhaps, away from his mother's influence, João might find it in him to behave as a true husband.

How she longed for that! In the five years since her marriage João had tried only half a dozen times to get her with child, but each occasion had ended in fiasco and had been followed by further acrimony and hatred, and she had been forced to bear in silence the barbed remarks of Dona Marguerita, who made no bones about blaming her for failing to produce an heir.

She had sometimes been tempted to follow the example of certain ladies in court and accept the attentions of a secret lover, and had little doubt that had a good tall nobleman come along he could have swept her off her feet without so much as a murmur of protest. But so many of the Portuguese looked and spoke and behaved like João – so many, in effect, were small and plump and effeminate – that she had come to detest their fads and fancies, their fawning boy-talk and their unending whisperings and anecdotes.

Here I shall live away from them all, she mused. I shall have my horses and my books, my maidservants and my gardeners. I shall try to find a little peace, a little tranquillity.

She turned back from the balcony and went through one of the large upper rooms to the inner balcony which looked down upon the entrance hall. There, Dom Fernando and her husband were laughing together and telling each other what good parties they would have up here at the Quinta de Piedade.

Seeing João throw his arm round Fernando's neck and kiss him idly on the cheek, she drew back quickly, but too late.

João's laughter echoed in the hallway. 'Now look, we've scandalized the Senhora!' he exclaimed, and deliberately held Fernando closer. 'What's the matter, Sarainha?' he asked in a hard, scornful voice. 'Am I not permitted to show affection to my dear friend? See, look – we kiss each other so, and so, and on the lips, so. Now what is wrong with that, may I ask? What is wrong with that?'

Three weeks later Sara moved with her servants Ana and Maria Candida from the Quinta de Santo António to the Quinta de Piedade, and a week after that João – having obtained a dispensation to break the official period of mourning for the King – gave a large dinner party for some of the most influential people in Lisbon.

Several former members of Sebastian's royal council were there, together with a number of writers, artists and *fadistas*. Many of the servants belonging to the previous owners of the household had stayed on, and in the days leading up to the banquet long hours had been worked in the house to decorate it to João's requirements. Now the table was laid with solid silver cutlery, the walls were hung with tapestries from the Orient, and on João's express orders the cherubs on the ceiling had had the pink of their cheeks freshened by the finest artist in Lisbon.

While the guests helped themselves to the piles of grapes and almonds, and serving girls moved up and down the tables replenishing goblets from the jugs of Estramadura wine, a one-eyed, wizened man in his fifties was reciting his own poetry in a voice charged with a passion born of many years of hardship and suffering:

> The sky, the earth, the soothing wind . . .
> The waves that run upon the sands

Listening to the poet, Sara was reminded of her father and Ireland, for here was a real man, a man who had sailed to the farthest corners of the world, who had fought in sea battles, been shipwrecked, imprisoned, given up for dead. Here was a man whose poetry vibrated with that unmistakable sincerity of genius, a man who had risen above the paltry traditions of Portuguese literature and hoisted it up to the level of Virgil and Homer.

She looked at the greedy, self-indulgent faces up and down the table and sighed inwardly for the Portugal for which this poet, Camões, had fought and voyaged and suffered, the Portugal her own mother had remembered, the Portugal Sara had confidently expected to find when she stepped ashore to meet her husband-to-be for the first time.

But that Portugal, that grand empire, was already wasting away and her champion-poet with his little beard and sightless eye, his bad teeth and deeply lined face, seemed to Sara to symbolize the decay of the nation whose heroic deeds and discoveries he praised.

He had come to the end of his recitation, and while the guests were applauding, João stood up to make a speech.

'Most excellent gentlemen and ladies,' he began, placing his spread fingertips on the table before him and moistening his lips with the tip of his tongue. 'First, permit me to extend to each and every one of you here present my warmest welcome to the Quinta de Piedade, and to express my sincere hope that this visit of yours will be but the first of many.'

This overture was greeted with polite applause, and João continued, in his own precise way, to eulogize several of the guests. Sitting at his side, Sara glanced up and down the table at the gently fluttering fans of the ladies and the wine-reddened cheeks of the men, and began asking herself which of all the men present she might choose (if she had the choice) as a husband.

There were her two Spanish brothers-in-law, Don Luis and Don Martin, but the one was almost certainly one of King Philip's intelligence agents and the other had no conversation save on the subjects of property, horses and wine. There was that infamous womanizer Otelo de Tavares, who was undoubtedly good-looking and taller than most, but Sara had no desire to join his circle of middle-aged admirers. Then there were the various members of the nobility with whom João was currying favour for one reason or another, but most of these had fat, bored wives and visited kept women in the city three times a week. No, the only real man present that evening was Camões, and he was clearly exhausted by the rigours of writing as much as those of his travels.

João had launched into one of his anecdotes. That afternoon he had been out riding with Fernando and had returned with some poor wretch he had picked up in the dunes behind the long, rough beach known locally as the 'Guincho', or the 'Screech' for the violence of the sea and wind often to be found there.

It was by no means the first time João had picked up young men from the beach, and Sara had ceased to take any interest at all in such activities. What João did and who he did it with were his business, and she had no wish to be involved in any way.

'. . . and why, you may ask, am I relating this to you?' João's dark eyes were bright with the surprise he intended to spring. 'What possible interest can a half-starved vagabond be to us gathered here to celebrate, albeit a little tardily, the fifth anniversary of my wedding to Dona Sara? Let me remind you, my excellent guests, of the time only a few months ago when it was announced, with deep regret, that I would be unable to accompany our late beloved King to Africa. You will recall, will you not, my ardent desire to bow to the royal command, but my equally strong obligation to bow to the wishes of my dear Little Mother and to observe the clear sign given to us by Saint Anthony. You will remember the devotions to Our Lady, the novena we kept and the earnest prayers that were offered up every day for a month for the return of the Santarém Madonna, that priceless family treasure whose possession or loss carries with it so dire a tradition.'

While João paused to take a sip of wine, the banqueting hall was hushed as the guests waited for him to continue.

'Ladies and gentlemen – it seemed, did it not, that our prayers went unheard and unanswered, and there were even those who murmured against me, saying that I had used the loss of that priceless medal as an excuse for not answering the call to arms.'

He paused again, but this time for effect, and after looking slowly up and down the rows of attentive faces, proceeded with all the solemnity at his command.

'This very day, those murmurs have been refuted and the sincerity of our intention vindicated. This day, we have received the clearest possible sign that we were indeed well advised by our dear confessor to pray urgently for the return of the Santarém Madonna before going on that ill-fated journey to Morocco. This day, most excellent gentlemen and ladies, through the intercession of Saint Anthony and the glorious and ever-virgin Mary, the Mother of God, our holy relic, our medal, was found upon the person of none other than the young vagrant we took in and fed and sheltered. And this evening, before you all, I can prove this miracle, for that is what it undoubtedly is – a miracle not only of finding that which was lost, but one of positive guidance from above, guidance which we followed humbly, guidance which has preserved our life, for had we gone with our dear, late Sebastian we should surely have perished with him.

'Most excellent nobles, gentlemen, ladies – ' (here a gasp went up, for João took from his purse the Madonna on its silver chain and held it up for all to see) ' – I now return the Santarém Madonna to where it belongs – the bosom of my beloved wife.'

As he slipped the chain over Sara's head, Padre Jorge began offering a prayer of thanksgiving to St Anthony, and many of the ladies present were sighing and crossing themselves.

But it wasn't the medallion Sara had seen drop into the sea. She knew that immediately, for during her brief ownership of it during that last summer in Ireland she had fallen into the childish habit of sometimes holding the Madonna between her teeth when she was reading, and the silver effigy of the Virgin Mary had been marked by the unmistakable imprint of her incisors.

This one, while showing signs of wear, bore no such indentation.

The guests stayed overnight and remained in the house the following day, eating and drinking and smoking tobacco with João while the servants tried to clear up round them.

Anxious to escape the futility of their conversation, Sara went for a walk round the property and found the manager of the quinta inspecting his vines.

Joaquim dos Santos was a man in his early forties, and not at all the sort of person she would have expected to find working as a *caseiro*, for he looked far too intelligent and civilized for the position. But he was clearly devoted to the estate, which he tended with loving care, and although they had only been acquainted for a fortnight she had taken an immediate liking to him and there was already growing up between them the beginnings of friendship and mutual respect.

He took off his cap to her as she approached, and she bade him accompany her along the neat rows of vines while she discussed her plans for the quinta. She wanted more orange trees planted, a greater variety of flowering creepers and a fountain in the formal garden.

'*Excellentissima Senhora!*' Joaquim exclaimed, smiling indulgently upon her as if she were his favourite niece. 'There are a hundred other tasks to be done first, and we are short of hands.'

'Then we shall find you more pairs of hands,' she insisted. 'I shall speak to the *patrão* about it. Now these vines, do we really need so many?'

Joaquim was appalled. 'These vines were planted in the reign of King Manuel, my lady, they are my life's work!' He reached down and lifted one of the tendrils in his gnarled hand. 'I love these vines more than I love myself.'

She glanced at him quickly. She had already wondered how and why he had come to work here, but whenever she had asked him about his past he had deftly changed the subject.

'In that case let us build more terraces and plant more orchards. Let us have flowers – and birds – and fruit in abundance, Joaquim. I want the Quinta de Piedade to become a second Eden, a land flowing with milk and – ' She stopped, listening. From the lower warehouse came the repeated sound of leather thongs on bare flesh. When she looked back at Joaquim, he had lowered his head so that she should not see his expression.

'What's going on in there?'

'My Lady – it's not a matter that will be of interest to you,' he said quietly, and his manner was oddly authoritative, and not at all one she would have expected from a simple *caseiro*.

'Everything that happens here is of interest to me,' she said, and without waiting to hear his reply, gathered her skirts and hurried downhill between the vines to the storehouse below the stables.

Flinging open the door she was greeted by a sight so bestial it made the vomit rise in her throat. João, with Fernando and a few other friends looking on, was whipping the young vagrant they had taken captive the previous day. The victim was bound naked to the wheel of an oxcart in such a way that he was bent double. His back and buttocks were a mass of weals and blood and his privates were tied back in the cruellest possible way. But when Sara managed to look again upon his face, which hung upside down between his legs, she recognized him immediately.

It was the fugitive who had escaped from one of the King's ships on the day Sebastian had sailed for Africa.

She walked into the *armazém* and held out her hand for the scourge, whose several thongs were studded with balls of lead.

'Give me that,' she ordered.

João smiled and shook his head.

'Give it to me!' she repeated, but again he shook his head, glancing back to reassure himself of Fernando's support.

'This is no business of yours, Sarainha,' he murmured. 'Please leave us to do what has to be done.'

She held her ground, but made no reply.

'Did you hear me, Sarainha? We're not playing games, we're trying to get the truth out of him. It's your medal he stole, after all.'

She heard Joaquim approach behind her. When she glanced back at him, he shot her a warning look. But she did not heed the warning, and turned back to face her husband.

'He did *not* steal it,' she whispered, 'and you know it.'

They faced each other for several seconds, each sizing up the determination of the other. Then, abruptly, João turned back to continue the torture.

'Wait,' Sara said. 'If you try to hit him once more I shall place myself in the way. Do you hear me, João? I shall take the blow upon myself.'

João shrugged in disbelief. 'That's up to you,' he said, and raised the leather scourge high above his head.

Later, she could not quite remember how it happened. One moment she was standing to one side, the next, as the leather thongs screamed, she had placed herself in the way of them, and was aware of a white-hot pain across her face, her neck, her arms, her bosom – and blood trickling down over her cheek.

But if she was stung physically, her moral hurt was far greater. Careless of her own bruises, she rounded on them all, her eyes blazing and her teeth bared.

'Now – you – ' she said to one of the menservants. 'Release him. Joaquim – go into the house and tell Maria Candida to prepare a room and a bed for him.' She took the scourge from João's hand. 'I will look after that, thank you, João.'

134

They were suddenly speechless before her like little boys who have been caught out by their nursemaid. João surrendered the whip without a word, and the menservants released the prisoner, who collapsed on the earthen floor. Fernando and one of the guests made to leave the storehouse, but Sara called them back. 'No – don't go. You can carry him into the house. Gently now, mind his head!'

She could hardly believe it – they were obeying her, actually obeying her! She went with them as they carried him past the stables and into the house; she led the way up to the first floor, and cautioned them to take care as they laid him face down on the bed; and when they were gone – when everyone was gone, even Ana and Maria Candida – she knelt at the bedside and gently began bathing his back, whispering prayers for his recovery and weeping over him for reasons that she did not understand.

He opened his eyes.

'It's all right,' she whispered. 'You're safe.'

He had thick, dark eyebrows, a short but unkempt beard and eyes the colour of a rough sea.

'Are you Spanish?' she asked.

He tried to shake his head, and winced.

'What then? French? Levantine? Italian?'

'Irish.'

She felt a sudden rush of affection for him, a need to look after him and care for him. She began to weep and laugh at the same time. 'Irish!' she whispered, lapsing into the old brogue of Corcaguiney. 'My soul from the Devil, if he isn't Irish!'

She gave orders that he was to be waited upon only by herself, and instructed Pepito to sit outside his room and prevent entry by any other person. She went to the kitchens to choose his meals, at first giving him gruel and honey, and later white fish, veal and lightly boiled plovers' eggs. Before João returned to Lisbon, she made it clear to him that from then on her authority at the Quinta de Piedade was to be unquestioned, hinting that if she had any further trouble from him she would seek an audience with the Archbishop himself and apprise him of all the evils that had beset her since she first set foot on Portuguese soil.

'And I shall be obliged if you will in future address me by my proper name and not call me "Sarainha". I am a grown woman, João, and I insist upon being treated as one.'

João swung himself into the saddle and rode off in a huff, and when he was gone, Sara called all the servants together and gave them a good talking to, saying that from that day forward they were to take their orders only from her.

Afterwards, she heard Maria Candida singing an old Irish song in the kitchen, something she hadn't heard once since the day she sailed out past Beenbeg Point and saw her father and brothers waving from the top of Ballymacadoyle Hill.

She went up to see how her patient was doing, and found him sitting up. She sat down on the bed as if it were the most natural thing in the world.

'Now then, let's be hearing all about you,' she said. 'What part of Ireland do you hail from, and how did you come to be taken as a galley slave?'

He was very thin – she could see his ribs – and his eyes were hollow with fatigue and that animal caution that comes from being on the run. But behind the hunted, hungry look she saw an honest face, and the body, though starved and beaten, was well formed and muscular.

The thought went through her mind that having saved his life, she could claim his fealty. It sent a little shiver of excitement through her.

'Let's be hearing from you then,' she said briskly, showing no sign of her thoughts. 'What's your name?'

'John,' he said quickly.

She waited for him to go on, but he remained silent.

She stood up and went to the window, which faced north-west and overlooked the patchwork of fields where oxen were plodding two by two and gulls were following the plough.

Without turning, she said in a deliberately hard voice, 'I can only help you if you tell me everything.' She turned. 'You can start by telling me where you come from.'

'Cork.'

'Is that a fact? I'm from Corcaguiney.'

He looked blank.

'It's terrible short of words you are, John, for a man of Cork.'

He tried to smile, but only succeeded in looking sheepish. She was wearing the medallion, and lifted it from its chain. 'And how did you come by this, may I ask?' The fear came back into his eyes, and she wished she hadn't asked him. 'Tell me honestly, and I'll believe you.'

He looked troubled. His expression reminded her of one of her father's wolfhounds: it was at the same time loyal, loving, sad, and trusting.

' 'Twere given me,' he said.

'Do you have the Gaelic?'

He shook his head.

'What's your second name?'

He thought a moment, then looked up. 'Kelly.'

'So you're John Kelly from Cork, and the medal of the Blessed Virgin was given ye, you don't have the Gaelic, and you've never heard of Corcaguiney, is that it?'

He was trying to look her in the eye, but could not. He nodded, and she said to herself, If you're John Kelly from Cork, my lovely man, then I'm Queen Elizabeth of England – and no sooner had she thought that than she began to guess the truth.

'Well John, and is it a good Catholic you are?'

'Aye,' he said in a voice not much more than a whisper.

'Then you can do me a small service, by way of a thank you for what I did for you. You can say a decade of the rosary for me. I've not been home to Ireland once in five years, and it'll warm my heart to hear an Irish voice again. Will ye do that for me?'

She knelt by the bed in a businesslike way and made the sign of the Cross. She looked up at him. 'So. Will you be starting, please, John?'

His mouth opened and shut. 'It's . . . a long time since I prayed . . . I'm only a mariner, see – '

She remained kneeling by the bed, but put her elbows on the coverlet and her chin in her hands. She stared directly into his eyes, and this time he did not look away but seemed to be appealing to her for forgiveness.

'You're not a Catholic, are you?' she said at length.

He hung his head.

'And your name's not John Kelly, and you're not from Cork.'

She waited, but he remained silent.

'Tell me the truth, then. You're English. Yes?'

She saw him swallow twice. When he looked up and nodded, she felt a strange feeling of relief.

'I've never been to England,' she said. 'You'll have to tell me about it.'

She got up off her knees and stood looking down at him. 'So which part of England do you call home?'

He gave a great sigh. 'Cornwall.'

'Is that in the south?'

'The south-west.'

'How long have you been away?'

'It's . . . more'n three years now.'

'And what's your real name?'

He looked troubled again.

'You can tell me,' she said softly. 'I'll not tell on you. And if you like, I'll – I'll tell you about Ireland, so next time, when you're asked, you'll know what to say.' She smiled. 'I'll teach you to say a rosary and be a good Catholic, too.'

She saw the trust coming back into his eyes, and detected a softening of his expression that triggered a further stirring of feelings towards him.

'What is your name, then? Your true name.'

He told her. She went again to the window and looked out over the valley.

'Tristram Pascoe,' she said. 'Tristão de Páscoa. You know what *páscoa* means in Portugal? It means Eastertide. And when we say someone has a "*cara de páscoa*" it means he looks cheerful. So will you promise to tell me no more lies, Tristram the Cheerful?'

'I promise,' he said quickly. 'I do promise.'

'May I know your name?' he asked. Although he spoke gravely and with sincere respect, she was sure she could detect a trace of humour in those steady, ocean eyes of his.

'Certainly. I am Dona Sara Hussey Valdez de Santarém.'

He was silent for several moments, but it was not an awkward or hostile silence: when he glanced up to meet her gaze, she had a strange feeling that she had known him for a long time, and they had always been friends.

She smiled. 'It's a long title, isn't it?'

He nodded and looked shyly at his hands. She felt a sudden need to put him at his ease – to stop playing the lady and treat him entirely as an equal.

She was just about to speak when he looked up, as if he had guessed her thoughts. 'Which of those names should I use?'

They were carrying on two conversations at the same time: one was spoken in words and the other silent, the language of which was through the sudden meeting of glance with glance.

' "*Excellentissima Senhora*" is my correct title. Can you say that? Listen: Shlenteessima Sen-yora.'

He repeated it carefully, and she laughed in spite of herself at his attempt, biting her lip to stop herself.

'*Excellentissima Senhora,*' he repeated. 'What does it mean?'

She felt herself blush. She was sure he already knew what it meant. 'Most excellent lady,' she murmured. 'But there'll be no need to use it when – when others aren't present. You can call me Dona Sara.'

'Dona Sara,' he echoed. 'The name is as excellent as the lady.'

It occurred to her that he was exceedingly composed for an escaped galley slave, and his presence was having a strange effect upon her. His deep, burring voice and those splendid eyes had already worked some magic inside her, so that her heart was pattering faster and her body seemed suddenly more alive, more aware of itself. She turned and went to the door therefore, afraid that if the interview continued much longer she might say or do something that would give her away and indicate to him the extraordinary effect he was having on her.

'I have other matters to attend to,' she told him. 'I may call in to see you again this evening, and as soon as you are fit I shall put you to work in the gardens. If you would like that – ' She stopped herself, realizing that she was already going too far.

'I would like it above all else,' he said gravely.

She smiled faintly, trying desperately to maintain her composure. 'Then we shall speak further of it in due course,' she said, and left the room.

She took the path by the river to the orangery. Strolling beside the swiftly moving water, she experienced a sudden sense of freedom. She was mistress of this quinta: there was no João or Maezinha to spy on her or interrogate her. Providing she was careful, she was free to do as she pleased. The thought of it – and the Englishman – left her with a strange, pleasurable ache. It was one she had never experienced before but recognized and welcomed, because she knew that it was the desire of sex, and it forced her to acknowledge that she was no longer a child.

A week after coming to the Quinta de Piedade, Tristram was put to work in the gardens under Joaquim. The river had recently flooded, and much of the embankment below the house required repair. Stripped to his waist, the weals on his back still livid and raw, he worked all day under the *caseiro*'s supervision.

He slept on a stone floor with the servants in a long low-roofed outhouse, but having survived the rigours of life aboard an Andalusian galley, his new life at the Quinta de Piedade seemed luxurious. In the evenings, when the sun was down behind the mountain, the servants gathered behind the outhouse and fresh sardines were cooked by the dozen over a large charcoal grid. Jugs of Colares wine were brought out from the kitchens, and they sat round in the dust, eating the fish in their fingers and flinging the bones to the lurchers.

The winter rains came. Mists swirled down over the mountain, and quantities of wood had to be cut for the fires. The vines had to be pruned and the oranges picked. In February the olives had to be shaken down from the trees onto sheets and turned into oil. The road had to be repaired after every rainstorm, and parties of visiting huntsmen accommodated at short notice.

Then suddenly, magically, it was spring, and the fields and hedgerows were ablaze with flowers – more flowers than Tristram had ever seen before. Brilliant songbirds courted among the orange and almond trees; orioles flew in pairs over the terracotta roofs of the Quinta de Piedade, and called to one another among the pines above the duckery – and sometimes at night, when the hunter's moon was high overhead and wolves were howling in the forest, Tristram would creep out from the stables and stand alone in this Eden, wondering, as he had wondered so often before, how he might make his escape and find his way home to Jennifer.

He had never forgotten her. In the three years since that day when he had been swept up half drowned on the coast of Spain, he had never once given up hope that he would one day be able to find his way home to England and make Jennifer his wife.

Claiming to be Irish, he had slaved in the boiling sun in Seville, had been pressed into service as a foot soldier and shipped across the sea to North Africa. He had deserted, been recaptured, interrogated, beaten and sent to the galleys. Guarding his precious Madonna with his life, he had hidden it, fought for it, had it stolen and had stolen it back; and when his chance came to desert he had had the audacity to leap overboard right under the nose of the King of Portugal on the day he was to sail for Morocco. For weeks after that he had lived like a wild animal, sleeping in hollows of sand up behind the cliffs to the north of Lisbon, trapping birds, eating gulls' eggs and stealing melons and love apples from the fields until, like a wild animal, he had been run to earth and captured, and brought to the Quinta de Piedade.

But Jennifer – no, he had never once forgotten Jennifer. He had prayed every day for her, gazed at the moon to send messages to her, ached constantly to return to her and to see his child who must now be three years old.

He had remembered those few short nights under the wall by the beehives, and the way she used to whisper to him: 'Tristram Pascoe, Tristram Pascoe, never, never let your lass go', and had convinced himself that if ever he gave up the struggle to return to her – to hold her again in his arms, to marry her and be her husband and the true father of their child – then his love for her must have been a sham, and empty: for love, he believed, was not love if it could be turned like a weathercock by the wind of fortune.

Working on the quinta – whether replacing the stone cobbles in the square or repairing the river banks or wielding the mattock in the fields below the bridge – his thoughts were seldom far from Jennifer, or the problem of how to escape back to Cornwall. So although he was grateful to Dona Sara for saving his life and although he could not fail to appreciate that she was indeed a most excellent lady, he was quite unaware that he had made any sort of impression on her, and would have been aghast if he had known how often her thoughts turned on him, and how many times she watched him secretly from her balcony.

It was strange, Sara often reflected, how much easier it was to imagine events than to make them happen. If, on that first day she spoke to Tristram, she had been told that a year would pass before she spoke privately with him again, she would not have believed it; and although her new life at Colares was indeed an improvement on her cloistered existence in Lisbon, she was still virtually a prisoner of the conventions and etiquette that attached to her status.

She rose each morning at dawn and heard Mass in the private chapel. When João was not present – and he seldom visited more than once a month – she ate her meals alone or with her confessor, Padre Bernado. During the day she would sometimes be seen sitting on her balcony reading, or she would take a stroll along the paths that led between the neat rows of vines. But although she presented an outward appearance of calm and serenity, her private thoughts were a turmoil of hopes and imaginings: of joyous reunions with her father and brothers, of returns to Ballingolin Castle, of improvements in her relations with her husband or – and this last ever more increasingly – of conversations with Tristram Pascoe.

On the face of it, nothing seemed easier than to make his acquaintance: she was undisputed mistress of the Quinta de Piedade, and had she sent for her 'Irish' servant he would have been brought to her immediately.

Yes, occasionally she had paused to speak with him when she passed him in the grounds, but such conversations were limited to lofty enquiries into his wellbeing on her part and gruff declarations of gratitude on his.

Why could she not force events further than that? She longed to speak with him, to ask him about his country and to tell him about her own. She knew instinctively that they were natural allies – in spite of the fact that he was English and a Protestant. She prayed secretly (and also asked forgiveness for thus praying) that God would somehow bring them together, somehow make it possible for the huge gap between them to be bridged.

But the weeks passed and turned into months, and the months turned into a year, and the *vindima*, the grape harvest, came round again before she could bring herself to make the first tentative approach.

João and his entourage arrived from Lisbon in the last week of September. Their coaches clattered over the cobbles and pulled up alongside the main entrance gate, and when the passengers had alighted, each carriage continued along the side drive at the end of which was a wide square for turning and parking in the shade of an ancient walnut tree.

Suddenly the Quinta de Piedade was alive with bustle and chatter and noise. Extra cooks were brought in from the village to cope with the mountains of food that had to be prepared; extra laundry maids were engaged to wash the mounds of linen in the Colares river, and as each gentleman and lady brought a string of personal servants and body-guards, the outhouses where they slept became impossibly overcrowded, with men, women, girls and boys jammed up together, snoring and chattering and swiping at the mosquitoes all the night long.

There was also the problem of the dogs, for nearly all João's friends had brought along their hunting dogs, so that these animals were to be found everywhere: panting in the sun, scavenging behind the kitchens, fighting over bones, howling at night and shocking the ladies by making free with each other whenever they felt the inclination.

These were the days when the lines of pickers – mostly young girls and old women – moved among the vines, cutting the heavy clusters of fruit off the tendrils, and calling out, *'Balda cheia!'* each time a wooden pail was filled. One by one, the huge baskets of grapes were carried down on the shoulders of the sweating basket-men to the awaiting oxcarts, and one by one the oxcarts made their way down the hill to the big, cool building that housed the *lagares*, the massive granite tanks where the grapes were trodden.

One evening João brought his house guests along to witness the treading. Leading the way, with Sara on his arm and Pepito following behind, he was welcomed by Joaquim, who doffed his cap respectfully and wished 'the patron' good evening.

'A good colour, Excellency, a good colour,' he said, glancing to Sara for moral support. 'Though the quantity of grapes is not quite what we hoped for.'

It was after midnight now, and the treaders were tiring: the women had been picking all day and the men carrying the baskets down the hill. Now, to the slow beat of a drum and the melancholy notes of a traditional song about a lover over the seas, the treaders were swaying from foot to foot, thigh deep in the must.

'Come, we must do better than this!' João said to all in general, and clapped his hands to stop the music. 'More happiness!' he ordered. '*Mais alegria!*'

The musicians obeyed immediately, breaking into a jaunty song about the smells and sounds of Lisbon which was popular at the time. The words were well known to João and his friends (they were full of puns and double meanings), and the rafters were soon echoing with the voices of the rich, who were full of good food and strong wine and determined to enjoy themselves.

In the *lagar* the village people stared incredulously as João tried to do a folk dance with his wife and, finding Sara quite unable to follow his banging of heels and twirling hither and thither, turned to her bodyguard and ordered him to be his partner.

Pepito was an excellent dancer. With a ramrod straight back, narrow hips and firm little buttocks that jiggled up and down in time with the beat, he and João captivated their audience so completely that the beat of the drum was almost drowned out by the people clapping in time.

When the dance came to an end, however, João was not satisfied. 'Come – we shall tread the grapes ourselves!' he said to his gentlemen guests, and without the slightest show of embarrassment removed his breeches and hose and leapt into the *lagar*, insisting that Pepito – as well as Fernando and Rui and Nuno and Otelo – did likewise.

But although most of the treaders were amazed and delighted by this performance, there was one who was not amused, and this was the servant, Tristram Pascoe. Sara saw him choose his moment and leave the *lagar* when João's back was turned and some time later, when the dancing in the grape must was reaching a frenzy (João was bouncing up and down with Pepito, to whom he had taken quite a fancy), Sara felt so sickened that she went out also.

She went down through the orangery, and came upon Tristram where the path descended between rushes to the river. The night insects were trilling loudly here, and a full moon was sailing overhead. He turned quickly at her approach, and she stopped short.

'You like to be alone, like me,' she said in a low voice.

He thought that she had come to fetch him back, and that he would be whipped for leaving the *lagar* without permission.

'Yes my Lady,' he mumbled in Portuguese, conscious of his bare legs, which were stained purple from treading the grapes.

'Tristão. . .' she whispered, and looked very directly into his eyes, so that he was left in no doubt as to her reason for following him down to the river.

He was aware of his heart thudding heavily. 'My Lady,' he managed, 'what is it that you require of me?'

She seemed unable to answer him. Her mouth opened to make a reply but no words came, and the look of longing in her expression touched something inside him, something that was very tender and which had not been touched since the last time he had held Jennifer in his arms.

For a few moments they stood gazing at each other, with the rushes whispering around them; then the sound of laughter came from the *lagar*, and immediately Sara turned, and having made a visible effort to compose herself, ran away up the path.

João left a few days later when the *vindima* was over, and he took his new favourite, Pepito, with him. Sara was therefore left without her bodyguard, and she wasted no time in sending for Tristram and informing him that he was to take Pepito's place.

His appearance had improved considerably in the year since his arrival at the Quinta de Piedade: he had changed from a skinny wretch with fear in his eyes to a young man slightly taller than herself, with powerful biceps, straight legs, and eyes that melted something inside her. 'I have directed that you be fitted out in the house livery,' she told him. 'From now on you will sleep outside my door at night, wait upon me whether at Mass or at my table and accompany me wherever I go during the day. Is that clear?' She relaxed a little and addressed him half-confidentially: 'You understand – I need – I need a companion as well as a guard.'

He looked quite bemused.

'You don't look very pleased, Tristão. If you are to be my personal servant, I don't want a gloomy face about me. Or have you forgotten how to smile?'

And then he *did* smile, and she experienced that same shiver of excitement he had caused in her the very first time she saw him, when he ran naked across the Palace Square and she had prayed secretly for his survival.

Suddenly, it seemed to Tristram that Jennifer was very far away. Having been present in his thoughts almost constantly since the day he struggled out of the surf and collapsed upon a beach somewhere to the south of Cadiz, the memory of her now receded, so that there were nights when he went to sleep without a thought of her and mornings when he awoke with a strange sense of expectation and happiness that he had never known before.

He was in no doubt as to the cause of this sudden change: he found it impossible to sleep outside Dona Sara's room, to wait upon her at table or to accompany her on her frequent walks about the quinta without being drawn to her, first out of gratitude for her kindness, later out of admiration of her character and finally out of an affection that was far stronger than anything he had known before.

He was afraid of the strength of this feeling at first, and tried to tell himself that it was simply the result of loneliness, and that he might easily have fallen for any other lady who had shown him similar kindness. But the more he saw of Sara the more convinced he became that this could not be so, because there were moments when he felt a great ache of love for her, a love that had to be disguised and hidden, because he was sure that Sara could not possibly regard him, her servant, with anything approaching the same fondness. So although she often encouraged him to talk and tried to draw him out about his past, a powerful sense of guilt over Jennifer and an equally powerful awareness of his own inferior station rendered him virtually tongue-tied in her presence.

Often, before going to sleep at night, he would tell himself that he must not allow himself to slip into the habit of fondness for his mistress. Lying across her doorway, he would resolutely force himself to think of Jennifer; but every time he tried to conjure up her face or recall those nights they had spent together under the wall on the Roscarrock estate, he would find his thoughts drifting away back to something Sara had said to him that day, or the way she had turned to smile at him on their way through the almond orchard, or her lovely voice singing in Irish when she was getting dressed in the morning.

After a while he gave up the struggle. However desperately he tried to keep loyal to the memory of Jennifer, he felt her slipping away out of his grasp. If he could have turned off his feelings for Sara as one might turn off the tap of a water butt, he would have done so gladly. But the love he now felt for Sara was far stronger than a trickle from a barrel. It was like the seething torrent of the Colares river after a rainstorm, and though he might be able to dam it and keep it in check for a while, he knew very well that sooner or later it must burst through, and he would be swept away for ever.

They went in single file up the steep path through the wooded slopes of the Serra da Sintra: Tristram first, with a strong stave in his hand, and Sara following. They climbed over lichen-covered boulders and toiled upwards among pines, corks, cedars and mimosa. Occasionally, when they came to a steeper part or it was necessary to climb over a fallen tree or negotiate a boulder, Sara would stop and ask for his hand, holding on tightly until they were past the obstacle.

On and on they went, sometimes pausing to look back on the way they had come, sometimes catching a glimpse of a more distant view until, towards midday, they broke out of the forest and reached the last slope before the summit.

Three hundred feet above them the ancient walls of the Moorish castle followed the contour of the peak, while below them, the coast from Cabo da Rocha to Cabo Espichel sparkled in the January sunshine.

Sara sat down and leant against a tussock of coarse grass. She put her head right back, and closed her eyes. For a few moments she could almost imagine herself back on the slopes of Ballysitteragh, with the bays of Dingle and Ventry below her, and the smoke rising from the farmhouse within the walls of Ballingolin Castle.

She sighed deeply and opened her eyes. Tristram was standing with his back to her looking out over the ocean, immersed in thoughts of his own.

'What are you thinking, Tristão?' she asked gently.

He turned.

'Of home?'

'Yes, Dona Sara, of home.'

He had been her servant for three months now, but in spite of her repeated attempts to break down the barrier of formality between them he was little more forthcoming than on his first day. This expedition of theirs was not her first attempt to advance their friendship, and like several previous, it had so far proved as uphill as the expedition.

'You can sit down if you like,' she said 'In fact I wish you to sit down. No, not over there, Tristão. Here.'

He obeyed like a big, clumsy puppy, and succeeded in making himself as uncomfortable as possible by perching on a stone.

She would have liked to order him to sit closer – on the grass beside her – but didn't want to frighten him off.

'Tell me about it, then. Tell me about your home.'

He looked down at his hands for several moments, and then turned his head away and looked down over the green mountain slopes.

'Well?'

When he looked back at her, she suspected that there were tears in his eyes, and the sight of them caused a tumult of feelings that were so strong she was similarly affected. For a moment, they stared at one another in silent amazement.

'I know what it is to be homesick too,' she whispered. 'I long to see Ireland again every bit as much as you long to see – what is the name of your village?'

'Polruan.'

'Tell me about it, then. Is it on the coast?'

'Yes.'

'Well? What is the coast like? Is it like this? Are there cliffs and beaches as we have in Corcaguiney? Do you live on a mountain or in a valley?'

Slowly, and with great difficulty, she began to break down his reserve. She asked him about his parents, his brothers and his sister; she drew him out on the subject of his early childhood, and heard about his days at the grammar school in Fowey.

'So can you read and write?' she asked, and was delighted to learn that he could, saying that in future, to improve his education, she would have him read to her from *The Lusiads*.

He told her about his apprenticeship at Knollys's shipyard, and how he had once hoped to build ships himself.

'Then why did you go to sea?' she asked.

He bowed his head, aware that she was leading him on and that he must now preserve his honour and declare his loyalty to Jennifer.

She reached out and put her hand over his. 'Don't be afraid, Tristão,' she whispered. 'You can trust me, I won't repeat a word of what you say.'

He was trembling visibly. 'It was – my father – '

'Yes? What about your father?'

He looked at her pleadingly, as if begging her forgiveness in advance. Then he said in a low voice: 'I got a lass with child, Dona Sara. But my father wouldn't allow us to be man and wife, and insisted that I accompany him on a voyage.'

She felt a thud of disappointment. 'What was her name?'

It was the first time he had spoken it to anyone since being capsized in the *Russell*'s cockboat.

She forced herself to repeat it. 'Jennifer. That's a good name.'

He nodded and looked away. She felt like crying out in anguish. This Jennifer of his might by now be the mother of his child. He was promised to her in loyalty and honour. No wonder he had been slow to respond to her advances!

She was careful to remain calm, to disguise her dismay. 'With me, it was my mother,' she said. 'It was she who arranged my marriage. My father would have preferred me to stay in Ireland.' She picked up a pebble and threw it down the slope. 'But perhaps it was for the best, Tristão, for if I had not come to Portugal we would not be sitting here, would we? Besides,' she went on, feeling a sudden need to hide her feelings by conversation, 'times are hard in Ireland just now, what with the Fitzmaurices and the Ormondes at each others' throats.' She glanced sidelong at him, and added, 'And I'm thinking Corcaguiney would be a much safer place to live in if it weren't for the English, too.'

He said nothing to that, but looked uncomfortable. Still hurt by his revelation about Jennifer, she felt an irrational urge to hit back. 'But that Queen Elizabeth of yours is going to have to watch out. There's an army on its way this minute, sent from the Pope himself with Fitzmaurice to advance the Catholic cause in Ireland and sweep every last English soldier from the land. Did you know that, Tristão?'

He shook his head, but said nothing.

'And I'll tell you something else, too. I've heard there's a Spanish admiral – the one who beat the Turks – who says that if he can have the Portuguese Navy to help him, he could take an *armada* up the Sleeve and land an army on English soil. And did you know there are more Catholics in England than Protestants?'

He looked at her steadily. 'I don't believe that.'

'It's what I've heard.' She lifted the medallion that hung on its chain round her neck. 'And even you yourself are more Catholic than Protestant, are you not? I think there are a good many people like you in England who are more Catholic than they think, Tristram Pascoe, and when the time comes and we send ships and soldiers up to London, there'll be plenty of men ·like you who would be only too glad to join forces with them and claim back England for the true Faith.' She looked at him. '*You* would, wouldn't you?'

His chin went out and he tilted his head back. 'I reckon I'd fight for my country,' he said in a low voice. 'I don't see why we can't be left to live and believe as we see fit. Just because we don't like taking orders from Rome doesn't mean we aren't Christian.'

'Then you should practise as you preach, and leave us poor Irish to live and believe as *we* see fit!' she burst out, and they were suddenly face to face, each filled with feelings of patriotism and love for their countries and yet, at the same time, each aware of a new respect and admiration for the other.

Some moments later she asked: 'Have I offended you?'

He shook his head. 'I've heard worse spoken of my country than that. And when all's said and done, there's good and bad in every nation.'

'I don't like those dour Lutherans much, though,' she said. 'Do you?'

He considered a moment, and when he replied there was a hint of a smile in his eyes. 'No more than those smooth-tongued Jesuits.'

She laughed. 'Let's climb up to the castle,' she said, and on the way up, she caught his hand and held it, not letting it go even when they reached the top, but interlocking her fingers with his and exchanging secret messages of affection.

He was a Protestant, an Englishman, a servant and the father of a bastard, and she was well aware that to conduct a secret affair with him would be to court disaster. But she couldn't stop herself: six years of an empty marriage to João had planted in her a deep need for true friendship and love, and having found in Tristram all the qualities that were lacking in her husband she was suddenly determined to let nothing stand in her way.

She knew that by encouraging him she was in effect denying her faith and descending into mortal sin. She knew that she should confess to

Padre Bernado, the 'singing priest' of Colares. She knew she was inviting Tristram to betray the trust of the girl he had left behind, and lay awake at night suffering agonies of guilt and jealousy over the rights and wrongs of it all.

But how could these floods of tenderness and love she felt for Tristram be 'sinful'? She could not believe it. And what was there, after all, to confess? That she had held hands with one of her servants? Surely she should first confess to all the frustration and bitterness and hatred João had engendered in her and which she had bottled up inside herself, ruling herself with an iron hand, never allowing herself to express her true feelings about him, always keeping a curb on her tongue, never allowing herself the luxury of hearing the asides made about him or showing any disloyalty to him.

So she did not confess, and instead began teaching Tristram Portuguese and made him read to her in the afternoons, and when they came to the ninth canto of *The Lusiads*, in which Venus rewards the gallant Portuguese discoverers on their way back to Lisbon, the last threads of reserve were finally broken, and they giggled like children over the sensual descriptions of hungry kisses, gentle caresses and rippling laughter.

' "Count nothing imposible," ' he read, reaching the conclusion of the canto, ' "he who willed always found a way. In the end you too will be listed on fame's scroll of heroes, and this Island of Venus will be yours." ' He looked up, blushing furiously, and when their eyes met, it was as if a magic force drew them together.

'Do you believe it, Tristão?' she asked softly. 'That "this Island of Venus will be yours"?'

He felt his desire for her mounting suddenly, and saw equal desire in the way she now looked at him. 'I believe that where there's a will, there's a way,' he replied huskily.

'So do I,' she murmured, and stood up. 'Let's take a stroll by the river,' she said. 'Please come with me, Tristão.'

He walked along a pace or so behind the swaying hem of her dress, knowing what was to come, half excited by it, half apprehensive. They went through the orangery and on along the narrow path that led between rushes. She stopped, and looked back at him. 'Is it safe?' she whispered.

He felt his heart hammering in his chest. He was hardly able to speak. 'I think so.'

She looked quickly back along the path, then took his hand and led him in among the rushes. They faced each other, each trembling for the other. She stood before him, her hands at her sides, silently imploring him to make the first advance and show his love by deed rather than word; and when the impossible happened, when he reached out and took her into his arms, all her feelings of guilt and uncertainty were finally dissolved.

She put her head back. He covered her face and neck with kisses. 'Sara!' he whispered. 'Sara!'

He explored further. His hand – warm, gentle – enclosed her breast. She gave a long, grateful sigh. Lying back against the supple canes, she pulled him down with her; and casting all other thoughts aside, she gave herself to him, letting out a shudder of happy pain as his love came flooding in.

'We must go back,' she whispered. 'Look at me – be my mirror. Am I red in the face?'

He gazed at her, still overcome by what had gone before.

'Tell me, Tristão,' she said. 'Will they notice anything?'

He brushed the leaves off the back of her dress and smoothed her hair, tying her ribbon with fingers made nimble from splicing rope and sewing canvas. In return, she picked a twig out of his hair and touched lips with him once more before they emerged cautiously from their hiding place and sauntered back to the house.

Joaquim hurried up and doffed his cap. 'My Lady!' he exclaimed. 'I've been searching everywhere for you! A messenger has arrived with important despatches from Lisbon!'

He led the way round the house to the square, where three armed horsemen were refreshing themselves from the drinking fountain on the outside wall of the house. On Sara's approach they straightened, and their captain came forward and saluted.

She accepted a letter from him and broke the seals. It was from João:

To: Her Excellency Countess Sara Hussey Valdez de Santarém

His Majesty has seen fit to confer upon myself the title of Count of Colares as a mark of gratitude for my loyalty and service to my country. We are therefore particularly desirous that you and all at Colares fully understand that to give shelter to any person or persons who are acting in support of the bastard Prior of

Crato will put their own safety in jeopardy as well as that of our beloved country. Long live Cardinal Henry, King of Portugal.
Salutations,

João
Count of Colares

Sara didn't know whether it was the pomposity of João's letter that had tickled her sense of the ridiculous or simply nervous relief after what had happened with Tristram; but whatever the cause, Joaquim and the despatch riders were amazed when she gave way to peals of Irish laughter.

She laughed until the tears streamed down her cheeks, and the sight of Joaquim and Tristram smiling and looking so happy for her and yet puzzled at the same time made her laugh all the more.

'But what has happened, my Lady?' Joaquim asked eventually. 'May we be allowed to know?'

She bit her lip and wiped her eyes. 'I'm a countess, Joaquim. Imagine! Me – a countess!'

It was the happiest time she had ever known, an idyllic interlude of peace and love. Every morning when she awoke she looked forward to her first meeting with Tristram that day, and every night when she lay down to sleep she recalled their conversations, their happiness together and their love. And although it was necessary to be watchful and to keep their liaison secret, the very necessity for secrecy added to the thrill. It was not all that difficult, either: over the past two years she had grown accustomed to keeping her own company, so that the sight of the lady of the quinta going for solitary walks with her bodyguard following a few paces behind was no novelty at the Quinta de Piedade.

Off they would go, through the orangery and along the path between the rushes to the edge of the Sintra woods; no word would be spoken between them for a quarter of an hour or more while they went up between the damp boulders and over the carpets of pine needles. And then, when Sara was sure it was safe, she would turn and wait for him; he would come to her and they would link hands; and slowly, relishing the moment, their lips would meet in the first wonderful kiss of the day, the prelude to so much more.

Ten days after João's elevation to the nobility, Cardinal Henry, King of

Portugal, died without issue, and the question of his successor threw Portugal into a new turmoil of uncertainty.

Lisbon was suddenly full of rumours, and the Quinta de Santo António busier than ever. A continual stream of councillors, officers, aides and secretaries called upon the Count of Colares, who had by now declared himself a staunch supporter of Philip's claim to the throne over that of the Prior of Crato. 'Do we want a king or a bastard?' he would say, and from her bedroom upstairs, his mother would shriek back, 'A king! A king!'

Dona Marguerita seemed quite indestructible. Lying all day in her huge, tapestry-draped bed, she gave audiences, issued instructions, listened to reports from her personal agents and conducted a relentless campaign to ensure that when the Spanish took over (as everyone knew they surely must) her son would have his rightful share in the government of the country. Her particular ambition for him was that, as the son of a sea captain, he should one day rule the Portuguese Navy, and to this end she set about pulling strings with Admiral Moitinho (who was comptroller of the fleet and had designs on Maria Teresa) to get João a directorate on the general staff.

The bustle and confusion at the Quinta de Santo António mirrored the chaos in the city at large. Having prepared the ground before the death of the Cardinal-King, Spanish agents and diplomats now set about bribing their way into power. Promises were made that when the Spanish took over no one appointed to office by Cardinal Henry would be dismissed; that the Portuguese would be treated as equals; that an attack upon Portugal would be seen as an attack upon Spain, and that the Portuguese possessions in Africa, India and the Orient would be afforded protection under the safe umbrella of the most powerful empire on earth.

There seemed no stopping Philip now. The monumental palace in the Escorial mountains near Madrid was nearing completion; his possessions in the New World were like horns of plenty, overspilling with fabulous riches; his army was in control in the Low Countries, where even some of the English aristocracy were deserting their Queen and changing sides, and with the Pope's blessing and the assistance of Fontana, the Apostolic Collector in Lisbon, a force had already sailed for Ireland to set her free from the English oppressor. Now, with the crown of Portugal and all her possessions about to fall into Spain's lap, it was beginning to look as though Philip might indeed embark upon the much-vaunted Enterprise of England, and win her back for Christendom.

But in the meantime it was necessary to cleanse Portugal of every last Protestant spy and Lutheran heretic, and with this in mind the Inquisitor-General issued instructions to his agents to investigate every smallest whisper of gossip and to leave no estate or quinta unvisited.

It was May again, and Colares was ablaze with flowers. Sara had spread her cloak inside-out on the moss in their forest hiding place: the mountainside was echoing with birdsong, and overhead brilliant slivers of sunlight pierced the umbrella of leaves.

'Four months,' she murmured. 'Yet I feel I have known you all my life.'

'Perhaps that's the way of love,' he said. 'Like a river, it has no beginning and no end: it's simply there, and the choice is ours whether we plunge in, or walk beside it – or turn away.'

She lay in his arms and they were silent for a while. One of the things she loved most about him was that he never felt any need to chatter.

He gave a little sigh. 'What?' she asked.

He hesitated. 'I think . . . I think Joaquim knows about us.'

She turned her head; they kissed gently. 'Why do you say that, Tristão?'

He smiled sadly and she felt a little pang of apprehension that their stolen honeymoon could not last for ever.

'He has been hinting . . . about the Inquisitor. You know they're in Sintra at the moment? Well, Joaquim said – ' He stopped.

'What did he say?'

'He said that we must all be on our guard.'

She relaxed a little. 'But that doesn't mean he knows about us, Tristão!'

'And yet it does,' he whispered, taking her hand between his own, 'for though he said nothing directly, I knew by his manner that he has guessed. He is a man of intelligence – you know that. He has a way of speaking without words, of giving a warning with nothing more than a glance.'

She knew exactly what he meant. 'But . . . do you think he was threatening to denounce us?'

'No. Quite the opposite. Joaquim is a friend, I'm convinced of it. And he's completely loyal to you, too. In fact I think it was more for your sake than mine that he sounded the warning.'

For a moment she recalled the memory of the adulteress at the auto-da-fé and the sound of her shrieks of agony as the flames enveloped her.

'He told me something else,' Tristram said suddenly. 'He said that if he were in my shoes, he would try to escape back to England. He said he knows a fisherman in Cascais who could provide a boat. He seems to think I could just sail it home on my own. But it's not as easy as that.'

'Could it be done, though?'

He thought a moment. 'It's not impossible. But it would be a lot easier with another pair of hands.'

'I'll come with you, then.'

He held her. 'If only you could.'

She was silent for a long time. 'Do you *want* to go back to England?' she asked eventually.

He took her hand in his. 'What I want and what I ought are quite different, Sara. What I want is never to be parted from you. What I ought is to return to Jennifer, marry her and take responsibility for my child.'

She held his hand to her cheek.

He continued slowly, quietly, as if to himself. 'And if – if Joaquim knows that you and I are . . . as we are, then sooner or later others will suspect it, and we shall be denounced. Isn't that so?'

'Yes, that is so, Tristão, but – '

'And if we are denounced, you will risk the punishments of the Inquisition. Perhaps even death.' He gripped her hands tightly. 'I couldn't bear that, Sara. I couldn't bear to think that I, who love you more than I can explain, could be the cause of your hurt or injury. So in one matter at least duty and desire are one, for if I can keep you from danger by leaving Colares, that is what I must do.'

She thought of the girl he had left with child in Cornwall, and felt a pang of guilt. 'Perhaps you should go, Tristão. But not for me. For Jennifer.'

He shook his head. 'The only reason I could ever be parted from you is for *your* sake. You must allow me that, Sara. You can't forbid me to love you or insist that I act for reasons which I don't feel. I can't pretend to motives that are not my own, so although I still have a deep sense of fondness and duty towards Jennifer, neither my duty nor my affection towards her can compare to my love and loyalty towards you.'

'I feel like a thief,' she whispered. 'I feel I've stolen you from her – '

'But you haven't! I was only a lad of sixteen when I knew her. Our love was the love of children – it was no more than a youthful experiment, an infatuation. I'm full grown now, Sara, and my love for you is full grown too, and far stronger than anything I knew with her. Whatever happens in the future – even if I go back to Cornwall – it will always be you who takes first place in my affections. I know that as surely as I know that Polaris marks true north or the sun stands highest at noon.'

They were quiet for a while, each aware that their conversation had been a turning point, the beginning of the end.

'So . . . will you take Joaquim's advice?' she asked eventually.

'The only advice I shall take will be yours. If you say I must go, then – I shall go. If you wish me to stay, I shall stay.'

She closed her eyes a moment, and in that moment it seemed that all the feelings of hope, love, conscience and despair flowed quickly through her. 'I think you should go,' she said quietly, and then added fiercely, the tears starting suddenly to her eyes: 'Yes, my darling one, go – but not for my sake or yours, not for Jennifer's sake or the sake of your child, but for all of us, Tristão, for the love and safety of all of us together and each of us separately. Will you do that?'

'If I must,' he whispered, and then she was in his arms and weeping without reserve at the cruel decision fate had forced upon them, and Tristram was staring at the tangled undergrowth of the forest, trying to look into the future, but seeing only darkness and confusion.

The sky had suddenly clouded over. They stood up and shook the moss from her cloak. A little while later, when they emerged from the trees and came down the path to the quinta, Sara was walking ahead as usual, with her bodyguard following five paces behind.

That evening she found Joaquim supervising the digging of a new irrigation trench beyond the bridge, and having sent Tristram back to the house she summoned the *caseiro* on the pretext of receiving a report of progress from him.

Respectful as ever, he lifted his cap to her and began a lengthy explanation of why a new ditch was needed and how it would enable him to grow a yet more varied and plentiful supply of fruit and vegetables for her table.

'Yes, I understand that,' she said eventually, 'but is it not something of a scar across our lovely valley, Joaquim?'

'Indeed it is, my lady – but its present appearance is only temporary. I shall plant shrubs and fruit trees along its banks, and within a few months it will be completely disguised.'

She smiled at his earnest manner and looked across the valley. 'I'm glad to hear that,' she said softly, then turned back to look him directly in the eye. 'I understand the Inquisitor will be paying us a visit one day soon, and it would be as well to have everything just so, don't you agree, Joaquim?'

'I do agree, my Lady,' he said gravely. 'That is of the greatest importance.'

'Tell me,' she said. 'You are in a position to know a great deal of what happens at Piedade. Is it your opinion that anyone of us here has aught to fear from the Inquisition?'

He looked back at her very steadily, and while he did so she remembered Tristram's remark about how he could speak without using words.

'My Lady,' he said, 'if any person has reason to fear the Inquisition, it is I.'

She presumed that his words were simply intended to reassure her, and his gentle manner and understanding look told her that she could open her heart to him, without fear. And she needed that, she needed it desperately. For years she had bottled up her private thoughts; now, she knew instinctively that she could turn to Joaquim and confide in him as she had once confided in her own father.

She heard her own voice, very strained, say: 'Myself no less, Joaquim, as I think you will have guessed.'

They walked in silence along the path to the almond grove. At length, she said: 'I am not afraid for myself. Only for him.' When he made no reply, she added: 'Please consider yourself free to speak of it, Joaquim. I shall value your advice.'

He considered for a few moments, then said: 'I am much more concerned for you, my Lady. You are in the greatest danger of all.' Then he surprised her by adding: 'And I am the chief cause of it.'

'You? Why you?'

While they continued along under the almond trees, he gave her his answer. 'There was a young priest at Braga,' he said quietly. 'He ran away from the seminary twenty years ago. Because . . . because he couldn't accept that it can be given to any man to remit sin, and he refused to sell indulgences. He ran away, he broke the laws of fasting and abstinence, he made false confessions, lived with his washerwoman, fathered children.' Joaquim sighed a deep sigh. 'And years later, he came to Colares and started work as a gardener.'

She stared at him. 'You mean . . . you were a – '

'I was a priest. Yes.'

'But is it likely that they would know you? After so long?'

'In normal circumstances, I would say no. But the Inquisitor in this area, so I understand, is Frei Bartolomeu Azevedo.' Joaquim laughed bitterly. 'I shared a dormitory with him in my first year at Braga.'

They stood together in the shade of the almond trees. From the kitchens came the sound of Maria Candida scolding one of the servants.

Sara thought rapidly. She was in no doubt now that all three of them were in great danger. Joaquim had guessed at her romance with Tristram, so it seemed likely that there might already be whispers of it among the servants. And when the Inquisitor arrived there was no saying what would be wormed out of them, or what chance remark might arouse their suspicions.

'You will have to leave,' she said. 'Both of you.'

'And what will you say to Brother Bartolomeu when he arrives here and finds that your *caseiro* and bodyguard have recently departed?' Joaquim shook his head. 'You will be in even greater danger, my Lady. No, what must be done is this: first you must dismiss your bodyguard. Today – as soon as you arrive back in the house. Then he must *escape*. And when the Inquisitor asks questions, you must say that the English boy was dismissed for insulting your modesty and ran away because he knew you would denounce him.'

'But how can he escape, Joaquim?'

'By boat – '

'But not alone, I have already asked him about this.' She glanced at him, acknowledging that Tristram had repeated his conversation with him. 'And besides – what of yourself? If they recognize you – '

'I shall draw their interest away from yourself, my Lady. I have had a good life – better than most. It is a service that I would be honoured to give.'

'No,' she said, suddenly decisive. 'There's a far greater service you can render me.' She turned to face him. 'You can help Tristão. Escape with him, Joaquim. By sea. To England.'

They wasted no time in formulating a plan and putting it into effect. That evening, with Joaquim's permission, Sara repeated their conversation to Tristram, and persuaded him that it was for all their good that he and Joaquim should abscond from the Quinta de Piedade. The following morning, having obtained from Tristram details of the sort of boat he would need and a list of stores and provisions, Joaquim was sent down to Cascais with a purse full of silver to obtain the use of a boat and to arrange for it to be made ready and left hidden in a small, sandy cove just north of the Guincho. On his return Sara called the whole household together and had Padre Bernado harangue the servants for over an hour on the importance of examining their consciences and preparing themselves spiritually for the visit of the Inquisitor. In this way she managed to strike terror into the heart of every last laundrymaid and pan boy, and effectively diverted attention from Joaquim and Tristram.

She awoke the following morning with a feeling of dread. This was to be Tristram's last day at Colares, and was the day when she would have to turn on him publicly and dismiss him from her service. Listening to the dawn chorus she looked back over the past months of happiness they had had together and wondered if there could ever come a time in the future when she could be as happy again. And then she saw the years of loneliness stretching out ahead and wept into her pillow, praying to God to watch over Tristram and to take him safely home and to give him all the happiness he deserved with Jennifer and his child.

But in the morning things did not go exactly according to plan. With Tristram in attendance as usual, she heard Padre Bernado say Mass in the chapel. Afterwards, she was just finishing her breakfast when there was a clatter of hooves in the square. A moment later, Maria Candida waddled in looking sweaty and pale. '*Minha senhora!*' she panted. 'It's him! It's the Inquisitor! He's outside with his assistant and escort!'

Frei Bartolomeu was a large, rounded man with yellow skin that hung in folds from his chin. He had a hawk's nose and very small eyes which moved ceaselessly, as if he were searching every corner of the room. His assistant, Frei Martim, was a younger man with an air of haughty insolence about him and a way of sighing from time to time, as if he were unspeakably bored.

'We are entirely at your disposal, Fathers,' Sara told them, and snapped her fingers imperiously at Tristram. 'Find the housekeeper and tell her to prepare rooms for our guests,' she said, 'and inform the *caseiro* that I wish a pig to be slaughtered in their honour. Don't stand gaping, you idle good-for-nothing – go!'

Tristram found the cooks and servants whispering nervously in the kitchens, the menservants and stableboys muttering outside, and Joaquim working alone with a hoe among his beloved vines.

'You know they're here?' he asked.

'Of course I know they're here!'

'Dona Sara told me to tell you to slaughter a pig.'

'In that case you can help me.'

'But I never help with slaughtering – '

'Do as you're told boy,' Joaquim replied, and led the way to the outbuildings to collect the rope and the knives, and to select the largest porker in the sty.

He saw to it that the killing took as long as possible and made a great deal of noise, and when the Inquisitor and his assistant came round on a conducted tour of the quinta with Padre Bernado and the Countess, both Joaquim and Tristram were so liberally splattered with hog's blood that they were hardly recognizable.

After the slaughtering the pork had to be bled, singed and spitted, and by the time all was complete and ready for Cook to take over, a rumour was going round the kitchens that the Condessa's bodyguard was in disgrace.

All afternoon and evening the household revolved round the visitors. The laundrymaids pummelled their creamy white cassocks in the river; the cooks and kitchenmaids slaved for hours to present them with a six-course feast; their armed escort was given a hearty meal and, on Joaquim's insistence, a surfeit of Colares wine, and Sara stretched her conversational ability to the limit to entertain her guests and delay for as long as possible the moment when they began their investigations.

And to her great relief, at the end of the afternoon, Frei Bartolomeu announced that he and his assistant wished to go up to their rooms for an hour in order to say their office and prepare themselves for the evening, and the moment they were gone Sara summoned her bodyguard to escort her while she walked through the quinta and said her rosary.

They went slowly down the path by the river, and crossing the bridge where convolvulus grew in a floral arch, they came to the orangery. 'Keep well behind me, Tristão,' she said softly. 'They may be watching us.'

Head down, her lips moving as if she were reciting her Hail Marys, she spoke to him for the last time.

'Wherever you go, my darling, whatever happens, always remember that I shall be thinking of you, that I shall never forget you, never betray you. And if you are one day reunited with – with Jennifer, you must learn to love her again, do you understand? You must be a good, gentle husband to her and a loving father to your child.' She pressed her hands to her face, stifling a sob. 'And – and will you promise me not to be sad, Tristão the Cheerful? Will you promise to remember me with a smile on your face and love in your heart?'

'I promise,' he managed.

They passed out of sight of the house behind a screen of rushes, and immediately she stopped and began to take the Madonna from her neck. 'Here – I want you to have this. Quickly now. It's rightfully yours – '

He shook his head vehemently and spoke in a whisper. 'No, Sara, I can't accept it. You must keep it for your own safety. I insist.'

'Then not for my safety, but only to remember you by,' she whispered.

And then she was in his arms and they were kissing fiercely, possessively, their tears mingling, their hearts breaking.

'Goodbye Tristão, goodbye my darling one,' she murmured, and with a choking cry she released him and turned quickly away to hurry back along the path to the house.

While the cooks and tablemaids waited upon the guests at dinner, Joaquim made his final preparations for departure, wrapping thick rags round the hooves of the two horses that had been left out in the field, filling four wineskins with fresh water – even applying a little olive oil to the hinges of the iron gates to ease them.

And then all that remained was to wait, and wait, and wait – for the dinner to be over, for the guests to go up to their rooms, for the servants to finish in the kitchens and the watchdogs to fall asleep; and at last, at that hour when the only sounds were the trilling of night insects and the croaking of frogs, the renegade priest and his English companion set out from the Quinta de Piedade.

They reached the coast before dawn and made their way to the tiny beach where the boat was ready and provisioned. It was no larger than the *Russell*'s longboat, with a stumpy mast and a lateen sail, and Tristram quickly discovered that although Joaquim was an excellent farm manager, he was no sailor.

Hissing orders to him to 'pull on that rope' and cursing him for not even knowing how to belay a halyard, Tristram eventually got the craft launched through the surf and the sail up, and after some vigorous rowing managed to clear the jagged coastline.

Now, eight hours later, they were rolling along in a brisk westerly with the mountains of Sintra dropping away astern.

While Joaquim hung miserably over the lee gunwale, Tristram sat up in the stern with the helm in his hands and the beginnings of hope in his heart. The wind was fair for a passage north; they had provisions and water. There was a long way to go, yes, but now, for the first time in four years, he began to see a glimmer of hope that he might at last succeed in returning to England.

He began thinking about all that had happened since the day he left Polruan, and breathing a prayer of thanks to God for assisting his escape, he tried to imagine the outcry at the Quinta de Piedade when it was discovered that they had escaped. But that brought his thoughts back to Sara, and thinking about her filled him with a terrible longing for what might have been, and fears for her safety.

He remembered the promise he had made her, but though his heart was still brim full of love for her, trying to think of her with a smile only brought the tears back to his eyes.

He blinked them away and faced grimly up into the wind, looking out over the tumbling waves. 'It's Jennifer you must think of now,' he muttered to himself. 'Because you'll never go back, you'll never see Sara again.'

Back from the Dead

For three days and nights, the wind blew steadily from the west and the coast of Portugal slipped by on the starboard beam. At first Joaquim was so overcome by seasickness that he had no time for fear and Tristram was so intent upon putting distance between them and Frei Bartolomeu that he went without sleep, clinging to the helm for hour after hour and, in the night watches, staring up at the Great Bear and the pole star upon which he steered.

When Joaquim was at last managing to keep some dry bread and water in his stomach, Tristram decided it was time he learnt how to steer.

'This is what's called a soldier's wind,' he told him, 'because it's right on the beam, and we can head in the direction we want to without having to beat to windward or worry about the sail gybing round.'

'On the beam . . . beat to windward . . . gybing round . . .' Joaquim muttered. 'How can I be expected to learn when you talk gobbledegook?'

Tristram tried again. 'Very well then – just take the helm and try to keep us pointing as we are. When you pull it up to you – like this – the bow bears away from the wind . . . so. And when you put the helm to leeward, up comes the head to the wind . . . so, until the sail flaps and we have to bear away again. So all you have to do is keep her steady, with the land over to starboard and the wind – ' He broke off, hardly able to keep his eyes open any longer. 'Just do the best you can, Joaquim,' he said, and the *caseiro* found himself with the helm in his hands and the boat surging along under his charge while his young skipper lay fast asleep on the bottomboards.

What an extraordinary turn his life had taken! Only a few weeks before, he had been content, secure – and happier than at any other time in his life. He had been able to look forward to seeing out his days at peace with himself and the world. His vines had been pruned and hoed, his orangeries blossoming, his beloved valley of Colares becoming more beautiful with each year that passed. He had built walls and arbours with his own hands; he had planted a variety of evergreens on the mountainside opposite the house so that their different shades would blend and make a pleasing pattern to the eye; he had served as a faithful *caseiro* and had set his subordinates a good example by attending Mass regularly on Sundays and holy days of obligation. Above all, he had become a devoted and loyal servant to Dona Sara, whose natural dignity and grace had captivated him from the moment he saw her dismount and gaze with undisguised admiration at his valley, his *terra*.

And now . . . here he was, Joaquim dos Santos, steering a cockleshell over the ocean with a boy of twenty for a captain, and his only real hope of survival lying in his trust that God would preserve him from evil.

He watched as another blue mountain of water reared up to port, and wondered again how the boat could possibly surmount it. But up they went, high over the crest, before sliding down its foam-streaked back, so that the land to starboard disappeared from view and Joaquim was left wondering, all over again, how they could possibly surmount the next.

When Tristram awoke it was already dark, and he was immediately aware that the boat's motion had changed and that the wind had freshened. The smack was plunging heavily now, and cold spray was thudding into the bilges with every downward lurch of the bows. Every so often the sail flapped noisily, and overhead the stars were jerking and gyrating, as if the eternal forces which kept them in their appointed places had lost all reason and order.

He struggled aft to the sternsheets, and found Joaquim clinging to the helm, his face white with terror.

'Thank God you're awake!' he yelled. 'I've been shouting at you for the past hour!'

Tristram took the helm from him, and looked heavenward for Polaris.

'What are we going to do?' Joaquim yelled.

'Do? What d'you mean?'

Joaquim stared in terror as another black wave towered above them, its crest breaking. 'We can't last long in this, boy!' he screamed. We shall be drowned!'

'*Bolas!*' replied Tristram cheerfully. 'This is only a little gale! It's just what we want! We'll cross Biscay in five days if we keep up this speed!'

'Cross Biscay! We're taking water, I tell you!'

'Taking water? A few drops of spray, more like! And if you're worried, there's a scoop up for'd so you can start bailing.'

Joaquim was hardly reassured. 'We said we'd go up the coast all the way, not straight across Biscay.'

'That was before we were sent this soldier's wind. We'd be crazy to go
into the Bay now. We've got water enough for a week, and that's all we
need.'

'But look at the mast! It'll break any minute!'

'Go and get some sleep, old man, and leave me to worry about the
mast.'

In the morning, when the sun came glimmering up out of the sea, there
was no land in sight, and the little boat was alone upon a wilderness of
wild blue water. They ate some bread, chewed some salted cod and drank
a little more of the precious water from the barrico.

'So, Joaquim, are you feeling a bit less fearful than you were in the
night?'

'Perhaps,' conceded Joaquim, 'but I'd still rather we went along the
coast. How are you going to find out where we are? We've no chart to
guide us, no compass – '

'We've the best compass there is! We've got the sun by day and Polaris
at night. And look – ' Tristram drew a piece of knotted line from his
pocket and held it out taut before him. 'I've made a makeshift cross-staff,
so I can calculate our northings from Cape Finisterre.'

Joaquim eased the helm as the bows topped a wave crest. He was
beginning to see that having thrown in his lot with Tristram, he could
have done a lot worse in his choice of boy-captain, and that he had no
alternative but to trust him.

So they sailed on across Biscay, and when it rained they lowered the
sail and used it to collect water, and one morning the fishing line they
kept trailing astern brought in three mackerel which they grilled over a
little charcoal stove Joaquim had insisted upon bringing with him the
night they set out from the Quinta de Piedade.

As the days passed and they stood watch and watch about at the helm,
each discovered qualities in the other which they had not previously
expected. Tristram found that the ex-priest was quick to learn and not so
much of a lubberish coward as he had first thought, and Joaquim
discovered that Tristram had a surprisingly old head on young
shoulders. The result of these discoveries was that they began to move
into that close friendship that can only be formed when men put their
trust in frail craft and sail out upon the ocean.

When they had been out of sight of land for four days the wind veered
north-westerly, and the sea became shorter. Sailing closer to the wind,
the boat lurched more heavily now, its bows thudding down on the waves

and the mast and lateen sail juddering repeatedly. Late in the afternoon, when Tristram was asleep on the bottomboards and Joaquim was at the helm, there was a sudden twang as the port backstay parted, and moments later a crack like a musket shot as the mast broke low down near the step, carrying the lateen sail with it into the sea.

One moment they were sailing, the next they were wallowing motionless.

Tristram had awoken, and was looking round in bewilderment. 'What've you done? What's going on?' He stood up and surveyed the wreckage of mast and sail that had gone overboard.

'Now what?' Joaquim said. 'I suppose we start rowing, is that right?'

'No, we get the mast and sail back inboard, and we make repairs.'

'Oh yes? What with?'

'We have a knife. And our hands. And a little cordage.'

But it was not so easy, as the yard of the lateen sail was jammed against the boat's side and holding the mast and sail rigidly out to starboard. They strained and heaved at it, but were unable to recover the gear. Eventually Tristram stripped and went over the side, ducking under water for seconds at a time to clear the forestay, which had snagged under the keel, and having to unlace the sail in order to remove it from the yard and recover it.

By nightfall they had the tangle of gear inboard, but were so exhausted that they collapsed in the bilges and slept like children through the night.

With a shortened mast it was necessary to reduce the area of the sail in order to make it possible to hoist it, and this operation, together with that of re-stepping the mast and re-lacing the sail, took most of the following day; and by the time they were finished and the jury mast and sail were hoisted it was nightfall again.

Tristram took the helm while Joaquim halved the last of the bread. They gnawed at it in silence for a while.

'You made a good job of it,' Joaquim said gruffly.

'If I'd listened to you, the mast wouldn't have carried away in the first place.'

'Why's that?'

'The backstay was slack, that was why the mast was moving. And the mast put more strain on it as it moved back and forth. So you were right, Joaquim, and I was wrong.'

Joaquim looked kindly at him. There weren't many who had the ability to admit to a mistake and give credit where it was due. 'It's mended now,' he said quietly. 'So all's well that end's well.'

'All won't be well 'til I set foot on Polruan Strand again,' Tristram muttered, and as Joaquim lay down to sleep, his thoughts turned again to his family, and Jennifer.

He had thought about her a lot since their first night at sea. It was not that he had forgotten Sara or ceased to love her, but rather that he was unable to forget the promise he had made to her about going back to shouldering his responsibilities as a husband and father. Now, with the pole star a point off the port bow and a pale moon flitting along behind the clouds, he was beginning to believe that he and Jennifer might actually be reunited, and the prospect of it filled him with apprehension.

It was four and a half years since he had seen her, and a lot might have happened in that time. Had she had her baby, and had the baby survived? Had his father succeeded in bringing the *Russell* back to Polruan? And what would have become of Matt and Jill and poor Nathan? Had they given Tristram up for dead, or were they still keeping a watch out, as some of the wives and mothers did when their menfolk were lost at sea?

There were harder questions yet, questions that he hardly dared think about. What if Jennifer were standing up on the clifftop when they arrived off St Saviour's Point? What if she were there, hardly believing her eyes, when the boat touched bottom off Polruan Strand, and he and Joaquim waded ashore? What if she ran into his arms, the same Jennifer that he remembered? Worse, what if she saw instantly that he had changed, and guessed that he had given his heart to another?

The wind was dying away now, and the boat moved gently on through the night. He dozed and woke and dozed again. At his feet Joaquim muttered in his sleep. The stars wheeled slowly and the sky paled in the east.

Joaquim awoke. He stretched, put his head up over the gunwale and scanned the horizon under the belly of the sail.

'Have you seen those rocks up ahead?' he asked suddenly.

It was Ushant, and for two days they were swept back and forth, becalmed among the islands, sometimes resorting to the oars to clear the dark rocks upon which the Atlantic rollers broke with such whitened fury. Then, when Joaquim was beginning to lose hope that they would ever escape the swirling tides and races and when the drinking water was all but finished, the wind picked up from the south-west and they were able to make an offing and set course for Cornwall.

'Thirty-five leagues, more or less,' Tristram said. 'We should make a landfall in a day or two, God willing. Don't look so gloomy, Joaquim! We're almost there!'

'All very well for you,' Joaquim said. 'You've got your woman to go to and a house to stay in. I've got nothing. I'll be arrested the moment I set foot ashore, aye, and hung for a spy most likely, if what I've heard about Queen Elizabeth's anything to go by.'

'I'll not see you hang, Joaquim. They'll have to hang me first, and that's my promise as an honest Cornishman.'

'Fine words seldom saved a humble neck,' Joaquim muttered, and shook his head.

'Then we must agree what we are to say about each other, so that they can't catch us out. I'll tell them the truth about you – how you helped me escape from the Inquisitor, how you saved my life.'

'When did I save your life?'

'Every day for the last sixteen days! I couldn't have made this journey on my own. And who supported Dona Sara when they were beating me? You did. I've a lot to thank you for, Joaquim, and I intend to speak well of you. I'll tell them that you're a good Christian, a true Protestant. But I think it'll be best not to mention that you were once a priest.'

'If you tell them that, I'm a dead man!'

'What shall we say you are, then? You must have some occupation, and they're bound to see that you're educated.'

'Unless I play the fool, and you treat me as a servant. That way at least I might have a chance. And isn't it the truth? Tell them I'm a servant. A lowly gardener. Tell them I'm *your* servant, and that you refuse to be parted from me. And in return – '

'Well? What?'

'In return, I'll serve you faithfully, and I'll never breathe a word of your love for Dona Sara.'

Tristram turned quickly away, and stared aft at the straggling wake. 'From now on, Joaquim, my love for Dona Sara must be forgotten. It must remain in the past. I have given thought to this. It would be dishonourable to take Jennifer as my wife while nurturing a secret affection. So if you wish to be of service to me, you will never again mention Dona Sara's name, nor remind me of the life we had at the Quinta de Piedade. From now on, the only person I can love is Jennifer Gristy.'

Joaquim smiled sadly. 'It's as I said then. I'll keep your secrets, you'll keep mine and we'll stay together, come what may. Here – give me your hand on it, Páscoa, and we'll pledge our loyalty.'

So with the little jury-rigged smack heaving along under a quartering breeze, they gripped hands and pledged themselves to keep secret what must be kept secret and to support and help each other always; and although from that moment they seldom spoke of Dona Sara, each was secretly aware of their joint devotion to her, and each pledged himself in the hope that they might one day have the good fortune to serve her again.

Towards noon the following day, they sighted land. Having learnt his lesson from their experience off Ushant, Tristram had been steering due north, calculating that the force of the south-westerly wind would take them down to leeward and fetch them up off Gribbin Head.

After several hours, when the smudge of land began to take shape and Tristram had been standing for some time in the bows, balancing with one foot on either gunwale to stare ahead, he announced: 'It's the Lizard. I'm sure of it.'

'Is that good or bad?' Joaquim asked.

'It's neither and both. It means that I know where we are, which is good, but it also means another night at sea.'

They had been two days without water, so this calm statement meant more to them than the words themselves.

They sailed on through the night, and in the morning found themselves only a mile or two off shore and able to bear away down past Falmouth and Deadman Point. But that afternoon, when they were barely ten miles off the Gribbin, the wind dropped right away and they were left becalmed, with the boat wallowing about, the ebb taking them westward again and fatigue and frustration fraying their tempers. Then, as the sun slipped down into yellowing clouds, a southerly breeze sent catspaws scurrying over the water, and they began making way again, the water gurgling cheerily under the forefoot and the phosphorescence sparkling in the wake.

Now that they were so near their destination, they found it suddenly difficult to speak easily with each other, for Tristram had always spoken in Portuguese to Joaquim, and he was now aware that he must soon start speaking English again.

'There're rocks two miles off the Gribbin,' he muttered to himself, 'and they dry at the first quarter ebb. So best go close inshore to avoid the strong current, though the cliff 'll take some of our wind. . . .'

And then, as if by magic, a waning moon came out from behind the clouds, and he saw the old familiar hump of St Saviour's Point, with the dark entrance of the Fowey just to the west of it, and the old windmill up behind St Kathern's Hill.

He stood in the sternsheets. The boat sailed slowly on in a following breeze. As the entrance came clear, the lights of Fowey became visible and the sight of them stirred Joaquim as much as Tristram.

They embraced, weeping with relief and joy.

'Thanks be to God who made Heaven and earth!' murmured Tristram and Joaquim echoed, 'Amen! Amen!'

Slowly the fishing smack crept in on the flood tide. Seeing the cliffs loom up above them, Tristram remembered Ralph Bryant and all the lessons in navigation he had given him; he remembered his friends and shipmates aboard the *Russell*: Davy Treffry, Nick Polwhele, Tom Rowe, Evan Goodall. . . .

St Saviour's was almost abeam. He could see the two old forts on either side of the entrance.

'Joaquim!'

'Yes sir?'

'We shall make our landing on a beach round to starboard, just after this fort here. We may lose the wind under the lee of the cliff, so we shall have to be ready to lower the sail and get the oars out.'

'Aye, sir!'

'Joaquim?'

'Sir?'

'Why do you call me "sir"?'

Joaquim looked like a wild animal with his thick beard. 'Because you have more than earned the title, and I'm proud to be your servant.'

They came round the point, and carried just enough way to beach the boat. Tristram insisted that they put the anchor out and lower the sail, and when they had done so he slipped down into the icy water and led the way ashore.

It was after midnight and the village was silent. They went along the beach to the stone quay and climbed up to the fish market. Having drunk deep at the horse trough by the Russell Inn, they walked up the steep, narrow street between the rows of sleeping cottages, whose thatched roofs overhung the latticed windows and whose low doors gave directly onto the cobbled street.

Going past one cottage they heard deep, resonant snores coming from inside and Tristram turned and whispered to Joaquim, 'That'll be old Mother Rashleigh – she always was one for snoring!'

But speaking in a foreign tongue in his own home village sounded oddly strange to his own ears, and he experienced again that feeling of apprehension – almost fear – of returning to Hill House.

They paused halfway up the hill and looked back over the harbour. Everything seemed just as Tristram remembered it: the same, but oddly different, as if it had somehow diminished in the time he had been away.

They went on up the hill between the high banks. When they came to St Saviour's Church Tristram stopped at the gate.

'Shall we go in?' he whispered.

He led the way into the dark church, and they knelt in silence on the stone flags, which seemed to heave under their knees like a long ocean swell.

On their way out of the church Tristram noticed a new tombstone that had been given pride of place in the graveyard, and bending down read the inscription:

ANN PASCOE
Died in Childbirth
4th November 1579
aged 39 years

He turned quickly away, bowing his head.

'Who?' Joaquim asked gently.

'My mother.'

Joaquim watched sorrowfully. When Tristram had controlled his grief, Joaquim took his arm and led him back to the lane.

They went on to Hill House. Gaunt as ever, it stood in the night wind, its windows shuttered like blinkered eyes. They stood at the latchgate, listening to the distant call of the owls down on the Roscarrock estate.

'I'm afraid, Joaquim. I'm afraid to go in.'

But Joaquim gripped his arm and pushed him forward. They reached the front door, and as soon as they knocked, dogs began barking.

'We never had dogs before,' Tristram muttered, and looked back at Joaquim. 'Everything's changed! I can feel it!'

He knocked again, and a minute later they heard the incoherent boom of a man's voice. 'Hollo! Who's there?'

'Nathan? Is that Nathan?'

'Who is it? Who calls?'

' 'Tis your brother come home, Nathan! 'Tis your brother Tristram!'

Candlelight appeared in the hall, and then Nathan's voice came to them through the door: 'Tistum?'

He felt as if his heart were breaking. 'Yes, it's Tristram! Open the door, Nathan, please open the door!'

The bolts were drawn back; the heavy oak door swung open – and there was Nathan in his old flannel nightshirt with a nightcap on his head and a candlestick in his hand.

'Tistum!' he bellowed, and turned to waken whoever else was still asleep in the house. 'Tistum's home! Tistum's home!' he cried, his voice cracking with excitement, then he turned back and peered closely at Joaquim. 'Who be him?'

'It's my servant, Nathan. Joaquim – '

'Joking!' Nathan brayed, and bellowed up the stairs: 'Mother! Tistum's home! Tistum and Joking!'

For a moment Tristram wondered if he had misread the inscription on the tomb, for a woman was coming down the stair, a woman in a nightgown like the one his mother used to wear, and because she carried a candle before her he could not make out her face properly. But then she stopped, and held the candle to one side, and stared down at him, and he looked back into the face of a person he knew was Jennifer but who was not the sixteen-year-old girl he had remembered and loved and struggled to return to.

He spoke her name. She stared back at him, shaking her head and whispering, 'No. . . no. . .' and when he went to embrace her, she recoiled from him as if he were a foul fiend come to haunt her.

He appealed to her. 'Jen! It's me! It's Trist!' He reached out again, but she put out her hand to ward him off.

'It's all right,' he whispered. 'You've only just woken up. It's not a dream, Jen, not a dream. I'm safe back home and I'll never leave you again.' He stopped. A child had started crying in one of the upper rooms. 'Is that – is that our child? Tell me, Jennifer, for the Lord's sake! Is that our child?'

She nodded an affirmative, but was unable to speak. He went on his knees to her, silently imploring her to recognize him, but in reply she drew back in such horror that he was suddenly filled with foreboding that the one possible event he had always striven to banish from his thoughts had taken place.

He stood up and went back down the stair, then looked back at her from the hall. She was crouching like a frightened animal, and the candle was on the step beside her, guttering in the draught from the open front door.

'Are you married, Jennifer?' he asked quietly. 'Is that it?'

When he saw her nod, he experienced a dull thud in his stomach. Why hadn't he guessed it before? How could she have been expected to believe he was still alive after four and a half years? What right had he to expect it of her, he who no longer wore the keepsake she had given him and who had come back with secrets of his own?

Of course she had married! What girl wouldn't have done the same? There were plenty of good lads in the village. Davy Treffry for one. Yes – it was bound to be Davy Treffry, and he would be away at sea now, and Jen would have come back to help Jill look after Nathan and keep house. . . .

He felt a little calmer. He must be gentle with her, forgive – no, not forgive her, for there was nothing to forgive. Understand her. Remain loyal to her, whatever the cost.

'Who was it, then?'

His question had the opposite effect on her to the one he had intended, for Jennifer took up the candlestick and ran away upstairs, and a little while later the child stopped crying and there was a terrible silence in the house, a silence that brought with it a creeping fear of the unknown.

He went up after her and found her in the bedchamber which had once been shared by his mother and father. When he entered, she was bending over a child's bed in the corner by the window.

He saw his son for the first time. The little boy stared fearlessly up at him in the candlelight, a thumb in his mouth, his thick, dark hair rumpled. He went to the boy and crouching down took his hand and looked him in the eye.

'So what's your name, my handsome?' he asked.

'Arthur.'

He nodded, smiling sadly up at Jennifer. 'I knew it would be a boy. And that you'd call him Arthur.'

Jennifer was weeping silently.

'Who was it you married, Jen? Was it Davy Treffry?'

She shook her head, and turned away to the window. The first grey fingers of dawn were already in the sky.

'Who, then?'

She seemed to choke. 'Your mother died last winter,' she began. 'She never gave up hope, Tristram. She used to go out every day to watch for you from the clifftop. We tried to stop her, but she always went – even when she was carrying her child. And then . . . when her time came – ' Jennifer put her hands to her face as if to erase the memory of it. 'It was stillborn, and she died the same day.'

She threw back her head. 'She was the only one of us who believed you were alive. She and our Nathan, that is, but he didn't understand anyway. Your father said . . . he said he'd seen your head go under, Tristram. He told us – over and over again. I had to believe him. What else could I do? And after your mother died . . . he was a changed man, a sad man. We were all sad. And then . . . Davy asked your sister to marry him. I was lonely Tristram . . . and your father was kind to me. We were both lonely. Your father said Davy and Jill shouldn't wait too long. He said your mother wouldn't have wished it. So . . . they were married at Easter and – and there didn't seem to be no choice. We couldn't go on as we were, the two of us in the house. It was – it was either marry, or leave, and I didn't have nowhere to go . . . Oh God! God forgive me!'

He felt a numbing chill. When she put into words what he already knew, it was as if the blood in his veins turned suddenly to ice.

'I'm your father's wife, Tristram,' she whispered. 'I'm Mrs Pascoe. We were wed only a month since. . . . '

A Gentleman from London

He stumbled out of the room and down the stairs, where he was met again by Nathan, with another 'Hollo Tistum!'

'Go back to your bed, Nathan.'

'Getting light!'

'Not time to get up yet, though.'

'Tistum won't go away again?'

'No, I won't go away.'

Nathan nodded wisely to himself and then, with a 'See you soon!' went clumsily up to his room leaving Tristram in the half light, and Joaquim already asleep on the floor in the hall.

He went quietly through to the kitchen and sat by the hob, leaning his back on the chimneypiece for the heat of the banked-up fire, and while a confusion of thoughts clamoured for his attention, candlelight crept in from the hall and a moment later Jennifer came in and sat down at the table, and they faced each other in silence, each too overcome for words, each gazing into the other's face and wondering how Fate could possibly have played them such a terrible trick.

'I never stopped loving you, Trist.'

He stared miserably at the floor, shaking his head. He knew that he should say the same to her, but was unable.

'What we going to do?'

'Run off somewhere?'

'I'm married, Tristram. I've given him my promise. Besides . . . there's Arthur.'

He looked at her. It was hard to believe that the slip of a girl he had known could have matured into the woman who now faced him.

'So what'll you do?' she asked. 'Stay on here at Hill House? Go back to Knollys's yard?'

'I don't know,' he mumbled. 'I don't know anything right now.'

'You know what they'll say in the village. They'll say it's a judgement on us, and maybe they'll be right. And if you stay here with Harry away, well – '

She rose from the table and came to him, and put her hand on his, and for a moment gripped it tightly, as if somehow she could pull them both back into the past, undo her marriage and make them one again. She whispered his name, and he whispered hers: for a few moments she struggled to resist an immense force that drew her to him – but knew that if she gave way to it, if she surrendered will to feeling, they would be swept away by a new and far worse tide of events.

She let go his hand and began to stoke up the fire. 'I'll make you some breakfast,' she said in a very matter of fact way. 'Gammon, eggs and a jug of fresh-drawn ale, all right my love?'

He watched her as she busied herself at the stove, and began to recognize the ways she had, movements of her arms and head, the way she held herself, all the little things that went to make her the girl he had loved.

He gave a sudden, humourless laugh.

'What was that for?' she asked, her back to him.

'I just thought – you're my stepmother.'

She turned quickly. 'Don't ever call me that, Trist. I couldn't bear it.'

She turned back and began breaking eggs into a pan. He tried to imagine her with his own father, tried to understand how she could possibly have allowed herself to be persuaded by him – and remembered a night in a Plymouth bordel, and the glimpse of his father in bed with a whore. He put his head in his hands, trying vainly to erase the memory of it, but was suddenly filled all over again with the same old hatred of that man, who had trampled his way over all their lives, who had bullied his mother into humiliating subjection, who had, if village gossip was to be believed, caused Nathan to be what he was by rough-handling him as a baby, and whose bull-headed obstinacy and self-will had been the very cause of the *Russell* becoming lost in the fog off the Spanish coast.

'Do you love him?'

He had not intended to ask that question. It came out of its own accord.

She went on frying the eggs and gammon. Do I love him? she wondered, and didn't even know the answer herself, for although she had had misgivings as she repeated after Mr Drew her promise to love, honour and obey, she had surprised herself on her wedding night, finding that Harry could be as gentle and expert as she could have wished, and that in spite of herself, she had responded to him and gained as much physical pleasure from their union as had he.

176

But was that love?

She shook her head, but did not turn to give Tristram his answer. 'I was sorry for him, Trist. And – and he was sorry for me. I can't explain. You don't have to have love to make a marriage work, everyone knows that. He's very good to me.'

Tristram looked at the candle on the table. It burnt on, although it was daylight. The flame was useless now. Just a waste of wax and wick.

'When's he expected back?'

She shrugged. 'You know how it is. Autumn sometime. We don't expect 'un 'till we see 'un.' She took down a plate that had been heating by the fire, and heaped the gammon and the four fried eggs onto it. She took a knife from the rack, and cut bread for him, then fetched his father's best leather tankard from the dining hall and filled it with ale from a firkin barrel kept in the larder.

'And is Matthew with him?'

'Aye, Matthew's with him. Says he's going to be a privateer captain himself, one day.'

She put the food before him and he ate ravenously, pausing every few mouthfuls to swill the ale down his throat.

Jennifer watched him. 'They've gone to Ireland, so I believe.'

'Ireland?'

'With the Queen's ships. They're having a rebellion over there, seemingly.'

'Matt's a bit young for war.'

'That's what folk said in the village. But there warn't no holding him – once – ' She stopped herself.

'Once Mother was gone?' Tristram prompted her, and the spark ignited a little flare of jealousy and anger in him. 'Isn't that what you were going to say? No, naught to stop him, nor my father, nor yourself neither, Jen, not with my mother in her grave and out of the road.'

She sat down at the table opposite him. 'It wasn't like that,' she whispered.

'Wasn't it? I'm not so sure. All I know is that if Mother weren't dead, young Matt wouldn't be in Ireland, and you wouldn't be Mrs Pascoe, neither.'

'It isn't like that!' she insisted. 'How was I to know you were alive? I asked everyone – I talked to Davy, and Jan Lanyon and even Bosun Rashleigh. They all said you didn't have a chance, Trist. They said – they said the best thing I could do was put you right out of mind. I even refused Davy because of you. Over a year ago, he come to me and asked me to be his wife – don't tell anyone this – but I knowed your Jill was fond on him, and I said no. I didn't want to make no one else unhappy, see? And when your father was left a widower, and him wandering about the house like he was lost. . . .'

He stared into the candle flame. 'When I was in chains aboard a slave galley, Jen, I used to look out through the ports and glimpse a star, and make myself believe that you were looking at that self-same star. And now – '

He reached across to the candle and blew it out. They were silent for a long time.

She said: 'What happened to the medal, then? The one I put round your neck with my own hands?'

He closed his eyes and saw it as he had seen it so often, lying upon Sara's breast. He remembered a crisp January morning when they had held hands and climbed the last slopes to the Moorish castle on top of Sintra Mountain. He remembered a secret place among the rushes by the Colares river. Haven't I been every bit as false as Jennifer? he wondered. Or are we innocent victims, both caught up in something too big to understand, some fast-running tide of circumstance that can't be stemmed, like the tide that swept our little boat back and forth round Ushant?

'It saved my life a dozen times Jen. They thought I was Catholic, and I didn't tell them otherwise. I made out I was Irish, see. But then I was caught near Lisbon, and – '

'And?'

'They said I'd stole it from them. They beat me to make me admit it, but I wouldn't. Then the lady of the house put a stop to it, and she was Irish herself, Jen. She found I was English straight off. She was good to me, she gave me work as a gardener with Joaquim.'

He felt himself blush, and wanted suddenly to tell her everything, to unburden himself, but knew that by doing so he would only make matters immeasurably worse; so instead he reached across the table for her hands and held them, and they were still gazing hopelessly at each other when there was a knock on the front door.

They leapt apart, and Jennifer went quickly out to answer it. At the back of the house the dogs began barking again. Tristram sat at the table and heard women's voices coming in through the hall, and a few moments later they came into the kitchen: his sister Jill, looking very much the neat wife now, and Marion Treffry, who had a basket of fresh-baked bread on her arm and the pink of early morning in her cheek.

They stood at the doorway and stared in at him; he rose from the table and went to Jill, embracing her. Nathan came downstairs, braying and booming and laughing his maniac laugh – and in the middle of all the chatter and excitement, Tristram caught Jennifer's eye, and it was as if their talk had been another farewell, another leavetaking, for each knew that any chance of opening their hearts to each other in the future must, through the demands of propriety, be slim indeed.

'We heard as how there was a boat found anchored off the strand, and being as Mr Mayhew's men are going through the village asking questions, and everyone's in a pother, I thought best to come up and see if Jennifer here was all right, see,' Jill prated. 'But I never expected –well – I never even dreamed it'd be our Tristram! Why, we all was sure as new-laid eggs was new-laid eggs you were dead, love! Oh, my grief! What a turnabout, what a turnabout!'

Jennifer set about making breakfast for Nathan, and Jill and Marion sat down at the table to hear Tristram's story; and while all this went on there was another knock on the door, and when Nathan went to open it, he found two of Justice Mayhew's men, old Addy Lanyon and Tom Carew, dressed up in their best leather jerkins with helmets on their heads and fresh-oiled pikes in their hands which they had drawn from the village armoury half an hour before.

'We be hinvestigating the harrival of furriners in the night,' Addy Lanyon announced importantly as Nathan brought them through to the kitchen, and then, on seeing Tristram, went white as a sheet and had to sit down.

' 'Sblood!' he said, blowing out his cheeks. 'I be too old for shocks like this!'

Jennifer cut bread and cheese for them, bade them take off their helmets and made Carew sit at the table too, and while all this was going on Marion, who was very fond of little Arthur and like an aunt to him, brought the child in as well, and the kitchen was so full of talk and questions and people that the arrival of one more went unnoticed.

'*Bom dia Senhores e Senhoras,*' Joaquim said gruffly from the door, and touched his forelock.

Jill screamed. 'Lord save us! Who's that?'

Carew and Lanyon sprang to their feet and wished they'd kept their helmets on.

'Joking!' boomed Nathan. 'Joking wants breakfast, Mother! Joking wants – '

'He's a Spaniard!' Jill shrieked. 'Merciful Father, he's a Spaniard!'

Joaquim backed away instinctively and the justices, thinking he was making a move to seize their pikes which they had left in the front hall, rushed him, seized his hands and twisted them up behind his back in a double-Raleigh arm lock.

'Right, this one's hunder harrest,' Lanyon announced.

'In that case I am too,' Tristram said, and going to them held out his fists together. 'Here: you can bind my hands with his, for without Joaquim, I wouldn't be alive today.'

'He's a papist none the less,' Jill said sharply from the other end of the kitchen. 'Anyone can see he's a papist.'

'Not so,' Tristram told her. 'Joaquim's as true a Protestant and Christian as any here present, and on that I'll stake my life.'

Carew looked at Lanyon. 'We'll 'ave to take 'un in, Addy. Mind what Justice Mayhew did say?'

They looked dubiously at Joaquim and longingly at their bread and cheese and jugs of ale; but the call of duty won in the end and they decided they must take Joaquim in charge and, because he insisted upon it, Tristram as well.

As the four men tramped down the lane to Moville House, where Mr Mayhew lived, Joaquim turned to Tristram with a wry smile and remarked: '*Mesma merda – outras moscas.*'

'What was that? What did he say?' Lanyon demanded.

Tristram grinned but said nothing because he decided that these two officers of the law would not take kindly to the translation: 'Same dung – different flies.'

'So you have definitely seen nothing at all?' asked Justice Mayhew for at least the fifth time that morning, and Sir Gregory Roscarrock, still hale but beginning to look his years now, reassured the magistrate on his honour as a knight and a gentleman that no one in the household had knowledge of any landing whatsoever.

They stood in the forecourt of Roscarrock Hall, the beeches creaking in the wind. This was not the first time Mayhew had had cause to question Sir Gregory. He was sure that the Roscarrocks could not maintain their estate and pay their pew fines without support from abroad, and that such support could only be earned in certain ways. Now that the rumours of foreign agents and invasion were multiplying at such an alarming rate, he was uncomfortably aware that this old and apparently gentle Catholic family might be furthering the papist cause under his very nose.

But the balance of equilibrium in the village was a very fine one, and Mayhew knew that if ever he decided to order a search of Roscarrock Hall (and there had been only two searches in the past ten years) he had to have a good reason for it, for every fruitless search caused a loss of face and put Sir Gregory and his son further on their guard.

'Very well!' he said now, and swinging himself up into the saddle, rode off down the gravelled drive and out between the high, iron gates.

As he came to the Y junction where one lane goes straight down past the fort to the village and the other goes across to Fore Street, he was met by Salvation Polwhele, the father of Pete and Nick, who looked very flushed and out of breath, having run all the way from Moville House.

'Justice Mayhew, zir!' he burred between gasps for breath. 'It were young Tristram Pascoe in the boat! 'E be come back with a Portingal, an' Addy Lanyon and Tom Carew got 'em in charge over by your place, zir!'

'Have they indeed?' replied Mayhew, and urged his mount into a canter, so that the gold chain he wore around his neck leapt and thudded on his chest.

He found the four of them waiting by the stables, and as he rode up, Lanyon and Carew stiffened to attention.

'We got 'em sir!' Lanyon said proudly.

'So I see,' said Mayhew and dismounted. He went over to Tristram. 'Well, well, Master Pascoe!' he exclaimed quietly. 'I never thought I would see this day!'

Mayhew had been widowed ten years before and now lived at Moville House in semi-seclusion, a man known for punctilious loyalty to the Crown, ardent support of the new English clergy, and close contact – principally by letter – with certain gentlemen close to the Queen. He was a great reader and classicist; he kept an excellent table and cellar; he spoke little, listened much, owed no one a penny and gave regularly, though not overgenerously, to the poor.

He had long ago given up any hope of making his mark in the world, having discovered from his study of history that such aspirations are seldom realized by those who are not prepared to dedicate their lives wholly to their ambition; and now, at fifty, he was content to fulfil his role as a Justice of the Peace and to contribute in a small way to the complicated machinery of law and order upon which England's peace and stability had come to depend.

'So,' he began, when he had seated himself in his study and Tristram Pascoe stood before him, 'I understand you arrived by boat in the night, is that correct?'

'Aye, sir.'

'And that you have brought with you . . . a Portuguese?'

'Sir.'

So the questions began, and within a very few minutes Justice Mayhew saw that the story Tristram had to tell was so long and his experiences so varied that a written record would have to be made and forwarded to the Lieutenant of the Hundred.

Tristram was ordered to bring up a chair, and Mayhew reached for pen and ink, and for the rest of the day the young man was quietly but thoroughly grilled on every town, village, port and gaol he had visited, every name he could remember and the exact circumstances of his escape and voyage back from Lisbon in an open boat.

The record of this interrogation covered six leaves of folio, and when it was finished, Tristram was required to read it through and sign it as being an accurate record of his adventures.

It was by now late afternoon, and Tristram was very short of sleep. 'Sir – what of my servant, Joaquim?' he asked. 'As I told you, he is a good man and I should not like to see him ill-used.'

Mayhew rang a bell, and when his manservant appeared sent for Joaquim to be brought in.

'Do you speak English?' Mayhew demanded, when Joaquim stood before him.

Joaquim shook his head.

'Sir,' put in Tristram, who knew that Joaquim's Latin was near perfect, 'I've heard tell that Portuguese is so close to Latin that if it is spoken slow, even the humblest peasant can understand a little of it.'

'Can they indeed?' replied Mayhew, and proceeded to conduct a conversation in Latin with Joaquim which Tristram did not understand at all, apart from seeing that Joaquim was careful to play a dumb-but-honest role that seemed to satisfy the magistrate.

The guards were sent for again, and Joaquim taken out under escort.

'Will he be allowed to stay, sir?' Tristram ventured.

Mayhew shook his head. 'No, he'll have to go to Launceston, as he's an alien.'

'Then I must go with him, Justice Mayhew,' Tristram said gravely. 'I owe my life to that man, sir. He's one of nature's gentlemen and I'll not see him treated ill. I'm willing to be held responsible for aught he says or does, sir, I swear it – '

And then he made what he saw afterwards was nearly a terrible mistake, for he had become so used to making the sign of the Cross to emphasize his words that his hand went quickly up to his forehead, and he stopped himself only just in time.

Mayhew gave him a very penetrating look, and Tristram had a feeling he knew very well what that sudden movement of the hand had been. Does he think I'm a papist? he wondered, and half expected to be clapped in irons and carted off for trial that moment.

But to his surprise, the magistrate gave way. 'Very well, Master Pascoe. If you'll give me your signature to that, and are prepared to answer for all and every one of his actions – '

'Sir – I'll gladly sign anything you ask if it will keep that good man out of gaol!'

So a further paper was signed and when the sand was blown off the ink, Mayhew sat back in his chair and asked the young man what he intended to do now.

'Why – pick up where I left off, sir. I'd like to see out my apprenticeship at Knollys's yard – '

'And where will you live?'

Tristram looked surprised. 'At home, sir. Where else?'

'In Hill House? No, lad, you can't stay there, not with young Jennifer you can't. You'd scandalize every wife and mother in the village, and justifiably so too, in my opinion. No, if you stay here in Polruan at all it'll have to be under another roof.'

'I don't know who'd have me, sir.'

Mayhew considered for a few moments. There was no doubt in his mind that Tristram was a most unusual young man, and he was beginning to think that his unique experiences since being lost overboard from his father's ship must fit him for some useful service.

'What about Mrs Treffry? She's a good soul, and has a room to spare now that her Davy's got a place of his own. As for that – that "servant" of yours, he can come and mend some of my walls to earn his bread. In the meantime, I suggest you go down to the Russell Inn, the pair of you, so that those who want to can hear your story from your own lips, and we don't fill the whole village up with gossip and idle talk.' Mayhew tossed a crown piece across to Tristram. 'There you are lad, something to start you off. And remember – don't you or your Portuguese friend try to leave this parish without my permission, understood?'

'Understood, sir! Thank you, sir! Thank you very kindly, sir!'

Mayhew nodded and dismissed him; and when he had gone returned to his desk and took out another sheet of paper, upon which he started a letter addressed to a gentleman of Greenwich which began:

Sir,

I have the honour to report to you the circumstances attendant upon the return to Polruan of one TRISTRAM PASCOE, a young man of this village who has recently escaped from slavery in Portugal, and who has accomplished the remarkable feat of sailing in an open boat back from Lisbon. In view of the nature of his experiences, and the special qualities of endurance and seamanship which this young man has displayed, together with the fact that he has a good knowledge of Portuguese and Spanish and is a loyal subject of Her Majesty, I have no hesitation in recommending him for special service in the defence of the Realm. . . .

The Russell Inn was crowded out that night, and many of the womenfolk broke with custom by accompanying their husbands into the ale parlour to hear Tristram tell his story. He sat on the bar fender with Joaquim, a long tankard of ale in his hand, and went over the whole odyssey again, so that by the time he had finished he was a local hero and for days after he was followed about the village by Polruan's children, who gazed upon him like a god or dared each other to run and touch him.

Mol Treffry was only too happy to invite him to stay, and so was her daughter Marion, who fell in love with the lodger overnight and soon began to nurse hopes of matrimony.

On the face of things Tristram and Joaquim seemed to be sitting pretty: Mr Knollys agreed to take Tristram back at the shipyard, and Joaquim – who was delighted with the simplicity of the church services at St Saviour's – settled down to rebuilding Mr Mayhew's walls and husbanding his orchard. Two or three times a week Tristram, Joaquim, Jill and Marion were invited up to Hill House for a meal with Jennifer; and these comfortable family evenings did a great deal to help Tristram to readjust to being a free man again.

In spite of his new easy circumstances however, Tristram soon began to be restless. Polruan was, after all, a very small village indeed and he could not summon much enthusiasm for the art of building hoys and crumsters. Though he saw Jennifer and his son regularly it was always in the company of Jill and the Treffrys, so he had no opportunity for private conversation with Jennifer, and knew that even if such an opportunity arose, there was little more that could be said on either side.

But there was a darker cloud on his horizon, and this was caused by the expectation of the *Russell*'s return before Christmas. When that happened, he knew the village would prove too small a place for himself and his father to live amicably, and that a further collision between them was inevitable.

Harry had come a long way in five years. After that first disastrous cruise into the Atlantic he had brought the ship home, refitted her, engaged a new navigator, called for fresh volunteers and set sail again in the spring with heavier armament embarked and stricter rules enforced. Taking a leaf out of Drake's book, he had trained and drilled his men to work the ship with ever-increasing efficiency, so that by the time they found their first prize off the Barbary coast they were able to sail rings round her and reduce her to a smoking, mastless wreck with no more than six broadsides from the brass sakers. Admittedly she was only a Spanish urca with a cargo of salt fish and olive oil, but the master and his gentlemen wore some fine rings and gold chains, and there was a small hoard of silver ducats in the ship's strongbox, so that by the time Bosun Rashleigh's boarding party had put the Spanish crew into their boats and set fire to the ship, Harry Pascoe had made enough profit to pay his crew, refit the *Russell* and leave himself very comfortable, thank you.

Two equally successful cruises had followed and Harry began to believe that he was on the road to fame and success. On learning that Ann was pregnant in '79, he sailed off to the Windward Islands sure that the Lord was smiling upon him and that when he returned he would be the father of another fine son like Matthew.

But when he arrived home Ann was dead and buried, and he was hurt far more than he cared to admit. Suddenly his habit of flirting with Jennifer turned into a desperate need for her affection, and when Jill announced her betrothal to Davy Treffry, Harry had little difficulty in convincing himself that it was his duty as a Christian to marry Jennifer and be a father to her son.

She had not been easily persuaded, however, and he had been obliged to use all the charm and gentleness at his command. But he surprised himself in this, and made the discovery that being gentle with a maid (or in this case, a young unmarried mother) could yield unexpected results, so that when Jennifer gave in and agreed to be his wife, he achieved that gratifying experience of pleasuring her more effectively than either of them had expected.

Suddenly, life was good. For three weeks after the wedding Harry Pascoe and his new wife scarcely emerged from their front door except to attend at St Saviour's on a Sunday morning. What did it matter what folk were saying down in the village? He had consulted with Justice Mayhew and Reverend Drew and had obtained their assurance that the marriage was legal and did not in any way violate the Church of England's new rules of kindred and affinity. He had signed documents to make himself the legal parent of Arthur, and if his nightly exercises with Jennifer were anything to go by, the chances were high that he could look forward to starting another family, and so increase his stature in society yet further.

But what gave him the most lasting satisfaction – a satisfaction deeper even than that achieved when his pleasure with Jennifer was at its height – was the fact that by taking her to wife he had not only retrieved the face he had lost when he had been tricked by Martha into losing her to Sam Gristy, but had also, in a complicated way, scored off the memory of his own son, and proved himself once more as a man.

Less than a month after his wedding day, in early July, Harry received news from Plymouth that an extra ship was needed to carry soldiers and supplies to Ireland, where Lord Grey and the Earl of Ormonde were engaged in suppressing the papist rebellion, and as he had long had an ambition to sail with the Queen's ships he lost no time in volunteering his services.

Like every other English shipmaster on the south coast, Harry knew very well that the peace with Spain which Queen Elizabeth went to such lengths to maintain was now a very fragile one, and he had no doubt that the illegal landing of a papal force under Fitzmaurice the previous year and the more recent arrival of the papal legate along with reinforcements under the command of San Giuseppe could be a Catholic foot in the door that would lead to an all-out landing upon English shores; so when he dropped anchor in Dingle Bay at the end of July, he saw nothing but good in the ruthless methods Lord Grey and the Earl of Ormonde were using to subdue the locals.

That summer of 1580 was a terrible time for the people of Corcaguiney, and it was only because Ballingolin Castle was on the far side of the bay that the Hussey family did not suffer as badly as some. Cattle were slaughtered; crops were burnt; stockades were broken down and women and children raped and butchered. Dingle was sacked and burnt, and the streets decorated with hanging corpses. The people began to die of starvation. Farmers offered up their wives and children to be slain rather than see their milch cows slaughtered, and it was rumoured that some of Ormonde's soldiers had chopped up babies and roasted their flesh, and that infants had been tossed among the soldiers like play-balls and caught on their sharply pointed pikes.

By the end of October much of the pasture land had been laid waste and the major part of the livestock slaughtered. The locals were existing in huts and caves, and some had taken refuge with San Giuseppe, who, along with Dr Saunders and six hundred men, had retired within the walls of the Fort del Oro. But their choice of refuge was not a happy one: perched on the edge of Smerwick Harbour in that beautiful fertile plain between the Three Sisters headland to the north and Mount Eagle and Slea Head to the south, the fort was an easy target from landward and seaward.

Admiral Sir William Winter's squadron arrived in the bay on a crisp, clear day in early November, and having anchored out of gun range of the fort, the shipmasters were summoned to a council of war aboard the flagship. Harry buckled on his sword and struggled into a stiff ruff. He put on a heavy gold chain and had himself rowed across in his longboat by a crew dressed in their best seamen's smocks for the occasion, but he was disappointed to find that he had to scramble up a Jacob's ladder to get aboard and that as the most junior captain present he had to stand at the back while the deliberations proceeded.

The habit of smoking tobacco was now much in favour among nautical men, and within a short time there was a blue fug in the admiral's great cabin where the council was held. Present in addition to Lord Grey and Admiral Winter were Walter Raleigh and Lord Grey's secretary, the poet Edmund Spenser, and it was the latter, during the discussion of tactics to be used for the bombardment of the fort, who put foward a novel method of pouring the greatest amount of shot into the fort in the quickest possible time.

'Should it not be possible, Sir William,' he said in a resonant voice that commanded immediate attention, 'for the ships to sail round the bay in line, so that as each ship brings the fort abeam, her guns may be discharged in broadside? In this way shall we not make best use of the physical shape of the bay, and ensure that the least time is wasted in reloading and manoeuvring?'

At dawn the following morning, Lord Grey's battery opened fire upon the landward battlements of the fort, and as soon as sufficient breeze had picked up, the English squadron weighed anchor and formed up in line ahead, so that San Giuseppe's soldiers soon found themselves under attack from opposite points of the compass.

On board the *Russell*, Matthew Pascoe enjoyed every minute of the two-day operation. This was his first taste of action, and it seemed to him to be a very pleasant way of earning a living. Standing at his father's side, he acted as messenger for Harry, bearing orders to Bosun Rashleigh upon the type of shot to be loaded and the number of pieces to be fired, instructions to Mr Lanyon on the trim of the sails, and exhortations to the men working 'tween decks.

In between times, while the *Russell* followed in the wake of the next ahead, putting about in the mouth of the bay and sailing down upon the fort on a starboard reach, Matthew stood on the poop with his arms folded and his feet braced well apart in the way he had seen Admiral Winter stand. Narrowing his eyes like a veteran, he watched for the p-p-p-puff of white smoke coming from Lord Grey's battery on shore and listened for the b-b-b-boom that followed it, nodding to himself in precocious satisfaction when he saw a further section of the fortifications crumble under the barrage.

On the second day, having pleaded at length with his father, he was given charge of his own saker and gun's crew, and as he already knew every gunner's order by heart he had no difficulty in gaining his men's trust and proving that he had the making of a gunner in him, even if he was only thirteen years old.

Really he would have liked that day to go on for ever: bawling out the orders to load, ram, run out and fire, he found himself in the grip of something he did not fully understand. His only previous experience that came anywhere near it was the time a year before when his father had taken him to the Russell Inn and he had drunk himself into a stupor for the first time in his life. Now, as then, he felt a strange sensation of being detached from himself – as if the rumble of the gun carriages, the oaths of the men, the crack and roar of the ordnance were in their own way as intoxicating as strong Malmsey wine.

Towards evening, when the papal banner fluttered down from the fort and two white flags were hoisted in its place; when Bosun Rashleigh passed the order, 'Cease firing! Sponge out – secure guns – return gear!' Matthew felt a positive ache of disappointment that the bombardment could not have lasted longer.

'So, lad,' his father said to him that evening when the crew had been issued with double rations of ale and the afterguard were celebrating in the great cabin. 'Your first crack at the Pope!'

Matthew was hoarse from shouting. 'And not the last, let's hope, Father!' he croaked, pleased that his voice sounded so manly.

Harry beamed upon the boy, of whom he was both fond and proud. 'We'll drink to that,' he said to his pilot and his gentleman adventurer, and the party of four rose to their feet.

'Queen Bess!' Harry announced, raising his cup. 'And a slow death to every papist!'

In the morning, after lengthy negotiations between Lord Grey and San Giuseppe, when the latter believed he had been offered pledges of mercy for his soldiers and all the local families who had taken shelter with him, the siege of Smerwick was lifted.

The Queen's soldiers entered, and having taken possession of the arms, ammunition and victuals, ordered the insurgents out; whereupon Lord Grey, who regarded this cosmopolitan collection of Catholics as the hirelings of Antichrist, and who did not consider himself to be bound by any promise of clemency, gave the order for bands of pikemen to advance, and seven hundred were slaughtered and their headless bodies laid out in neat lines on the fine white sands of Smerwick Harbour.

Harry put in at Plymouth to collect payment for his services to the Crown before returning to Polruan, and took Matthew ashore with him to see the city. When they entered the front parlour of the Pelican Inn there were few other customers present, so father and son were able to find places at a settle and drink their mulled muscadine by the fire.

Harry enjoyed his youngest son's company, because Matthew was always ready to listen to him air his views on world events, and it wasn't very long before he was back on his favourite subject.

'What he's done,' he was saying, 'is to make one of his bulls. You know what a bull is, don't you, Matt?'

'Aye, Father.'

Harry winked at a bald, urbane-looking gentleman who had come in just after them and whose white bull terrier was now stretching himself contentedly before the fire.

'What is it, then? Let's be hearing from you.'

'Marry, Father – it's a kind of paper, isn't that so?'

'Writ on paper maybe, but more than that. It's an order he sends out to all the miserable wretches who call him "Father" and hold to the heresy that he's Christ's vicar on earth.' Harry spat into the fire. 'It's like an order to his people, Matt, that's what a bull is. And what he's said in this one is that although our good Queen's excommunicated and accursed – aye, that's what he says – although her Majesty's a heretic by his lights, he says that the Catholics of England are allowed to obey her until the day *he* sees fit to call them to rebellion. Now what d'you make of that?'

Matthew had already heard a lot of talk about Pope Gregory's latest bull, and was as anxious to parrot his knowledge as his father was for him to do so. 'I reckon he's made every last papist into a secret traitor, Father.'

'Right indeed, lad, right you are indeed!' said Harry, delighted to have given his son the opportunity to shine in public.

He glanced at the gentleman in the corner, who obligingly caught his eye.

' "Out of the mouths of babes and sucklings",' quoted the gentleman, and his refined accent told Harry immediately that he was from London, and quite possibly the court.

Harry lost no time in making his acquaintance. 'Allow me to introduce myself, sir,' he said, putting on the manner he used when he wanted to impress. 'Henry Pascoe, shipmaster and owner of the bark *Russell*, lately returned from the Queen's service in Ireland. And this is my son Matthew, who has sailed with me and had his first whiff of gunpowder.'

'At your service, sir!' Matthew said, having got to his feet in order to bow in the way his father had taught him.

The gentleman seemed mildly amused at this, and said he was pleased to make the acquaintance. 'Just back from Ireland?' he asked Harry. 'With Admiral Winter's squadron, were you?'

This gave Pascoe just the chance he wanted to give the gentleman – and any other of those present who cared to listen – a blow-by-blow account of his exploits, but as the *Russell* had been the last of Admiral Winter's flotilla to return to Plymouth (Harry had gone seaward of the Blaskets and the Scillies) his story held little interest for the few regulars in the bar, who smiled behind his back and remarked that anyone would have thought this Cornish dolt was Drake himself, and just back from a circumnavigation.

The gentleman from London was far more obliging however, and kept Pascoe supplied with a flow of questions and promptings and restrained exclamations of surprise, so that by the time Harry had explained the

ingenious new method of bombardment in Smerwick Harbour – which
he hinted had been his own idea – he was sure he was making a markedly
favourable impression upon someone of position and influence.

'And – er – who have I the honour of addressing?' he asked eventually,
realizing that he didn't even know the fellow's name.

'Wray,' replied the other. 'William Wray.'

'So what brings you to the south-west, Mr Wray?' Harry asked, and
winked quickly to his son when Wray wasn't watching.

Wray explained that he was acting as an agent for the Crown, and was
engaged in inspecting ships being built in the west country for the
Queen's service.

Harry sat up and looked interested. 'Are you indeed?' he said, and
ordered the serving girl to refill Mr Wray's tankard. 'You should come to
Polruan in that case, for our Mr Knollys builds as sturdy ships as you'll
see anywhere, and I can prove my word if you like, for he built the *Russell*
for me twenty years ago.' Harry had a sudden idea. 'Would you care to
see over her, Mr Wray?'

Wray looked gratifyingly solemn and interested. 'I would indeed, Mr
Pascoe.'

They finished their drinks and stood up to go. 'You don't mind if
Hobden accompanies us I suppose?' Wray asked, indicating a tall man in
his forties with thinning hair and the precise air of a civil servant. He had
been sitting nearby throughout their conversation, but Harry had hardly
noticed him.

'Not at all!' he replied, feeling a little put out as he had just winked at
Matthew for a second time behind Wray's back and was sure Hobden
must have seen.

'And of course Barty must come too, because Barty is an expert on
ships,' Wray said, and called to his bull terrier, who stretched and
yawned and got to his feet and wagged his whip-like tail against his
master's legs, snuffling and grunting through his nose as he followed
them out of the door.

'And what of the rest of your family, Mr Pascoe?' Wray asked as he sat
with his yeoman and his dog in the sternsheets of Pascoe's jollyboat. 'Is
Matthew here your eldest?'

'No, my eldest boy was lost at sea nearly five years back. Matthew's my
youngest, and he has an elder brother and sister.'

'So you are a true family man, Mr Pascoe. What a fortunate man you
are, and how fortunate your good wife must be!'

Harry looked at Matthew and explained quickly that he had lost his first wife just over a year before. 'But I have taken another wife, happily, and will be home to see her afore long.'

The boat went alongside, and when Barty had been hoisted aboard in a canvas bag, Harry gave a conducted tour, during which he dropped several hints that he was looking for a backer to finance the building of another ship at Knollys's yard. Mr Wray listened to him with grave attention, and seemed genuinely appreciative of everything he saw. He also had the tact to make no remark upon the foul stench that rose from the ship's ballast.

'I would much like to meet this shipwright Knollys,' he remarked when Pascoe had brought them back to his cabin and a servant was pouring Spanish wine taken from the Fort del Oro. 'How far is Polruan by road?'

'By road – a day's journey, and one filled with hazard for the traveller, withal,' Harry said. 'But if you care to take passage aboard my ship, Mr Wray, we can sail at dawn and be in the Fowey's mouth by nightfall.'

Wray turned to his yeoman and asked if they could spare the time. Hobden bit his lip and looked rather mournful. 'We have to visit Falmouth and Bideford yet, sir. . . .'

But Wray decided, on balance, that he was so impressed by Mr Pascoe's ship and the reputation of Knollys's yard, that the diversion was worthwhile.

'In that case, you are my guests!' Harry announced, and having given orders to Mr Lanyon to have the ship in all respects ready for sea by first light the next day, he took Mr Wray, Mr Hobden and Matthew ashore again and treated them to a slap-up meal in the city.

There was frosty fog the following morning and little more than a breath of wind, but Pascoe decided to warp out nevertheless as he knew Plymouth harbour well, so with the oars of the longboat creaking and the leadsman singing out the depths from the forepeak, the *Russell* slipped out past the Hoe like a grey ghost in the mist.

In spite of Harry's predictions of a quick passage, light winds prevented much progress that day, and by nightfall the *Russell* was still off Rame Head, with the fog coming down again and the sails barely filling. At the dinner table that night, with the lantern swinging gently over their heads, William Wray asked about the circumstances of Tristram's death and Harry put on a suitably grieved expression and told the story he had told so often before, about the loss of his pilot and the terrible mistake of navigation Tristram had made, and how, but for his own seaman's instinct, they would have been dashed upon the coast of Andalusia.

'And this young man's following the family tradition, is he?' Wray asked, looking at Matthew.

'Aye, sir!' replied Matthew. 'I'd like to serve in the Queen's ships one day, sir!'

'With Frank Drake, like every other keen young blade in the west country, I've no doubt!'

'And he may yet, Mr Wray,' Harry put in, 'for he has the makings of a master gunner in him, isn't that right, Matt?'

Matthew grinned proudly at this, but the conversation was interrupted when Davy Treffry – who was now captain of the foretop – came down to report that the wind was veering north-west and freshening, and Harry went up on deck to take charge.

In the morning, when Wray and Hobden came up on deck, the ship was hove-to off the entrance to the Fowey and final preparations were being made for entering harbour. Harry was pacing up and down with Mr Lanyon at his side, and Barty, who had been tied to the mizzen for the night, was barking and howling for his master.

'Good morning, good morning!' Harry said briskly. 'We shall be entering within the hour.'

'Launches coming out now, sir!' shouted Davy Treffry from the forecastle.

When the courses and topsails had been brailed, tow lines were passed down to the launches and the *Russell* proceeded in through the mouth of the Fowey. Watching the operation from the aftercastle, Harry was just thinking about Jennifer and the welcome she would have ready for him, when Treffry came up the ladder and reported to him.

'Mr Pascoe, sir!'

He turned. His son-in-law was nearly as tall as he, a heavily built young man with an honest look and a thick, blond beard. But at that moment, there was something in his expression that was akin to fear.

'Well?'

'Sir – we've just had it from the men in the tow-boats that your Tristram's alive. He's come back, sir – back to Polruan, and awaits you this minute.'

Harry felt as if his heart had for a moment stopped beating. He turned away quickly and stared up at the gulls wheeling and gliding astern.

'Bad news, Mr Pascoe?' enquired Wray – and behind them, Hobden turned away to conceal the flicker of a smile.

The news that the *Russell* was off the harbour entrance had spread through Polruan by dawn, and soon afterwards Jennifer went along the cliff path below St Saviour's.

The sun was a pale disc behind the mist, and a gentle swell was slapping lazily on the rocks. No one else was on this part of the cliff: the womenfolk and families always gathered by the fort when the *Russell* came in.

A little to the east of the headland, the path descended into a dip before going on along the cliff edge, and as Jennifer went along it she saw Tristram. He was watching as the *Russell* struck her sails and was taken in tow.

He turned at her approach. She climbed the remaining yards and stood with him, staring wordlessly up at him. They had not spoken privately since that first early morning of his return. Now, each was aware that this was their last chance.

'Shall we go on a bit?' he asked quietly, and she nodded, as anxious as he to avoid being seen alone with him.

They went down between brambles and gorse, and climbed up again to the cliff above Washing Rocks. She took his hands and faced him. The *Russell* was out of sight.

'I'm his wife,' she said. 'I can't pretend otherwise. You do understand that, don't you?'

He nodded. Below them, gulls circled, crying mournfully.

'Whatever happens I want you to know that you're the only one I ever loved, Trist. There's no one else but me in this world as can make you happy. It's still true, isn't it?'

'Aye, it's true, Jen,' he mumbled, but knew very well that it wasn't, and that neither he nor Jennifer was speaking from the heart.

And then she begged him to hold her – 'just for a minute, Trist, like we used to' – and they stood sadly together, she with her head under his chin and he looking southward to the horizon, while the waves broke gently on the boulders a hundred feet below.

'Time changes people, Trist,' she whispered, and smiled to him through tears.

'I know,' he said. 'I know.'

194

Half an hour later, when Jennifer had gone back to the house, Tristram was on the stone quay in Polruan harbour when his father came ashore, and most of the village had turned out to welcome home their loved ones and witness the reunion of father and son.

Sitting up in the sternsheets with his two guests, Harry stared ahead while the boat came alongside. Then he leapt up onto the quay, and stood face to face with his son.

'Father – ' Tristram started, and came towards him; but although they embraced and tears came to Harry Pascoe's eyes, Tristram was immediately certain that in spite of Jennifer's words, time had changed nothing, and the same old enmity lurked between them.

There were twelve for dinner at Hill House that night. They sat at the oak refectory table in the hall, Harry at one end and Tristram at the other, with Jennifer, Nathan, Hobden, Davy and Jill on Harry's right, and Mol Treffry, William Wray, Matthew, Joaquim and Marion on his left.

Harry had insisted that as he and Davy were still newlyweds they should have their brides sit beside them, and he went out of his way from the start to show who Jennifer belonged to by paying her compliments, putting his arm round her waist, kissing her cheek and making one or two sly remarks about joys to come. Jennifer took this in good part, but was careful never to look in Tristram's direction, and as the evening went on and Harry proceeded to get himself drunk, Tristram was not often to be seen looking up from his plate.

Inevitably, most of the talk was about Harry's doings in Ireland and when Tristram heard Dingle mentioned he looked at Joaquim, who now understood some English and who had also heard the name of Sara's birthplace.

'What was that town – Dingle – like, Father?' he asked.

'A good enough anchorage,' Harry replied, 'and a pretty enough place withal, if you care for barren mountains and windy shores. But as for the town – that's in cinders, burnt by your Earl Ormonde.'

'And what of the people?'

'The people of Dingle?' Harry winked at Matthew. 'We didn't speak with many people, did we Matt?'

Matthew laughed and helped himself to more cider. 'Marry, father, we did not!'

'And you know why?' Harry looked round his audience. 'Go on Matt, tell 'em why!'

Matthew grinned and showed a set of yellow teeth. 'They be hung, mostly. Hung up by the neck on every street corner for to put the fear of God into they papists.' He turned to Tristram, whom he was clearly anxious to impress. 'But sacking the fort at Smerwick was better sport, Trist. Firing broadsides all day long we were, all day long for two days, so there weren't no more than a couple of barrels of powder left at the end, and the roundshot was all but used up. And afterwards, when the papists were done for, I took the cockboat ashore and their helmets were like cockles on a beach and I took one for a prize, and I got 'un on board. And one of they soldiers of Lord Grey's regiment let me fire his harquebus an' all, and they'd strung up the papists' heads for targets, and when you hit 'un, 'e goes like that – pfffsh! – like an old rotten egg!'

Having spent the night as guests of Mr Mayhew, Wray and Hobden visited Knollys's yard in the company of Harry Pascoe the following morning. Mr Knollys was nearing seventy now and very bent and frail, though his eye was still as good as ever and the crumster that was nearing completion on the stocks was proof of his shipbuilding skill.

With his bull terrier snuffling along at his heels, Wray took a keen interest in this and several smaller contracts that were on hand. He spoke kindly to the old artisans who wielded handsaws, spokeshaves and adzes, and when he returned to the drawing office where Tristram was engaged in designing a hatchcover, he quizzed Knollys at some length on the maximum size of ship that could be built in the yard.

'Marry, zir,' Knollys mumbled, smoothing the oak grain of the drawing table with a gnarled hand, 'I reckon we'm talking about a hundred tons or so, zir. Mebbe hundred and twenty. Limited by the keel length we are, see zir.'

Wray glanced at Hobden, who looked as poker faced as ever. Then he turned to Pascoe. 'We had bigger ships in mind than that, Mr Pascoe, did we not?'

'You'll get bigger ships built over Fowey side, zir,' Knollys put in. 'Bigger, aye, but not better, mind.'

Wray nodded to himself for some seconds, and gazed out of the drawing-office window, which commanded a view across the river to the small forest of masts along the Fowey foreshore. 'Then – I'm greatly obliged to you,' he said suddenly, as if taking a final decision; and ignoring Pascoe's look of dismay, he headed for the door.

As they were leaving the drawing office however, Wray appeared to have an afterthought. 'I'd like to hear more from that son of yours, Mr Pascoe,' he said.

'You mean my youngest – Matthew – '

'No – this one here. Tristram isn't it?'

Pascoe laughed. 'I don't think Master Tristram can be of much interest to you, Mr Wray. He's spent the last five years pulling on an oar in a Spanish slave galley from what I can make out. Now my Matthew – there's a real lad for you, Mr Wray. Young Matthew's got the makings of a – '

Wray cut him short. 'Ask the young man to come up to Justice Mayhew's before noon,' he told Hobden, and Harry lapsed into a sulky silence as they walked back into the village.

Tristram approached Justice Mayhew's door a few hours later with mixed feelings: at dinner the previous evening Wray had ignored him and he had had the impression that Mr Hobden was keeping him under some sort of surveillance, so whatever it was they wished to see him about he could not believe that it was likely to be for his own benefit.

The door was opened to him before he could knock and instead of being shown into Mayhew's study he was taken straight through the house and down some steps to a small outhouse which had once served as a dairy. There, Wray sat behind a small table with Barty asleep at his feet and Hobden standing at his side.

'Sit on that milking stool, Mr Pascoe,' Hobden said, and Tristram obeyed.

Wray lifted some leaves of folio, which Tristram recognized as the statement Mayhew had taken from him some months before.

'We've read your account,' he said quietly, 'and very interesting reading it makes, too.'

Tristram waited. Wray glanced through the pages again and seemed just about to ask another question, when Hobden snapped: 'What was the name of the village in which you stayed before escaping by sea?'

'Colares, sir.'

Wray leafed through the statement, then nodded.

'And the name of the family which employed you?'

'Santarém, sir. Valdez de Santarém.'

'And had the master and mistress issue?'

'No sir, they were childless. The Count lived in Lisbon most of the time, sir, and his lady at the quinta in Colares.'

There was a silence. Then, abruptly, Hobden's questions began again:

'How did you come to fall overboard from your father's ship?'

'We were towing off, sir, having made a close landfall in fog. I was in a boat and we were capsized.'

'Did no one try to save you?'

'We were still very close under the cliffs, sir. And – '

'And what?'

'Well – I was left astern, sir. I suppose they couldn't run the risk of stopping for me.'

'Have you spoken to your father about it since his return?'

'No sir.'

They both looked at him.

Wray said gently: 'Why not, Tristram?'

He felt himself blush. Since that first gesture of paternal love his father had shown him on the quay the day before, Harry had hardly spoken two words to him.

'I – didn't feel it my place to ask him, sir.'

Wray nodded; there was another pause. Just when Wray seemed about to frame a question, Hobden started on a new tack.

'And your stepmother. What were your relations with her before you went to sea?'

He flushed again and felt sweat breaking out.

'Are you not the father of her child?'

'Sir – I beg you – please – spare me questions to which you already have answers!'

Hobden crossed and stood behind him. The silence went on so long that Tristram began fighting to prevent himself bursting out a demand to know why he was being interrogated in this way; but he had been questioned many times before, and knew that it was best, always, to answer as briefly and honestly as possible, and never to volunteer information.

Wray leant forward and joined his hands on the deal table. 'Was there not . . . a keepsake you used to wear? A silver medallion?'

He had said nothing of that in his statement, and wondered for a moment if they or Justice Mayhew had obtained the information from Joaquim; but then, his mind racing on every possibility, he realized that the crew of the *Russell* had known about the Madonna and that there had been five years in which to gossip about that and every other aspect of his absence. And hadn't Wray and Hobden crossed from Plymouth with his father? What else might they have found out while they were on board the *Russell*? Who else had they talked to? Had they come to Polruan to arrest him? He was beginning to wonder if he might have done better to stay at Colares and face the Inquisition.

'Aye, sir.'

'What sort of medallion?' Hobden put in.

He felt suddenly angry and careless of his own safety. 'It was a Madonna,' he said, and for the first time his impatience came through in the tone of his reply.

Wray took up the questioning again. 'And it was given to you by Jennifer Gristy, Tristram, is that right?'

'Sir.'

'And where did she get it? Wasn't it from her mother?'

'I believe that to be so, aye, sir.'

He saw Wray glance at Hobden behind his back, and a moment later the yeoman put his mouth close to Tristram's ear and asked in a loud and very hard voice: 'Would you be a secret papist by any chance, Mister Pascoe?'

He denied it and continued to deny it, however many times he was asked and however many ways Wray and Hobden contrived to lead him into an admission. But they were not satisfied with simple denials: they wanted reasons and explanations, detailed accounts of the simplest little incidents, verbatim reconstructions of conversations; word pictures of ports he had visited, fortifications he had seen and ships he had voyaged in, whether as a pressed soldier or miserable slave.

Their questions followed no logical order: they leapt about in time, from the circumstances attending the death of Mr Bryant to exactly why Joaquim had agreed to accompany him on so dangerous a voyage.

This last point pressed him harder than all the others, for he had promised Joaquim never to divulge that he had once been a priest.

The interrogation lasted all afternoon and continued without a break until long after dark. Finding himself led into a conversation upon the subject of the Portuguese succession, and unaware that Philip had already been proclaimed King, he told them that as far as he knew, the great mass of Portuguese regarded Philip of Spain as the inevitable choice.

'And will that stand Portugal in good stead?' Wray asked.

He shrugged. 'I think it must do, sir. From what I have heard – from Joaquim and others – it will be greatly to their advantage, as much of the country's wealth was squandered on the expedition to Morocco and the people are left all but leaderless.'

'And Spain – how will she benefit?'

Cleverly, Wray had taken over the questioning, and had relaxed him, so that it was as if he were having a pleasant conversation rather than being interrogated.

'Why, sir – from the ports and harbours and the Portuguese *armada* itself! Nobody is in any doubt of that!'

'And how do you suppose Spain will make use of her new possession?'

The answer was such an obvious one that Tristram feared a catch.

'Well, sir, I've heard tell that they plan an invasion of England. And – and with Portugal theirs, and the Netherlands also, there may be no stopping them. I heard – I heard say that some people in Portugal believe England to be more Catholic than Protestant, and that it would not take too great a force to tip the balance and spark a rebellion.'

'And that would please you mightily, no doubt – ' Hobden remarked drily.

He had been answering their questions honestly, patiently, carefully for nearly six hours. Now, his temper exploded.

'That is a stramming injustice on me, sir!' he exclaimed. 'No one calls Tristram Pascoe a traitor and gets away with it!' and standing up he seized Hobden in a Cornish wrestling lock and put him quickly down on the stone flags. This woke up Barty, who with a snarl leapt at Tristram, and buried his powerful jaws in his rear.

Wray, who could hardly stop himself smiling, called his dog off, and Hobden got to his feet and dusted himself down. Ignoring the pain in his backside Tristram stood ready for a counter-attack, expecting that Hobden would draw the dagger he carried at his side; but Hobden made no move to do so, and when Barty was safe back under the table, his thick purple tongue hanging out as he panted in satisfaction of a duty well done, Wray turned to his yeoman and said, 'I think we've heard enough, Mr Hobden, don't you?'

'I think we have, sir,' Hobden replied ruefully.

Wray looked at Tristram. 'Sit down, Pascoe,' he said briskly. 'I've a proposition to put to you, and I want you to consider it carefully.'

After parting company with Wray and Hobden, Harry went out to his ship to put in hand the business of offloading the stinking ballast, and spent most of the afternoon discussing with Mr Rashleigh the repairs required to fixtures and fittings before the spring, and it was late evening before he returned ashore and went up to the Russell for a few ales.

The Treffrys had taken over the inn a year before. When Harry entered, Marion had only just come in and Harry (who had a soft spot for her) was quick to see that her eyes were red from weeping.

Accepting his special tankard from her hands, he punned: 'I know who's aled me, lass, but what's ailing thee?' and winked at the yokels who nodded into their jugs by the smoky hearth. 'Crossed in love are we, maid Marion?'

'Oh, Mr Pascoe! Haven't you heard, sir?'

'Haven't I heard what?'

'About your Tristram, sir! Been took into custody, he has, by Justice Mayhew and they gentlemen from Plymouth you brought in yester-morn.'

'Oh aye? Who says?'

She was untying her cap strings and taking off her cloak. 'I just come from next door, sir, an' Davy and Jill had it from Addy Lanyon. Seemingly they've cancelled the cliff patrol for the night so's guard can be mounted on your Tristram and the Portugal up at Moville House.'

Four of the local fishermen came in while she was speaking: hearty, red-faced young men like Harry had been when he used to fish for pilchards with Sam Gristy.

'You heard aught about my Tristram being kept in custody, lads?' Harry asked.

The ones in front looked back at those behind them, none wishing to confirm the bad news. 'I did hear something to that effect, aye,' one said, and they went through to the other end of the parlour for a game of shovegroat.

Harry looked back at Marion. 'On what charge?'

She shook her head miserably and dissolved into tears. Her mother, a comfortable body if ever there was one, came out from the back kitchen to comfort her, and she had to tell her news again.

'But why, love, why should Justice Mayhew do a thing like that?' Mol asked her.

'They say – they say he be a papist!' Marion sobbed. 'They say he's come back with that Joking man for to spread sedition and plot against the Queen!'

Harry waited to hear no more, but strode out of the Russell and up the hill to Moville House.

He found Mayhew entertaining Wray and Hobden to dinner. They all looked up as he entered. He dispensed with all the niceties, and pointed at Wray.

'You took passage aboard my ship under false colours, sir, and I demand to know what's going on and on what charge you're keeping my son.'

Wray glanced at Mayhew who, in answer to an unspoken question, nodded his agreement.

'Captain Pascoe,' Wray said, and even then his use of the title gave Harry a little fizz of pleasure, 'I fear we do indeed owe you an apology, but our task is never an easy one and too often we find that news of our intended arrival travels ahead of us and prejudices the outcome of our activities, so we find it necessary, from time to time, to resort to the sort of subterfuge which we practised on yourself at Plymouth. As to your son and his Portuguese friend – you must prepare yourself for bad news.' Wray glanced at Mayhew before continuing. 'They are required for further questioning. We intend to have them removed from Polruan tomorrow morning, first thing.'

'Further questioning? On what charge?'

Wray sighed and spread his hands. 'Mr Pascoe, you must understand that there are some matters affecting the safety of the Monarch and the defence of the Realm upon which I am not at liberty to speak – not even to the father of the person concerned.'

Harry lowered his head and grunted.

Mayhew said: 'We need your cooperation, Mr Pascoe. It will require patience on your part, but we have confidence – '

'To Hell with your confidence!' Harry foamed. 'And to Hell with my patience! If you can't say it, I'll say it for you. He's a papist, isn't that the sum o' it? A papist and a traitor, and if I'm right, you're welcome to him. String him up with his scurvy Portugal alongside him, but don't talk to me about patience!'

Matthew, Nathan and Jennifer were sitting round the fire in the back kitchen when Harry arrived back. Jennifer jumped to her feet as he entered.

He jerked his thumb. She went upstairs immediately.

'Tistum!' boomed Nathan, a dribble of saliva going down his chin. 'Where's Tistum? Why's Tistum – '

Harry fetched him a clout over the head. Nathan whimpered and was silent.

A candle was burning on the landing. As he went by, his own shadow rushed past him, elongating on the wall. He pushed open the door to the bedroom at the end of the passage.

She turned as he entered. She had undone her hair but otherwise made no further preparation for bed. He had told her, soon after they were married, that he liked to watch her undress, and as this fad of his seemed quite harmless she had always been careful to oblige him. So while he stood leaning back on the door, she unpicked her fastenings and discarded her shift, glancing across the room at him, her white breasts rising and falling, a shiver running down her back.

He went to her and put his hands on her shoulders and she stood looking up at him in just the same way she had looked up at Tristram on the cliffs above Washing Rocks the day before.

He was already convinced that Tristram's arrival home had altered her attitude towards him. Looking down into her coal-dark eyes, he thought: I can see through her like glass. She married me because she had to, because there was nothing else she could do. I'm second best to her, just as Ann was second best to me.

'Have you heard about – ' He stopped himself. He didn't even like to mention Tristram's name. 'Have you heard the news?'

She shook her head.

He was glad about that, and watched very carefully for her next reaction. 'Your cousin and his Portugal friend've been arrested.'

He waited, but her expression hardly changed.

'Don't you want to know the charge?'

She was breathing through her mouth. Her eyes looked down, then back up into his.

'Popery and treachery,' he said softly, enjoying the fall of the words. 'Popery and treachery. . . .'

She turned away from him, but immediately he spun her back to face him.

'You shall see him go, Jennifer,' he said softly. 'You shall come with me, at first light tomorrow, and see for yourself what has become of 'un.'

She was shivering visibly, and her breasts were covered in goose pimples. Quite deliberately, and without any trace of affection, he stroked her nipple back and forth until it stood up and came to a point under his thumb.

'I don't love him, Harry,' she said, very low. 'If that's what you're thinking. I don't love him at all. Fact – I don't think I ever loved him proper.'

But he saw her eyes go from side to side, and he was sure she was just saying that for her own protection.

'It's you I love,' she whispered. 'Honest to God, an' I won't never look at another man so long as I live.'

He pushed her back onto the bed and began unbuckling his belt. 'It's me you love, is it?' he muttered. 'Then let me see you show it, Mistress Jennifer. Let me see you show it right and well.'

By dawn a crowd had already gathered outside Moville House. They stood at the gate, the women chattering and gossiping among themselves, the men in a separate group, glancing in the direction of Mayhew's stables where Tristram and Joaquim had been kept under guard all night. Outside these stables, feeling conspicuous and self-important, Tom Carew stood 'at ease' with a pike in his hand and a well-polished helmet on his head.

The four constables from Fowey came marching up in single file and the spectators separated to let them pass. Justice Mayhew appeared briefly at his front door, acknowledged the salute of the constable in charge and handed over a commital order to authorize the removal of the prisoners to Launceston gaol; and when Mayhew had returned inside his house and the front door was shut, the stable door was opened and the two were brought out.

They were roped together, and their hands were bound.

The people crowded round the gate, whispering among themselves and looking at Tristram Pascoe with new eyes. The escort formed up: one went ahead and two followed behind, with the constable in charge walking a safe distance from the pair to avoid being the accidental target of any missiles that might be thrown.

The people filled the narrow street as they followed the prisoners and escort down to the harbour, and when Nance Rashleigh leant out of her window and shrieked 'Papist!' it was as if that single accusation had been a key to unlock the sluice gate and allow a flood of abuse to rush out.

The first rotten apples found their mark, and the first jeers and cries of 'Traitor!' and 'Iscariot!' went up. For a minute or so the constables stood to one side, as if temporarily handing over the rule of law to the people and allowing them to reach their own verdict in their own way.

At length the chief constable stepped forward and held up his hand for the barrage to stop, which it did. Smeared with filth, and yet still keeping their heads up and their dignity intact, the prisoners were pushed at pike's end into a boat, and the escort embarked with them.

It was then, as the oars were being shipped and the boat pushed off from the granite landing stage, that Harry Pascoe came down to the harbour with Jennifer on his arm.

The village people fell silent. All eyes were on the couple who descended to the beach: Harry red-faced, his eyes blazing in undisguised hatred, Jennifer looking small and slight at his side, her face white and drained of emotion, but composed nevertheless.

The oars dipped and as the launch moved away, Harry raised his fists above his head.

'Bloody traitor!' he bellowed, his voice echoing back over the calm water from Fowey Castle and Poleeth Point. 'Bloody papist heretic! I disown you, d'you hear me?' He grasped Jennifer's hand and held it aloft, to demonstrate that she was one with him. 'We disown you and curse you! You're no longer a Pascoe, no longer my son, no longer kin to your family!' He paused, breathless in his fury. The boat continued on across the water, heading for Fowey. 'May God and Queen Elizabeth see justice done! May you go straight from the gallows to the fires of Hell!'

And then, for the first time, Tristram and Joaquim turned to look back and for a few moments there was a strange silence, during which the echoes of Harry's shouting died right away and the onlookers glanced one to another, shocked by the curse he had called down and afraid that the evil of Tristram's treachery might somehow rebound upon themselves.

Later that day two horses were delivered to Moville House by the ostler at the Russell Inn, and William Wray and his yeoman rode off, with Barty, the white bull terrier, running along behind them.

8

Penance

The Inquisitor's voice shook with pious fury.

'So do you still insist, Countess, that the Santarém Madonna fell from your neck into the *sea?*'

It was the fourth day of the inquisition. Since the disappearance of Joaquim and Tristram five months before, there had been hardly a day's respite for Sara from the questioning and probing of Frei Bartolomeu and his various agents and assistants. João had been summoned from Lisbon; Sara had been confined to the house and every servant and slave had been subjected to close interrogation.

Now, in order to avoid scandal, João had succeeded in persuading Frei Bartolomeu to convene the inquisition in private at the Quinta de Piedade, and Sara had been arraigned on charges of making false confessions and receiving the sacraments while in a state of mortal sin.

Frei Bartolomeu was sitting at the head of the table in the banqueting hall, with Frei Martim and Padre Bernado on his left and Count João and Padre Jorge on his right. At the far end, two secretaries kept the official record. Facing the table, dressed in black in accordance with the custom, Sara sat straight-backed on a stool.

For four days they had tried every trick to lure her into an admission, whether of superstitious practices, immorality, witchcraft or failure to fulfil her religious duties. Obliged to be confessed secretly by several priests in turn, she had incurred their anger by denying any knowledge of the *caseiro*'s religious inclinations. Throughout her ordeal she had remained faithful to Tristram, to Joaquim and to herself. Steadfastly she had refused to admit; steadfastly she had refused to denounce.

'I have already explained it to you, several times, Frei Bartolomeu. I moved my head suddenly, the chain broke – '

'And yet your husband has affirmed under oath and before witnesses that the Madonna was later found upon the neck of a vagabond, the selfsame Irishman at whose chastizement you personally intervened, with the support of your gardener. Are you saying that your husband is a liar?'

'No, Frei Bartolomeu, I would never suggest such a thing. But – '

Frei Bartolomeu pointed a finger at Sara. 'Is it not a fact that the day you set foot in Portugal you lied about the manner in which that priceless heirloom was lost? Is it not a fact that you have been lying daily about it ever since? Can you deny that you have misled and deceived every member of the family and household that took you in and fed you, welcomed you and treated you as an equal? Can you now, in the presence of us all, make the sign of the Cross and swear that you played no part in the escape of your heretic gardener and his Irish accomplice? Can you swear before the Saviour, His Holy Mother and all the Saints that you are innocent, that you have made no false confessions, taken no sacraments unworthily, never once profaned the name and sanctity of our Blessed Lady, the Immaculate Ever-Virgin Mother of God?'

There was a silence. From outside, behind the kitchens, there came a sudden demented clucking and squawking which ended as abruptly as it had started.

Sara drew herself up and spoke quietly and with complete control. 'As God is my judge, Frei Bartolomeu, I swear before you that my conscience is clear.'

The Inquisitor took out a large silk handkerchief and pressed it against his forehead and the soft folds of skin that hung under his chin. His dark, grape-like eyes moved sideways to the left and then sideways to the right.

Sitting at some distance from their table, Sara watched and waited while these corpulent dignitaries conferred. She saw Padre Jorge whisper at some length in her husband's ear and João nod gravely; she saw João conferring in turn with the Inquisitor, cupping his hand to his mouth as he did so. She saw Frei Bartolomeu consult with his assistant and turn back to make some sort of whispered bargain with João and Padre Jorge. Then, after several more minutes of whispered consultation, they came to a decision.

Frei Martim looked at Sara and addressed her rather as a master might address a tablemaid: 'Stand up and listen carefully to what the Inquisitor tells you.'

She obeyed, frightened now, because she was sure that her denials had been to no avail and that having failed to extract an act of faith and repentance from her, Frei Bartolomeu would direct that the admissions they sought should be burnt out of her publicly in Lisbon.

She joined her hands and prayed inwardly for courage and strength. She thought of Tristram again, wondering if he had survived his sea voyage, still sure in her mind that what she had done was not in any way evil – and still thankful, in spite of all the consequences, for the brief time of happiness and love they had shared.

'So, Countess,' Frei Bartolomeu said. 'Having regard to your title and reputation, and taking into consideration the past generosity of your husband and his family to the Dominican Order, we have decided upon a course of great leniency. But because there is no doubt in our minds that your soul has been deeply immersed in the slough of mortal sin, we are persuaded that, for the expiation of such sin, much penance is necessary. It is therefore our decision that you be removed immediately from the Quinta de Piedade and returned to Lisbon under the charge of Padre Jorge. Until further notice, you are to be forbidden the sacraments. For the period of one year in the first instance, you are to be confessed and required to offer up the Holy Rosary and the Stations of the Cross twice a day for your sins. You are to be belted and shaved and are to wear only a single shift of coarse cloth, so that you will be constantly reminded of the low station to which you have brought yourself by your deceits and misdeeds. You are to be given a discipline with which to chastize yourself, and it will be well for you if the marks of your self-punishment are renewed morning and evening. You are to be deprived of servants and kept separate from all persons except your confessor. You are to eat only slaves' food, so that you may be reminded of your slavery to mortal sin. This is your penance, Countess – these are the wages of the sin you have so obdurately refused to admit. And if, at the end of one year, your confessor is able to report that you have convinced him of a genuine contrition and desire for forgiveness, your case will be reviewed and the possibility of a return into communion with our Holy Mother the Church will be considered. But if such a report is not forthcoming, we shall have no alternative but to apply to His Holiness for the authorization of the ultimate measure, so that you may have one last opportunity to offer up your vile body in a true act of faith. Now may God grant you the will, through penance, to save your mortal flesh from the temporal fire, and your immortal soul from the eternal fires of Hell. In the name of the Father, and of the Son, and of the Holy Ghost. Amen.'

She was led out to the front courtyard where a closed carriage was waiting. She was pushed inside and was followed in by Padre Jorge, who drew curtains across the coach windows so that she should be prevented from looking back, like Lot's wife, on the scene of her downfall.

She heard the shouted commands of the coachman and the crack of a whip, and then the carriage jerked and moved forward.

But although the Inquisitor could take control of her body and her physical behaviour, he was unable to order her thoughts and imaginings, and in the semi-darkness, as they went up the steep, winding hill out of Colares, Sara comforted herself by picturing in her mind's eye a last glimpse of her beloved Quinta de Piedade. She saw the formal gardens, the orchards, the paths by the river and the neat vine terraces which Joaquim had tended so lovingly.

And then – almost as if she were seeing a vision – she was aware that Tristram was thinking of her at that very moment, and she imagined his face so clearly that she gave a little gasp of happiness. Suddenly she was quite positive that his love for her was unchanged and that he was safe.

The carriage went slowly on up the hill. She leant back in the seat and closed her eyes. Whatever happened now, whatever discipline they imposed on her, she knew she would be strong enough to bear it, and that her suffering was not in vain.

Through the Fire

Tristram and Joaquim were transported under guard, their hands bound and their ankles linked by two short lengths of chain. At the end of each day, when they were required to get out of the cart and walk to the cellar or dungeon in which they were to spend the night, they could only shuffle in step like a pair of performing bears. Thus chained, they travelled, ate, slept and even answered the calls of nature together, so that each came to regard their closeness during the voyage from Lisbon as nothing compared with this new enforced intimacy.

On passing through a town they would lie down and cover themselves with sacks to avoid being seen by the people. Their various guards, believing them to be traitors, treated them with brutality and contempt. They slept in their own filth at night, were given nothing but dry bread to eat, and when they needed drink were led like animals to the nearest horse trough.

They saw the insides of the gaols at Launceston, Exeter, Dorchester and Winchester. If word got out that traitors were being taken through a village or town, they were showered with bad eggs, refuse and slops. But in spite of all these ills Tristram never lost confidence in William Wray's promise that he and Joaquim would be taken to London in order to be trained for the Queen's service.

'He told me that before we could be of any use to her Majesty, we must be tempered in the fire like steel, and proved as a blade is proved when it is bent in a circle so that the point touches the hilt,' he told Joaquim.

'That's all very well,' grumbled Joaquim, 'but I'm not a young man any more, and if anyone tries to bend *me* double, I shall snap.'

'How many times must I say it? Mr Wray gave me his personal assurance, as a gentleman and a man of honour, that you will come to no harm. I insisted from the start that I refused to be separated from you, Joaquim. That was the basis upon which I volunteered our services to the Queen.'

Joaquim looked gloomily at the bleak, marshy pastures that went all too slowly by. He was hungry, filthy, cold and dog-tired into the bargain. There were sores all over his body; he had a hacking cough and his head ached. He was also unconvinced that on their arrival in London he would not be immediately put to death as a traitor, and was by now convinced that Tristram had been duped.

'We'll be separated soon enough,' he muttered, 'whether by plague or distemper or the hangman's noose I know not and care less.'

'It's stopped raining,' Tristram said, hoping to lift Joaquim's morale. 'Look – the sun!'

Joaquim looked at the pale, wintry sun that had come out between steel-grey clouds. 'You call that the sun? Is that the best you English can do for a sun?'

'*Paciência*! We're in midwinter, and it rains even in Portugal at this time of year.'

'Not this icy cold rain, though.' Joaquim sighed despondently. 'And who will prune my vines? Who will manage the vintage, and tend my orange trees and collect my almonds? Ah – what would I give to make this the Colares river!'

Tristram raised his head above the side of the cart to look out. A little way ahead, a wide, brown river, swollen by the winter rains, was winding its way through marshy pastures where cattle stood knee-deep in ooze.

'A river indeed!' he said. 'I think it must be the Thames, Joaquim, and that means we're nearing London.'

While he spoke there came the sound of a great number of wings beating the air with a throbbing hum, and a moment later they were treated to a magnificent spectacle: a hundred or more white swans were flying overhead, their necks outstretched, their great wings making a magical 'hew-hew-hew' as they circled and prepared to land; and then, splitting up into families of half a dozen or so, they came gliding down with their black webbed feet thrust out before them to alight upon the water with a swish.

'How wonderful to be able to fly!' Tristram breathed. 'And see how proudly and majestically they stem the river's flood! What a fleet! What a navy! Ah, if only I could fly like that, if only I could spread my wings and fly away to – to – '

Joaquim glanced at his young companion. 'To Portugal?' he suggested. 'To Colares and Dona Sara?'

That night there was a light fall of snow, so when they reached the capital the following afternoon, the spires, towers and steeply sloping gables were clad in white.

Neither had seen London before, and each had expected something grander. If Lisbon, with her royal palaces, her seven hills, her domes and spires and castles, could be compared to a great lady of declining years, then this bustling waterfront was more like a busy wife who had not enough hours in the day; but although Joaquim at first snorted contemptuously at the rows of dirty warehouses, the wharfs and the continuous clatter of wagons and carts, he could not fail to be impressed by the sheer activity of the place: by the number of argosies, hoys, crumsters, hulks, wherries and barges upon the river; by the sideshows, market stalls, vendors and brawling apprentices on the streets, and even more particularly by the great volume of woodsmoke that rose from a thousand chimneys and hung like a pall over the city.

When they approached the great bridge they were provided with a stern *memento mori*: over the fortified gate the skulls and recently severed heads of traitors were raised in their dozens upon poles.

Joaquim tapped his forehead. 'I wouldn't be surprised if this one joins that lot before long.'

'You won't be much surprised at anything if that happens,' Tristram rejoined.

The cart joined the queue of vehicles for the bridge and entered the long tunnel formed by the houses which rose four stories high on every span, and on emerging from this tunnel it plunged into the heart of the city. Tristram and Joaquim fell silent now: each was aware that they were nearing their destination, and each was attacked by stronger misgivings than before.

The cart entered a yard and stopped. From a single opening in the stone wall came the sound of piteous cries, and as Tristram watched a hand was thrust out between the bars, the fingers waving and grasping at the air as if trying to snatch at freedom itself.

'What did I tell you?' Joaquim muttered. 'What did I say all along?'

'He gave me his word!' Tristram whispered. 'He told me on his honour that – ' He stopped: a gaoler and four trusties had come out to take over their charges.

The fetters were taken from their ankles and they were separated.

'That one,' ordered the gaoler, a huge, bald man in leathers with keys at his belt. He pointed at Joaquim. 'That's the Dago, that's the one we want.'

'No!' shouted Tristram. 'We must not be separated! You must take me also!' He struggled against the two guards who held him, but his hands were still tied and he was powerless. 'Joaquim!' he shouted as the Portuguese was frogmarched across the yard to the prison door, 'I never betrayed you, Joaquim! You must believe me!'

Just before he entered, Joaquim turned to look back at Tristram for the last time.

'I do believe you!' he called – and with that he was immediately hustled inside, and the great door banged shut behind him.

On a crisp February morning, several weeks after Tristram Pascoe's ignominious arrival in London, Thomas Hobden arrived by boat to call upon his master at his home in Greenwich.

William Wray's house stood close – but not too close – to the river's edge, and its latticed windows afforded a perfect view of the comings and goings on London's river. As it had its own landing stage, visitors to the Wray household usually arrived by boat, so that the outside world seldom knew the identity of the nautical gentlemen who came ashore there from the galleons at anchor in midstream or the wealthy merchants who came down in their barges from the city; and as the Queen was in residence less than half a mile from his front door, Wray was also conveniently close to the centre of affairs, and readily available for consultation with the members of her Majesty's privy council.

His role as a Crown agent had brought Wray into close contact with certain of the Queen's advisers, and some years before he had been invited by the Queen's Secretary to take a special oath of allegiance, and so become one of a small élite, whose members were dedicated to protect her Majesty as much from her own womanly whims and weakness as from the several popish plots to overthrow her and put Mary Stuart on the throne.

Slowly, and with great finesse, Wray had worked himself ever closer to the inner sanctum. When Walsingham commissioned him to prepare a plan for the protection of the Queen against the Catholic League, he proposed the formation of a new echelon of secret agents and counter-spies, maintaining that only by using stealth to combat stealth could the Queen's safety be assured and England afforded adequate protection from the servants of the Pope.

Placed at the head of the new secret service, he pursued his aim with such dedication that he eschewed all public acknowledgement of his work, refusing a knighthood when it was offered him and insisting that Walsingham and his personal secretary, Thomas Phelippes, take full credit for every successful operation. 'For if I were to do so,' he would say, 'my service to the Sovereign would be made public, and I could not hope for such successes in the future.'

He stood at his window now and watched the tall, slightly stooped figure of his yeoman come striding up from the river, and when Hobden had been shown in, Wray wasted no time upon the niceties.

'Well?' he asked. 'What progress, Mr Hobden?'

Barty wagged furiously round Hobden's legs to welcome the man who had so often (and so diplomatically) slipped him tidbits under the table; but Hobden ignored the animal and looked as dour as ever.

'Our Mr Pascoe continues reluctant to afford us his cooperation sir,' he reported. 'He still insists upon being brought before you and refuses to answer questions until his request is granted. I begin to wonder if he is as well suited to our purposes as we at first presumed.'

Mrs Tripp, Wray's housekeeper, bustled in with a jug and two tankards which she set down on the oak table, and the conversation was continued only when she was out of the room again and the door shut.

'What have you told him?'

Hobden withdrew a poker from the fire and plunged it into his ale so that the brew hissed and gave off a curl of vapour. 'Simply that he finds himself in a position of great privilege, and that if he wishes to serve his country he must accept our decisions without further croaking. But he insists that he will obey no one until dos Santos is restored to him.' Hobden glanced at his master. 'He clearly sets great store by what you told him, sir.'

Wray warmed his back at the fire and flexed his shoulders. 'And does he believe dos Santos dead or alive?'

Hobden considered. 'I think . . . alive, sir, though I have seen the first signs of doubt in his manner. When I questioned him yesterday he told me that if dos Santos must hang, then he wished to be hung with him.'

'Very creditable,' Wray murmured, 'but hardly useful to our purposes, eh Tom?'

'Hardly, sir,' Hobden agreed, and smiled thinly.

'And is he well looked after? Is he clothed and fed?'

'He is, sir. Your instructions have been carried out to the letter – though of late he has refused food.'

Wray crossed to the window and looked out through the lattice at a heavily laden barge that was being towed downstream on the ebb.

He turned. 'Very well. I think it time to grant him his request. Bring him here tomorrow at nine o'clock. I'll break his fast and his silence at one and the same time.'

He had been given a shirt, hose and jerkin to wear; his hair and beard had been trimmed; he had had regular meals until choosing to put himself on a fast, and had been given water to wash himself and keep himself clean; so when he was brought up to Wray's house in the morning he looked more like a gentleman's son than a prisoner, and the knowledge that he was at last to have a chance to speak to Mr Wray had put him in good heart.

The house was full of the delicious smell of Mrs Tripp's baking, and when Hobden ushered him into the hall he found Wray awaiting him and the table set for breakfast.

'My boy!' Wray exclaimed as if welcoming a favourite nephew, and shook Tristram warmly by the hand. 'You'll have some breakfast, I hope. My housekeeper has surpassed herself this morning, so I trust you will do justice to her skill.' He waved Tristram to sit down at the table, and nodded to dismiss Hobden.

Tristram sat down, then stood up again. 'Sir – I've promised myself not to eat until I hear news of Joaquim dos Santos – '

Wray held up his hand. 'And I have promised myself that you shall hear nothing from me until you have broken your fast, Tristram. So – eat first, talk later. I insist upon it.' He lifted a silver cover from a dish and revealed poached eggs, beef and two baked fruits which Tristram did not recognize. 'These are potatoes,' Wray explained, 'and very nourishing they are too, especially if taken with a little salt and butter. Go on, lad, help yourself! I shall say nothing more until I've seen you eat!'

So Tristram complied, reluctantly at first, but with increasing relish on tasting Mrs Tripp's cooking and sampling his first baked potato, and by the time he had had second helpings and had drained half a yard of finest London ale, he was feeling very much better disposed to the world in general and Wray in particular.

'Now – as to your sometime companion,' Wray began, and lighting a tabaco, leaned back in his chair and blew a cloud of smoke. 'I think, if you are sincere in your wish to serve your Queen and country, you must first put all thoughts of Joaquim dos Santos from your mind.'

He listened to Tristram's protestations courteously but remained quite unmoved by them. He never once raised his voice or showed any sign of being ruffled in any way, but at the same time made it clear that nothing Tristram could say would change his mind in even the smallest degree.

'You see – there is a difficulty,' he said. 'Before you can become a useful servant to your country, I must be satisfied that we have your complete trust and loyalty, that you have been entirely open with us and that we know everything there is to know about you. And while you remain unwilling to grant us this trust, you are of no use to us at all, Tristram, and you might as well go with your friend to the gallows.'

'So he *is* condemned!' Tristram burst out.

Wray smiled. 'And now you are jumping to conclusions. That is a mistake you will have to learn to avoid at a very early stage.'

There was a silence, during which Wray got up from the table and threw more logs on the fire, before which Barty lay warming his pink belly.

'You should also realize,' he continued, 'that you have already been made privy to matters which must remain secret. That places a further burden of responsibility on your shoulders. It means, in effect, that there is no going back. Do you understand what I'm saying to you?'

Tristram felt suddenly drained of all the optimism with which he had been filled only half an hour before. 'I understand it, aye, sir.'

'I wonder if you do, Tristram. It means that if you will not cooperate with me here this morning, if you will not agree now to tell me the truth – the whole truth – about dos Santos and yourself and the full reasons and means of your escape from the village of Colares, then there is no alternative open to me. I am bound, in duty to my Sovereign, to have you taken from this house today and hung and drawn for treachery. And we shall ensure, furthermore, that before you hang, you are made to watch the execution of your friend, so that he will go to his death believing himself betrayed by you, and you will go to yours knowing that it was within your power to save him.'

Tristram looked across the oak-panelled room at the quietly spoken, bald man who stood at the window and, perceiving for the first time something of the massive weight of authority which he wielded, was in no doubt that Wray meant every word he said and that he was entirely capable of putting it into effect.

How proud he had been to be invited to enter the Queen's service, and with what innocence! It had seemed to him, then, that here was an easy way to escape the tiny world of Polruan and the petty hatred and jealousy of his father; to make a new life for himself, a life that would be worthwhile, one that would use his abilities and experience to the full; but he saw now that in volunteering he had exchanged his birthright of freedom for a ruthless bondage, in which his new masters would control not only his physical person but his mind and destiny also.

Wray was speaking again, and now he adopted a sharp, uncompromising tone. 'Perhaps you would care to start by telling me about dos Santos,' he rapped out. 'Where did he learn to speak Latin with such fluency, for instance? In a seminary was it? What is he – a Jesuit?'

Tristram sighed deeply, and bowed to the inevitable. 'He was a Dominican,' he said in a low voice – and hearing those four words, Wray knew that the victory was his and that he had secured total control over another recruit.

The relief at being at last free to unburden himself was tremendous. Going over his story all over again, he found himself admitting to all sorts of secret hopes and fears. He spoke of his teenage love for Jennifer and of how he had been caught on the Roscarrock estate; of the clashes with his father from his earliest years; of the dilemma he had found himself in after Bryant's death, and of his conviction that his father could, without hazarding the ship, have sent a boat back to pick him up had he genuinely wished to save him from drowning. He explained about the silver Madonna, how it had led him into posing as an Irish Catholic, and how that pose had been discovered by Sara.

Of Sara, he tried at first to say as little as possible, but Wray led him back and back to her, asking where she came from and of what family, what her opinions were of her husband, her country, Portugal, Spain and England. He wanted to know how often Tristram had attended Catholic Mass, and could not prevent his eyebrows going up in surprise when Tristram told him that he had attended daily throughout his time as Sara's bodyguard.

'And can you be sure that you have not been tainted in any way by so close a connection with popery?'

'Sir – you may hang me for a heretic if you will, but I am of the opinion that there be Christians in both camps, and I know in my heart that Dona Sara is one such.'

'And was she greatly enamoured of her gardener ex-priest?'

Tristram coloured. 'No sir! Not enamoured. She treated him well, and they often talked together about – about the management of the quinta and – and other things too, no doubt. But the affection between them was at all times proper, sir, I am quite convinced of it.'

'But can you be sure? Isn't it possible that they were secret lovers?'

'Quite impossible, sir! I could not entertain such a thought! Dona Sara is quite beyond reproach in such matters. She is the most gracious, fair and wise person that I know, and – and – '

'And, it seems to me,' Wray said very gently, 'that she has quite captured your heart, Tristram Pascoe. Indeed – I would even go so far as to guess that you made her your mistress. Am I right?'

Tristram tried to speak, tried to find words to express the torment he had suffered since returning to Polruan and finding Jennifer and his father married; but unable to meet Wray's penetrating stare or to deny what he had kept secret for so long, he bowed his head and covered his face with his hands.

'It's better thus,' Wray said when he had regained control. 'You must have no secrets from me, no secrets at all. Only in this way can you be proof against calumny and betrayal; so if there is any other secret, any other hidden alliance or affection of which you have not told me, now is the time to do so.'

'There's nothing more to tell, sir,' Tristram replied, and Wray accepted his word on it without further question.

Outside, sleet had begun to fall. Tristram felt as though he had aged more in the past hour than during his five-year absence from Polruan. He could not know what lay ahead, but only that a man of Wray's rank and office would not have taken so much trouble over him if he did not intend some special service. He understood now what Wray had meant by having to go through the fire, and knew that he had been thus tested, and had not been found wanting.

'Sir – may I know what has become of Joaquim?' he asked.

Wray smiled. 'He is alive and well, Tristram.'

'Then – '

'No, you may not see him. You must trust me in this. It's for your own good. I shall tell you nothing more, because there are certain things which you do not need to know and which might prove dangerous to you, to England and to Joaquim himself if you did. That is another important lesson you must learn straight away, and you will do yourself and your friend a service by putting him completely from your mind. Can you do that?'

'Then he will not be hanged?'

'I will say it but once more. You must put him from your mind. You must trust us in order that we may trust you.' Wray waited for Tristram's assent, and on receiving it, picked up a hand bell and rang it, and when a servant appeared sent for Hobden; then, while the sleet pattered on the window and Barty snored before the fire, the Great Bible was taken down from the shelf, and Tristram repeated before them the oath of allegiance to Queen Elizabeth and the cause of Protestantism.

'And now,' Wray said when the Bible had been put away, 'we must see about your education.'

He was provided with lodgings in Westminster, and started receiving private tuition in the classics from William Camden, an earnest, academic man with a quietly ironic wit who had recently been appointed as second master of Westminster School.

Camden was also an ardent diarist and follower of current affairs, and he employed Tristram as trainee secretary and amanuensis, so that within a short time he became well versed in the burning issues of the day. Three afternoons a week Tristram would report himself to his tutor in his school house, and when he had construed passages from Seneca, Livy or Thucydides, Camden would discuss with him the latest news from Europe or Scotland, or whether Queen Elizabeth should take the Duke of Anjou for her husband.

This last topic was one that was being hotly debated in the alehouses of the city, and hardly a week went by without a new broadside or ballad being published on the subject.

What it all boiled down to, as far as Tristram could make out, was that without a marriage between Elizabeth and Anjou there could be little hope of a league offensive with France against Spain, and without that, no one could be sure which way France might jump, for the Duke of Anjou might be tempted to look to Spain for a wife instead. And if Parma's army succeeded in subduing the low countries, Spain might then be in a position to launch an invasion across the Sleeve into Kent – and England would be plunged into another round of civil wars every bit as damaging as those between the Yorkists and the Lancastrians a hundred years before.

For a year, more or less, the Queen kept her subjects in suspense as to her intentions, and when at last she agreed to make the match, no expense was spared in the hospitality offered to the large embassage of earls, seigneurs and barons that arrived from France. Arrangements as to dowry, a pension for the Duke and the succession order for progeny were neatly tied up, and for a few weeks it seemed that England was to have a King again and a Catholic one at that; but before the contract was finally exchanged, and partly because of the outcry that was already going up in London against the proposed marriage, the Queen insisted, at the last minute, upon adding one vital reservation:

'But Queen Elizabeth is not bound to consummate the Marriage, until she and the Duke shall thoroughly satisfy one another in certain points. . . .'

The Duke of Anjou was annoyed by this example of fickle femininity, and Walsingham had to be sent to France to explain. The trouble was that France was now in a state of hostility with Spain, and the Queen saw that if she agreed to consummate the marriage, far from achieving peace and tranquillity for England as had been her wish, she could do further damage to her relations with Philip and the forces allied to Rome.

So the marriage was on, then off, then on and then off again, and there was hardly one of Elizabeth's subjects who didn't hold an opinion on the matter. Some said she had a duty to provide a successor to the throne and must go through with it; some fervently hoped that she would not, and prayed secretly that she would be overthrown and supplanted by the Scottish Queen; while many believed that she would serve her country best by abandoning further thoughts of matrimony.

'So what is your opinion on the matter?' Camden asked one day. They had just returned to his chambers after witnessing the bloody amputation in Westminster market-place of the right hands of an author and a publisher, whose book had argued the puritan case against the Duke of Anjou, and had been declared libellous by the Queen.

Tristram had learnt by now to weigh his answers to Mr Camden carefully: these conversations they had together were not for entertainment, but to test him and strengthen his grasp upon matters of the moment.

'I think it impossible to make a rule on the subject, sir,' he said. 'While I agree that there are dangers in her marrying a subject or a stranger, and I acknowledge that the unhappy experiences of her sister and her grandfather Edward must be taken into account, I can't see that it should be at all inevitable for her to suffer the same unhappiness. If – if she truly loves Anjou and he her, then only good can come of a union between them, for in *my* opinion, sir, if love alters, then it is not true love.'

Camden smiled whimsically at this little lecture, and made a mental note about the ingenuous nature of youth.

'And this be-handing that you have seen today. What do you make of that?'

'Why, sir – the deed revolted me!'

'Whether or not you were revolted is beside the point. What matters is the effect – the political effect – it achieved.'

'But – you were there, sir! You saw how the people stared in silence! A deed like that can only harm her Majesty's reputation!'

'Perhaps the Queen was not thinking of her public reputation. Perhaps she was thinking that the puritans must be shown that their foaming sermons and fiery broadsides have no effect upon her, and that she will balance all equally and make up her mind for herself.'

'In that case, sir, should she not also stop this flood of priests that is creeping in under her front door and undermining her authority with the Bull of Pius Quintus? Should she not arraign that Jesuit Campion in Oxford who is openly saying that he would stand for the Pope should he send his forces against her?'

'Perhaps she will – perhaps she will,' Camden sighed, and smiling enigmatically, he invited Tristram to open his Greek grammar and revise his pluperfects.

After a year under Mr Camden's private tutelage, Tristram was sent to Cambridge to learn how to pinch a wench's bottom and drink a quart of ale without taking a breath, and it was here, on the misty banks of the Cam and in the smoky alehouses of the city, that he made the acquaintance of some of the rising stars in the firmament of literature and the arts.

There was Chris Marlowe, a drunken young tearaway with whom he shared lodgings in Corpus Christi; Bob Greene, one of the sizars at St John's who was always in debt or in love; Tom Kyd, who spent most of his time away from Cambridge and who Tristram suspected was also in the service of Mr Wray; Tom Nashe, at St John's with Greene – and besides these there were Baines, and Skeres and Poley and many more hangers-on, most of whom were caught up in the new enthusiasm for writing and versifying and dusting off old stories and turning them into plays, and all of whom had strongly held ideas about religion and politics.

These young men visited each other's lodgings, disputed in the alehouses over the existence of God, fell asleep in Gabriel Harvey's tutorials, wrote plays, made rhymes and kept the peace-loving inhabitants of the city awake by their late-night revelries and carousings.

Two more years went quickly by. From time to time Pascoe was excused from his studies in order to travel to the Continent on secret government service, whether as a temporary secretary to the ambassador in Paris or as Queen's messenger to the English forces under Sir John Norris in the low countries, so that he developed not only a good grounding in the classics and the ways of young gentlemen, but also first-hand experience in the field and a firm grasp upon the situation on the Continent, where the Duke of Guise was pressing Rome for an invasion of England, and the bloody struggle against the Spanish in the Netherlands dragged on interminably.

Towards the end of 1583, however, the pace of circumstance quickened. Plots to free Mary Stuart and overthrow Elizabeth were being hatched and despatched almost every week; letters were being intercepted, traitors were being denounced, priests run to earth and rumours uncovered that the Catholics in the north were preparing to rise against London and join forces with a Spanish invasion of England.

For Tristram matters came to a head early in the following year, when a coded message was delivered to his lodgings in Corpus Christi ordering him to repair immediately to Greenwich.

He travelled all day and all night, and arrived at Wray's house before dawn. He was now nearly twenty-five years old: tall, with the build of an athlete, a high, well-shaped brow and watchful eyes that missed little and gave nothing away.

Since going to Westminster as Camden's pupil three years before, he had never once mentioned Wray's name or seen his face; he had received a regular and generous allowance, and had obeyed his master's anonymously delivered directives without question. Throughout that time he had been conscious that this period of education was a preparation for special service. Now, as he entered Wray's oak-beamed hall and was greeted like a long-lost friend by the white bull terrier, he knew that his training was over.

Wray rose from his table and gripped Pascoe's hand. 'Are you fit?' he asked.

'For all and anything,' Pascoe replied, and Wray smiled at his enthusiasm.

'You'll have some breakfast?'

'Thank you, sir, I will.'

Wray looked with approval upon his protégé. During the past three years he had received regular reports on him from Camden and Harvey and had seen certain despatches from Paris and Antwerp in which Pascoe's service had been mentioned. Now, there was no doubt in his mind that Tristram had matured considerably since he had last seen him, and had acquired just that grave brevity of speech and honesty of manner he liked to see in a man.

'You've heard of the Mendoza affair?' he asked, referring to the recent dismissal of the Spanish ambassador.

'Aye sir, I have.'

Hobden took a seat opposite Pascoe, and Wray waited while Mrs Tripp set a plate of lean beef and scrambled eggs before the guest.

'You know he's gone to Paris?'

'Yes, sir, I heard that.'

'What else do you know of him?'

Pascoe glanced up from his plate, and spoke with authority. 'He's a dangerous and clever man, sir – a man with a grudge. That he was in alliance with Throckmorton I have no doubt. His wrath at being ordered out and his protestations of innocence are only a smoke screen to cover his guilt and the anger he feels at having his plans frustrated.'

Wray nodded his agreement and glanced at Hobden, who met his gaze poker faced.

'And . . . this "Enterprise of England"?' Wray asked. 'What is your opinion of that?'

'Unless Philip can be shown that it cannot succeed, I believe it to be inevitable, sooner or later, sir.'

'Why?'

Tristram smiled. Only two nights before, he had had a drunken argument with Marlowe on the subject, in which Marlowe had insisted that Parma's invasion plans could only be put into effect when the low countries had been subdued, and Tristram had maintained that the low countries could not be subdued until England had been successfully invaded.

He counted off the reasons on his fingers: 'First, because Philip can no longer afford to allow Drake to plunder his treasure ships on the high seas; second because the Marquis of Santa Cruz now believes that he can win a battle with our navy, and third because the Pope wishes it, and is promising the certainty of eternal bliss to people like Mendoza and Allen who further the cause.'

'I see,' Wray said, pleased at Tristram's analysis and amused at the

223

passion with which he presented it. 'So do you agree that we should be gathering as much information about their intentions as we can?'

'I do, sir – and quickly. There may not be much time left.'

'And that the Spanish will be at pains to inform themselves about our capabilities and intentions?'

Pascoe cocked his head on one side, frowning. 'No doubt they will, sir, but that's little concern of ours. What is more important is the furnishing of a fleet capable of matching theirs. When I landed in Chatham two months ago the shipmasters and privateers there were complaining about the lack of ships, brass cannon and trained men, and though I grant that some building is going ahead, I must agree with those who contend that it is not going ahead fast enough. Indeed, if we are to – '

Wray held up his hand. 'The strength of our forces is no longer your concern, Tristram.' He went to the window to look out at the frosty fields on the other side of the river. 'We have a more important task for you. We need information about Spanish intentions, and similarly the Spanish need information on ours. We intend that you shall fulfil both needs at the same time.'

When he turned back, Tristram was staring at him in amazement.

'*Both* needs, sir?'

Wray glanced at Hobden. 'You will perform the one diligently and accurately for your Queen and country, and the other misleadingly and confusingly for Spain and the Pope.'

Tristram grinned suddenly. 'You mean – inform the one and mislead the other.'

'Exactly,' Wray replied, and in the silence that followed Barty, who had got too hot in front of the fire, stood up and took himself to the far corner of the room where he flopped down on the cool floor.

Tristram took a draught of ale and set the pewter tankard gently down on the table.

'How does the idea strike you?' Wray asked.

'It's – it's an excellent one, sir. If it'll work.'

'You will make it work, Tristram,' Wray said, and without further preliminaries, Hobden began giving him his orders.

'You are to make a single-handed passage across the Sleeve and land at Gravelines,' he said. 'You will be contacted by someone who will recognize you and introduce you. He will vouch for your loyalty to the papist cause, and from the moment you set foot on French soil you are to become, to all appearances, a Catholic. On arrival in Paris you will be

introduced to Mendoza's circle as an English recusant who is an expert
on English ships and sea warfare. For obvious reasons, you must not on
any account return to Lisbon. Apart from that you will be at liberty to
travel as you see fit – to Paris, Rome, Madrid – anywhere necessary to
collect and pass back information.'

Hobden enlarged in some detail, then turned to the question of
despatches. 'We shall give you an address in Paris to which they are to be
sent. I take it you are familiar with the royal codes?'

'Completely – '

'That's just as well, but you shouldn't have to use them overmuch. We
wish you to make all your reports in the form of sonnets.'

'But I am the world's worst versifier!' Tristram objected. 'I can't turn a
sonnet to save my life!'

'I was aware of that,' Wray said drily, 'so I commissioned a bard to run
off a couple of dozen. Commit them to memory and send them as the
occasion arises. Each sonnet can be used on its own for a pre-planned
purpose or, if you wish, you may write further information in invisible
ink between the lines. Now – your aim. It is this: to penetrate the Spanish
organization and if possible become a part of it. Your knowledge of
pilotage and shipbuilding will be useful to them, and they will be
interested in our coastal defences – '

'But I am no expert on that, sir – '

'So much the better. Your task is to mislead, not inform. It may be that
you will have to provide them with some useful information in order to
win their confidence; if this is the case, you must use your discretion. As
to the information we require, we need to discover their plans, their
strengths, their strategy – but most important of all, the date upon which
they plan to launch their enterprise. We could have an army three times
the size of theirs and still lose the day if they catch us ill-prepared, so if
you succeed only in giving us early warning, you will have served your
country well.'

There was a silence. Although Tristram had suspected for a long time
that he was being prepared for a mission of this sort, now that it had been
described to him he was aware of a sense of unreality, half expecting
Wray to tell him that it was just another test of his ability, and that he
could now go back to finish his studies at Corpus Christi.

A muffled explosion came from the direction of Woolwich, where
another batch of gunpowder was being tested at the arsenal.

'When do I cross to France?'

Wray looked steadily back. 'Immediately. We've put it about in Cambridge that you are a recusant, and that you fled from there because you received warning of the charges against you. So you are *persona non grata* in England now, and the constables will be on your trail at this minute. You have six hours of ebb tide to get clear of the Thames, and a northerly breeze to take you across the Sleeve.' Wray glanced out of the window. 'And I suggest you take warm clothing.'

'And my contact when I land – '

'He will approach you and make himself known to you. There is no need for you to know more than that.'

Wray continued with more detailed orders. On landing in France Tristram was to make his way to a rendezvous in a small chapel built on the beach near Gravelines. 'There, you are to wait until you are contacted. We have made good arrangements, and with God's help you should have no difficulty in getting to Paris and entering the diplomatic circle. Mendoza is the key: he is in contact with the Spanish court, Dr Allen in Rome and the Duke of Guise. Gain his trust, and you will have theirs as well.'

'And when should I return?'

'When your task is complete.'

'But that may be years – '

Wray appeared not to hear him. He went to the sideboard and took a small scroll of papers from a drawer. 'The sonnets. Commit them to memory as soon as possible, then destroy them. There's also a plenary indulgence in your name together with some of Campion's writings which may be useful if you are questioned on your loyalty to the Catholic cause.'

'And if ever you have to use invisible ink we prefer cow's milk to lemon juice,' added Hobden laconically, 'as the taste of citrus remains on the paper and can be easily detected on the tongue.'

'Money,' said Wray, and handed over a purse that clinked with gold coin. 'There's enough there for you to travel and dress as a gentleman for a month or two, and by that time you should be in the pay of Rome or the King of Spain, or both. Now is everything clearly understood?'

He would have liked more time, but knew that had he been granted it, the contemplation of his task might have weakened his resolve. He tried to think of questions, but knew already that Wray would have planned for every eventuality, and that the best hope of success lay in following his instructions to the letter. And besides – the tide was already on the turn, and every minute counted.

For the first time since he laid eyes on Hobden, Tristram saw in the yeoman's grey eyes a hint of respect. 'May God bless your endeavours, sir,' Hobden said, and gripped him firmly by the hand.

'God for England and Queen Elizabeth!' Wray murmured as they shook hands.

'God for England and Queen Elizabeth!' Tristram replied – and then he was going quietly out of the house and down the slope to the landing stage; he was getting aboard the boat which had been prepared for him, and within the hour he was scudding away past Woolwich and on towards Gravesend and the open sea.

The chapel was perched upon rocks above the high-water mark. The thick stone walls were salty and damp, and the north wind moaned and whistled at the entrance. Over the altar, illuminated by a single candle, a plaster Christ hung upon a cross, the brow bloody from the Crown of Thorns, the eyes cast down, the side pierced. As the candle flame moved in the draught from the door the shadow of this crucifix moved with it, as if the plaster image were struggling against the nails in its feet and wrists.

Another, larger shadow elongated upon the wall, and this was the shadow of the man who knelt in silent prayer before the altar. Tristram had entered the chapel five hours before and remained on his knees ever since. Now, as a cold February dawn sent grey light in through the small windows, he was wet and cold and close to exhaustion.

With the coming of first light the shadows blurred and became fainter. The candle burned on, but the faces of Christ, the Blessed Virgin and St Joseph seemed to lose the life that had been theirs during the night, and turned back into man-made images, with sightless stares and chipped alabaster features.

He heard a movement behind him, and was aware of others entering the chapel. There were no more than a dozen of them: simple peasants for the most part, the women in black shawls, the men in smocks and home-spun breeches. They knelt in the pews behind him, and rose to their feet at the tinkle of a bell.

A priest entered, attended by an altar boy. Feeling himself to be very obviously a stranger, Tristram kept his head down as they went up to the altar and prepared for the Mass.

Bowing down at the foot of the altar, the priest made the sign of the Cross from his forehead to his breast and started the preparatory prayers. '*In nomine Patris et Filii, et Spiritus Sancti,*' he murmured, and the server replied, 'Amen.'

'*Introibo ad altare Dei.*'
'*Ad Deum qui laetificat juventutem meam.*'

To God who gives joy to my youth. . . . Hearing those words, Tristram was reminded of mornings at Colares, when he had attended upon Sara at Mass. He wondered what had happened to her since his escape from Portugal, and breathed a private prayer for her safety and wellbeing.

The priest continued with the *Judica me*, the *Confiteor*, the *Introit* and the *Kyrie Eleison*, and while he did so, Tristram gazed at the close-cropped grey head and wondered if Wray's plans were going to work and whether he would indeed be contacted. It had been a long and bitterly cold crossing from England, and it was only through a piece of sheer luck with the tides that he had managed to land within a few miles of this rendezvous.

He stole another look round at his fellow worshippers, wondering if perhaps his contact was among them.

'*Sequentia sancti Evangelii. . .*' intoned the priest, and signed himself with his thumb on forehead, lips and breast before reading the Gospel.

It was the first time he had turned back to the people, and when Tristram recognized the intelligent, humorous face and the dark, kindly eyes, it was as much as he could do to prevent himself gasping aloud.

William Wray had kept his promises after all. The priest was Joaquim.

The End of a Honeymoon

Fotheringay Castle, 18 February 1587

Suddenly she was in their midst: Mary Stuart, granddaughter of Henry VII, Queen of Scotland and Queen Dowager of France. Dressed in a black gown and linen veil she came in on the arm of an officer of justice. Followed by her physician, her surgeon, her apothecary and her waiting women, she mounted the three steps to the platform and sat down upon the black-draped seat placed for her.

Her faced was framed in the perfect shape of a heart and her hands were pressed tightly together. There was a hush: she looked round at the assembled gentlemen in their velvet cloaks and tall hats, and a smile puckered her lips, as if she were surprised at the fuss.

Beale, the Clerk to the Queen's Council, read out the death warrant. She had been found guilty of incitement to insurrection against the life and person of her cousin Queen Elizabeth. While the words of condemnation echoed about the chilly hall she sat straight-backed in her chair, her eyes turned towards Beale, her fingers clutching a crucifix of ivory, the rosary beads slipping one by one past her thumb as she said her last Hail Marys.

When Beale had finished, Dean Fletcher began an oration concerning her condition in this world and in the world to come, but he had barely started when she interrupted him, saying that she had no intention of being perverted and would die as she had lived, in the true and holy Catholic faith; and when he said prayers for her soul, she added a few more of her own for the people of England and her cousin Elizabeth. Kissing the crucifix and making the sign of the Cross she cried out, her voice echoing under the rafters: 'As Thy arms, O Christ, were spread out upon the Cross, so receive me with the stretched out arms of Thy mercy.' Then she turned to her women-in-waiting to be helped off with her over-gown, and a moment later there was a gasp as she stepped forward in an underbodice and petticoat the colour of blood.

Covering her face with a linen handkerchief, she knelt down and whispered twice over: 'Into Thy hands, O Lord, I commend my spirit'; then she laid her neck upon the block.

The executioner glanced at Mr Beale, who nodded his head. The blade went halfway through on the first blow, and on the second the head thumped down upon the boards. The Dean cried out, 'So let Queen Elizabeth's enemies perish!' and the Earl of Kent answered, 'Amen!'

But the solemnity of the occasion was spoilt when the executioner bent to pick up the head and raise it aloft in accordance with the custom, because all that remained in his hand was an auburn wig, and the close-shaven head that lay at his feet looked more like a martyr's than that of a traitor-queen.

The news of what had happened that February morning in Fotheringay Castle travelled down England like fire down a fuse. Bonfires were lit on village greens and bells were pealed in village churches. Mary was dead, Elizabeth was secure. The dread that a Catholic monarch might turn the clock back to the bad old days of massing priests, papal bulls and the burning of heretics seemed finally banished, and the fear of civil war that had lingered in so many minds receded. England was for the English after all, and in authorizing Mary's execution Elizabeth had proved that she was indeed the defender and champion of the Faith.

On the Continent the reaction was one of outrage. The shock waves radiated first to Paris, where the court went into full mourning; then to the palace at El Escorial, where King Philip lived in monk-like seclusion and administered his empire from a small, blue-tiled study; then to Rome, where Dr Allen, the head of the English College, redoubled his efforts to persuade the Holy Father to give financial support to a full-scale invasion of England. From pulpits in Salamanca, Valladolid, Cordoba and Seville, bishops, monsignors and parish priests reviled Elizabeth, the murderous Whore of Babylon, and the irresistible cry went up: Arise, Lord, and vindicate Thy cause.

The demands for an invasion rose to hysterical pitch, and when King Philip finally bowed to the pressure and gave orders for the Enterprise of England to be launched with all despatch, a great sigh of relief went up in Spain, and every able-bodied man of spirit considered it his pious duty to offer his services.

Dorothea de Palacios Salazar y Vozmediano de Esquivias had a small face, swimming brown eyes and a quantity of golden curls. She talked very fast and she was very well connected. Her uncle was a general, her elder brother was a herald at the royal palace, one of her aunts was an abbess in Salamanca, and she had any number of cousins who were lieutenants or ensigns in the Castillian fleet. She was a rising star in the social firmament of Madrid. She never lacked an escort at the comedia or the masque; she was continually in demand at the banquets of the wealthy, and anyone who had had the good fortune to be invited to the new palace at El Escorial knew that the face of one of the angels in Zuccaro's 'Annunciation of Our Lady' was that of Señorita Dorothea.

Good looks and family connections have their drawbacks, however, and like so many bright young things before her, Dorothea was to fall foul of an unscrupulous suitor, who took what he wanted from her before taking a bride with a better dowry.

Ashamed of her lost innocence and terrified of being denounced to the Inquisitor, Dorothea went into a sharp decline. She removed herself abruptly from Madrid society and buried herself in the country. She stayed with a succession of aunts and cousins, and eventually landed on her sister Catalina, who was married to a struggling writer called Miguel de Cervantes Saavedra.

They lived just outside the capital. For nearly three months Miguel and Catalina endured Dorothea's depressions, tantrums and hysterical outbursts. To restore her to normality, the services of a sympathetic confessor were enlisted, an astrologer was consulted and apothecaries were called in – but all to little avail. In place of the vivacious young lady who had captivated every man who laid eyes on her, Dorothea was now a thin, listless creature, with dark commas under her eyes and little interest left in life.

'What you need, Thea,' Catalina said one afternoon when they were pickling olives together on the patio, 'is company. It's not good for you to stay so long in the country. You're the sort of person who needs people round you. People who can amuse you and make you laugh.'

'I've forgotten how to laugh,' Dorothea replied miserably. 'I have forgotten how to *live*.'

'That's heretical nonsense,' Catalina said rather sharply. 'We are all on this earth for a purpose, and it is a sin to despair. Sooner or later you will have to re-enter society, and the longer you leave it the harder it will become.'

'Perhaps I shall enter an Order,' Dorothea mused. 'I could go to Salamanca and become one of Aunt Agatha's postulants.' She gazed across the valley. A donkey was plodding round and round the well and the bucket chain was making a devilish squeaking sound; in the field below the windbreak negro slaves were turning the red soil with mattocks.

There was a clatter of hooves on cobbles and a moment later the master of the house arrived on horseback.

Miguel was nearly twenty years older than Catalina, and had lost the use of his left hand ('to the greater glory of the right,' as he used to say) at the battle of Lepanto. Taken prisoner by the Turks a few years later, he had spent five years in slavery in Algiers before being ransomed, and these experiences together with a chronic inability to live within his means had sent him prematurely grey and given him a world-weary look. Always short of money, he had married Catalina principally for her dowry, which had consisted of a few vineyards, some sticks of furniture, four beehives, forty-five hens and a rooster.

He dismounted, saluted Dorothea with a sweep of his hat, embraced his wife generously and began chewing an olive.

'And how is our damsel in distress?' he enquired. 'Has no knight in armour come by today?'

'Please don't tease me, brother-in-law, you know I don't like it.'

'Yes you do, yes you do!' Miguel answered cheerfully. 'You women are all the same, never content unless your dreams are coming true, that's what. Well, I'm going to make your dreams come true, my little Señorita of the Palaces. I'm going to take you down to Andalusia to stay with your Uncle Pedro in Cadiz.'

Catalina shot him a warning glance. It was all too easy to reduce Dorothea to tears, and she didn't want yet another scene.

'Now there's no need to look at me like that, my sweetness,' he said, and turned back to Dorothea. 'Cadiz! Ah – my dear, just think of it! All those strapping young hidalgos and squires! All those military banquets and naval fandangos! And of course your uncle the General will be in the thick of it! Your feet will hardly touch the ground!'

'Now Miguel please just be serious for a minute!' Catalina told him. 'If you think I'm going down to Cadiz with you, you're mistaken. And how you think you can afford to take Dorothea all that way is quite beyond me. Really sometimes I begin to wonder – '

'Wonder no more, dearest heart! You see, I have been appointed with immediate effect to a government post in Seville.'

They stared at him. 'Seville!' Catalina laid a white hand upon her bosom. 'Why Seville?'

'Because, because, because!' chortled Miguel, and strutted up and down importantly in the way he did when he wished to make fun of authority. 'Because, my dear, you are now speaking to the commissary-designate to his Majesty's Invincible Armada!'

'Heaven be praised!' exclaimed his wife. 'Is the pay good?'

The road south was full of travellers and mule trains that spring, and the wayside inns were packed out. Minstrels and strolling players were putting on performances in the villages, and every gentleman on the road seemed to regard himself as being charged with a holy mission to win poor little England back for Christendom.

To pass the weary hours of each day's travel Miguel made a point of falling in with others on the road, and regaled his companions with lengthy stories about damsels in distress, ill-used servants and broken hearts; and in the evenings he sat up late with a candle to scribble notes about some of the more unusual characters he had met.

Cadiz was in a ferment of excitement. The streets were full of gallants; ships were arriving every week, and the talk in all the inns and lodging houses was of the Enterprise of England. But as Dorothea's Uncle Pedro was away at sea when they arrived at his city house and only his ageing mother was in residence, Miguel agreed to stay on in the city for a few days to see Dorothea settled.

Early on the third morning after their arrival, the galleass *Napolitana* arrived from Rome. When sail had been struck and salutes exchanged with the guardship and the harbour battery, the long sweeps dipped in unison, and the great ship slid in past the Punta Candelaria and came to anchor among the other ships of the fleet.

Within minutes the oars were being stowed and a flotilla of tenders and barges was taking off stores and ferrying the officers and passengers ashore.

Among them was Tristram Pascoe.

He was dressed in cloak, buff leather jerkin, velvet venetians and buckled shoes, and was accompanied by Joaquim, who had trained at Douai during Tristram's time in London and Cambridge, and who wore the simple gown and sandals of a Jesuit. It was three years since they had made their rendezvous at Gravelines, and since then both had assumed their false roles so completely that there had been occasions when each had had to remind himself that they were not acting for Mendoza, King Philip or Spain, but for William Wray, Queen Elizabeth and England.

Advice of their arrival had been sent in advance, so when they stepped ashore at the landing stage below the city battery, an ensign on the staff of General de Valdes was there to meet them and escort them to their lodgings.

Though it was still early the city was bustling with activity. Morning sun was streaming down between the adobe buildings, and the narrow alleys were full of street traders, donkey carts, washerwomen and slaves. In the market-place, hundreds of chained negroes were being herded, groaning and wailing, into enclosures for the auction to be held that day, and a strolling minstrel was tuning his instrument and looking at his scores. Ensign Rodrigo, a young man with a silky moustache and fawn's eyes, smiled nervously at Tristram. 'You like our city?' he asked.

'It's very beautiful,' Tristram reassured him in near-perfect Spanish.

'We are very busy these days,' the ensign said slowly, unable to believe that the Englishman could understand his language. He made a gesture. 'Everywhere – full. Many people. Many, many people.'

They crossed the city and reached the cathedral square. Inland, a veil of mist lay like gossamer on the Andalusian hills, and to the south the long white beaches glittered in the morning sun. When the cathedral bell clanged as they passed by, Joaquim dropped to his knees, and Tristram followed suit, making the sign of the Cross in perfect time with his confessor. The ensign looked on, somewhat abashed at this outward show of piety and reluctant to kneel in the dust for fear of spoiling his best silk hose.

The consecration over, Tristram and Joaquim signed themselves again and got up from their knees, and after walking a few hundred yards more arrived at the house where they were to take lodgings.

They were admitted by a slave and brought into a roomy, tiled hall that was hung with tapestries of classical scenes and furnished in the most ornate Spanish style. Their arrival threw the household into confusion: voices were heard speaking rapidly behind the scenes for several minutes before a grizzled-looking man with a crippled hand appeared.

'Miguel Saavedra,' he said shortly and held out his good hand. 'Whom do I have the pleasure of addressing?'

Tristram bowed, introduced himself and Joaquim, and produced letters from the Spanish Ambassador and the head of the English College in Rome, together with a signed blessing from the Holy Father.

'Another knight in shining armour, I suppose,' Saavedra muttered, but his eyebrows went up when he saw the papal seal. He handed the letters back. 'So you're to be billeted here, is that it?'

'Sir,' said Tristram, who towered over him like a giant, 'we have been sent to assist the Holy Enterprise in any way we can, and need only the humblest accommodation. If our arrival here is in any way – '

He stopped. An old lady was entering assisted by a doll-like señorita in white with a tiny face, a quantity of golden-brown hair and a bosom that commanded his undivided attention.

There was now a considerable amount of bowing and scraping, for the old lady was the mother of Don Pedro de Valdes, General of the Andalusian Squadron. She was also very deaf.

'English!' bellowed Saavedra.

'English?' she repeated, horror-struck, and turning to Tristram pointed a finger. 'Your Queen is a whore and a murderess!'

Tristram was having difficulty keeping his eyes off the señorita. He bowed again. 'I am not of her party, Señora,' he shouted. 'I have come with my confessor as a servant of the Holy Father, and as a sincere believer in the one, true, Holy and Apostolic Faith. We are here to join the Great Enterprise and win England back for Spain and the Blessed Virgin.'

The old lady turned to the girl who supported her. 'Can you understand what he says, Thea?'

Dorothea repeated what had been said, and reminded her great-aunt of the request to provide them with lodgings.

'Lodgings?' squawked the old lady, her fingers clutching the girl's arm. 'What does he think this is? A boarding house?'

'It's because of the Enterprise, Great-Aunt! Everyone in the city is taking lodgers, and this gentleman and his confessor have been sent to stay with us!'

'Enterprise? What enterprise?'

Dorothea turned to Tristram with a look that left him weak at the knees. 'There will be no difficulty. We have plenty of room for you, Lieutenant, and for you, Father. But you must understand that my great-aunt is old and frail and does not take well to disturbance.' Again her dark eyes flashed in Tristram's direction. 'And perhaps . . . if your confessor could afford us his services during your stay, that would ease our burden, as the family confessor is at present abroad with the General.'

Joaquim – who had an inborn loathing of all things Spanish – smiled faintly and said that he would be only too happy to say Mass daily in the family chapel, at any times convenient to the mistress of the house.

'Allow me to complete the introductions,' Saavedra put in. 'May I present my sister-in-law Dorothea de Palacios Salazar y Vozmediano de Esquivias.'

But Tristram had hardly heard the introduction, for Dorothea's white bosom was rising and falling in such a hypnotizing way that it wasn't until he received a sharp dig from Joaquim that he managed to pull himself together.

'Señorita,' he said, and bowed low. 'I am greatly honoured to make the acquaintance.'

'And I yours, Teniente,' Dorothea whispered faintly. 'And I yours.'

When Joaquim had said a Mass of thanksgiving for their safe arrival, he and Tristram were joined by Miguel Saavedra for a light breakfast of spiced sausage and pickled olives, and in the course of conversation Saavedra learnt that the Inglés had been a slave like himself.

An immediate rapport was established between the old veteran and the young lieutenant: stories and anecdotes were swapped and punishments and privations compared, and when Tristram expressed an interest in the Armada, Saavedra let drop that he would soon be taking up an appointment as commissary to the navy in Seville.

Tristram could hardly believe his good luck. He drew Saavedra out about the size and composition of the invasion force, and agreed enthusiastically when it was suggested that they take a stroll along the city walls to view the fleet.

There were three anchorages: one off the city, one just inside the mouth of the inner harbour, and a third in the approaches to Puerto Real.

'What a truly magnificent sight!' Tristram said quietly.

Saavedra gave a little snort of contempt.

Tristram glanced at him. He had noticed already that this Lepanto veteran had a somewhat jaundiced outlook on life. 'Do you have doubts that the Enterprise will succeed?'

'I believe it *can* succeed, certainly. But our task would be a great deal easier if the powers that be listened more to Don Alvaro and less to the Duke of Parma.'

'Don Alvaro?'

'You would know him as the Marquis of Santa Cruz, but I fought with him at Lepanto under Don Juan of Austria, and can only think of him as Don Alvaro.'

'Ah,' said Tristram, and looked again at the great ships, wishing that he could get aboard some of them to see the state of their readiness for war.

'No, it's all very well calling this Armada "invincible",' Saavedra was saying, 'but to my mind that's tempting providence. The time to call a fleet invincible is when it has been tested in battle.'

'Do you have so little faith in the power of Our Lady and all the saints?' Joaquim put in earnestly. 'Our cause is a holy one and blessed by Christ's vicar on earth. If God be for us, who can be against us?'

Saavedra glanced heavenward, and seeing him do so, Tristram suggested tactfully that Father Joaquim might prefer to return to the house for his customary time of prayer and meditation.

Joaquim took the hint, and when he had gone Saavedra brightened considerably. 'Now then, I know just the place for oysters, and if we go early we shall avoid the rush,' he said, and they descended from the walls and plunged back into the city.

While they sat over their meal Pascoe plied his guest with wine, and Saavedra obligingly mounted his hobby horse and held forth about the shortage of provisions for the Armada, the lack of organization, the mistake that was being made in splitting the invasion between Parma and Santa Cruz, and the acute paucity of funds to provide adequate power and shot to take on El Draque, as he called Francis Drake.

'But that's the way of the world, my friend,' he sighed. 'And the lot of every military commander since time began. They won't learn, will they? Expect us to get a gallon out of a pint pot, and then put the blame on the soldiers when things go wrong. Look at that attempt on Ireland, for instance. What a fiasco that was! And all because of bad organization and not enough ships and men. And matters are not much better with this venture. Don Alvaro asked for twice as many ships as we're getting. He asked for a hundred and fifty great ships alone, do you know that? And we'll be lucky to scrape together ninety. We'll do our best of course, but the way things are going I wouldn't be surprised if the whole enterprise has to be delayed another year. . . .'

Late that night Tristram made his first report from Cadiz. It was in the form of a sonnet, between the lines of which were invisibly written, in cow's milk, coded intelligence of great interest to Her Majesty's Secret Service:

> That thou hast her, it is not all my grief,
> XXII GREAT SHIPS LYING AT CADIZ

And yet it may be said I lov'd her dearly;
PREPARATIONS HINDERED BY LACK OF FUNDS
That she hath thee is of my wailing chief,
SANTA CRUZ DEMANDS ARE NOT BEING MET
A loss in love that touches me more nearly.
PLANNED DEPARTURE DATE IS END OF JULY
Loving offenders thus I will excuse ye:
SHORTAGE OF STORES MAY CAUSE FURTHER DELAY
Thou dost love her because thou know'st I love her,
FLEET UNREADINESS INVITES SURPRISE ATTACK
And for my sake even so doth she abuse me,
SIX GALLEYS DEFEND THE HARBOUR
Suff'ring my friend for my sake to approve her.
THEIR GREAT SHIPS ARE OVERMASTED AND CUMBERSOME
If I lose thee, my loss is my love's gain,
FEW SHIPS ARE MANNED OR GUNNED FOR WAR
And, losing her, my friend hath found that loss;
THEIR PEOPLE SLEEP ALL AFTERNOON
Both find each other, and I lose both twain,
COASTAL SHIPPING IS UNDEFENDED
And both for my sake lay on me this cross.
FEW OF THE CITY'S CANNON BEAR ON THE HARBOUR
　But here's the joy: my friend and I are one;
SQUADRON OF GALLEONS COULD WREAK MUCH DAMAGE
　Sweet flattery! then she loves but me alone.

This sonnet was sent with the royal mails to Madrid for onward transmission to one of Tristram's lady friends at court in Paris, who passed it on to the English Ambassador, who sent it by hand of the Queen's Messenger to Mr Wray in Greenwich.

After that first day he saw tantalizingly little of Dorothea, who lived in a separate part of the house and who seemed hedged about by her duenna, her servants, her slaves and her great-aunt. But on those rare occasions when they did meet – whether at Mass in the family chapel, at confession or by chance in the high-ceilinged passages of Don Pedro's city residence – Tristram was always conscious of her moist glances and pale fragility, and thoughts of her began to occupy more of his time than was fitting for an agent in the pay of Queen Elizabeth.

　A week after their arrival, Saavedra left Cadiz to take up his appointment in Seville, but before he left he introduced Tristram to the Camp Master in charge of city defences. Through him, and on the strength of his letters of introduction from Rome, Tristram was seconded to the General Staff as an adviser on English pilotage and naval tactics, and became a member of the officers' mess at the headquarters in the Castillo de Santa Catalina, where he spent much time in conversation with the various staff officers and made it his business to become acquainted with senior officers earmarked for command in the Enterprise of England.

Once a week meetings were held in the great hall of the fort to discuss the logistical problems, allocate ships to the squadrons and continue the endless discussion of tactics to be used against the English fleet.

All the old guard put their faith in the well-tried methods of close-quarters fighting, insisting that the only way to beat an enemy was to grapple and board him.

'If he won't come to close quarters we may not beat him, but we won't be beaten either,' declared the fiery Don Hugo de Moncada, who seemed likely to take command of the galleass squadron. 'And our ships can row rings round theirs, no one can deny that.' He looked round at his listeners and mopped his brow with a large handkerchief. 'Just let me get close to them, and I'll take them on two at a time.'

Another captain, Martin de Bertendona, turned and craned his neck over the heads of those who stood behind him. He pointed at Tristram Pascoe. 'You. What's your opinion?' he asked. 'Let's hear what the Englishman has to say.'

Aware that all eyes were on him, Pascoe chose his words carefully. 'My Lords,' he said, 'I agree that if the English keep their distance they will be able to do little damage against the strong timbers of our ships, but I have personal knowledge of English shipbuilding methods and I know that their hulls are every bit as stoutly constructed as our own. Therefore, I say, we must engage them as closely as we may, and as soon as possible too, so that by the time we make our rendezvous with the Duke of Parma's fleet of barges we shall have put every last one of Drake's galleons to flight – or to the bottom of the sea.'

'But you agree, do you not, that our galleys and galleasses are in every way superior to their galleons?' insisted Moncada.

This was a much-discussed topic: Pascoe was already aware that many of the General Staff had misgivings about sending galleys built for work in the Mediterranean out into the Atlantic.

'Under oars they are undoubtedly faster and more manoeuvrable than the galleons,' he said, 'but the voyage from Cape St Vincent to Scilly is a hundred and fifty leagues of deep water and rough weather, and we shall do well to ensure that the slaves are kept well fed and watered if they are to fulfil our expectations of them.'

'That's just a question of supplies,' Moncada retorted dismissively. 'I think we can leave that to the provisioners.'

Walking back along the front after the conference, with the sun sparkling on the sea and the ladies promenading with their duennas, Tristram reflected on the strange succession of circumstances that had led him to this city. Could it really be that those scented gentlemen actually intended to invade England? How calmly they talked of it, and with what assurance! And yet what a surprise must await them when they first met English ships upon the high seas, and how dearly he would like to be aboard one of Drake's ships on that day and to see the likes of Hugo de Moncada eat his words!

He was still reflecting on these things when he caught sight of a group of people coming towards him. It was Dorothea, out for a stroll in the city with her duenna, her maid, young Ensign Rodrigo and a couple of slaves.

A caged bird was singing for all it was worth; children were playing in the dust, and a fish wagon drawn by a mule went clattering by. But he was only dimly aware of these distractions, for his whole attention was now fixed upon the slight figure of Dorothea as the distance between them dwindled and he saw her look of happy recognition.

He took off his cap and bowed. 'Señorita,' he murmured.

'Teniente! What an unexpected pleasure!'

He could hardly speak. 'The pleasure is entirely mine. . . .'

She gave a sudden giggle and glanced sidelong at her duenna. 'Would you care to walk with us, Teniente?'

'It would be a great honour,' he managed; and falling in beside her, he listened enthralled as she told him about her society life in Madrid, while at the same time sending him secret messages with her lovely, liquid eyes.

Joaquim was taking a siesta in their sitting room and was flat on his back on a bench when Tristram entered. He opened his eyes, but did not sit up.

'You have an admirer,' he announced.

Tristram had not expected Joaquim to discover his secret quite so quickly. 'Oh yes? Who would that be?'

'Don't try to pretend you don't know, boy! Tiny Thea of course.'

'And how do you know?'

'I heard her confession this morning. She's been having impure thoughts about you.'

Tristram strolled to the window. 'What penance did you give her?'

'The Stations of the Cross.'

'That was a bit harsh.'

'Not at all. We don't want her getting ideas.'

'No, but we don't want to put her off, either. She's a useful contact.' He turned. 'Besides, I've just walked round the town with her.'

Joaquim sat bolt upright. 'You did *what?*'

'You heard me, Joaquim. I met her on my way back from the *estado maior*. I couldn't very well avoid her, and it would have been the height of bad manners to refuse to escort her.'

Joaquim snorted. 'You could have, if you'd had a mind. These young things that walk in the town don't do it for the fresh air, you know. They're out trapping foolish lieutenants to turn them into husbands.'

'I can look after myself,' Tristram replied, feeling oddly happy. 'After all it's in the line of duty isn't it? And she's a pretty little piece.'

'It's the prettiest little pieces that make the ugliest little scenes in my experience.'

'Well there's nothing ugly about Dorothea, I assure you. She's had a very difficult time, do you know that? Her father was killed at Lepanto and she was badly used in Madrid – '

Joaquim's patience snapped. 'For God's sake open your eyes, man! This isn't Paris. The Andalusians take their love seriously. If you cross our little Thea you could find she has sharp claws. You could even end up being forced into marriage, do you realize that?'

Tristram laughed. 'Aren't you taking it a bit seriously? All I've done is stroll round Cadiz with her. And even if she were to trap me into marriage, I could hardly ask for a better disguise, could I?'

Joaquim looked at him in silence for several seconds. 'The truth is, you want her for her sex, nothing more.'

Tristram went to the balcony and looked out over the glittering sea. 'And what if I do?' he said quietly. He bowed his head, overcome suddenly by a desperate sense of loneliness and isolation. 'I didn't choose this life, did I? Or at least, I didn't know what I was letting myself in for. Neither of us did. If I could go back now to Polruan and live as – as a fisherman maybe, with no cares in the world and a wife to go home to at night – ' He broke off, shaking his head. 'Yes, I want her for her sex. She's warm and she's loving and what's more she's a woman.' He turned.

'You're a good friend, Joaquim, and always will be. But you're not a woman.'

She had a seductively doleful expression, and talked almost incessantly in a rapid, lisping delivery, seldom pausing to take a breath but frequently glancing adoringly in Tristram's direction to ensure that he was paying attention. Over the course of a fortnight's promenading after siesta each day, she told him her entire life history three times over.

Usually they walked two-by-two: Dorothea and Tristram first, then the duenna and Dorothea's maid, and finally Ensign Rodrigo, who acted as liaison officer between the family and the military headquarters, and spent most of his time running errands for Dorothea, whom he adored.

Trotting along at the head of this little procession was Bamba, a little black slave boy whom Dorothea kept on a collar and lead and treated like a pet.

At first she had particular difficulty with Tristram's rank and name, which came out as 'Teniente Trithtan' and sent her into fits of giggles. Later she abandoned his name and addressed him as 'Teniente' or 'Inglés'.

After ensuring that he knew all about the sad loss of her father in the wars against the Infidel and her mother's later death of a broken heart, she launched into the vast complexity of her private life, entrusting to him petty confidences about past suitors and their dastardly treatment of her.

'But you will not use me thus, Teniente,' she lisped. 'You are too fine, too much the gentleman. When we walk thus, each day, I look at others with their suitors and I see that it is you who are the most handsome gentleman in all Cadiz.'

'You flatter me Señorita – '

'No, no! I do not flatter, Teniente, I never flatter. I am the most honest of people. If . . . if I found any fault in you I could not keep it to myself. Perhaps you think me a chatterbox, but let me tell you this: never before have I confided so much in a gentleman.'

He began losing sleep over her. He had been starved of female affection for too long, and now he lay awake night after night thinking about her, longing for her, imagining how it would be to make love to her. It seemed to him that they were made for each other: every time he looked at her he felt an ache of desire, and when they took their promenades in the city together he was often convinced that she was thinking exactly the same as he and that her longing for love – her physical desire – was every bit as strong as his own.

In the month since his arrival at Cadiz, he had sent two more intelligence reports back to England: more ships had joined the assembling battle fleet, and some further progress had been made in storing the ships and preparing them for war. Parties of conscripts were being herded down from the villages inland to be kept prisoner in the fort before embarking, and the sale of slaves in Seville had been halted in order to provide a pool of manpower available at short notice. Every morning the people of Cadiz awoke to the sound of trumpets, and hardly a day went by when there wasn't some parade or military exercise.

Out in the harbour the galleys were changing the guard. White puffs of smoke leapt from the bow minions as salutes were exchanged, and gaily coloured banners fluttered from the mastheads. The shouted commands of the galley-masters could be heard, and the sweeps dipped in precise unison, sending the long, sleek hulls cutting through the calm water in an impressive display of speed.

'What fine ships!' Dorothea breathed. 'What grace and power is theirs! Does not the very sight of them fill you with pride, no?'

They had managed to manoeuvre themselves so that there was a tree between them and her duenna. She was gazing up at him: her breath was coming in sudden little gasps, and her breasts were rising and falling, rising and falling. Suddenly, after a quick look from side to side to make sure they were still unobserved, she snatched his hand and thrust it into her bosom, so that he felt the point of her nipple, hard beneath his palm.

'Bless me Father, for I have sinned.'

Joaquim was hearing the weekly confession of each member of the household. After making the sign of the Cross and murmuring a blessing, he turned his ear to the grille.

The list of venial peccadilloes wafted, upon a cloud of Dorothea's bodily odours, about the confessional. She had given way to gluttony by eating cakes for breakfast on Tuesday; her attention had wandered during Benediction on Wednesday; she had inadvertently caught sight of her own flesh while being bathed by her maid on Thursday, and had experienced unbidden desires on awaking from a siesta dream on Friday.

For a few moments the stream of self-accusation dried up, and Joaquim became aware that she was weeping.

'My child,' he whispered. 'If there is any other sin upon your conscience, you must confess it now, that your distress may be eased and your soul cleansed.'

She struggled to control her tears, and when eventually she succeeded, the words flooded out in a rush, tumbling over each other in an almost incomprehensible torrent.

'It is the Teniente, Father, the Teniente Trithtan. He – I – Oh Mary most pure forgive him! – he hath made an impure touching of me, Father. He hath touched me and hath looked upon my person as if – as if we were already betrothed, as if he had carnal knowledge of me. And in my dream, Father, the dream I have already confessed, he had knowledge of me, knowledge of the most intimate kind, so that I can no longer look upon his face because I know that in his mind he hath taken from me what is only for a husband to take, and that only through betrothal can my conscience be set at ease.' She dissolved into another flood of tears.

Joaquim thought rapidly. 'My child,' he began, 'it is not at all unusual for a maiden to dream, and there is no sin in experiencing that which, of our own volition, we do not – '

'You do not understand, Father! He hath made an intimate advance upon my person, he hath signalled an invitation, and if he doth not now ask for my hand I must in Christian duty denounce him as one who hath trifled with my innocence.' Dorothea gave way to renewed sobs. 'But – but I cannot do that, Father, because he is my life, my everything! Oh – Father, Father! I have been so cruelly used in the past! Can it be that I am to be misused once more? Speak with him, I beg you! My poor heart cannot bear to be broken again! Tell him how he may heal the wound he has made in me! I do not wish to denounce him – no! But – but what else am I to do if he doth not quickly make clear his intentions to me? I cannot continue thus with him. If he is the gentleman I believe him to be he must no longer trifle with my innocence but declare himself openly just as I have declared myself openly to you!'

'So there it is, my friend,' Joaquim said when their door was shut and they were able to speak in private. 'Either you ask for her hand or we leave. There's no alternative. I warned you, but you wouldn't listen.'

'In that case I shall ask for her hand,' Tristram said.

'In *that* case, you're a fool.'

'Yes – yes, I'm a fool. I admit it. I love her, Joaquim, and love is foolish.'

'Love? Ha! Lust more like. The only part of you that loves that little flibbertigibbet stands up between your legs, my friend. This won't be a true marriage. It'll be a fiasco. You're as ill-suited as it's possible to be. You think in different ways, you speak a different language, you owe allegiance to different powers. You're chalk and cheese, Protestant and Catholic. Even your bodies are unsuited. It's not good that so large a man be joined to so small a woman.'

'I think we can leave beam, draught and tonnage out of it, can't we?'

'Nevertheless – '

'Nevertheless nothing! There is every reason why we should get married. We were attracted to each other from the first moment of meeting. She is an honourable, patriotic person – and a Christian, in her own way. And quite apart from anything else, marriage to her will enable me to serve my country more effectively. When her uncle arrives back I stand a good chance of finding a place on his staff. Yes, I admit that I shall have to deceive her in some ways, but they will only be small ways, and when we have this Armada beaten I shall take her back to England where I – '

'To England?' Joaquim laughed bitterly. 'Listen – whether the Armada is beaten or not, you will never go back to England. Never. If you went back to Polruan you would be reported at once – even by your own family. You would be arrested, and questioned, and racked, and your Mr Wray would not lift a finger to defend you. There is no place on earth where we can be safe, Tristão. We are outlaws, fugitives, condemned to wander this earth making believe to others that we are what we are not, and to ourselves that we are not what we are – obliged by our accursed occupation to turn everything that is good and just on its head, to feign love for those we detest and profess a faith that we abhor.'

'I do not entirely abhor it,' Tristram said quietly. 'I oppose it, but I do not abhor it.'

Joaquim went to the balcony. 'And what about Sara? Or have you completely forgotten her?'

For a few moments Tristram made no reply, and when Joaquim turned back to face him he was shocked to see that his lips were tightly compressed and his eyes full of tears.

'Forgotten her? You ask me if I've forgotten her? What sort of person do you think I am, Joaquim? Have we worked together all this time for you to know so little of me? Do you think I haven't hoped and prayed and wondered about Sara every day and night since we left Colares? I can

245

never forget Sara, never. But for you to ask "what about Sara?" is as meaningless as to ask about the wind. Sara is there, always there, but I have no claim on her. I shall never see her again, let alone marry her. Even to hope for such a thing is like the torture of Tantalus to me. She is my past and my present, yes, but I have been forced to accept that she can never be my future.'

Joaquim shook his head. 'I just don't understand you,' he muttered.

Tristram smiled sadly. 'Dona Sara would. And anyway, it's very simple. I'm going to marry Dorothea, Joaquim. That's all there is to it.'

Twenty miles inland from Cadiz, two hills with contours as smoothly rounded as a maiden's breasts rise gently from the plain, and perched at the top of the western of these two hills, Medina Sidonia sleeps her way through the centuries.

Built on the topmost slopes of the hill, the town is full of narrow cobbled alleys, low-roofed houses with sagging gables, lichen-covered tiles, unexpected hencoops, dozing donkeys, brawling children and duennas who peer at you from upper windows before moving swiftly out of sight into the shadowy recesses of their darkened chambers.

This is a town where time seems to glide in lazy circles like the eagles that soar all day on upcurrents caused by the hot, terracotta roofs and the billowing smoke from charcoal stoves. It is a town still touched by the moorish influence of bygone centuries, a town where the women are scarcely out of purdah, where monks and nuns live secret lives ruled by bells and breviaries.

It was here, in the church of Santa Maria la Coronada, that Tristram Pascoe came to be married to Dorothea de Esquivias.

They had travelled up with an armed escort the previous day. Dorothea's great-aunt owned estates in the locality, and one of these had been put at the bride's disposal as a dowry.

Tristram and Joaquim had taken lodgings in the town the night before the wedding and now, as the sun rose majestically above the Ronda hills, they climbed up past clumps of prickly pear to stand upon the rounded summit and savour the peace and beauty of the morning.

Joaquim broke a long silence. 'We shall not be seeing so much of each other after today, my friend.'

'No,' replied Tristram. 'But that will not prevent us from working as well together as we have in the past.'

Joaquim smiled and glanced across. 'You'll have to be a regular penitent.'

Tristram nodded, and they fell silent again. Far away in the distance there was a faint 'boom!' as the galleys in Cadiz harbour exchanged salutes. Bells rang in the Convent of Misericordia. Overhead, the first eagle soared upward, balancing upon ragged wings.

'I must go down,' Joaquim said eventually. 'I promised the Abbess I would say Mass.' He turned to Tristram and grasped him suddenly by the hand. 'If I were a true priest I would give you my blessing,' he said, and Tristram saw with a shock that there were tears in his eyes. 'As it is, all I can do is hope that you find happiness, and that my fears are ill-founded.'

He turned quickly and went away down the hill. Gazing westward to Cadiz and the sea beyond, Tristram was filled with a sudden sense of foreboding. It was as if the distant, sparkling horizon were the very edge of time, and beyond it a vast armada of events were sailing inexorably towards him, and must soon come into sight.

The church of Santa Maria la Coronada had been completed forty-five years before, and its tiled dome, graceful pillars and intricate stonework were the pride of Andalusia. Thousands of ducats had been donated by the aristocracy towards its construction. The several altars were faced with solid silver; angels, painted in gold leaf, hovered over the worshippers, and behind the high altar a superb golden image of the crowned Madonna was the centrepiece of a massive wooden carving in which one hundred and sixty-eight other images portrayed the various scenes of Christ's life and death and the assumption of His mother into Heaven.

Bowing down before this multiplicity of graven images, the close relations and influential friends of Dorothea de Palacios Salazar y Vozmediano de Esquivias witnessed her marriage to the man who had become known as Teniente Don Tristan Pascua Inglés.

Tristram was dressed in all his military finery, and when he brought his new bride out into the brilliant sunshine no one could deny that he made the most handsome groom. Some ungenerous souls even whispered that Dorothea had done better than she deserved.

The newly-wedded couple led the crowd of guests down the hill to the house on the northern slopes of Medina Sidonia and embarked upon a twelve-course banquet under the almond trees. Almost the whole of Andalusian society attended, and Dorothea pointed out every single important person to her new husband with that hushed reverence peculiar to the compulsive name-dropper.

Miguel Saavedra was there, his hair even closer-cropped than before, his face wearing the same ironical look; many of the military commanders of the Armada were there, each with his aide and his lady; even a few of Dorothea's acquaintances from Madrid were present, including the playwright Lope de Vega, who had been banished from the capital for improper conduct and had come south to offer his services to the Enterprise. But at the top of the order of precedence came the Duke of Medina Sidonia himself, a quiet, elderly gentleman who, in spite of a bad cold in the head, had travelled from his orange groves in San Lucar for the wedding in place of the Marquis of Santa Cruz, who was attending to more serious matters at the Escorial Palace.

And when it was all over, and the sun was descending in a blaze over the sea; when the last eagles were swooping away from the hill top and returning to their eyries; when the door was closed and the bride and groom were alone at last, the alchemy of youth and good looks worked its magic, and if either partner had had any misgivings about the rights and wrongs of the marriage these were now quickly abandoned.

Tristram had not enjoyed a woman's favours since his days in Paris over a year before, and Dorothea had remained chaste since her crisis the previous autumn. The long nuptial Mass, the banquet, the speeches and the music and dancing had had their effect. Now, as they started their first intimate explorations, each was surprised, for where Dorothea had expected gauche clumsiness she found gallant confidence and where Tristram expected the natural obstacles presented by inexperience and virginity, he found a wanton expertise that shocked and delighted him.

So they were united, and afterwards when Thea lay milky white in his arms with her thumb in her mouth and her limpid brown eyes moist with the romance of it all, Tristram felt a surge of affection for her.

'My lovely new wife,' he whispered, smoothing her shoulder with his palm.

She rubbed her breasts back and forth against his chest.

'More?' she purred.

That single question, 'More?' would have served as Thea's motto, for however ardently Tristram performed his husbandly duties during the first few days of their honeymoon, she always demanded more.

But this was not the glorious boy-and-girl love he had known with Jennifer, nor was it the spiritual plateau of love he had ascended to with Sara. This was love in its basest form: love that could be kept alive only by experiment and variation, love that was never the same twice and yet always the same, because it was flawed by deceit. And though Tristram at first revelled in Dorothea's brazen sensuality and Dorothea wore her Inglés like an ornament; though it seemed to both that no two people could possibly make love more energetically or imaginatively than did they, each became increasingly aware of a feeling of dissatisfaction and of being short-changed.

Something was wrong, something was missing; and it began to dawn on Tristram what that something was. Joaquim had been right all along: his love was not love, nor was his marriage a marriage, but simply a means to an end, a vehicle for lust.

'You make me sound like your aunt,' she said. 'My name's not Tia, it's Dorothea, and if you must call me Thea at least try to pronounce it properly.'

It was the fifth day of their honeymoon. They were at breakfast under the patio arches.

He grinned amiably and promised to do better.

'And I wish you'd smarten yourself up a bit, Inglés. You look awful in that shirt.'

'We are in the country, Thea. A ruff in high summer isn't the most comfortable of garments.'

'I didn't say you had to put on a ruff. Just change your shirt. What the servants think of you I can't imagine. You look like a sort of – pirate.'

Only half an hour before, they had been scaling the heights of passion together. It amazed him that they could descend from those heights so quickly.

He put his hand over hers. 'All right. I shall change my shirt if you will change your temper. Do you agree?'

For a split second – so brief a moment that he was hardly aware of it – her eyes were like black bullets. Then she softened and smiled and moved her body in that magical way that so fascinated him, and her eyelashes fluttered, and her eyes went moist, and her little white hand sought his and held it very tightly and he thought yes, yes, perhaps we do love one another after all.

He changed his shirt, but if she changed her temper it was for the worse. She became increasingly irked by little things: by the simple dishes prepared by the cook, by the rural slowness of the domestics, by the failure of the washerwoman to press her petticoats properly and the inability of the chambermaid to make the bed the way she liked a bed to be made.

Tristram was saddened by her petulance and irritability. He was already coming to love this rambling farmhouse and the huge estate, and would have gladly taken it in hand and made it his home. There was so much to do: the stables were falling down; the vineyards going to seed and the orchards needed pruning and replanting. With Joaquim's help he could have turned the estate into an ornament on the rounded slopes of Medina Sidonia, and with Dorothea as a loving and obedient wife he could have established himself as the head of a family.

A family – wasn't that what he wanted most of all? To have sons and daughters to care for and love; to sit at the head of his own table, to own a little land – perhaps take a hand in local government and work to better the lot of the people. . . .

But it was a dream, that was all – a dream to obscure the uncomfortable reality; a dream to help him forget everything that he held most dear: England, Polruan, his family, Jennifer, his own son Arthur – but most of all Sara, whose face he could conjure up even now as he rode up the hill to the farmhouse, where Dorothea awaited him in the arched courtyard.

He dismounted and handed the horse over to a stable hand. Dorothea came to him with a letter. 'This arrived,' she said. 'They want you to go back to Cadiz.'

She had already opened the letter, although it had been sealed and addressed to him personally. It was from the Maestro de Campo in Cadiz. It informed him that his position on the staff would have to be reviewed if he did not return to his duties within the week.

'So we shall have to make a move,' he said, pleased that the decision had been taken for him.

'I don't see why,' Dorothea said.

He sensed trouble ahead. 'Don't you want to see a bit of city life again?'

'Yes, but not smelly old Cadiz. If we go anywhere it'll be to Madrid, Teniente. I can get you a post in Madrid as easily as I can in Cadiz. My cousin is a herald at the palace of San Lorenzo, didn't I tell you that?'

'Yes, you did. But it makes no difference. I was sent to Cadiz by the Holy Father. I can't leave until the Enterprise is ready to sail.'

She stamped her foot. 'You are married to *me*, Inglés, and you will not leave here until *I* am ready.'

He followed her into the house.

'And yet I must go,' he said quietly. 'You will have to accept it. It's my duty.'

'Then I shall arrange matters so that it is no longer your duty.'

'Well – we shall see – ' he began lightly, but she slammed the flat of her palm down on a table.

'No, we shall *not* see, Teniente! I have told you that you are not returning to Cadiz, and it is *you* who will have to accept it! Do you hear me? I won't have you ordering me about! This is *my* estate and *my* dowry – and – and you are *my* husband!'

He laughed deliberately – and condescendingly. 'Dearest,' he said, chuckling still. 'You are the most beautiful creature when you are angry! But it doesn't alter the fact that I shall have to return to Cadiz!'

She went quickly out to the courtyard, where he found her in tears.

'Dorothea,' he started, reaching out to her. 'Listen to me. You are the dearest person on this earth to me – '

She whipped round to face him, snatching her arm away. 'How can you say that? How can you? You would never cross me in this way if you loved me! No, don't touch me, don't ever touch me again!' She backed away from him, and there was a black malevolence in her eyes that revealed a Dorothea he had never seen before but which he now recognized had always lain dormant beneath her seductive chatter. 'You thought – you thought you could use me like a toy, didn't you? Well I am *not* a toy, Inglés, at least not your toy, and you aren't the great lover you think you are, either, you know that? You're nothing to the suitor I had when I was in Madrid. He was a true Spaniard and a gentleman. He knew how to behave – '

'That wasn't the story I heard,' he put in coolly. 'The story I heard was that he jilted you, and I can see why now – my God, I can certainly see why!'

She gathered her skirts and ran weeping into the house. Remaining in the courtyard, Tristram stared down at the unweeded flags. He was already regretting his words, and was painfully aware that much of what she had said had been deserved.

She stayed away from him all that day and slept apart from him that night, but the following afternoon when he came back from a long, solitary ride she was waiting for him on the patio, and her pale face and doleful expression told him immediately that she wanted to make friends.

She said nothing at all to him, but simply took his hands and leant her forehead against his chest, her body trembling like that of a terrified animal in a snare.

He embraced her gently and she gazed up at him. But he could find no words to say to her, for the stark truth had now dawned: he knew that their marriage was no more than an empty hull.

'Will you siesta with me, Trithtan?' she asked in a small voice. 'Please?'

He nodded and they went up to the bedchamber. She shut the door behind them and pressed her lips against his in a desperation that aroused his sympathy but not his desire.

'You do love me, don't you?' she whispered, and began unpicking his shirt.

He nodded.

She pressed herself closer. 'Tell me, then. Tell me.'

He managed: 'I love you,' though it was harder to say those three words than it had been to swear allegiance to the King of Spain.

She put aside her modesty with her petticoats. 'Come to bed, then. Don't keep Thea waiting.'

There was a rumbling boom in the distance. He turned, listening.

'Thunder,' she said.

He threw open the shutters. It could not have been thunder: the whole dome of the sky was a brilliant blue.

Thea sat bolt upright on the bed, her golden-brown curls falling over her shoulders.

'What are you doing, husband mine?'

He narrowed his eyes against the blinding sunlight and stared westward. There was another distant boom.

'It's gunfire,' he said quietly.

'Rot,' she said. 'Come to bed. I want you.'

But the honeymoon was over: Tristram was already struggling back into his hose and throwing on his shirt, and within ten minutes, in spite of all Dorothea's protestations, he was in the saddle, and the finest mount from Don Pedro's stables was taking him fast along the flat, dusty road to Cadiz.

PART III

CONFRONTATIONS

Face to Face

Though he had never ridden a finer horse, nor ridden a horse harder, the journey seemed to take an age. Cursing himself for being absent from the city at so crucial a time, he would have been just as impatient had his mount spread wings and flown.

As he neared the city and the two bays of the inner and outer harbours came into view, the sound of gunfire became more intense and he saw the first swathes of smoke rising above the clustered ships berthed off the city batteries, and as he approached the Puente Suaca, which linked Cadiz Island to the mainland, he caught his first glimpse of the battle that was raging. Yes: those were English galleons, from whose bluff sides poured broadside after broadside into the Spanish fleet; yes, they had already put the six galleys to flight, and yes they were here in numbers, a whole fleet of them – how many? twenty? two dozen? – and they were creating a smoking havoc that far exceeded his greatest hopes or expectations.

'Drake, it's Drake!' he shouted aloud. 'It must be Drake, it must be!'

The hooves thundered upon the wooden boards of the bridge and he spurred the animal to get the last ounce of effort out of it. And now he came upon the first panicked townspeople, the peasants and fisher folk who were carrying their belongings in bundles over their shoulders and driving their livestock – pigs, cattle, mules, goats – out of the city and away from the rape and pillage that would surely follow when the city fell to the English and El Draque sent his sailors on the rampage.

Bellowing to the people to keep clear, he rode through them, scattering them left and right. He went on along the long, sandy strip that led up to the walled city and at last entered by the south gate.

The scene that met him was one of total confusion, total panic. Orders were being issued and countermanded. Soldiers were running hither and thither. Women were standing in doorways holding their children to their aprons, their eyes full of fear. Every bell in every church, cathedral, convent and monastery was tolling.

In the cathedral square, Captain Gregório de Chinchilla, a red-faced

255

barrel of a man, was trying to take charge of a squad of harquebusiers. Dressed only in satin venetians and a frilly shirt without a collar, he was insisting that the men muster in three ranks before marching up to the walls to defend the city.

'Sir!' a terrified corporal was shouting at the top of his voice. 'We must return to the armoury, we have powder but no ball!'

Chinchilla looked as if he were on the brink of apoplexy. 'Arrest that man!' he shrieked in a sudden falsetto, and the almost hysterical corporal was immediately grabbed by two of his subordinates and frogmarched away.

Tristram forced his way through the crowds to the fort, intending to volunteer his services and prove his loyalty to Spain. But as he neared it he found his horse surrounded by a solid mass of women and children, in the middle of whom was Ensign Rodrigo with Dorothea's great-aunt.

'Thank God you're here, sir!' Rodrigo shouted. 'The city magistrates have ordered all women and children into the fort, but the fort commander has shut the gates on us! If you can possibly – '

There was a sudden, deafening roar of gunfire: a Levantine argosy which had been unloading in the harbour – one of the few vessels to offer the attacking fleet any resistance – had been set upon by four of Drake's galleons, and a thunderous barrage was being exchanged. The effect of this new engagement on the civilian population was immediate: the crowd surged forward, people screamed and stumbled, and women and children were trampled underfoot.

This stampede of terror subsided as quickly as it had developed, and left behind it, like driftwood on a beach, a scattering of bodies, mostly female. Mothers and daughters were shrieking and wailing, and a little girl who could have been no more than four or five years old was cramming her fists into her eyes and crying piteously: 'Mama! I want Mama!'

But her mother was dead. Tristram had dismounted from his lathered horse and was carrying her lifeless body in his arms to place it with the others under the trees by the fort.

The attack continued. Having put the galleys to flight with their superior firepower, Drake's ships swept through the harbour to the inner bay where another flotilla was anchored.

All through the night guns roared, magazines exploded and ships turned into massive torches of flame; and when the dawn came, they were still at it: the pinnaces were busy plundering stores from the hulks and urcas, prizes were being taken in tow, and more ships were being set alight.

Tristram had at last gained entry to the fort, and had volunteered his services. The defensive batteries had been designed to protect the city from an assault on the seaward beaches, and the cannon and basilicos on the walls were pointing in the wrong direction and were of too short a range to reach the English ships in the harbour. To rectify this a long-range culverin weighing nearly three tons had been dragged from the city gates and was now being hoisted by a hundred or more chanting black slaves to a position on the walls from which to hurl roundshot at the intruders.

Gentlemen, officers, soldiers and slaves were working shoulder to shoulder now, and Tristram was among them as they cheered and heaved, cheered and heaved, and the great gun rose inch by inch up to the battlements.

They had the culverin positioned and firing by mid-morning and within half a dozen shots had got the range of a sizeable galleon that had remained at anchor while the majority had gone on into the inner harbour.

The culverin roared and roared again and the crew cheered: a direct hit had been scored on the English galleon, which looked to Tristram as if she belonged to the second-in-command, by the banners and flags she was flying.

For a few seconds there was a lull and during it, across the water, came the sound of a man screaming in agony.

Hearing this, one of the gun's crew, a thickset man with tight black curls all over his body and a massive black moustache, turned to his mates and remarked, 'We've got one bloody Lutheran in the bollocks, anyway!'

The wind dropped away towards midday and after another skirmish between galleys and galleons in which the English ships anchored and warped themselves back and forth to bring their guns to bear, much of the fighting stopped for the afternoon, with ships lying becalmed on the glassy water. More guns were brought up to the walls and three thousand troops arrived to reinforce the city. But still the English remained, and when the defending galleys set fire to some ships in the hope that they would float down on the tide and do some damage to the invaders, the harbour was for a while busy again, with Drake's pinnaces and long boats taking the fire-ships in tow under oars in order to haul them clear.

Darkness fell, and the ships remained becalmed. In the city, people began to ask why it was that the galleys, the pride of the Mediterranean Fleet, were so powerless against these sailing ships of Drake's, and the first whispers of dissent spread among the townspeople.

Soon after midnight a breeze sprang up, and the English made a move: following Drake's stern lantern they slipped out one by one, and as they went their crews shouted and cheered and sang songs of farewell to their unwilling hosts.

Tristram watched them go: lightheaded from lack of sleep and filled with pride at the way his countrymen had acquitted themselves in battle, he at first longed to be able to shout and wave and cheer; but later, standing there in the quiet after the battle, the sound of those jubilant west-country voices coming across the water caused in him a sudden homesickness, a longing for England and the fireside, for a winter's tale, roast beef, and a jug of best ale served by Marion Treffry in the old Russell Inn.

A council of war was held a few days after the attack, and most of the General Staff of the Invincible Armada attended. The Marquis of Santa Cruz took the chair, and was assisted by his generals and captains, among whom was Don Pedro de Valdes, Dorothea's uncle, who had returned to Cadiz the previous day.

Though de Valdes had not witnessed the attack he was in no doubt as to the causes of the English superiority.

'Artillery,' he declared with complete authority. 'Their ships carry more guns, and their point-blank range is longer. Our galleys were not taken by surprise. They were simply outgunned.'

Several heads, including those of the Marquis and Don Martin de Bertendona, nodded in agreement, but Hugo de Moncada, his lips working furiously as he mentally prepared a defence of his beloved galleys, shook his head violently.

'Not so,' he countered vehemently. 'We were simply outnumbered, that is the beginning and the end of it. Had the harbour defences been provided by the proper, balanced fleet of galleys and galleasses which I have repeatedly advocated over the past year, El Draque would never have got further than the sandbar. How many times must it be said? The galley is our fastest and most effective ship of war, but it is not suited to harbour defence unless complemented by the galleass.'

'If it's not suited to harbour defence I don't know what it *is* suited to,' Miguel de Oquendo remarked. 'No, the answer's quite obvious as far as I'm concerned, and it's this: we've got to learn, once and for all, that the English fight dirty. They have less sense of honour than rats on a raft. The only way to beat them – mark this, gentlemen – the only way to beat them is at close quarters, and if our six galleys had gone straight in, rammed, grappled and boarded, we wouldn't be sitting here today asking what went wrong.'

'My Lord! My Lord!' exclaimed Moncada. 'I object most strongly! There is no question but that our galleys fought magnificently and courageously. . . .'

On and on it went, each senior officer mounting his hobby horse and riding it for all it was worth, each rising in defence of his own pet theory, each anxious to convince the Marquis of his own personal bravery, loyalty, perspicacity and dedication.

In the body of the hall Tristram listened to the arguments with inner satisfaction, and couldn't resist wondering if the intelligence reports he had sent back to England had played any part in Drake's splendidly daring attack.

At length the Marquis raised a finger for silence, and a lengthy argument concerning the significance of the English galleons' ability to dip their lugsails was halted. 'Gentlemen – I beg of you,' the Marquis said in a weary voice. 'We cannot undo what has been done. We must stop nursing our wounded pride and start sharpening our wits instead. We have incurred losses, yes, no one can deny that. We have had our beards trimmed, but trimmed beards grow back thicker than before and we must see to it that ours do so as quickly as possible. I have already sent word to his Majesty that the Enterprise will have to be delayed for at least three months to give us time to make good our losses and reorganize. And I am sure that we agree on one point at least, namely that this harbour is not easy to defend, nor is it well suited to our purposes as a starting point for this great venture. I have therefore decided to move my headquarters to Lisbon – ' (there was an immediate buzz of surprise at this and Tristram, who was standing among the ensigns and lieutenants, had the impression that the Andalusian traditionalists were quite appalled) ' – to move my headquarters to Lisbon, which has a larger harbour, deeper water, better wharferage and the added advantage of being geographically closer to our objective.' Santa Cruz paused to take a sip of wine and water, and in that pause looked suddenly old and tired. 'Now,' he continued, 'in the light of that decision, there are certain steps we must take to safeguard ourselves against further losses at the hands of the English. Firstly, all argosies and carracks en route for Cadiz are to be held at the Azores until we are sure Drake and his fleet are clear of our coasts. Secondly, no effort must be spared to hasten the production of high-quality brass pieces for our ships. Thirdly, with immediate effect, coastal trade with stores for the Armada is to be diverted to Lisbon.'

'My Lord!' interjected a distinctive voice from the back of the hall, and Tristram recognized it as Saavedra's. 'It may not seem an important matter on the face of it, but may I point out that one of the urcas that was burnt to the waterline last week carried a full load of barrel staves? We are therefore acutely short of this particular item, and as the representative of the Provisioner General I would recommend that a high priority be given to ensuring that replacements are made available at the earliest possible opportunity. Thank you, my Lord.'

'Thank *you*, Saavedra,' the Marquis replied tiredly, and his tone occasioned a certain amount of nudging and chuckling in the hall.

'Stupid old fool!' whispered one of the cavaliers standing behind Tristram. 'Why doesn't he go back to writing stories?'

As soon as the meeting was over, Ensign Rodrigo elbowed his way through the crush and caught Tristram as he was about to leave. 'Sir!' he said in awed tones, 'General de Valdes commands your presence on the instant!'

Tristram followed him back through the groups of officers who were still discussing the new plans and their implications. At the head of the hall the Marquis was surrounded by his senior commanders, and Ensign Rodrigo motioned to Tristram to wait with him at Don Pedro's elbow until a suitable moment offered itself for him to be presented.

'I understand Captain Chinchilla mentioned you favourably in his report on the defence of the city,' Rodrigo whispered earnestly. 'So that will be a feather in your cap, Inglés.'

Pascoe murmured his thanks, and a few moments later he found himself face to face with his uncle by marriage. Rodrigo stammered out a formal presentation; Tristram bowed low, and Don Pedro, a fine-looking man with large black moustaches, a receding hairline and the manner of one who has long been accustomed to being obeyed, looked him up and down. 'English, I understand,' he barked.

'By birth, but not by inclination, sir. At least – not while that Queen Jezebel of theirs remains upon the throne.'

'And what did you think of Drake's little adventure last week?'

'It is as General Oquendo said, sir, they have less honour than rats on a raft. But I think they've taught us some useful lessons, and their little jaunt, for all the pain it has caused us, may rebound against them, for now we know their tactics and will be better able to counter them.'

Don Pedro nodded his agreement at this, then changed the subject. 'And I understand you are staying under my roof at the minute?'

'Yes, sir, and I am more than grateful – '

'And what news of my niece?'

'She has remained at Medina Sidonia for the present, sir. I thought it unwise for her to come to Cadiz until we are certain that El Draque will not return.'

'And where will she go when you travel to Lisbon?'

'Sir?'

'Are you deaf, boy? Where will Dorothea stay when you journey to Portugal?'

'Sir – I was not aware – I was not expecting to go to Portugal. His Holiness sent me to Cadiz, and – '

'His Holiness sent you to Cadiz because that was where the Armada was assembling, Lieutenant. And I'm sending you to the Tagus as my staff officer for the self-same reason. Well? Will you take your new wife with you or leave her behind?'

'Sir – I haven't given the matter a thought – '

'In that case I'll do your thinking for you. You are to assume command of the escort for my baggage train and take Dorothea with you. Overland. And as I'll be travelling to Lisbon within the month, you'd better start out before the end of the week so that you can have my headquarters prepared by the time I arrive. Clear?'

Joaquim had returned to Cadiz from Medina Sidonia two days before, and when Tristram returned to his quarters he found his collaborator hearing confessions in the family chapel. Anxious to keep up appearances, he jumped the queue of penitents, and when the old housekeeper came out, crossing herself repeatedly and mumbling the prayers she had been given as a penance, he entered the confessional and muttered the customary opening.

'What's happened?' Joaquim whispered, sensing by Tristram's manner that something had gone wrong.

'I've just met Don Pedro. He's taken me onto his staff and wishes me to escort Dorothea and his baggage train to Lisbon.'

He heard Joaquim's slight intake of breath. 'Didn't you decline?'

'How could I? Don Pedro's not a man who takes no for an answer. To refuse would have brought immediate suspicion on us both.'

'If we go to Lisbon, we shall risk far more.'

Tristram bowed his head in his hands. 'Either way we are at risk,' he whispered. 'But if we go to Lisbon we shall at least be able to do the job we've been ordered to do. Once the General Staff moves from Cadiz, there'll be little more than society gossip to report here.'

'But we were specifically warned not to return to Lisbon.'

'I know that. But the situation's changed, hasn't it?'

Joaquim spoke in an almost inaudible whisper. 'You realize the price we may have to pay?'

'Of course. But isn't the risk just as great if we stay? These people aren't fools, Joaquim, whatever you may think of them. I can't refuse a general's order and expect to get away with it.'

'We could escape now. We've done excellent service already, and we might yet be of service elsewhere – '

'Unlikely. Besides, there's much more to do in Lisbon. I shall be at the very hub of things on Don Pedro's Staff. I can't miss a chance like this.'

'You sound as if your mind's already made up.'

'It is. I'm going to Lisbon. If you don't want to come too, that's up to you. But my duty can only be to keep close to the central Staff and continue making reports to England until the Armada sails – or the Enterprise is abandoned or I'm drawn and quartered.'

'And . . . Sara?'

'If we're lucky, she'll be living out at Colares still, and we shan't even hear of her.'

'And if we aren't?'

'We shall just have to be careful.'

Joaquim was silent for a long time. Eventually he said: 'This wouldn't have happened if you hadn't tied yourself to that – '

'I know,' Tristram muttered. 'You don't need to remind me of it.'

At that moment he would have welcomed the chance to make a genuine confession to Joaquim. Since breaking off his honeymoon so abruptly he had seen nothing of Dorothea but had received one letter from her in which she bewailed her isolation up in Medina Sidonia while completely ignoring the terrible blow to Spain. Away from her, he had had time to reflect. Joaquim had been quite right – he acknowledged that now. He was saddled with a wife for whom he felt not the smallest affection. Worse: by using marriage to satisfy lust, he had been guilty of a cynical betrayal of himself and all the standards of behaviour which he held in highest regard.

But dimly, at the back of his mind, there was another reason for going to Lisbon: there was now present in him a need to place himself in the greatest danger in order to win back some shred of honour and self-respect. It was as if all that had happened had been pre-ordained, and that Lisbon were drawing him back by some mystical force. To oppose that force would have been not only futile but disloyal – to his country, to Queen Elizabeth, but most of all to himself.

'I must go,' he whispered. 'I must go.'

'And I with you,' Joaquim replied, then raising his voice added, 'and for your penance say three Pater Nosters and three Ave Marias. *Absolvo te in nomine Patris et Filii et Spiritus Sancti.* Go in peace, and say a prayer for me.'

'I will. Thank you, Father.'

Six days later, when the morning sun was glittering on the sea beyond the Punta Candelaria and trumpets were braying out over the city battlements, Don Pedro de Valdes's baggage train set out from Cadiz under the command of Teniente Tristan Pascua Inglés. It consisted of six horse-drawn wagons escorted by twelve foot soldiers and several slaves.

Dorothea was very subdued now: riding in a carriage with her little black slave boy sitting beside her, she raised no objection at having to sleep under canvas, never murmured about the rigours of travel, the delays, the heat, the flies or the mosquitoes; and whenever Tristram spoke to her she would look at him in an injured way that almost – but not quite – aroused his sympathy.

In order to obtain further intelligence, he took the coast road along the southern Portuguese seaboard instead of following the more direct inland route over the Sierra Morena to Grandola. After staying a night at Ayamonte they crossed the Guardiana river and set out along the straight, flat road which led between almond orchards and orange groves to Tavira, and towards dusk the caravan clattered to a halt outside the coastal fort of Cacela Velha, whose granite walls rose steeply on an escarpment overlooking a tidal lagoon of oyster beds.

As they approached the hamlet they became gradually aware that tragedy had befallen it: several of the little dwellings had been gutted by fire; the chapel bell was tolling, and mourners were standing in the graveyard.

The wagons filled the cobbled square outside the fort, and Tristram dismounted. Children stared at the armed newcomers and ran to their mothers' aprons for protection. By the well a donkey hee-hawed as if it carried all the cares of the world upon its crossed back.

A corporal appeared at the gate, and although he addressed Tristram with respect, his manner made his dislike for these smart Spanish soldiers abundantly clear.

'What's been going on here?' Tristram asked him.

The corporal gave him a sullen look and led him to the wall overlooking the lagoon. Drawn up on the beach were the cindered remains of a dozen fishing boats.

'Drake,' said the corporal. 'That was the Drake.'

All along the coast they heard the same story. Drake, it seemed, was everywhere. Villages were being sacked, fishing boats burnt at their moorings, coastal traffic plundered. Though the city of Lagos had acquitted itself well and had driven Drake's landing party back to their ships, every other town and village thus visited had been left with its boats burnt and its stores of salted fish confiscated or spoiled.

'If only I could speak with him!' Tristram whispered one night to Joaquim. 'If only I could tell him about the far greater prizes off the Azores that are his for the taking!'

'Why don't you?' Joaquim returned. 'We've got plenty of time. We can go as far as Cape St Vincent if necessary. And as you're not sharing a tent with your wife these days, she's unlikely to miss you if you take a night off.'

So they pressed on westward along the coast, and after an uncomfortable night near the village of Salema, Tristram heard local reports that Drake's men had recently occupied the fort of Henry the Navigator and that his ships were at anchor nearby.

The following night, when the moon was down and Dorothea had retired into the privacy of her tent, he slipped away down to the beach and pushed off in a little cockleshell boat; and within an hour he was approaching the shape of an English galleon, whose aftercastle towered over him in the darkness.

The lamplight from an after cabin played on the water as the great ship rolled gently at her anchor. He lay on his oars and allowed the boat to drift closer.

'Hulloa!' he called out quietly. 'God for England and Queen Elizabeth!'

There was an immediate cry of alarm from the watchkeepers. Within seconds a lamp was swung out on a boom over him and a soldier appeared with a longbow at the ready.

'Who calls?'

'A friend. A Cornishman. I'm unarmed and I have important intelligence. Will you let me board?'

While the watchkeepers held a further brief conference the bowman took aim on Tristram's heart and held the weapon at full stretch. Then a new voice, the voice of authority, said: 'Stand up in your boat and be recognized.'

He obeyed, expecting an arrow in the chest at any moment. Instead, a rope thudded heavily on the bottom boards at his feet, and he was ordered alongside.

He swung himself over the bulwark and jumped down to the deck. Immediately he was grabbed by the arms. A lantern was held aloft, and bearded faces peered closely at him.

'Cornish did you say?' a swarthy old-timer challenged. 'Which Hundred?'

'Powder. And if any Cornishman aboard like to converse with me, let 'un ask anything he please, and prove me.'

They conferred for a few moments, and messengers were sent – one for'd, one aft. While he waited, Tristram looked about him, admiring the galleon's lines and the evidence of a well-run ship: the uncluttered decks, the taut halyards, the clean guns.

'Ah, mates!' he murmured. 'If only you knew what it's like to be aboard an English ship again!'

One of the messengers returned with a black bearded giant who looked so obviously Cornish that Tristram almost laughed aloud. The man was still half asleep, and took a while to understand what was required of him. When he at last understood, he looked hard at Tristram and recited: 'Vizzery, vazzery, vozery, vem.'

He could hardly believe his ears. The Cornishman had started the first line of a chant he hadn't heard since the days he played lippety-lap on Mother Russell's front doorstep.

'Vizzery vazzery vozery vem,' the mariner repeated, clearly confident that he had Tristram beaten.

'Tizzery tazzery tozery tem,' Tristram replied.

'Hiram jiram cockrem spiram.'

'Poplar rollin gem.'

'There stands a pretty maid in a black cap.'

'If you want a pretty maid in a black cap – '

'*Please take she!*'

This last line was shouted in unison, and as soon as it had been uttered the mariner turned to the others. 'Aye, 'e be Cornish right enough,' he said, and stumped off back to his slumbers.

'Lay him aft, then,' a voice said, and Tristram turned to see a lieutenant standing on the break of the aftercastle looking down at them.

He was taken to the ladder and an escort of two followed him up. He found himself face to face with a man of about his own age, who looked at him closely.

'What are you, an agent?' he said very quietly.

'Aye. With important intelligence.'

'What sort?'

'Of Spanish treasure ships. And Armada preparations.'

The other nodded, then turned to the escort who stood a few paces apart. 'Hold him here while I go below,' he ordered, and Tristram was left waiting among them again.

The ship rocked gently at her anchor. Hearing English spoken again had already moved him more than he had thought possible, and now the thought occurred to him that if this interview went well, he might at the end of it request to be allowed to stay aboard and take passage home to England. Joaquim would understand, he knew that. Perhaps he even expected it.

The lieutenant returned within a minute or two, and Tristram was ushered down a ladder and into the great cabin, where a swarthy man with a pointed beard sat with the *Mariner's Mirror* open at his knee and a clay pipe smouldering at his elbow.

'Wait outside, Mr Bodenham,' he said. 'I'll see him alone.'

The lieutenant withdrew. Tristram felt his heart hammering in his chest.

'What's your name?'

'Sir – I would rather not divulge anything that might – '

'Answer!' the Admiral rapped out, and there was no question of disobeying him.

'Pascoe, sir. Tristram Pascoe.'

Drake fixed him with blue, slightly bulbous eyes. 'Have we met before?'

'No sir. That is . . . in a way, yes sir.'

266

'When?'

He swallowed. 'In the Pelican at Plymouth, sir. Twelve – nearly thirteen – years back.'

The Admiral pointed a finger. 'Pascoe. . . So would your father be master of that little bark . . . what's her name?'

'The *Russell*, sir.'

But even this was not enough, for Drake continued to stare at him suspiciously. 'Very well, Mr Pascoe,' he said eventually. 'Answer me this. Who's Barty, and where does he live?'

He laughed with relief. 'Why – he's a bull terrier, sir! He lives at Mr Wray's house in Greenwich!'

That seemed to satisfy the Admiral, who then proceeded to quiz him on every aspect of the Spanish Armada. He wanted to know details of the damage done by the English attack on Cadiz, the effect of the raids along the Algarve coast and the whereabouts of Recalde's Biscayan flotilla; he was interested to hear that since the raid on Cadiz, the Spanish were placing less reliance upon the galley and the galleass, and pleased that they still favoured close-quarters fighting. He listened intently to Tristram's assessment of the sea-keeping qualities of Spanish and Portuguese galleons and his report on the shortages of culverins and demi-culverins. He asked about Spanish supply routes from the Orient and the Indies, and when Tristram told him that treasure ships bound for Lisbon and Cadiz were being held at the Azores until the English were clear of the area, the Admiral shot him a quick glance, and touched the wart on the side of his nose as if an idea had just that moment taken seed.

'Is there aught else?' he asked eventually, when Tristram had been answering his questions for nearly an hour.

'Naught that I can think of, sir.'

Drake nodded briefly. 'Mr Bodenham!'

'Sir – ' began Tristram.

'What?'

'I was wondering, sir . . . if there might be any possibility of my taking passage home to England – '

'None whatsoever,' said the Admiral crisply, and looked up as the lieutenant put his head in. 'I've finished with him, Mr Bodenham. He can be put back in his boat.'

There was no word of thanks, no handshake, no sign even that Tristram was regarded as fighting in the same cause. One minute he was face to face with Drake, the next he was jumping down into the skiff.

After casting off the painter he sat and allowed the boat to drift aft on the tide, his mind still full of all that had been said in the past hour; and while he did so he overheard part of a conversation on the high aftercastle of the *Elizabeth Bonaventure*. Drake was pacing his quarterdeck with his lieutenant before turning in for the night. Their words carried quite clearly over the calm water:

'. . . one or two useful scraps of information, Jonas, but I'd guessed most of it already. And these spies. . . they're all the same. You can never really trust them, can you? And they always set too high a value on their own importance.'

'Too much sun and soft living, that's what does it, sir.'

'The fellow even looked like a Don Diego!'

Then they laughed, and Tristram – half blinded with tears of outrage – seized the oars and rowed noisily back to the shore.

They arrived at the gates of Lisbon five days later, after a long, hot journey over the rolling plains of the Alentejo. Neither Joaquim nor Tristram had seen the city for over seven years, and returning after so long and in such altered circumstances was a strange and unnerving experience.

There was no doubt that the city and harbour were busier. Galleons, galleasses, urcas, pataches and zabras lay at anchor off the Palace Square, and the market-places were packed. But the City of Ulysses had changed in another, subtler way which Tristram could not easily define, and it took Joaquim to put into words exactly what had happened.

Riding beside Tristram at the head of the baggage train he looked about him in silence for some time before he turned to his companion and said, 'See what these Spanish have done, my friend? They've got us poor Portuguese organized at last!'

On making enquiries at the military headquarters, Tristram was met by a harassed Portuguese adjutant, who clapped a hand to his forehead and groaned when he read Don Pedro's letters of introduction and requisitions of accommodation for his staff.

'I can make no promises, Lieutenant. I shall try to arrange lodgings for you and your General, and provided your men take their turn on the city guard rota they can doss down and eat with the *infanteria*. But don't expect luxury, because this city is already bursting at the seams, and we just have to fit you all in as best we may.'

'And the General's headquarters?'

The adjutant, a small, wiry man with black hair that stood on end, laughed. 'Headquarters? I can't fix miracles, you know. If anyone wants to set up a staff headquarters in Lisbon these days, he'll have to make his own arrangements.'

'But General de Valdes has given orders – '

'My friend – everyone is giving orders. Even my spaniel bitch is giving orders! And what is being done? *Nada! Nada, nada, nada!*'

They were interrupted by the sound of Dorothea's animated chatter, and when Tristram turned he saw her entering on the arm of a dashing-looking Spanish gentleman, upon whom she was bestowing the same misty looks of admiration she had once used to captivate Tristram.

'Husband, husband!' she chirruped excitedly. 'See who I have met! Don Martin Alvarez of all people!' She turned to Don Martin. 'This is my husband, Don Tristan Pascua. He is Uncle Pedro's lieutenant and we are here for the Great Enterprise! Ah, my dear Martin, how glad I am to see you!' She turned to Tristram. 'You must forgive me, husband, but Martin and I played games together when we were little – remember, Martin? Remember how Aunt Agatha scolded you for climbing on the roof, and the day I fell in the mill pond?'

Don Martin was almost as excited as Dorothea. He glanced admiringly at her, amazed that she should have grown up into such an attractive young woman. He returned Tristram's bow and said he was honoured to make the lieutenant's acquaintance.

'Uncle Pedro, you said? Would that be Don Pedro de Valdes? Ah – of course! I knew those colours were familiar! So you will be here until the *Felicissima Armada* sails? In that case you must stay with us. No – I insist. It will be a great pleasure to play host to dear Dorothea and her most fortunate husband.' He bowed again. 'A pleasure and a privilege! A pleasure and a privilege! And it will be a further honour to put my house entirely at the disposal of the General and his staff. If you would care to follow me I shall show you the way. We're up in the Mouraria.'

They went out into the sun, and when the soldiers had been mustered in two ranks and turned into column, the baggage train set out up the steep hill to the neat suburbs of the Mouraria where the wealthy lived in their separate estates, each with its walls, its main house, its servants' quarters, stables, chapel and gardens.

Riding up the hill past the Franciscan monastery and the palace of the Duke of Bragança, Tristram felt considerably relieved – not only that he had been able to find quarters for himself and his General, but that they would not be guests of the Portuguese aristocracy, and would therefore be at less risk of meeting any member of the Valdez de Santarém family.

If he and Joaquim could only last out a few more months. . . .If they could just stay unrecognized until the fleet sailed. And then what? He remembered what he had overheard Drake saying about spies and – not for the first time since that half-hour on board the *Elizabeth Bonaventure* – he longed to be unburdened of his duty and set free to seek a more honourable occupation. But how could that be done? Could he escape back to Paris and thence to Greenwich? Would it ever be possible to persuade Mr Wray to relieve him of this continual strain, this unending awareness that at any moment he might be denounced, arrested or stabbed in the back? But I must not plan too far ahead, he told himself. I must just take each day as it comes. . . .

Don Martin led the way beneath an arch to a cloistered square decorated with blue tiles and a fountain. Overhead, hundreds of white doves cooed and fluttered and strutted on the jumbled roofs. The servants were summoned to meet the new arrivals, and arrangements were put in hand for stabling the horses and quartering the soldiers, servants and slaves.

Joaquim was introduced to the family confessor, and Tristram and Dorothea were shown upstairs to rooms overlooking the inner square.

While Dorothea went into the bedchamber to be undressed by her maids and bathed in fresh lemon-water, Tristram, hearing ladies' voices in the square below, went to the balcony of their private sitting room and looked down.

A guest was just about to depart. Settling herself in the seat as the carriage moved away, she glanced upward at the balcony.

He felt as if he had been struck suddenly in the chest. It was Sara.

Sara

It was not Tristram because it could not possibly be Tristram, and yet it was because it could not possibly have been anyone else. That half rueful, half apologetic look of his, that hint of roguishness, his shape, his build, his size – even his very Englishness – all these shouted only one name, the name Tristram Pascoe.

And yet – how could he possibly be here in Lisbon?

All the way back through the city Sara tried to convince herself that she had been mistaken, and all the way back a voice insisted that she had not.

The silly thing about it was that seeing him (or whoever it was) had made her want to cry. Memories of Tristram that she had long since pushed away into the back of her mind kept leaping out at her, so that moments with him at Colares – whether walking in the gardens or climbing up to Sintra or meeting secretly among the whispering canes – came vividly back, and brought with them all the ache and emptiness she had suffered after his departure with Joaquim.

Seven years! How quickly they had passed, and how little she had to show for them!

As the four bays plodded slowly up the last steep hill to the Quinta de Santo António she recalled that spring morning when she had been obliged to inform the Inquisitor that her *caseiro* and bodyguard had absconded.

Remembering her own inner terror at Frei Bartolomeu's anger, she broke out in a chill sweat.

João and his mother had expected her to break under the strain of her year of penance, but their expectation drove her to prove them wrong. Keeping the memory of Tristram always in mind, she had beaten herself daily with whips, crawled round the chapel on her knees, chanted prayers, said rosaries, made novenas and bought every indulgence that was on sale, so that when the twelve-month was up, Padre Jorge could only make a good report of her, and the Inquisitor was persuaded that she should be allowed to grow her hair again and resume her position as the Countess of Colares.

Her reinstatement had taken place nearly six years ago now, but although João had allowed her a gradual increase of personal freedom, he had been advised by Padre Jorge against ever allowing her back to her beloved Colares on her own, so she had been forced to remain a virtual prisoner at the Quinta de Santo António, and it was only in the past few months that she had been allowed the privilege of making calls in the city.

The carriage went under the tiled arch and entered the inner courtyard, and when it drew up outside the front door Sara remained in her seat for a few moments more, staring up at the brilliant potted geraniums on the balcony, half expecting a vision of Tristram to appear to her again.

Her thoughts were interrupted by Maria Candida, who came bustling out of the house in a flather. '*Minha senhora, minha senhora!*' she panted. 'A letter! A letter from Ireland! *Ai, minha senhora*, I thought you would never return!'

As she entered the cool, tiled hall, Sara heard João's catarrhal voice. 'Fish?' he was saying. 'What sort of fish?'

Since being appointed as Recorder General to the Most Happy Armada, the Count had given over almost the entire ground floor of the Quinta de Santo António to offices, and his days were now taken up in compiling the *relación*, the account of who and what was to be embarked in the ships of the invasion force.

'Why – fish of all kinds, sir – '

'Then it must be changed. We must make an accurate *relación* or no *relación* at all, Rui, and when we list fish we must list each sort of fish. Salt fish, dried fish, smoked fish, *Bacalhau, linguado, roubalo* – '

'But sir that is an impossible task – '

'Don't argue with me, *rapazinho*. Nothing is impossible. Do what you're told. . . .'

A moment later the secretary, who was not a '*rapazinho*' at all but a man of nearly fifty, came out of the office, his face pale with fury; but on seeing Sara he softened immediately, bowed twice and wished her *boa tarde*.

'May I enter, Rui?' she whispered. 'I believe the Count has a letter from Ireland.'

'Of course, my Lady – if you will wait one moment – ' He tapped again on the door, and João's voice came impatiently out to them: 'Now what?'

She entered at his command, and found him sitting at his writing table studying a list. João liked lists: they gave him a warm, comfortable feeling. He had lists of provisions, lists of ships, lists of seamen and soldiers, *gente de mar* and *gente de guerra*. On the walls of his office hung great parchment lists of military commanders and naval captains showing the chains of command for all the various departments. He liked keeping accounts, too: he set great store by a column of roman numerals with a sum total at the bottom. He liked XXII and XXII to make XLIV, and frequently used a small ivory-beaded abacus to make sure that they did.

'Well?' he demanded. 'What do you want?'

'Maria Candida tells me that mails have arrived from Ireland and if there is a letter for me, I would like to see it.'

He lifted a letter off the table and handed it across. She thanked him and was about to withdraw when he stopped her. 'No – there is no need to take it away with you. You may read it here.'

She unfolded the stiff paper and her heart lifted at the sight of her father's chunky scrawl. It was the first letter she had received from him in over a year.

'Well?' João snapped. 'Don't keep it to yourself, woman! Construe it for me!'

But Sara was already choking back tears, for Gerald Hussey's letter to his daughter told her that hard times had come yet again to Corcaguiney: that there had been an unprovoked attack on Ballingolin, that the farmhouse had been burnt to the ground, that her mother was dying and that her beloved brother Niall, to whom she had been so close in the days of her childhood, was dead.

Having told João of it, she stood before him and allowed the tears to flow freely down her cheeks. Coming so soon after the shock of seeing Tristram, it was almost more than she could bear.

'João,' she whispered. 'Grant me this one favour: allow me to return on a visit to Ireland. Allow me to see my family at this time.'

He snorted derisively. 'Go to Ireland? When every other ship on the high seas is an English man-of-war? Have you gone mad, Sara?'

She struggled to contain her grief. 'João – I beg you – let me go. My father has asked me – see, these are the words here – he has asked me to return if only for a few weeks. You know how I long to see my family again. My father is old, and my mother is dying. If I don't go now I may never see either of them again. And – and I am not afraid to travel alone. There is no need for you to escort me. There are ships plying between Lisbon and Dingle still – I know it for a fact. If I go soon, I shall be back before the autumn gales. Please – my dear – if you grant me no other request, allow me this one. Surely you of all people know how much I long to go back, to see my people, to see Ireland – '

'Ireland, Ireland, Ireland! How many times must I tell you that your home is not Ireland, Sara?'

'But my mother – '

'Yes, your mother is ill, we know that. My mother is ill, too. Has it not occurred to you that had I not been bound in duty to Maezinha I would have been the first to volunteer my services to the Enterprise? We all have our duty, Sara. Each has his place. Mine is here in Lisbon, and yours is at my side.'

She would gladly have struck him. She knew very well that he had never had any intention of sailing with the Armada, and that he had leapt at the office of Recorder General in order to avoid having to go to sea. She knew he was terrified of water, knew that his mother's illness was a convenient fabrication and – she touched the Madonna that hung at her neck – she knew the reason why.

'Do you not understand, woman, what is happening down there in the harbour?' João was saying. 'Have you no idea of the momentous times in which we live? Here in Lisbon we are caught up in what may prove to be the last chapter in the history of mankind.' He swept a limp hand round the room at the wall charts, the lists, the sheafs of paper. 'The battle for which these ships and soldiers are gathering may prove to be the great Armageddon, the last conflict between the Powers of Light and the Powers of Anti-Christ! We, the Portuguese, are privileged to play out our part in this great venture! Your husband, the Count of Colares, sits at the very hub recording for posterity the means by which God's Holy Cause will be effected! And you come bleating like a nanny-goat about going to Ireland!'

Ignoring the contradictions in his argument, and not trusting herself to speak further with him, she turned and hurried from the room. She went outside into the blinding afternoon sunlight; she crossed the courtyard and went down the hill to the very limit of the quinta, where fig and loquat trees hung over the boundary wall; and there, she allowed her thoughts to go home to Corcaguiney: she went back to Ballingolin and stood again on the castle ramparts; she looked out over Dingle Bay, listened to the cheerful voices of her brave brothers as they returned from the hill, heard the cattle lowing in the fields, saw smoke rising from the chimneys in the town and winding its way up Ballysitteragh, where the heather was coming into bloom and the cloud shadows moved upon the mountain.

Sara was not kept long in suspense about the identity of the visitor at the Casa de Boa Vista, for her three sisters-in-law were frequent visitors at the quinta and new arrivals in Lisbon society came high on the gossip list. Nevertheless, hearing 'Don Tristan Pascua' referred to by name for the first time came as a shock, and learning that he was married to a Spaniard of high birth awoke in her all the anguish and jealousy she had once felt over Jennifer.

But her discomfiture over Tristram's marital state was of less concern to her than his very presence in the city: it did not take a great deal of thought to see that he had placed himself at risk by coming to Lisbon, and she could hardly believe that he would take such a risk without weighing it carefully.

So why had he come? The question intrigued her increasingly, and the harder she tried to find a comfortable answer to it, the more convinced she became that he must be a spy.

Her convictions were largely confirmed by her first meeting with Dorothea. They were introduced one afternoon when Sara, Teresa, Graça and Iñes had met for a chatter at the Quinta de Santo António. Though Sara detested these afternoon hen-parties, she had become resigned to them, having decided that it was better to have some social life than none at all. So two or three times a week the wives got together and sat about in each other's chambers fanning themselves and exchanging society news; and on this occasion Dorothea, as the new arrival, dominated the conversation.

She was the youngest of the group, and obviously considered herself the most alluring. Fluttering her long eyelashes at her audience, she told them of her society life in Madrid, of her gallant brother-in-law and of the many artists, courtiers, generals and playwrights she knew personally. Whispering behind her fan, she disclosed intimate details about private lives at court, and her rapid, lisping chatter held the three Santarém sisters spellbound.

Sara was not quite so easily impressed. 'And your husband,' she asked when Dorothea paused to nibble a fig with her slightly protruding front teeth. 'How did you come to be betrothed to El Inglés?'

Dorothea gave a little peal of laughter. 'I might ask how you, who are Irish, came to be betrothed to Dom João, Countess! No – I shall be serious. My husband is a very strong, a very passionate man. He is a champion of the Holy Cause, a good soldier in the army of the blessed and ever-glorious Virgin Mother of God. And you know something? He was sent to me with the personal blessing of the Holy Father, so I was quite sure from the start that here was the sort of man well suited to be the husband of the daughter of the great family of Salazar y Vozmediano de Esquivias, a family that is destined to shape history and whose name I know will be perpetuated for many generations to come.' She sighed. 'Yes, he is a good, a véry good man and a kind and loving husband to his Dorothea, but sometimes I wish that he did not work quite so hard and had a little more time for things other than the Armada.'

'But what does he do all day?' Sara asked.

Dorothea threw up her hands. 'Why, don't you know? He is my uncle's principal adviser! He is highly esteemed, highly esteemed. They say that no one in Lisbon knows more about English ships, English seas and English ways of fighting than my husband!'

'He works with *my* husband a great deal also,' Teresa put in. 'The Admiral is using him as his consultant, but of course it's very hush-hush like everything else these days.'

'Isn't it terrible?' Dorothea agreed. 'Why – Cadiz was nothing like this, nothing at all. We knew how to enjoy ourselves in Cadiz, but here everyone goes about with a long face like Father Joaquim!'

'Father who?' Sara asked rather too quickly.

'Father Joaquim, our confessor.' Dorothea sighed and fanned herself. 'What a holy, holy man is Father Joaquim! But he is Portuguese of course, and you know how solemn you Portuguese can be with all your *saudades*! Why – since we have come to Lisbon, Father Joaquim has scarcely been out of the house or off his knees! Of course he is one of these new Society of Jesus priests, and they are very devout. I am only glad that we have such holy men on our side!'

Maria Iñes turned to Sara. 'Are you not feeling well, *cunhada*? You have quite lost your colour.'

Sara laid a hand on her bosom.

'It's nothing. Just a little vapour, that's all.'

There were reasons for long faces that summer, for as time passed and the Armada preparations became increasingly feverish, hardly a day went by without some new delay, crisis or shortage being reported.

One day the city was astir with the news that Drake's ships were sailing up and down between Cascais and the entrance of the Tagus, and many of the wealthy families moved out to their country estates until the scare was over. A few weeks later, news came through that Drake had captured a most valuable Portuguese carrack, the *San Felipe*, off the Azores and speculation increased that the English Dragon was in league with the Devil and had magical powers which enabled him to see over the horizon.

Then there were the shortages: shortages of fish, shortages of oil, shortages of flour, of meat and of wine, the cause of which was always said to be the Armada. Not only were there thousands of extra soldiers, sailors and slaves to be fed in Lisbon, but provisions had to be stockpiled for the invasion force. Even provisions that were in plentiful supply were often held up in the delivery because the army was commandeering horses and wagons in every town and village, and an acute transport problem was developing.

Ships continued to arrive in the Tagus, and the city was full of soldiers, mariners and monks. The bawdy houses and brothels did a brisk trade, and there were frequent murmurings and mutinies among the men because of poor rations, disease and lack of pay.

Slowly, as October approached, it became increasingly apparent that the Armada would not be ready in time. A whisper went round that there was such a dire shortage of powder and roundshot that if the Armada met the English on the high seas, they could only prosecute an engagement for half a day, after which time they would be powerless in the face of the English guns. The strain began to tell: illness and apoplexy became a commonplace among those who were charged with bringing a semblance of order to this vast, chaotic collection of ships and men.

When the Captain General at last bowed to the inevitable and informed the King that the departure date would have to be postponed, the decision was received with great relief, and hailed as proof that those charged with leading the Enterprise were men of compassion and humility whose decisions were guided by God.

João was particularly relieved: his task of producing the official *relación* had developed into a nightmare, with nominal lists and inventories having to be amended every day as sickness took its toll and provisions rotted. Now that the sailing date had been officially delayed he felt as if he had been granted a stay of execution.

'We shall have a celebration,' he told Sara one afternoon when he had called her to his chambers. 'We shall have a proper vintage party up at Colares like we used to. We'll take the whole family and enjoy ourselves for a change. We'll get Maezinha up to the Quinta de Piedade in a litter, and Graça, Iñes and Teresa can bring their children. And let's ask that young couple staying with Don Martin – the little señora with the English emigré for a husband.' He rubbed his hands together. 'Let's have a bit of fun again, Sarainha!'

'Have you heard?' Tristram whispered through the grille. 'We've been invited to Colares for the vintage.'

Since coming to Lisbon, Tristram and Joaquim had been careful to spend as little time as possible in each other's company, and these whispered conferences in the secrecy of the confessional had virtually become their sole means of communication.

'I'm trying to find an excuse for not accepting. So if you have any ideas – '

Joaquim coughed. He was becoming increasingly troubled by bronchitis. 'What about Dorothea?'

'She's accepted on my behalf. Don Pedro has also been invited, and Dorothea has persuaded him to release me from my duties. So – what do you think? Do I accept?'

'I think you'll have to.'

'But I may already have been recognized by Dona Sara – '

'She won't betray you. Quite the reverse – she'll protect you. You'll have to be careful not to make her task any more difficult by remaining either too aloof or allowing yourself too close.'

'I am . . . I am terrified of meeting her, Joaquim. Terrified and yet drawn on by some mystical force, as if our paths have been destined to cross from the beginning of time.'

'Perhaps that is the case,' Joaquim murmured.

'And the Count – I dread the moment when I first have to look the Count in the eye. He saw little of me at Colares admittedly, but he may have seen enough. As for yourself, I don't think you can possibly show your face at the Quinta de Piedade. You're too well known there.'

'I shall commit myself to a week of solemn prayer and meditation for the speedy departure of the Armada, and remain here. But you must accept. There's already been gossip here about your reluctance to be seen in public, and you won't talk Dorothea out of going. Besides – the risk is perhaps smaller than you imagine. You must forget that you were a servant, and see all with new eyes. Hold your head up, speak in a loud voice and make friends with the Count, and no one will connect you with the miserable wretch you once were. It's a matter of confidence, boy. Act suspiciously and you arouse suspicion; act confidently, and you win confidence.'

'And if I'm recognized?'

'Deny it immediately – for Sara's sake if no one else's. If necessary threaten to denounce Dorothea if she doesn't stand by you and pull strings.'

'Denounce Dorothea? What for?'

'You'll think of something. She tells me she's been having impure dreams about Ensign Rodrigo.'

'And if that doesn't work?'

'You can try denouncing Count João. I don't have to tell you on what charge.'

'And if I'm brought before the Inquisitor?'

Joaquim gave a chuckle. 'I'll do my best for you boy. And we can always wave to each other through the flames.'

Early October can be the most beautiful time of year in Portugal. The sun has lost its harsh heat; the diurnal *nortada* has stopped making dust and sand storms every afternoon; the sea is calm again after the equinoctial gales, and at night the heavens seem the more crowded with stars, and the fiery harvest moon hangs over the eastern horizon like a golden orb after sunset.

These gentle, early autumnal conditions prevailed when the Count of Colares took his household to the Quinta de Piedade for the vintage.

They travelled in convoy with an armed escort, and to save her from the jars and joltings of wheeled travel, the elderly Dona Marguerita was carried all the way in a litter borne by eight slaves, who toiled barefoot up the hill as the caravan went out through the walls by the Porta da Mouraria and descended along the old Roman road that runs straight as an aqueduct to Sintra.

Sara made the journey in a state of considerable apprehension. She was quite childishly excited about seeing Colares again, and the thought of actually meeting Tristram had tied a knot in her stomach, so that she had hardly been able to eat since João's casual announcement the previous week.

Up into the mountain they went, the carriage wheels creaking, the horses snorting and straining, the harnesses jingling. Up – and down – and round a corner and up again; and down again, and round another corner, and down through a forest . . . and up again – and around another corner –

And there was the village of Colares, with the little dwellings clustered round the church of the Assumption of Our Lady. There were the sloping vine terraces, the wooded skyline, the humble roofs nestling amid the trees; and – yes – there it was, the Quinta de Piedade, with the Colares river running down past it, and the gardens, the walls, the shaded walks and arbours which Joaquim had tended with such care and which, through him, she had come to love so much.

Suddenly her eyes filled with tears. Why was she so moved? This wasn't Ireland, after all. Was she unusual in making such strong attachments to mere places? What was this yearning she felt inside her – this yearning for what the Portuguese called their *terra*, their earth, their land?

Glancing at the trees that grew beside the road she noticed one in particular whose gnarled trunk was scarred heavily by the pruning and lopping of branches, and whose sinuous roots had been partly exposed by the rains. Perhaps that is what I long for most of all, she reflected. Perhaps, when I was here at Colares, I began to put down roots of my own.

They clattered on through the village and made the wide sweeping turn round to the right, approaching the quinta along the almond avenue Joaquim had planted nearly thirty years before. The carriages drew up one by one to allow the passengers to alight before going on to the cobbled square under the lime trees.

'Right! Right!' João exclaimed, beaming at his nephews and nieces, who were already running off to explore. 'Welcome, everybody! Welcome to the Quinta de Piedade, and may I be the first to wish you all a *boa vindima!*'

But Sara could not share her husband's glee: looking about her at the goats grazing in the formal gardens, the fallen river banks and the weeds growing out between the *azulejos*, she felt a pang of sadness that her *terra* should have been so badly neglected.

'Come Sara!' João muttered at her side. 'Do your duty, the General's arriving!'

She stepped forward to welcome the guest of honour, who rode on horseback and was accompanied by his lieutenant.

Tristram had grown his moustaches longer and looked every inch the aide de camp. He clicked his spurs and bowed in the style favoured at the

Spanish court. 'It is my honour to present General Don Pedro de Valdes, Commander of the Andalusian Squadron of his Majesty's Invincible Armada,' he announced stiffly – but at the same time managed to send Sara a secret glance to reassure her that nothing at all had changed between them.

The guests stayed for five days, and most of that time was spent eating, drinking and talking. João was in his element: surrounded by people of influence, he gave full rein to his talent for witty conversation, and the long table under the vine trellis where he entertained his guests was constantly enlivened by his anecdotes, aphorisms and compliments; and while the merry-making went on and the rich enjoyed themselves, the common men and women of Colares sweated in the fields, picking the grapes, filling the stone *lagares* and treading out another year's harvest.

Inevitably, each member of the houseparty found himself or herself becoming attracted to others, and as the days passed and the formality of the first evening was dispersed by mounds of rich food and lakes of sweet Colares wine, these secret torches glowed brightly and – here and there – burst into flame.

Thus, while Tristram and Sara yearned inwardly for each other without giving any outward sign of their affection, Dorothea began making eyes at Rodrigo; the General admired Maria Iñes, and João was captivated by Rodrigo's adolescent charms.

On the last evening, when a saffron moon was turning the River Colares into a pale pathway between the old walls of the quinta, the whole party sat down to a gargantuan banquet, after which, with faces flushed and bellies full, they went singing and laughing down to the candle-lit *lagar*. There, João insisted upon jumping in and dancing in the grape-must. He jigged up and down with his hands above his head, and the guests clapped and roared with delight.

Catching Tristram's eye, Sara knew immediately that he, like herself, was remembering a similar evening years before when he had slipped out in disgust and she had followed him down the path to the river.

'One in, all in!' João shouted, and beckoned furiously with his little hands. 'Come along Rodrigo – off with your hose and earn your dinner!'

'Go on!' Dorothea told Rodrigo, and the ensign was obliged to obey. 'And you too, Lieutenant!' The Count ordered, and Sara, seeing Tristram's discomfiture, urged Don Martin and Don Luis to follow suit, so that within a short time all the younger gentlemen were thigh-deep in oozy purple grape juice and the ladies were clapping in time as they cavorted and pretended they were peasants.

Suddenly there was a shriek: Dorothea, flushed with wine and ardour, had hoicked up her skirts and joined the men in the *lagar* – something so completely unheard of that for a moment there was a startled silence; but this was quickly followed by a cheer from Ensign Rodrigo who, full of wine and courage, insisted on taking her hand and doing a flamenco.

The building echoed to the clapping in time and roars of aristocratic laughter. Dorothea's sweeping gestures and snapping fingers became increasingly exaggerated: the rhythm mounted to fever pitch; she twirled back and forth in the grape sludge, and João – who was by now panting for Rodrigo – tried to join in and make it a threesome.

But Rodrigo's expert flamenco dancing had by now lit the flame of Dorothea's desire and she wanted him all to herself, so she took Tristram by the arm and tried to partner him off with the Count instead. When he declined, she rounded on him.

'Don't be dull, husband! That's the trouble with you English – you don't know how to enjoy yourselves!'

It was then – for a split second – that Tristram found himself face to face with João, and in that moment he saw in the Count's expression a vague suspicion, a question mark, as if João was asking himself where he had seen this face before.

Sara saved the situation. 'Now then,' she said, turning to her sisters-in-law, 'we can't leave the gentlemen without their partners, can we?' and climbing into the tank she faced João and began snapping her fingers like castanets and tossing her head in the Spanish style so that he was obliged to dance with her.

Later that night Dorothea and Rodrigo slipped out of the *lagar* for a walk by the river, and when she eventually returned to her room, she found Tristram preparing for bed.

'If only you knew how stupid you looked,' she giggled sleepily. 'When you were trying to do that flamenco. Christ, you looked stupid! Christ!'

'I'll thank you not to blaspheme,' he replied, playing up to the image of a solemn Englishman she had created for him. 'And I'll also thank you to be a little more discreet in future. It was obvious to everyone what you were up to with Rodrigo this evening. Besides – the back of your dress is covered in leaves.'

She stood swaying and giggling while a Portuguese maid helped her remove her sodden clothes. Not bothering to go behind the screen, she allowed herself to be revealed quite naked, her legs stained purple right up to the small black triangle which she called her little baa-lamb.

'Who cares?' she mumbled. 'It's about time I had a bit of fun for a change. Christ – you English don't know what a party is, do you? Why – when I was in Madrid, we had parties that were real parties, you know that? You thought you were a great gallant, didn't you? Well I've got news for you, Mister Inglés. I've had a man for a lover who makes you look like a schoolboy in bed. I've had Zuccaro, you know that? Frederigo Zuccaro, who painted the picture of the Annunciation that hangs in the palace of San Lorenzo, and I was one of his angels, but you wouldn't understand that because you're not an artist, you're just a dull English fool!' And with that, she fell onto the bed, put her thumb into her mouth and dropped quickly off to sleep.

Tristram lay awake for a long time, untouched by Dorothea's revelations because he had a secret of his own. Just as the party was breaking up, when Dorothea and Rodrigo had still not returned and João and some of the other gentlemen had gone down to the river to wash their feet, Sara had stood beside him and had spoken to him privately for the first time since his arrival for the vintage.

He had been puzzled at first by her manner: she had seemed to pretend that they were no more than distant acquaintances. She had commented on the sorry state of the gardens, and had continued: 'It grieves me when I think how much work was done here, but we have been badly in need of a good *caseiro* for some years now, and our best workers are all required for service with the Armada. It's much the same at the Quinta de Santo António. Our wall at the bottom of the property is also quite dilapidated. Sometimes, when I'm sitting down there in the siesta hour, I wonder if we ought to repair it.' Then she had turned to face him, and he had seen with a glorious shock that her lovely eyes held a secret sparkle, a hidden message that was for him alone. 'There's a hole big enough for a man to pass through under the fig trees,' she said. 'It's a disgrace. But of course, it can't be seen from the house, and as I'm the only person ever to go down there, nothing ever gets done about it.'

The moonlight stole in through the casement and glittered palely upon the wall tapestries. Dorothea was stirring in her sleep. 'Christ!' she muttered. 'Christ!'

The rains came soon after the vintage. Day after day, night after night it bucketed down from heavy, leaden clouds. The Tagus flooded; the hovels by the river were washed away and hundreds were made homeless. A river of mud raced downhill, carving through quintas and gardens to leave a brown watermark behind it on the whitened walls of the buildings in the Mouraria and the Alfama. Inland, fields were submerged and roads blocked by fallen trees, and the unending caravan of wagons bringing stores for the Armada became bogged down in a sea of mud.

When it was over and the summer of St Martin began at the beginning of November, Lisbon put on her loveliest autumn clothes. The sky was paler blue; the air pleasantly cool; the sun was lower in the sky at midday; the city was full of the aroma of roasting chestnuts – and Sara was able to spend the siesta hour in the garden again.

The first time she went down with a book and sat below the wall to look out at the ships in the harbour, she felt that every member of the household must be watching her, but as she had often walked alone in the gardens before and João, Dona Marguerita and all the servants snoozed from two to four, her daily visits to the lower part of the quinta went unremarked.

After overcoming her fear that she would be watched, and when she had sat alone for an hour every afternoon for a week, she became terrified of a new possibility – that she might not have made her invitation clear, or that Tristram might fail to respond to it because he feared discovery, or did not trust her, or did not wish to meet her.

How she longed for him to keep this rendezvous! There had hardly been an hour since that first glimpse of him on the balcony at Don Martin's when she had not thought of him, prayed for him, watched for him, ached for him.

Sitting on a low bench, a volume of Horace open on her knee, she wondered if perhaps she had allowed her too-vivid imagination to take over, and that her remarks about the broken wall had been lost on him.

But he is not so obtuse, she reflected. Why – at Colares it was clear that he had changed completely from a mere slave boy to a gentleman, and an educated one at that.

She stared out over the busy harbour, watching as a boat under oars took a ship's anchor away in order to bring her to her moorings in the precise spot ordered by the harbourmaster.

And why is he here in Lisbon? she wondered, not for the first time. How can he possibly have changed so much, have turned against his country, become a convert, won favour at court – even secured letters of introduction from the Holy See? And Joaquim – how could he have taken orders as a Jesuit? Can it be that they would risk the Inquisition without good cause?

She shivered, unable to keep the possibility from her mind that they might be spies. After all, João was always talking about spies and saying that Lisbon was full of them. And what if they are? she wondered. What should I do, denounce them?

She bowed her head and pressed her hands to her face.

Perhaps I should go back now to the house and never come down here again. Perhaps I should avoid all contact with him, for his sake as much as my own. Perhaps –

She lowered her hands and opened her eyes: a branch of the fig tree was shaking gently, and yet there was hardly a breath of wind. Then a face looked cautiously out – his face – and suddenly all her fears were gone.

She ran down to the wall and ducked under the umbrella of faded leaves. For a brief moment, they stood face to face; and then they were in each other's arms and there was no need for words, because all that mattered now was that they were together, and the long years of wondering and hoping were over.

The Edge of Destiny

They sat under the umbrella of leaves, Sara's dress spread out round her and Tristram sitting cross-legged before her with her hands in his.

'You were my lodestar,' he was saying, 'the centre of my firmament. Without you, without the memory of you, I would have been lost a hundred times. . . .'

'I used to whisper your name, Tristão. I used to look up at the heavens from my window at night and whisper my love to you. And sometimes I knew – I *knew* that you were thinking of me at that very moment. . . .'

'Sara – I have so many difficult things to tell you. I never dreamt that I would ever return to Lisbon. I gave up hope long ago of ever seeing you again. That was why I married. It wasn't because I stopped loving you – '

'I understand, Tristão. I understand.'

'My marriage is – is an empty, meaningless thing. She was an infatuation, Sara. . . Joaquim tried to persuade me out of it, but I refused to listen to him – '

'Tristão . . . there's no need to explain – '

'But there *is*. There's something else you must know, straight away. I have to tell you this, Sara: I'm not acting for Spain, but for England. I'm in the service of Queen Elizabeth. Do you understand me? I'm a spy. So if – if you consider it your duty to denounce me, then you *must do so*. I've nothing else to live for now. I've deceived so many people – my whole life has become a lie. But I can never deceive you. I'd rather die than misuse you or put you in any sort of danger.'

He bowed before her and kissed her hands, and when he looked up his eyes were full of tears.

She reached out to him and put her arms lovingly about him. 'I could never denounce you, Tristão,' she whispered; and then they held each other for a long time, while the noise of the city continued below them and the leaves of their fig-tree tent rustled gently overhead.

Though each was aware of the risk they ran, they met two or three times a week after that, and over the course of several secret rendezvous, each told the other what had passed since the night he and Joaquim had escaped from the Quinta de Piedade.

She told him of her inquisition and the terrible penances and disciplines that had been imposed on her. She shared with him her longing to return to Ireland. She listened in admiration to his account of the voyage he and Joaquim had made to Polruan, and saw in his expression the anguish he still suffered over his father's marriage to Jennifer. And although she couldn't help feeling a little frightened by the knowledge that he was now a trained spy and dedicated to the defeat of the Armada that was assembling in the harbour, hearing his story helped her to understand how and why he had become what he was.

She found that he had matured considerably as a result of his years of preparation for the secret service. Though she had loved him deeply, first as the vagabond she had rescued and later as her bodyguard at Colares, she now discovered in him a man she could love more fully as her equal in conversation and intellect, and she enjoyed listening to him enlarge on the new philosophy he had learnt at Cambridge.

'To say that some things are of God and some are not is a contradiction,' he said one afternoon, 'for if something is not of God it cannot be a part of Him; and if some things are not part of God, God is not God, but a being less than infinite. And if God be infinite as we believe, we cannot also believe that He will side with one army or another, whether Christian or Pagan or Infidel, for to do so would be dividing what is indivisible. And from that, we may conclude that a Spanish invasion of England is no more a holy cause than a Portuguese campaign against Africa or an English campaign against Ireland.'

She loved to listen to him speak his deepest thoughts and beliefs, and yet she had a way of bringing him back to practicalities.

'And what will you be doing when this un-blessed Armada of theirs has sailed, Tristão? Can you answer me that?'

He reached forward and kissed her lightly. 'It depends. If you could get that husband of yours to go off to England with it, perhaps we could make off somewhere.'

'And what would you do about that wife of yours?'

'I know what I'd like to do. I'd like to send her back to Andalusia with her paramour.'

She flushed suddenly. 'Do you know, Tristão – there are times when –

when I want to scratch her like this with my fingernails. And when – when she talks about all the lovers she's had and boasts about you in the same breath, I long to scream out that you are *mine, mine*, and that all her claims on you are false.' She appealed to him. 'It is so, isn't it? She has no claim on you does she?'

'No, she has no claim,' he whispered. 'If I were to be told today that I would never see her again, it would be the best possible news I could hope for.'

'And yet . . . you have been lovers. You have given yourself to her.'

'But never out of true love, Sara! Never in the way we love. And much as I'd like to be rid of her, I can't escape the fact that she's my wife, and I must continue to behave as her husband until this Armada sails.'

'Yes, I know,' she said softly. 'And I understand. But – she's still like a knife in my side, Tristão. I can't help that.'

'I suppose there's no hope that the Count will sail with the Armada?'

'None. My dear João will never go.' She made a face. ' "My place is at Maezinha's side." Brazen liar that he is. The fact of the matter is, he's terrified of getting his feet wet.'

'We shall have to plan another escape. There are islands off the coast of Africa – '

'I'd rather go back to Corcaguiney, Tristão.'

'Then we shall go there. I shall turn into John Kelly and work as your *caseiro* like Joaquim. It'll be enough for me simply to see you coming out of your castle in the morning and to be able to wish you good day.'

She hugged him. 'That would not be enough for me, my darling man.'

They rocked back and forth together, whispering their love, making impossible plans.

'If I can lay my hands on a tight ship and a few loyal souls for a crew – '

'I shall be your crew. I'm a very good sailor, you know. I was never sick once coming over from Ireland.'

'We shall sail away, just you and me and the sea. . . .'

'Cities on Vesuvius.'

'I know, I know.'

'I'm so afraid for you, Tristão.'

'There's no need. . . . '

'But if you're discovered – '

'I won't be discovered – '

'Promise me this, then. If ever you are arrested, you must denounce me. I mean it. If we can't live together, let's die together.'

'But I couldn't betray you – '

'It won't be a betrayal. It will be – it'll be a marriage. Hell won't be Hell if we're together, and if we are to burn, let's burn side by side. Tristram! I burn for you already . . . there – am I not already aflame?'

There were dogs barking, drums beating in the city, a distant gun. She saw leaves, patches of sky, his face. They were together: her head went back, she whispered his name. For a few minutes, in the secret shade of that fig tree by the wall, they were in paradise.

The leaves fell from the fig tree; their meetings became less frequent; the Armada preparations became ever more chaotic. And then one terrible day Tristram gave Sara the news that Dorothea was to have his child.

Since the vintage party at Colares, Dorothea – anxious for the patronage of Count João – had become a frequent visitor at the Quinta de Santo António and, in spite of Sara's attempts to keep her at a distance, seemed bent upon making friends. She broke her news a few days later when they sat together in Sara's room, and went into raptures about the wonders of motherhood and the privilege that was hers.

'And you know something?' she went on, 'Uncle Pedro told me only today that when the Invincible Armada sails, my husband will go as his adjutant, with his own command of twenty soldiers! And when he returns we shall make our home in Andalusia and there enjoy the blessings of the land and the fruits of our labours! Ah Countess, what a happy woman I am!'

Sara was fully conscious of the hypocrisy and deceit that lay behind this declaration, and knew that the only thing Dorothea loved about Tristram was his influence and prospects of advancement; but she had not yet heard that Tristram was to sail with the Armada, and the news came as a shock.

She turned away to look out of the window at the ships in the harbour. 'I think your husband is indeed fortunate,' she observed faintly. 'My poor João would dearly like to sail with the Armada, but I am unable to help him have his wish because he knows that his higher duty lies at his mother's side, and unless she personally releases him from the vow he has made to stay with her, he will for a second time be prevented from going upon a Holy Campaign.'

'For a second time?'

'Eight – no, nine years ago, he was similarly prevented from accompanying our beloved King Sebastian, of happy memory, on his ill-fated adventure to Morocco.' Sara touched the Madonna that lay on its chain upon her breast. 'But that was before the Santarém Madonna was recovered.'

Dorothea nodded gravely: she had heard the strange story of the Santarém Madonna from Maria Iñes.

'It's a great tragedy,' Sara was saying, 'that he is to be once again prevented from fighting for Christendom.'

'Wouldn't it be possible to speak with the Archbishop? Surely Dona Marguerita could be persuaded to see that her son's honour should come before her wishes?' Dorothea's eyes sparkled suddenly at the thought of being able to pull strings and engineer a favour. She laid a white hand on Sara's arm. 'Leave it to me,' she whispered. 'I make no promises, Countess, but I'll see what can be done.'

The season of Christmas came and went, and still the ships lay in the harbour waiting for more guns, more powder, more provisions, more barrels, more men and above all more leadership. The mountains of paper grew daily in João's office; every morning seemed to bring with it fresh conflicts, whether with the Provisioner General, the Minister of Justice, the generals in command of squadrons or even poor António Alvarez, whom João was relying upon to print the completed *relación* at least one week before the Armada sailed.

'Excellency, Excellency!' Alvarez whined, cringing in the doorway and wringing his hands. 'How can I print the list if the list is not complete? How can I make a start upon it until every last detail has been added? Don't ask the impossible of me, Excellency! I have a wife and eight children and I cannot work miracles!'

João (who had a natural aversion to fathers of large families) was becoming increasingly concerned that if Alvarez failed to bring out the *relación* on time, he himself might be tainted with blame; but although the bare bones of the list were already complete, the exact numbers of soldiers, sailors, servants and slaves, along with the quantities of provisions to be embarked were still little more than a shot-in-the-dark guess.

'Why can't you set it up for printing and leave gaps for the figures?' he demanded. 'Won't that save time? I shall let you have the figures as I receive them, so you can set up and print each page as it becomes complete.'

But this was not possible, as Alvarez went to great pains to explain. In order to leave gaps it would be necessary to know the length required for each gap, and as it was physically impossible to set up a page of print without every smallest chink of it being wedged full of metal type or wooden furniture, the time taken to cut the furniture to fill the gaps would far exceed any time saved later.

'Then lay out the type as far as you can. Lay it out, page by page on a table – '

Alvarez threw up his hands. 'Excellency – I would rather risk my life than do such a thing! All that would be needed would be for the table to be jogged or for a cat to jump on it, and I should have a printer's pie!'

'Listen, fool!' screamed João, who now cast all thoughts of secrecy to the winds. 'The Armada must sail next month, do you understand? February the fifteenth! The King himself has ordered it – even if only forty ships sail. The Armada must go, so that the army in the Low Countries can make their crossing into Kent. And this *relación* must be complete a week before the first little patache pokes her bows out past the Torre de Belem. So you have three weeks. And if you let me down I shall make a personal recommendation that you be excommunicated. Now do you understand? You have three weeks! Three weeks!'

The drive to get the Armada ready for sea turned into a frenzy. Stores arriving by wagon train were offloaded into the first barge available and dumped higgledy-piggledy into the first ship willing or able to take them. Mountains of biscuit went mouldy in the warehouses. Soldiers and sailors were dying and deserting. Some ships had more than their full complement of cannon but no roundshot, others were loaded to the gunwales with ball of too great a calibre for their light falconets or sakers. There was still a severe shortage of barrels, and the squadron provisioners were now competing ruthlessly to hoard as much rice, oil, wine and bacon as possible – even if that meant turning some of the warships into freighters, with the powder and shot stowed far down in the lowest holds, and the foodstuffs piled on top.

But although some people in high places were beginning to doubt whether even a reduced Armada would be ready to sail by mid-February, no one was prepared to risk his career by saying so, and it was much easier to go along with the view that as God must be on the side of the Enterprise, He would not allow it to fail, and that if a miracle were needed for success, a miracle would be provided.

Early in February, when the sailing date was scarcely a week away, the

Count of Colares held a formal dinner party at the Quinta de Santo António to celebrate Dona Marguerita's birthday. The guest of honour was General Pedro de Valdes, and all João's sisters and their husbands were invited. The dining hall was cleared of desks and papers, and it was quite like old times again, with a black slave standing behind each chair as the party took their seats, and the candlelight glimmering on the silver salvers and goblets at each place setting.

Dona Marguerita had spent most of her afternoon and evening being dressed for the occasion, and she now sat on her son's right looking like a grotesque doll in a bejewelled gown and a glossy black wig.

Countess Sara was more simply dressed: she sat at the far end of the table with the General on her right and her brother-in-law, Admiral Moitinho, on her left. Further down the table, in places suited to their lower station, Tristram and his adorable, pregnant young wife sat side by side.

After dinner João made a speech. 'My dear Maezinha makes no pretence of her great age,' he announced. 'For she is today celebrating the seventieth anniversary of her birth, and it is well to remind ourselves that she was born just a few months after the heretic Luther first nailed his Theses to a church door in Wittenberg. Thus, my sweet mother's life has spanned the whole course of the Protestant evil which has beset Christendom and which, through the intercession of Our Lady, will so soon be overthrown by our most happy and glorious Armada. . . .'

When the toasts had been drunk the conversation turned to the imminent departure of the Armada and the probability of its success. Only a few days before, it had been reported that the Marquis of Santa Cruz was suffering from exhaustion and had been ordered by his doctors to rest, and although it would have been akin to heresy even to hint that another delay was likely, all present were anxious to have some reassurances from Don Pedro's lips.

He was at pains to calm their fears. 'There is no doubt at all that the time is ripe,' he told his fellow guests. 'We heard only two days ago that the invasion force is ready in the low countries and that the new canal from the Scheldt to the Haven of Dunkirk is complete. All the Duke of Parma requires now is the support of our fleet. As soon as we have arrived off the coast of Picardy he will send his invasion barges across to England.'

'And I heard it from the Nuncio that his Holiness has promised a million ducats to his Majesty the King on the day the first of our soldiers sets foot on English soil,' João put in.

'And with good reason, for the Holy Father knows very well that once we are ashore, England will quickly fall. Our army is without doubt the finest fighting force in the world. It has been well tested: it has defeated every army it has met in the field of battle. Once we set foot on Margate shore, you will hear Elizabeth sing a new tune, my friends, for her army is no more than a rabble, her cities are but weakly fortified and her people are still Catholic at heart, and will readily turn their backs upon the satanic heresies into which she has led them these thirty years past.' Don Pedro fingered his moustaches and looked round at the attentive faces of his fellow guests, meeting the beady eyes of Dona Marguerita who stared solemnly at him from the far end of the table. 'How I look forward, most Excellent Lady, to that day when first we sight the English on the horizon! For make no mistake – our mighty fleet will drive them from the seas like a great Andalusian bull that lowers his deadly horns for the charge! And what an honour it will be to march in triumph to London and bring the Jezebel of England to justice! What a – '

He stopped in mid sentence: there had been a sudden clatter of hooves in the courtyard, and now Ensign Rodrigo burst in looking very flushed and out of breath and still wearing his hat.

'Sirs – Excellencies – Admiral – General – ' he panted.

'Calm down, boy, calm down!' Don Pedro told him. 'Now what is it? What's happened?'

Remembering his manners, Rodrigo swept off his hat, bowed low, and delivered the news that Don Alvaro de Bazan, Marquis of Santa Cruz, hero of the battles of Lepanto and Terceira and Captain General of the Invincible Armada, was dead.

For a fortnight, all Spain mourned the passing of the man who had won so many glorious victories and whose confident promise to win back England for Christendom had spurred King Philip into authorizing the assembly of the mightiest armada the world had ever seen.

In Lisbon, bells tolled all day; masses for the repose of the Marquis's soul were said in every chapel and at every altar, and while the admirals, generals and Staff officers whispered nervously to each other in the halls and corridors of their temporary residences, preparations for the Enterprise – for which the late Marquis had worked himself literally to death – came to a complete halt.

Having frequently discussed the rights and wrongs of the Enterprise with Tristram, and having listened to any number of João's colleagues voicing their opinions, Sara viewed the state of petrified chaos that followed Santa Cruz's death with inner relief, for she was already convinced that the conversion of England would never be achieved through force of arms, and now hoped that good sense would prevail and that the whole expedition would be cancelled.

But the preparations were too far advanced for the Armada to be dispersed, and King Philip, who had delayed so long, was now afire with enthusiasm to press ahead. The fated year of 1588 had come at last, and all Europe waited with bated breath for the cataclysm which Regiomontanus had predicted a hundred years before.

So Sara's hopes were dashed: one morning Dorothea called upon her in a state of excitement to say that she had heard a whisper from Rodrigo, who had overheard it from Don Pedro, who had read it in a letter marked Private and Strictly Confidential, that a new Captain General was being appointed to take over command of the Armada.

'And you know something?' Dorothea chirruped, skipping from foot to foot like a seven-year-old, 'He was at my wedding! We are distantly related! He is Don Alonso Perez de Guzman el Bueno, the Duke of Medina Sidonia! Ah, Countess, what a good, kind, gentle man! What a godly and deeply religious man!'

A few days later the news was made official, and Sara attended the parade in the palace square when the new Captain General arrived in Lisbon and reviewed his army. But the man she saw was not at all the sort of person she had presumed would be put in command of such a huge campaign. Instead of the bluff military type she had expected, the Duke of Medina Sidonia looked exactly what he was: a self-effacing, elderly country gentleman, unused to war and all too conscious of his inadequacy to carry the great burden of responsibility the King had persuaded him to shoulder.

He also had a runny nose, and the story was being put about by some of the anti-Spanish *Lisboetas* that the new Captain General of the Spanish Armada always caught a cold when he went in a boat.

The Duke of Medina Sidonia brought an altogether different approach to the business of preparing the Armada. Where Santa Cruz had imposed his will upon his subordinates, Medina Sidonia, who was the first to admit his inexperience in naval tactics, was much more inclined to defer to the wishes of his senior staff. While Santa Cruz had stamped his personality upon the Armada, Medina Sidonia was content to allow the Armada to stamp its personality upon himself.

This change in the style of leadership filtered all the way down to the humblest foot soldier and manservant, and its effect was to alter the whole mood of the Armada, which became less of an armed invasion and more of a Holy Cause in which religious fervour was held in higher esteem than military efficiency.

For João, the news that the Armada's departure had been put back until April came as a great relief: now that he knew that the unforgiving eye of the Marquis of Santa Cruz would never scan his records, he decided to adopt a new policy towards the compilation of the *relación*. From now on, he would no longer strive for accuracy in recording the quantities of men, weapons and ammunition embarked in each ship, but simply use the figures in the original plan, estimating where necessary to fill the gaps. The heavily amended draft which had caused him so many sleepless nights was put aside, and a new list was drawn up – a list that bore little relation to fact but fitted exactly with the ideal, so that if Don Diego de Leyva had covenanted a hundred and fifteen soldiers to sail aboard *La Rata Santa Maria Encoronada*, that figure was entered regardless of how many had since deserted or died; and if the Provisioner General's target for bacon was six thousand five hundred quintals, the target was presumed to have been achieved.

Quite suddenly – some said miraculously – order began to grow out of chaos. Spring was coming, the books were being made to balance, the soldiers were being paid, and several new additions to the fleet had arrived, swelling the total number of hulls to something in the region of a hundred and thirty.

What did it matter if many of the great ships were rotten below the waterline? Who cared if the provisioners in the Portuguese squadron had amassed more than the appointed quantities of rice and fresh water for their ships? What point was there in arguing over who served in which ship, when the Captain General himself would have willingly surrendered his command to an abler man?

Nobody had time for details any longer: it was already more than a year since the Queen of England had had her cousin beheaded and all Christendom was impatient for Spain to avenge that wrong. The sailing date had been fixed for the end of April; the last consignment of newly cast brass pieces had been delivered, and for the first time since Drake's attack on Cadiz, the Happiest Armada was beginning to look like a fleet that was getting ready for sea.

Dorothea's affair with Rodrigo had not gone unnoticed in Lisbon society, and some of her early popularity among the wives had diminished. In particular, Don Martin's wife, Maria Iñes, had become suddenly more possessive of her husband's affections, and was now looking forward to the day when the Armada would sail and her guests would be off her hands. The one house where Dorothea still felt welcome, however, was the Quinta de Santo António. Hardly a morning went by now when her little carriage didn't clatter into the enclosed courtyard, and because Sara was a good listener and was adept at disguising her feelings, Dorothea had come to regard the Countess as one of her closest friends.

The two women were complete opposites: one was a chatterer and a social climber, while the other enjoyed reflection and simplicity. Listening to Dorothea enlarge upon her life in Madrid, her acquaintances at court or her most recent dream (Dorothea was always having the most complicated dreams) Sara sometimes reflected that Dorothea would have made a far more suitable wife for João than herself.

Of Tristram, she now saw very little. The fig tree was still bare of leaves, and the spy mania in Lisbon had reached such a height that they had agreed not to risk further rendezvous for the time being. And although Tristram had spoken to her of his hopes of deserting from the fleet at the last moment and escaping with her to Ireland, the chances of such a plan succeeding were so small that they had agreed that he should sail with the Armada and that they would try to make contact – somehow – when the Enterprise was over.

'But we mustn't lose touch, Countess,' Dorothea was saying one afternoon in early April. 'As soon as we're finished with this English campaign, you must persuade the Count to bring you on a visit to Andalusia. It's so beautiful, my dear! And the weather is so much better than in this wet, windy city of yours!'

Sara was just about to point out that Lisbon weather wasn't usually as bad as Dorothea had seen it, when a distinctive sound of panting outside the door announced the arrival of Maria Candida.

'*Minha Senhora! Minha Senhora!* Her Excellency Dona Marguerita! She's had an attack! Padre Jorge says you must wait upon her in her chamber immediately!'

Sara ran along the balcony, and Dorothea, determined not to miss a thing, ran after her. At Dona Marguerita's door a knot of servants stood wide-eyed and whispering. On entering, Sara found Padre Jorge administering the last rites, and João on his knees.

Dona Marguerita's limbs were shaking, her eyes were rolling back into their sockets and she had been violently sick.

Sara went quickly to the bedside. Another convulsion came, and another. Padre Jorge anointed the old lady with chrism and spoke rapidly in Latin. Behind the Count, Dorothea had dropped to her knees and was saying the rosary aloud, her eyes tight shut, her face turned towards the gilded angels on the frieze.

Dona Marguerita seemed to rally. 'Son,' she muttered. 'Listen. Listen to your mother. I want – ' but already another fit of convulsions was beginning, and she spoke with the greatest difficulty. 'It is my last wish – '

João's shrill sobs could be heard all over the house. 'Yes Maezinha? What is it? Tell me! In the name of God, tell me and I will do whatever you ask!'

The old lady made a supreme effort: her fists clenched tightly; the muscles in her neck tautened like cords of rope.

'*Vai!*' she whispered. '*Vai – com – a – Armada!*'

The body shook, the eyes stared upward, the throat rattled, then the old head sank back into the pillow and the soul fled away into eternity.

Dorothea got up off her knees and crossed herself. 'What a blessed, blessed release!' she whispered. 'And what a noble last wish to make!' She went to João and touched his arm. 'Count,' she murmured, her dark eyes swimming with tears, 'your wife has already spoken to me of your secret desire to sail with the Invincible, and it is clear that this was also what your dear mother was trying to say. May I beg the honour to be permitted to apply on your behalf to my uncle to seek a position for yourself aboard one of the ships in his squadron?'

João's mouth opened and shut.

'But of course – you are too stunned by your bereavement to think of such things,' Dorothea prattled. 'So you may leave it entirely to me, Count. I shall consider it a great honour to perform this small service for you.'

She was as good as her word. That same day she approached her uncle and persuaded him to invite the Count of Colares to sail as a gentleman adventurer with the Andalusian squadron, and João – obliged out of duty to his mother's memory – accepted on the condition that his confessor and his best friend, Fernando, be permitted to go along too.

Now that spring was well advanced, Sara had resumed her custom of spending her afternoons in the lower part of the grounds, but as each day passed and Tristram failed to appear, she became increasingly worried that he might not be able to meet with her before the Armada sailed. She was therefore relieved to see him at High Mass in the cathedral nine days before the date fixed for the Armada's departure. After the service, when the worshippers stood chatting in the sun on the cathedral steps, she left João talking to Fernando and went over to speak to Dorothea.

When greetings had been exchanged and Dorothea had gushed about how splendid all the men looked in their new military outfits, Sara turned to Tristram. 'You must have been working hard these last few weeks, Lieutenant?'

He bowed formally. 'Yes indeed, Countess. The days have not been long enough to do all that has to be done, let alone all that we should like to do.'

She smiled, and hoped that her agitation was not too obvious. 'As I am well aware! I sit in the grounds every afternoon, and I have never seen the harbour busier than it is now! The Count and I hoped that we might entertain both of you to dinner one evening, but I fear time is running very short.'

'What a very kind thought,' Tristram replied. 'But I fear my duties have become so demanding that I am unable to accept such invitations.'

And then – mercifully – they were joined by General de Valdes and Rodrigo, together with Maria Teresa and her elderly husband, Admiral Moitinho, and Dorothea turned her attention to what she was sure would be a more interesting conversation.

For a few moments the chatter of the people around them enabled Sara and Tristram to speak privately. They seized the opportunity.

'When can I see you, Tristão?'

'I don't know. . . .'

She raised her voice. 'And which ship will you sail in, Teniente? The *Rosário*, isn't it?' Then she added quietly, 'João has asked me to keep an all-night vigil for him in the chapel on the eve of his departure. He may stay up some of the time with me, but I think he will wish to spend his last night elsewhere. I'll try to go down to our place. But it may be very late – well after midnight – '

'I shall be there if at all possible – ' She saw his eyes shift their attention as João and Fernando came up with Padre Jorge. 'Now if you will excuse me, Countess, I must rejoin my wife and the General.'

João turned to Fernando. 'Do you know, dear boy – each time I set eyes on that young man I am the more convinced that I have seen him somewhere before.'

Fernando gave a whinnying laugh. 'That's not surprising! These Englishmen all look exactly the same!'

'Yes – don't they, Fernando?' Sara remarked lightly, and with her heart thundering in her bosom she took João's arm and reminded him that as they were expected at the Bishop's Palace, perhaps they ought to be making a move.

The last wagon trains of provisions, arms and munitions were being loaded into barges; the last contingents of slaves and foot soldiers were arriving in the Palace Square, and the last horses and mules were being hoisted aboard. As the day of departure – 25 April – drew nearer, the atmosphere of expectation in Lisbon became almost tangible.

Every day long queues formed at the confessionals in the churches and monasteries. The Duke of Medina Sidonia had ordered that every man who sailed aboard the Armada must do so in a state of grace, having confessed his sins and received the Holy Sacrament. No women were to be permitted aboard any ship, no blasphemous or foul language was to be allowed and immoral conduct of any sort was to be punished severely by the nine-score priests and friars who would be embarked.

This was a most dangerous time for Tristram. He had been sending regular intelligence reports back to England since his arrival in Lisbon, and was all too conscious of the distrust and suspicion that was now rife in the city. He had seen the beginnings of recognition in João's eyes, and knew very well that as an English emigré he was probably being kept under surveillance by Spanish agents. But in spite of these risks he could not bear the thought of departing without seeing Sara once more, and in the secrecy of the confessional sought Joaquim's opinion on whether to keep their hastily arranged rendezvous.

'If you take my advice, you'll not attempt it,' Joaquim whispered through the grille. 'We've done well to last so long here, and there's no need for you to see her again. Besides – that wife of yours would be only too pleased to find an excuse to denounce you. I wouldn't be surprised if she's having you watched already.'

'And yet I must see Dona Sara once more, Joaquim. I must. . . .'

Joaquim thought for a while. 'Very well, here's what I suggest. Do what every other husband with a pretty wife is doing. Make Dorothea swear a vow of chastity until your return.'

'What good will that do?'

'Tell her, at the same time, that you have already sworn yourself to celibacy until the successful completion of the Enterprise. Say you haven't the self-control to keep away from her on the last night unless you sleep in another room. Make her promise not to come to you, and give your word in return that you won't come to her. In short, say anything you like to convince her that it'll be safe for her to have one last night of bliss with her little ensign.' Joaquim paused, then added with some emotion in his voice: 'And – and if you manage to see Dona Sara, please convey to her the respect and duty of her old *caseiro*.'

Tristram approached Dorothea on the morning of their last day together. She was sitting idly in her room slapping a closed fan into her palm and gazing out at the pigeons strutting on the roofs across the courtyard. Since the beginning of her affair with Rodrigo the previous autumn, Tristram had deliberately played up to the role of a solemn husband, and he now harangued her at some length about the importance of constancy during his absence. When he finally proposed that she make a vow of chastity, she accepted the idea without a murmur.

'Why should I not make such a vow?' she said. 'After all, it will make little difference to me, for being married to you these past months has been like having a monk for a husband.'

'My dear,' he said gravely. 'I have always been at pains to behave towards you as a husband should behave.'

She laughed. 'Perhaps you should not have tried so hard, Teniente.'

He looked wounded. 'I am sure you didn't mean that seriously, Thea. But – as I was about to say – I have already made my vow. So I shall not be at your side tonight.'

She inclined her head.

'I shall also be grateful to you if you will promise not to tempt me by coming to my room.'

She gave a dry little laugh. 'Oh yes. You can certainly rely on that.'

He took her hands. Even now, he disliked having to deceive her. One grew into the habit of lying so easily. . . .

'It will be different, won't it Thea, when I return?'

'Yes,' she said coldly. 'I expect it will be very different.'

At about the same time on that last day João called Sara to his office, and a rather similar exchange took place.

'Will you miss me?' he asked when certain domestic arrangements had been agreed.

'The house will certainly seem empty and quiet when you have gone,' she replied carefully.

He nodded at this, and then she was surprised to see his eyes fill suddenly with tears and his lips begin to wobble. 'You will not miss me at all. No one will miss me. You will all be glad to see the back of me, isn't that a fact? Well isn't it?'

She looked at him very closely, and for the first time felt a shred of sympathy for him. Really he had never grown up, that was the trouble with João. He was still a little boy who liked other little boys and thought little girls were silly. What he wanted from her – she saw it quite clearly – was the comfort of a mother, not a wife. He wanted her to take him on her knee and beg him not to go – or to fall desperately ill in order to give him an excuse for staying behind.

'I cannot pretend to feelings that are not mine,' she said quietly.

He turned to face her. 'I may be killed. Do you realize that? I may – ' But the vision of his own death was too horrible, and he was unable to continue.

'We all have to die at some time,' she said. 'And if that is to be your fate, you will at least know that you do so in the worthiest of causes, and that you have obeyed your own mother's last wish.'

This seemed to help him a little, and he regained control. 'Will you do one thing for me, then?'

'What is that?'

'Give me back the Madonna to wear.'

Her immediate instinct was to refuse. Though she had never had any great liking for the Madonna which João had sent over to Ireland, this one meant much more to her because of its link with Tristram, and although she disbelieved the superstition about it, giving it back to João seemed to her like a betrayal.

But he must already have seen her falter, and she was terrified of arousing his suspicions in any way. 'Of course,' she said faintly, and with hardly the smallest hesitation took the medallion from her neck. 'There,' she whispered, holding it out to him. 'And may it give you courage, João, to face whatever may lie before you.'

'Will you not put it about my neck?'

She would never have expected herself to feel so strongly about a mere possession: the very act of putting the chain over his head was like tearing something out of herself.

'Now kiss me, Sara, and wish me a safe return.'

'May God grant you . . . a safe return,' she murmured, and with an effort forced herself to place her lips upon his cheek.

It seemed that all Lisbon went to bed early that night. The inns and bawdy houses closed up soon after sunset; the gaming rooms were empty, and the brothels and *fado* houses stood silent. In the churches and family chapels womenfolk kept silent vigils of prayer, and in the harbour the only sounds to be heard were the plash of oars as the guardboats did their rounds, and the rhythmical frapping of halyards against masts.

Well after midnight Tristram slipped out of a back door of Don Martin's house in the Mouraria. Keeping to the shadows of the city walls he hurried across the city on foot to the narrow street that ran along the lower boundary of the Quinta de Santo António.

This was a street where a gentleman would not normally go without an escort, a street that ran uphill from the Alfama district towards the Castle of St George. It was a street where cats yowled at each other in the darkness and beggars slept in rags.

Out of breath from the fast climb, he paused for a few seconds, crouching at a corner to make sure he was not being followed; and then, silent as the bats that wheeled overhead, he made a final dash for the part of the wall that was crumbling, and crawling quickly through a gap entered the black shadow of the fig tree on the other side.

Sara was already there, waiting for him. As soon as he straightened, he felt her touch. She took his face between her hands and kissed him slowly and lovingly on the lips. 'Don't say anything, my darling,' she whispered. 'Just hold me.'

But it was necessary to say much during those last precious hours together, for although they had often talked whimsically of an escape together, neither had any firm plan for the future. Though they could perhaps have risked an elopement then and there, to do so would have condemned Joaquim to almost certain death; and though Sara was willing to travel to England in order to be with Tristram, Tristram could not be sure that he would ever be safe in England, whether under

Protestant or Catholic rule. Nor could he ever risk a return to Portugal, for whatever the outcome of the Enterprise, both were now convinced that it was only a matter of time before he or Joaquim would be denounced. The only remote possibility lay in making a rendezvous in Ireland after the Enterprise had run its course, for in Ireland Sara could seek refuge with her family, and Tristram could perhaps find the anonymity he needed to survive.

When she told him about the Madonna he said that they had no need of keepsakes or charms. 'It never worked for Jennifer, nor for her father, come to that. No – the only beauty it had for me was because you wore it, Sara, and without it – ' he kissed the spot where it had lain ' – without it you are the lovelier.'

'Nevertheless, I hated giving it to him. I couldn't help remembering the foul way in which he acquired it, and how sorely you suffered at his hands.'

Far in the distance a rooster began to crow as the first fingers of light crept into the eastern sky. He said: 'I must go soon,' and she, choking on her tears, whispered back, 'I know.'

He held her in his arms a little longer, comforting her. 'Whatever happens, Sara, wherever you go and however long you may live, always believe that I am yours,' he told her. 'Always believe that we shall be reunited, someday, somewhere.'

'I believe it,' she whispered. 'I do believe it.'

'At least we have had this much,' he murmured. 'At least we have known what love is.'

She nodded, smiling through tears. A little later she said, 'You must go, Tristão. It's getting light.'

He stared at her, trying to fix her face in his memory so that he would never forget this moment.

'Please go now,' she whispered. 'Go quickly and – and think of me.'

They held hands very tightly. He said: 'I can't let you go.'

'Go!' she whispered again, and gave a sob as she released his hands.

Then he was gone, and waiting no more than a few moments longer, she bent double to emerge from the umbrella of leaves and made her way quickly and silently back to the house, entering the chapel by a side door in order to resume her vigil.

The banner bore the Arms of Spain between Christ Crucified and His Holy Mother, and beneath it were the words that had been quoted so often since the beheading of Mary Stuart: *Exurge Domine et vindica causam Tuam.* It was placed before the high altar of Lisbon Cathedral for the Mass of Farewell, and the Duke of Medina Sidonia knelt before it at the head of a vast congregation of generals, admirals, noblemen and hidalgos. In a ceremony lasting over two hours the Archbishop of Lisbon, assisted by an array of priests, friars and acolytes, and accompanied by treble choristers whose voices sent shivers up the spine, turned the bread and wine into the Body and the Blood and offered them up with such emphatic devotion that even the most hardened sceptic present was forced to admit that God must at least feel inclined to respond to the Armada's motto – to arise, and vindicate His cause.

After the last blessing forty heralds formed a guard of honour on the cathedral steps, and a tremendous fanfare of trumpets greeted the sacred banner as it was brought out into the windy sunshine of that April afternoon. Slowly, reverently, it was borne down the hill between lines of kneeling sailors, and the common people bowed down as it passed by.

The Duke of Medina Sidonia accompanied it into a barge; oars were tossed and shipped in frightening precision, and the solemn embarkation began. The wind was fair; the ships were clean and brilliantly painted; the armorial crests, indicating whose soldiers manned which ship, were in place along the bulwarks of every last patache and zabra. Not since the grand departure of King Sebastian nearly ten years before had Lisbon seen such a sight. Crowds lined the waterfronts. Messengers rode out of the city with the optimistic news that the fleet was already sailing. Mothers, sisters and daughters wept and prayed for the safe return of their menfolk.

But then there was a delay. The embarkation had taken longer than was anticipated, and there was too little of the ebb tide left to make departure possible that afternoon.

The crowds melted away. The following morning the Armada was still at anchor off the city quays. A wagon train of powder and ball arrived and, as it seemed absurd to sail without this important consignment, arrangements were made to have it embarked.

Another day passed, more provisions arrived, more conscripts – late arrivals – were embarked. Longboats and barges plied busily between the ships as officers and gentlemen paid and returned courtesy calls (though none was permitted between ships and shore) and as more days passed it seemed that there were now two independent cities on the mouth of the Tagus, one ancient and built of stone, the other gaily painted, brand new and afloat upon the river.

A fortnight went by, and still the Armada had not sailed. The people of Lisbon began to wonder why. Furious messages were rumoured to be emanating from the Escorial Palace. 'What is the delay?' the King wanted to know, to which, the city wags reported, the answer went: 'There is no delay, we always take this long.'

There were other, more serious rumours going round: that the Duke of Parma was not fully prepared for invasion, that the support of France could not be completely guaranteed and that the expected rebellion of Catholics in the north of England had yet to materialize. But although some were inclined to laugh at what seemed to them to be a débâcle, most thinking people regarded the workings of Destiny as a huge piece of divinely directed clockwork, in which many interconnected wheels marched and countermarched across the civilized world, and saw the presence of this huge fleet in Lisbon as the coiled spring that drove the whole movement and kept the clock hands turning on towards Armageddon.

At last, on 9 May, the ships started weighing anchor and moving downriver past the Torre de Belem.

But the people who came out to wave farewell to the Armada were to be disappointed again. A north-westerly gale was screaming in through the narrow entrance channel, and huge breakers were exploding in white spray upon the sandbar off St Julian's Fort. To sail the fleet in such weather was not only out of the question – it was impossible.

It was the worst May in living memory. Day after day, gales and storms lashed in from the Atlantic, and day after day – for another twenty days – the departure of the Invincible Armada was postponed.

Dorothea's baby was expected within a month now and as Maria Iñes was leaving Lisbon to visit her husband's family in Madrid, Sara felt obliged to invite the mother-to-be to stay at the Quinta de Santo António.

She moved in immediately with six servants and a wagonload of baggage, and was installed in Dona Marguerita's rooms, whose windows commanded a view of the harbour entrance. Every morning she sat in her window noting the movement of every smallest fly-boat in the harbour and watching for any sign that the Armada might be about to sail.

'If only they would *go*!' she exclaimed one day. 'If I see them swinging round their anchors out there much longer I shall go mad!'

'They will sail,' Sara murmured, forcing herself to play the good companion. 'And within a few short months they'll return as heroes.'

Dorothea went to her and clasped her hands. 'My dear Countess! You're such a friend to me! Please – let's always stay friends! Let's share our hopes, our fears, our love for our husbands! Let's stay here, together, until the Invincible returns! Let's use our husbands' absence to bind us close, and be for each other a support and consolation in the hour of our need!'

Sara smiled and agreed with as much warmth as she could muster: although she had already grown weary of Thea's chatter, she was determined to put up with it, for only by remaining close to her could she hope to have early news of Tristram.

Dorothea had returned to the window. 'Countess!' she exclaimed suddenly. 'Look!'

Sara joined her and looked down the Tagus towards the entrance. Right at the head of the fleet, three – four – five of the Portuguese vanguard galleons were already under full sail, and as they watched, dozens more sails were bellying out from the forest of masts and spars.

They turned to each other, and now Sara's eyes were as full and overflowing as Dorothea's. Suddenly they were in each other's arms, weeping and praying, terrified yet proud, overcome by the moment, and humbled by the knowledge that they were witnessing the beginnings of the greatest enterprise ever undertaken by man.

'I must go,' Sara whispered. 'I must go down to wave them farewell.'

'I'll come with you! We'll take a carriage!'

Calling to the servants, they had the carriage made ready and the horses harnessed, and within twenty minutes they rode under the tiled archway, down through the city, out by the Corpo Santo gate and along the Roman road known as the Marginal, which ran along the coast to St Julian's fort.

Hundreds went with them: crowds of children ran along the beaches, waving and screaming to the massive ships as they plunged steadily along no more than half a mile from the shore. Carriages, horses, mules and wagons of every description jammed the road.

It seemed, that day, that there was not a dry eye in the whole of Lisbon. All along the sandy coast women stood weeping and screaming out their prayers and their blessings, gathering their skirts to move along the shoreline, trying to keep pace with their menfolk's ships for as long as possible.

Hour after hour the fleet continued to sail out in single file through the narrow entrance channel: first the great Portuguese galleons, next the Biscayan squadron, after them the Guipuscoans and Castillians and behind them the Andalusians – the great flagship *Nuestra Señora del Rosário*, in which Tristram and Joaquim were embarked, the *San Francisco*, the *San Juan Baptista*, the *San Juan de Gargarin* and the *Duquesa Santa Ana* aboard which somewhere, amid all those brightly clad soldiers and grandees must be João.

Hour after hour the people watching from the shore waved and wept and wondered at the great spectacle – the very turning of the wheel of destiny – that was taking place before their eyes, and finally, when darkness had fallen and all that could be seen of the fleet was the stern lanterns of the senior ships as they led their squadrons out to sea, the people began walking back to their homes to light votive candles in their houses and to keep prayerful vigils for the safety of the Most Happy and Invincible Armada, the Armada that God would not allow to fail.

Four miles off the coast Don Pedro's flagship, the *Nuestra Señora del Rosário*, was labouring into heavy seas and making little progress to windward in the north-westerly gale. Strung out over a wide area, the other ships of the Armada were still attempting to take up their stations in the cruising formation that had been planned months before departure.

Don Pedro himself was pacing up and down his aftercastle, beating a fist into the palm of his hand.

'Not good enough, not good enough at all!' he kept repeating. 'Why is the forecourse tack flapping? What's that rolling about in the waist, and why was it not properly secured for sea? Where are the lookouts and why have they not yet been posted? Not good enough, not good enough at all!'

Further aft, watching the lights of Lisbon dwindle on the horizon, Teniente Pascua Inglés was joined by his Jesuit confessor.

'So,' Joaquim remarked. 'It's happened at last.'

Tristram nodded, but continued to stare at the shoreline without saying a word.

Joaquim glanced at him. 'Try not to think about her, lad,' he said quietly. 'You'll only make it hard for yourself by dwelling on what's over and past.'

It was late when Sara and Dorothea eventually returned to the Quinta de

Santo António, and when they arrived Maria Candida met them with a
letter addressed to Dorothea that had been delivered from the fleet that
morning.

She broke the seal quickly and unfolded the stiff paper, her lips
moving as she read the scrawled lines, her neat, black brows knitted
together as she tried to decipher a word.

'It's from my Trithtan,' she lisped. 'He's on board the *capitana*. And
look! He's sent me a poem! It's in Latin! Here – perhaps you can make
head or tail of it.'

Sara looked at the lines of a sonnet headed 'To My One True Love'.
'It's not Latin,' she said. 'It's English.'

Dorothea laughed shrilly. 'Well that's a lot of use! Why does he write
to me in English when he knows I don't understand a word of it, the silly
man?'

But Sara wasn't listening, for the lines she was reading were
indescribably beautiful, and though she could not know that they had
not been composed by Tristram or that they had once been intended by
William Wray as a coded message to report that the Armada would not
sail, she had no doubt that they were addressed to her, and that they were
Tristram's special way of bidding her farewell:

> Let me not to the marriage of true minds
> Admit impediments. Love is not love
> Which alters when it alteration finds,
> Or bends with the remover to remove:
> O, no! it is an ever-fixèd mark,
> That looks on tempests and is never shaken;
> It is the star to every wand'ring bark,
> Whose worth's unknown, although his height be taken.
> Love's not Time's fool, though rosy lips and cheeks
> Within his bending sickle's compass come;
> Love alters not with his brief hours and weeks,
> But bears it out even to the edge of doom:-
>   If this be error and upon me proved,
>   I never writ, nor no man ever loved.

'Why Sara, you're crying!' Thea exclaimed. 'Whatever can it mean to
move you so deeply?'

Sara struggled for control. 'It means – it means that his love will never
alter, Thea. And – and I'm weeping because I couldn't help reading these
lines as if they had been addressed to me, for I know that João's love for

me is in every way equal to that of the Teniente for yourself.'

Dorothea turned away. 'Well it's double-Dutch to me, so if you like it that much, you can keep it.'

Armada!

It was June, and the Royal Navy was ready. Lord Howard had arrived from Chatham in his flagship the *Ark Royal*; Drake had hoisted his flag as Vice-Admiral aboard the *Revenge*; Frobisher had come west with the *Triumph*, and Henry Seymour was raging up and down in the *Rainbow*, furious that he had been ordered to remain on patrol in the Narrows instead of joining the battle fleet that was now gale-bound in the Cattewater.

High on the greensward of Plymouth Hoe, William Wray, accompanied by Lord Howard, was taking Barty for a walk.

'Timing, my Lord Admiral,' he was saying. 'It is timing that is of the essence. So far, wisdom, through the good providence of God, has prevailed. We have persuaded her Majesty to resist the calls to keep the fleet at readiness through the winter, and have saved the exchequer thousands of pounds by doing so. We have continued negotiations with the Duke of Parma, with the result that much of his fiery determination to invade has been assuaged. The Armada has sailed, yes, but it has not yet arrived off our shores, and our latest intelligence from the Groyne indicates that gales on the passage north from the Tagus scattered their fleet, sank several hulls and have forced a further delay on the Duke of Medina Sidonia – who has little enough stomach for this enterprise already. Now, of all times, we must not lose our nerve. If we were to send the navy out to meet them on the high seas or to beard them in the Biscayan harbours as Drake and Hawkins would have us do, we should run a three-fold risk: first that we might succeed only in wounding them and thereby strengthen their resolve to fight, second that we would, by declaring open war with Spain, secure for her the wholehearted support of France so that the size of their Armada could be doubled within a few weeks, and third that we might miss them altogether and allow Philip to slip his right arm into the Sleeve unhindered.'

They paused for Barty to catch up, and faced into the southerly gale that was whitening the sea to the horizon.

'You must forgive me if I speak bluntly, my Lord. But I hear too much criticism of her Majesty's caution, and not enough praise for her wisdom.'

Howard listened but made no comment: though he had been acquainted with this urbane, balding gentleman for many years and knew that his position under Walsingham was one of great power and secrecy, he had never fathomed him out or discovered the exact extent of his influence.

He looked down at the assembled ships, in whose rigging the wind shrieked and whistled, and felt a surge of affection for those oaken hulls and a pride in the people who manned them. To serve as Lord Admiral of such a fleet and at such a time was surely the greatest honour an Englishman could aspire to.

'What ships!' he mused aloud. 'Do you know, William – there is not one of them in which I would not take passage to the Americas? Indeed, I would more cheerfully live in the company of these noble ships than in any other.'

Wray followed his gaze. They were indeed fine ships: designed and built on commission by John Hawkins; newly caulked, careened, scraped and tallowed, and now manned by cheerful, tough English sailormen who were for the most part as eager for the fight as Howard and his admirals.

'Yes, a fine fleet, my Lord,' he observed. 'But the finest fleet in the world is of no service at all if it is not in the right place at the right time.'

Still discussing the defence of the realm, they went on down to the harbour, while Barty the bull terrier – spry in spite of his ten years – trotted importantly at his master's heels, his whippy white tail wagging nonchalantly from side to side.

Harry Pascoe was in no mood for nonchalance. He was up to his shins in mud, and was cursing under his breath as his knife point sank into a rotten strake under the *Russell*'s counter.

He had brought his ship back from the Baltic a week before, and now that the ballast had been off-loaded and the yards removed for repair, he had had the ship careened for a bottom scrape and recaulking. As was his custom he had come down to inspect the ship's hull as soon as the spring ebb allowed, and while the labourers of Knollys's shipyard attacked the barnacles, he had explored every square foot of the exposed side of the hull.

He had made a sobering discovery: wood rot had taken a hold upon the timbers of the *Russell* since her last careening and if she was to be made tight and seaworthy, several strakes would have to be replaced. He was just pondering the implications of this discovery when he heard a shout.

'Father!'

Bending double, he moved out from beneath the stern. Matthew was standing on the slip.

'What?'

'Message from Justice Mayhew.' Matthew grinned, and Pascoe saw in that confidence and swagger a picture of himself thirty years before. 'He'd like a word as soon as you've finished.'

Pascoe knew very well why: on his arrival at Polruan, Mayhew had forewarned him that as he was in arrears in payment of the taxes being levied in the Hundred for defence against invasion, it was now expected of him to make the *Russell* available for the Queen's service to serve westwards with the Royal Navy in the event of a Spanish invasion.

He waded back through the mud to the slip.

'I reckon it'll be about the Queen's service, Father – '

'Never you mind what you reckon,' Harry cut in, and when he had washed his boots at the water butt, set off up the hill to Moville House without another word.

In the past year Mayhew had taken responsibility for drawing up the Muster Roll, which was a detailed inventory of horse, armour and weapons available in the parish. In his barn were now stored quantities of pikes, longbows, corselets, morions and almain-rivets, and here in his study he kept lists of every able-bodied man and boy in the parish, with his designated duty in the event of invasion. He had also been responsible for the manning and rearming of the defensive fort on the Polruan side of the entrance to the Fowey, and had ordered the building of the beacon on St Saviour's Point which was part of an early-warning network that was being set up across the length and breadth of England to sound the alarm when the Spanish fleet was sighted.

He was standing at his window looking out at the steeply sloping orchard when Pascoe was shown into his study, and turned immediately to welcome his guest.

'Ah – Mr Pascoe. Have you inspected your ship?'

Harry stood with his arms loose at his sides, an incongruous white-haired giant in this room with its book-lined walls and paper-strewn writing tables. 'Aye,' he said. 'I have.'

'And is she sound?'

'Sound?' he said. 'Aye, she's sound enough. Mind you, there's a bit of work to be done on her if you want her ready in a hurry.'

'What sort of work?'

'Recaulking. New strakes. New mizzen braces. New running rigging. New forecourse and spritsail. And of course there's the fresh ballast, stores, victuals, roundshot – '

'So when will she be ready? In a week?'

Pascoe laughed. 'A week! Four, more like, and then only if I can find some cash from somewhere, which isn't very likely. There's three hundred pounds' worth of work there and I can't afford that sort of money, not at short notice. Young Knollys doesn't give credit the way old John did, God rest his soul. It's cash on the nail with him, and the most I can run to right now is fifty sovereigns.'

Mayhew suppressed his impatience.

'There's precious little Crown money available, Mr Pascoe, and I'd be deceiving you if I promised anything more than repayment of victuals and your crew's wages. If you care to take a trip across the river, you'll find Mr Rashleigh fitting out the *Frances* at his own expense, and he has the whole of Fowey's respect for doing so.'

'My name's not Rashleigh,' Pascoe retorted. 'And I haven't got Richard Grenville's patronage. I tell you straight, Mayhew – I haven't the funds, and if I don't get them, we shan't be sailing, because I can't pay with money I haven't got. If Queen Bess wants to borrow my ship, Queen Bess can pay for the privilege.'

'*Yours* is the privilege, Mr Pascoe,' Mayhew said quietly. 'Yours is the privilege to defend this realm. Make no mistake about that.'

Harry's temper ignited.

'Oh is that so? Well those are fine words, but it's the likes of yourself who use them most often, in my humble experience, Mr Mayhew, and if you care to sample the privilege of salt beef and mouldy biscuit and making your bed under a leaky deckhead, aye, and standing twelve-hour watches in a tempest, then you'll be a most welcome guest aboard the *Russell*, and any one of my regular crew'll make room for 'ee. But until the day you take me up on *that* offer, I'll thank you not to talk to me about privilege.'

Mayhew spread his hands. 'So . . . do I understand that you are unwilling to put the work in hand?'

Harry glared at him. He had a nasty feeling he was being outflanked.

'Not unwilling, unable,' he said grumpily, and was just about to add a little softener when Mayhew cut in with his customary cool precision.

'So when the invasion comes to these shores, Mr Pascoe – and I think even you will agree that that event is now quite possible – am I to take it that you will make no contribution to the defence of your country? And what answer should I give to the good people of this village when they ask me what part Polruan will play at the hour of England's greatest need? No – don't trouble yourself to reply, Mr Pascoe. The door is behind you, and I shall be obliged if you will use it.'

Jennifer heard the front door bang, and knew immediately that her husband was in one of his tempers.

She was a busy woman these days: since her marriage to Harry eight years before she had presented him with three dark-eyed daughters: Bridget, Ann and Jessica; and to keep herself occupied during Harry's long absences at sea, she had turned Hill House into a profitable small-holding, with chickens, geese, pigs, three milch-cows, half a dozen beehives and a dovecot. Determined not to repeat her aunt's mistake of becoming a slave in her own house, she had insisted on domestic help and had given employment to Susan Rowe and her daughter Faith, the widow and orphan of Tom Rowe, who had gone overboard from the *Russell* with Tristram twelve years before. So, with her only son Arthur and her three daughters for company – as well as Nathan's brute strength for protection – Jennifer had 'made good' in Polruan, and if the villagers whispered about Mrs Pascoe behind her back nowadays, it was more often to commend her for her energy and the way she was raising her children than to hark back over old misdeeds and alliances.

She had also worked wonders with Harry. She had refused steadfastly to be bullied by him, and had persuaded him that he would be a happier man in himself if he bullied no one else. She kept a warm, welcoming house for him, and demanded in return that he turn himself into a warm and loving husband; and Harry – who was now fifty-four – had been at least partly tamed. He had given up his privateering adventures on the high seas and had instead plied a steady trade up and down the Channel and across the North Sea, settling for a reasonable income honestly earned in place of the uncertain hope of making a fortune out of piracy.

But for all that, a man is a man, whatever effect his wife may have on him, and Jennifer was by now well used to the unchanging order of Harry's moods that ran their course after his return from sea, and the slam of the front door told her quite clearly that the new moon of bonhomie was over and a gibbous, hump-backed phase of surly bad temper had begun.

She knew better than to ask him what the matter was and had enough work to do as it was without having to listen to him holding forth about the latest chip on his shoulder, so while Harry sat smoking his pipe with a face like thunder in the front room, Jennifer took the children out to the barn and fed the hens before visiting all their various nests to collect the eggs, which Bridget carried back in a basket to Mrs Rowe in the kitchen; and when she had milked the cows and poured off the cream to set for skimming, she returned to the house to make sure there was enough wood for the kitchen fire and that Mrs Rowe was getting on with the ironing. Then Arthur came back from school, and soon after that Nathan came in from the beacon on St Saviour's Point (he had been made a daywatchman, and took his responsibilities extremely seriously) – by which time the delicious aroma of spit-roasted lamb was filling the house and the three youngest were having their bread and milk before Faith took them up to bed.

Matthew came in as supper was going on the table, having stopped off for a jug at the Russell Inn. He took his place beside Jennifer and passed up the dish of carved meat to his father; and as he knew very well why Harry had the grumps, he made a point of starting the conversation on a light note.

'So Nat – what's the latest?' he asked easily. 'Seen any old armadas today, have you?'

'No Armada,' boomed Nathan seriously, and recited his day's sightings like a litany in a low monotone: 'Fisher boats, and the *Jonas Fortune* and Rashleigh's pinnace and eight bound east and five bound west and Mr Mayhew come up and I seen a ship he couldn't make out and he says I 'ad sharp eyes and give me a pat on the back!'

'Mr Mayhew himself? Well – that was a feather in your cap!' Matthew turned to his father. 'What did he have to say to you, Father? There was talk in the Russell you'd fallen out with 'un.'

Harry gave a snort of disgust, and Jennifer saw Arthur looking quickly from Harry to Matt. Eventually, after a minute or two's silence, Matt – who was the only one of the family who could talk to Harry when he was in this sort of mood – tried again.

'Give you a hard time, did he, Father?'

'What he wants,' Harry growled at last, 'is to have his cake and eat it.

There's three hundred sovereigns need spending on that ship, and he'll not give a penny towards it.' He snorted again. 'And if that's the way they think they can defend England, then I reckon they'll deserve what's coming to 'em.'

Jennifer looked up from her plate. 'Now, Harry,' she said quietly. 'You don't mean that.'

Matt leaned back on the bench and flexed his shoulders. 'What did you say?'

'Not much. He started telling me it was my privilege to defend the realm. I told him he could have the privilege of serving as a younker in my forepeak any day of the week.'

Matt laughed obligingly and supped his ale. 'So you put him in his place, eh Father?'

'I did too!'

Nathan, who had been following the conversation with great attention, let out a booming guffaw. 'You put 'im in 'is place!' he echoed. 'You put – '

'That's enough, Nat,' said Jennifer, and put her hand on Nathan's arm.

'Still,' Matthew remarked. 'I doubt if it'll get any cash out of the old skinflint. Though I was speaking with Davy Treffry and Addy Knollys just a half-hour past and they were saying that all at the shipyard'll work for half-wages to ready the ship, and there's plenty of good lads in the village willing to volunteer for service, so we'll not lack a crew, even if half of them don't know a cat from a crow's-nest.'

Harry grunted noncommittally at this, and in the ensuing silence Arthur – who was already dreaming of a life as a sailor – said: 'Miss Drew says that if the Armada comes, we should all have to be papists and pay Jesuits to forgive our sins.'

'I don't think anyone's going to let that happen too easy, love,' Jennifer said quietly.

'Miss Drew says it might, though. And Mr Drew thinks so too, because I heard 'un talking to Mr Mayhew after church, and Mr Mayhew was saying as how the Lord Admiral was at Plymouth and – ' He stopped short, warned by a glance from his mother.

Matt turned to his father. 'So what do you say? Make a start first thing, will we?'

'Make a start? I'm not making a start till Mayhew puts cash on the table.'

'But there won't *be* no cash on the table, Father!'

'In that case Mayhew won't have my ship.'

Matt was pushing a hunk of bread round his plate to soak up the gravy, but his father's words brought this operation to an abrupt stop, and he stared incredulously.

'What – you mean you'd leave the *Russell* sitting out there on the mud – '

'She's my ship. I'll do what I like with 'un.'

'But Father! We can't miss out on this! Why – every shipowner from here to the Narrows is readying for service!'

'And they're the fools for so doing,' Harry muttered. 'There's no profit in it, Matt, no profit at all!'

'Who cares about profit!' Jennifer remarked tartly. 'Not me, any road – least, not while there's Spanish papists sniffing round our shores!'

'Of course,' Matthew added as if to himself, 'if the Spaniard does come up the Sleeve I reckon there could be a few prizes for the taking.' He looked quickly across at his father to see if the idea had changed his mind.

Harry was unimpressed. 'That's as maybe, but it won't be the likes of me that'll have 'em. It'll be your fancy privateers like Fletcher and Fenner that Drake's got eating out of his hand. All they want the *Russell* for is to ferry out their powder and ball for them, aye, and ferry back their dead and dying and their empty beer barrels for refilling. If Mayhew expects me to pay for that privilege then Mayhew can think again, as I told him this afternoon.'

He glowered round at them, challenging anyone to argue further.

After a silence Jennifer accepted the challenge. 'So the *Russell*'ll be swinging round her anchor in Polruan Pool will she, Harry, and you'll be home with us while every other shipmaster's out chasing Spaniards? Make a change, I suppose, though I never reckoned on seeing you cut your nose off to spite your face.'

Matthew looked away and suppressed a smile, and Arthur wondered what his stepfather would look like without his nose.

Harry was beginning to see that he had argued himself into a corner. 'There won't be no Spaniards to chase! They won't let that blessed Armada near these shores. Soon as this gale eases Drake'll be off again, you mark my words, and the next thing we'll hear'll be that the scare's over. And then all your fine friends who've been beggaring themselves to tart up their ships and take on crews'll be wondering why they bothered.'

He returned to his roast lamb, which he shovelled into his mouth, pausing to swill gulps of ale down while his family stared at each other as if each were expecting one of the others to take up the battle.

'I can't hardly believe it was you said that, Father,' Matt said eventually. 'And – and I'd be a liar if I said I'd go along with it, too, 'cause I won't. In fact – if you won't put the work in hand first thing tomorrow, I'll do it myself.'

A dribble of gravy ran down Harry's chin. He shook his finger. 'You just try doing that, boy. You just try!'

'I will too Father – and I'll raise the funds if need be. I wouldn't be able to hold my head up if the old *Russell* doesn't do her bit – and no more would you, come to that. Know what they'll say? "Like son, like father," that's what. They'll drag it all out – aye, we all know what I'm talking about – they'll drag it all out and we'll have the women down on Polruan Strand yammering about us behind our backs again like in times past. Is that what you want? No, Father – the name of Pascoe's been shamed enough in this village, and I'll not see it shamed again, whatever you may say.'

There was a sudden tension across the table – a tension Jennifer hadn't felt in years, and one which Nathan and Arthur sensed as acutely as anyone else.

'I'm right, Father,' Matt said quietly. 'And you know I'm right. So as I say – if you won't put the work in hand, I'll do it myself, and – and I'll skipper her too if need be, and you can stay in-a-door like an old man.'

Looking up from his plate, and seeing them all waiting for his reply, Harry felt suddenly old and tired. He had never really intended to withhold his ship. It was unthinkable that he, Harry Pascoe, should not play his part when every other able-bodied Englishman was arming himself to defend his country.

'God damn it all to Hell!' he muttered. 'So be it. Have it your way.'

Matthew lost no time in putting the word round the village that the *Russell* was to be fitted out for the Queen's service, and the news was like a breath of fresh air among the people of Polruan, some of whom had been croaking about the Armada and saying it was invincible.

Once the decision had been taken however, the village was suddenly united and the *Russell*'s refit went ahead at full speed, with men working through the short summer nights and the womenfolk bringing their meals down to them at Knollys's shipyard, where young Adam was now in charge of shipbuilding and repairs. Meanwhile, across the water at

Fowey, John Rashleigh's ship the *Frances* was also being fitted out, and it wasn't long before the people of Polruan determined among themselves to see to it that their ship would be better finished, better crewed and better sailed than Fowey's; and although everyone privately knew that this would be quite impossible because Harry Pascoe wasn't a quarter as rich as John Rashleigh, it did no harm to pretend, and the common cause served to end old enmities and give the villagers a new-found pride in what they came to regard as 'their' ship.

Prompted by Matthew's enthusiasm, Harry began to catch the fiery mood of expectation that was spreading through the west country. He began to share that peculiarly insular feeling of outrage that another nation should dare to send her fleet to invade English shores; and as his outrage grew and he saw his ship being turned from a battered old coaster into a respectably armed bark, some of his old zest returned, and with it a new surge of protectiveness and affection for his wife and family.

As the work proceeded the rumours circulated. Some said the Armada had been wrecked in storms off the coast of Spain; some held that Queen Elizabeth was so terrified that she had been frozen into indecision, while others pointed out that if only the astrologers had been listened to years before, the inevitable catastrophe that was now approaching might have been averted.

Then, in mid-July, word came from Plymouth that the Navy had sailed to intercept the Spanish, and for a week Polruan – like every other port and harbour along the south coast – held its breath.

On the Saturday evening at the end of that week, when the *Russell*'s refit was complete, Harry Pascoe called a meeting for all those who had worked on his ship and who had a mind to sail in her, and so many turned up to drink his ale that there wasn't room for them all, and the door and windows of the Russell Inn had to be opened so that those who couldn't cram in under the oak beams could stand outside and listen to what he had to say from the street.

Davy Treffry called the meeting to order. 'Right lads, let's have a bit of hush!' he shouted over the chatter, and the buzz of conversation and laughter ceased as Harry stood up.

'We've just had word,' he started, looking about him at the intent faces, 'that the Queen's ships have returned to Plymouth from the Groyne without a sighting of the Spanish.'

There was a further buzz of excitement at this announcement, which quickly died down again as Harry continued. 'Now as I see it, that means

Frank Drake's lost his last chance to deal with 'em in their own ports –
and what *that* means is that the Spanish Army may be paying us a visit
after all. Now it's possible we'll never see so much as their topsails on the
horizon. But it looks more than half likely now that they'll make a try at
coming up the Sleeve, and if they do, well I reckon we're going to have a
job on our hands.'

There was some amusement at this understatement, and while his
audience whispered and nodded to each other, Harry paused to take a
draught of ale.

'Now as I've no wish to take on the whole Armada single-handed when
I sail out past St Saviour's, I've decided to delay no further and take the
Russell over to Plymouth on tomorrow's tide, and to offer my ship to the
Lord Admiral to use in any way he sees fit. Whether that'll mean fighting
or ferrying or fly-boating I know not. But you can be sure I'll see to it that
we'll make a profit out of the venture, whether by payment from the
Crown for services rendered, salvage or maybe the taking of a prize. So
the time's come for volunteering, lads, and if I know the people of this
village there won't be no hanging back. I need two score and ten mariners
and eight gunners minimum, and every one an able-bodied man who's
not afeared of a fight. My son Matthew will serve as my lieutenant, Davy
Treffry here'll sail as my bosun and Jan Lanyon over there says he'll
make this his last voyage as coxswain – '

'And I as a volunteer!' an educated voice said from the back, and all
heads turned in amazement towards Amyas Roscarrock, who stood in
the doorway. 'That is if you'll take me, Mr Pascoe,' he added. 'For
though I be a baptized Catholic, I am yet an Englishman, and I oppose
the invasion of our shores as strongly as any here present and beg the
honour to prove my loyalty to her Majesty Queen Elizabeth.'

Harry was dumbfounded by this turn of events, and was at first
inclined to reject Roscarrock's offer of service; but there were still many
in the village who retained a filial respect for the old family which had
once been so powerful in Polruan, so he decided it might be prudent to
accept. 'Thank you, sir,' he replied with a slight bow, and coughed in
embarrassment. 'Now then, my lieutenant's ready with quill and paper,
and I'll be obliged if every man willing to serve in the bark *Russell* under
my command will now step up and give his name and add his mark, for
which he'll receive one shilling of the Queen's money tomorrow mid-
forenoon, when, God willing, the *Russell* weighs her anchor.' He picked
up his jug of ale again and held it up. 'So here's to the *Russell*, say I – and
God save England, and Good Queen Bess!'

Matt immediately stood up and raised his tankard to the ceiling. 'God save England and Good Queen Bess!' he shouted, and the volunteers gave a cheer and drank off the toast, and the Russell Inn was suddenly full of Cornish talk and laughter as men and boys came up one by one to the table to be signed on for the defence of their country.

Harry was a quiet man when he came home that evening, and over supper Jennifer noticed more than once that he was looking down the table at her in a gentle, loving way. Now that he had signed on his crew and had brought forward the sailing date, the threat of invasion had become suddenly real, and she found herself reflecting on all those things that were most precious in her life: her husband, her children, her home and the peace and safety of this little fishing village of Polruan.

Not many people in the south-coast ports of Devon and Cornwall slept easily that night. Husbands and wives lay awake tossing and turning; girls whispered prayers for the young men they had grown up with; landowners reviewed yet again their plans for the distribution of weapons and the defence of their shores, while up on the headlands and cliff paths a volunteer army of old men and boys kept watch for the approaching invasion and stood ready to light the warning beacons. For the first time in over five hundred years – since the day King Harold fell at the Battle of Hastings – there was a real fear among the people that their country might be overrun and that they might be subjected to a new slavery, a new Doomsday.

A little before dawn Jennifer woke Harry and reached out to him for comfort.

'I had a dream,' she whispered, and nestled down into his arms so that her still-dark hair spread out across his chest and her forehead was soft against his chin.

'Oh aye? What did you dream, then?'

'I was walking down in Pontpill woods, and I saw a man – '

He smoothed her shoulder reassuringly.

'But I couldn't – I couldn't make out who it was. He – he kept flitting away just out of sight ahead of me, Harry. And every time I ran to catch 'un up, he just kind of melted away into the trees – and then suddenly I was at a banquet with Justice Mayhew and he was trying to make me drink something out of a silver goblet – and – and it was blood, Harry – it was real blood!'

She clung to him, and her body shook. 'Harry!' she whispered. 'Please don't go, please don't leave us!'

But they did go: as soon as the last anthem was over and old Drew had given the blessing from the chancel of St Saviour's, the men of Polruan came out of the church and walked down to the harbour in the company of their dear ones, and though there were plenty of red eyes and wet handkerchieves among the womenfolk, there was little outward weeping or wailing, for Reverend Drew had said that as good Christians they must trust in the Lord to preserve them from evil and give them victory if that were His will.

So the boats went back and forth between shore and ship, and for upwards of an hour after the last swabber had been embarked, the *Russell* remained at her anchor while the crew stowed their gear and were put into watches and told their parts of ship; and towards the end of the afternoon when the last of the ebb was flowing, the women and children and the old men who waited on the shore saw the longboat being manned and heard the throaty voices of the men on the windlass as the anchor was hove up; and slowly the *Russell*'s bows turned seaward, and with sails brailed and the men waving from the tops and standing on the yards, she moved out past the fort as she had moved out so often before; and as she cleared the entrance a single gun salute spoke out to the people who stood waving from St Saviour's Point; and then the spritsail and mizzen bellied out; the younkers crawled on the yards and the main and forecourse were set; and turning before the south-west wind, the little ship set course eastward for Plymouth.

Plymouth! The harbour was jammed with ships and the city alive with bustle and people. Though the Queen's galleons had stood up well to their week of rough weather off Ushant, several of the merchantmen that had sailed westward with Drake had sprung leaks, and many of the men had gone down with sickness from scant rations and bad ale.

And now there was a panic on: Drake was appealing to Howard for fresh recruits, better ale and more munitions; Hawkins was snatching every tide to careen and rummage the ships that were leaky or foul, and Howard was writing urgent letters to Walsingham begging him yet again to persuade her Majesty to release more money, so that the fleet would not go short of essential stores.

Old Will Hawkins, the Lord Mayor, had taken responsibility for repairs and replenishments to the fleet, and the guildhall was packed with seafaring men – mostly masters, paymasters or bosuns – who queued up at tables where harassed-looking officers and clerks registered the ships for the Queen's pay and noted requests for recruits and stores.

'Ship?'

'Bark *Russell*.'

'Master's name?'

'Harry Pascoe.'

'Ship's tonnage?'

'Hundred ton.'

'Number of souls?'

'Sixty-six.'

'Armament?'

'Four sakers, two minion, one falconet, two fowlers, six longbows and two harquebus.'

'Powder and roundshot?'

'No more than enough for twenty rounds a gun. I reckon we'll need three times that, minimum.'

The clerk pointed to a queue at another table. 'You must ask over there for munitions, but I doubt if you'll be granted anything more'n what you've got. Are you well acquainted with pilotage in the Sleeve, Mr Pascoe?'

'I should be – I been sailing up and down 'un these past thirty years!'

'Then you'll be sailing under the charge of the Vice-Admiral with the west-o ships.' He pointed again. 'That gentleman over there – the one scratching his head, that's Mr Poole, master of the bark *Bond*. I'd advise you to speak with him, Mr Pascoe, as he's already served westward with the Vice-Admiral and knows the ropes. Come back tomorrow and we'll have the commissioning warrant ready for 'ee. Thank you, sir. Next gentleman please!'

Mr Poole was a jolly man, very Devon in his way of speaking and very fond of his ale, as Harry Pascoe and his son found out that afternoon in the Pelican. He had joined Drake three weeks before and had accompanied the Vice-Admiral on the fruitless sally into the Bay of Biscay. Now, he had been given the task of getting to know the masters of the smaller ships and acquainting each with the gun signals and other conventions used in the fleet, as well as explaining the secret contingency plan for sailing of ships at short notice.

The Pelican Inn had by now become the daily meeting place for the shipmasters, and because there wasn't room inside for everyone, many of the captains took their jugs outside and sat on the benches under the latticed windows that faced south over the Sound; while on the bowling pitch adjacent to the inn the admirals and captains of the Queen's galleons met every afternoon to discuss the latest developments and – by affecting to play bowls – to present to the world an outward air of calm and control while at the same time being on hand to react immediately to any news of the approaching invasion.

'First off then,' Poole said when Harry and Matt had joined him on the bench outside, 'is the golden rule, and that is, follow the senior ship's movements. If the Admiral weighs anchor, you weigh anchor. If he makes sail, you make sail, if he wears – you wear. You're bowline-rigged I suppose?'

'Aye, we are – '

'And we can dip the mizzen lug,' Matt added.

'That's a mercy. If there's one thing the Admiral insists on it's ships that are handy to windward and can put about quick and clean with no hanging in stays or paddling with oars. Right. So far so good. Rule number two: never cross the Admiral's bows, nor take his wind, nor sail betwixt him and the foe, not if you don't want eighteen pounds of culverin roundshot up your arse, that is. That goes for all the Queen's galleons. What else? I know – croaking. We've had a bit, and a few deserters too, and the only way to stop it is stamp on it first thing. Flogging, that's the thing, and no quarter given. And that goes for anyone caught telling fortunes or reading palms or playing with the Tarots or dabbling in popish superstitions or any other sort of mumble-jumble. We don't know how long we're going to be kept waiting here, and the less whispering and murmuring among the men the better. Keep 'em busy, Mr Pascoe. There's always something to be done aboard, you know that. Keep 'em on the go from sparrowfart to pipe down, and you'll have a fresher company of men with more fight in 'em when the time comes. And until we sail, there's to be no shore leave, right? Else we'll have more deserters yet, and we're short enough of souls as it is.'

'What about pay?' Harry put in. 'We've seen no more than four-score shillings of the Queen's money – '

'Keep accounts – it'll all be tallied up later.' Poole winked. 'Least – that's what they tell me. But don't bank on it, Mr Pascoe, will you? I'm not, and if you take my advice, you'll follow the Admiral and mess six-on-four until we see how things are shaping.'

'Six-on-four?'

Poole laughed and drained the last of his ale. 'Six men to four men's rations. You never heard of six-on-four? Oh – and another thing. If ever you find yourself separated from the fleet, you keep fighting, right? No surrender. If your ship can keep one Spaniard busy, so much the better, and chances are you'll be helped out sooner or later.'

'Chances are,' Harry muttered. 'And what if chances aren't?'

'Then you go down fighting and die like good Englishmen. Now then – my throat's quite dry from all this talking, so if you were thinking of recharging our jugs, Mr Pascoe, I'll not say no to another quart of Mr Adams's best Devon ale.'

The *Russell* had entered Plymouth on 25 July – a Monday – and each successive flood tide thereafter saw the arrival of further volunteer ships, which crowded into the Cattewater and berthed in trots of four, so that the little haven became almost solid with ships. Crammed up alongside each other in this way, each ship's company found itself the close neighbour of three or four others, and as the men went about their work, hoisting stores and munitions out of barges and stowing them below, splicing fresh sheets and bowlines, cleaning guns, swabbing decks and – for many of the pressed men – learning the ropes, they were able to look across at the ships berthed ahead or alongside or astern and see their opposite numbers making the same preparations and undergoing the same training; and once a day, in the forenoon, one of the admirals made it his duty to be rowed round the fleet to inspect the ships and review the readiness of each, so that even the humblest swabber had a chance to see the faces of those who were to lead them.

Tuesday, Wednesday and Thursday passed thus, and with each day the atmosphere of anticipation in the fleet became more tense. Up on the Hoe, butts had been set up for archery practice, and the old fortifications on Fisher's Nose built during Henry VIII's reign swarmed with soldiers who had been drafted in for the defence of the city. On the headlands, coastguards stood watch day and night, anxiously scanning their horizons for the first glimpse of the invasion fleet. Rumours circulated freely; the master of every humblest hoy or crumster that put into harbour was questioned as to whether he had seen any sign of the Armada, and every bosun and master gunner had his own pet theory on what the Lord Admiral should or should not be doing.

Then, on the Friday afternoon, when the shipmasters and gentlemen volunteers of the barks *Bond*, *Bonner*, *Hawkins* and *Russell* were standing outside the Pelican with their pewter jugs of ale, a little fifty-ton pinnace rounded Rame Head and came flying up the Sound under full sail, and within a few minutes she had been recognized by the watchers on Plymouth Hoe as Tom Fleming's scouting pinnace, the *Golden Hind*.

Her fast progress up the Sound was the subject of immediate interest, and the Pelican emptied as Mr Adams's customers spilled out onto the greensward to watch her come in past St Nicholas's Island and drop anchor off the entrance to Sutton Pool. On the bowling pitch, Lord Howard's game with Drake, Frobisher and Hawkins had been briefly interrupted by Lieutenant Preston of the *Ark Royal*, who crossed the green to advise the Admiral of the arrival.

Ten minutes later Fleming came striding up the hill accompanied by his bosun. Both men had that look of rugged exhaustion that comes from days spent at sea in brisk weather, and both ignored the stares and questions of the shipmasters as they went on past the inn to report to the Lord Admiral.

They watched: the bosun had hung back, but Fleming was speaking personally to Lord Howard, and Drake was close by, making a show of continuing his game while at the same time listening and commenting. The Lord Admiral was questioning Fleming, who was speaking fast and at some length, and clearly reporting more than a fruitless mission.

Bill Poole turned to Pascoe and the other shipmasters who stood with him. 'I reckon this is it, lads,' he remarked softly, and his words voiced the opinion of them all.

The game of bowls continued, but now Lieutenant Preston was busy running messages for the Lord Admiral, and while the shipmasters waited and speculated outside the Pelican, several of the senior captains – Sir William Winter of the *Vanguard*, Lord Sheffield of the *White Bear*, George Beeston of the *Dreadnought* and Edward Fenton of the *Mary Rose* – were summoned by the admirals for a council of war; and there they stood for some while, conferring gravely and calmly, nodding in agreement, deferring to one another – until the onlookers grew impatient and began wondering whether the Armada had been sighted after all.

Then Amyas Preston, a polished and ceremonious young man who was the Lord Admiral's flag lieutenant, came down the hill to speak with them, and they crowded round him, hanging on his words.

'Gentlemen,' he said, 'the Spanish fleet has been sighted. Mister Fleming found their Armada hove-to off the Lizard – '

He was immediately bombarded by eager questions. 'How many ships?' 'What of their armament?' 'When do we sail?'

Preston held up his hands for silence. 'Gentlemen – gentlemen! You shall have your answers soon enough. In the meantime, the Lord Admiral directs that every master and officer repair to his ship and place her under sailing orders. You know the order of departure well enough and we shall hold to that. The tide will remain foul until a little before nine o'clock, and the Lord Admiral intends that the *Ark Royal* shall lead the fleet to sea, commencing at the last quarter-hour of the flood. He wishes it to be impressed upon all that our departure must be orderly and seamanlike. It will be necessary to tow and warp out against this wind, and all ships' boats will be required to assist the operation. Above all, I am desired to impress upon you the need for a calm, orderly departure. We have plenty of time gentlemen – indeed, as you can see, the Vice-Admiral is insisting upon finishing his game. So let us avoid a headlong rush, and set our people an example of calm determination by so doing.' Preston nodded briefly to conclude his briefing. 'I wish one and all Godspeed, success in our endeavours, and victory with honour.'

'Amen to that!' Harry Pascoe exclaimed, and several others echoed: 'Aye, amen to that!'

One by one the galleons were warped and towed out of the harbour and into the Sound: the *Ark Royal*, the *Elizabeth Bonaventure*, the *Golden Lion*, the *White Bear*, the *Vanguard*, the *Revenge*, the *Victory*.

All through that night, from the beginning of slack high water to the end of slack low, the work went on. Ropes splashed down into the waters of Sutton Pool and the Cattewater. Heaving lines thumped down into longboats. Hawsers were passed across and made fast to sampson posts before the coxswains ordered, 'Give way – together!' and the banks of oars dipped and the Queen's ships turned slowly seaward and gathered way through the lamp-lit water.

The wind had dropped away with the coming of darkness, and the Devon voices of those who were nonchalantly performing this feat of seamanship echoed across the harbours. Bosun called to bosun; boats' coxswains gave orders to their crews; captains exchanged words of quiet good humour as their ships passed within feet of each other, and the few townspeople who were aware that the Royal Navy was slipping out of harbour stood in silence and awe, watching from the foot of Plymouth Hoe as these ships, which were the very soul and pride of England, put out to sea.

After the galleons went the pinnaces and smaller ships of war, and after them went those private merchantmen that were ready for sea – ships like the *Roebuck*, the *St Leger* and the *Virgin God Save Her*; so that when the damp Saturday dawn came up over the city of Plymouth, the forest of masts in the Cattewater and Sutton Pool had diminished to nothing more than a copse, and the fleet could be seen off Cawsand Bay.

The *Russell* left harbour on the first of the forenoon ebb, and by midday was close hauled on the starboard tack and heading south-south-east out of Plymouth Sound with every inch of canvas straining. A few miles ahead, the main body of the Lord Admiral's flotilla was standing out towards Eddystone, while on the starboard beam to the north-west, some of Drake's ships were hugging the shoreline and beating into a fresh west-south-westerly to weather Rame Head. Harry was watching them closely and when Matt joined him on the aftercastle, having done rounds of the ship to check that all gear was secure, he acknowledged his son's arrival with a nod.

'All well 'tween decks?'

'Aye, all well, Father.' He nodded in the direction of the lee bulwark over which Amyas Roscarrock was hanging with a face like tripe and onions. 'Though our gentleman volunteer doesn't look too happy.'

Harry grunted again, his mind on more important things. The *Russell* had been ordered to join up with Drake's ships on leaving the Sound, and several other of the small armed merchantmen had already tacked astern.

'Standing out for the tide?' Matthew asked.

Harry nodded. 'The ebb runs faster out here. I'm in no hurry to put about. Better to make three long tacks than six little 'uns.'

For nearly an hour, he held on out to sea. As the ship came out of the lee of Rame Head, the westerly swell began to make itself felt, and from time to time the *Russell*'s larboard gunwale was buried in white foam. The wind sang in the stays and bowlines; up on the fore and maintops, lookouts stood scanning the western horizon. Now that the night's work was over and the business of putting to sea and making sail was complete, the hands on deck – like the master and his son who stood up by the whipstaff – had time to reflect upon events and to wonder what the next day would bring.

This short lull, this temporary easing of the tension that had been mounting so steadily over the past days, was broken when Harry passed the word to his bosun to put about.

'Bowlines in hand, man the lee braces, ready about!' bawled Treffry, and immediately the decks were alive with men and boys running barefoot to their stations as the whipstaff was put over, the bows came slowly up into wind and, as the ship payed off on the new tack, the yards were sweated as far round to starboard as they would go, the mizzen lug dipped and the sheets hove in.

Gradually the two halves of the fleet drew apart, the main body under Howard standing out into the Channel to the south, and a dozen or so of Drake's ships beating laboriously inshore; and towards mid-afternoon the lookouts on board the *Russell* reported sighting the smoke of the warning beacon alight on St Saviour's Point.

Now that it was known that the invasion fleet had been sighted from shore, all eyes on board the *Russell* strained for the first glimpse of the enemy. Men clung to the shrouds and climbed out along the bowsprit to gaze westward, squinting against a watery afternoon sun which had appeared from beneath a bank of cloud.

The flood tide was making now, and running against them. Following the Admiral's movements, Pascoe beat back and forth all day into wind and current, making little progress against either, so that it took an age to pass Polperro and bring St Saviour's Point closer, and he began to wonder if the Spanish had given Drake the slip after all.

And then, when the sun was no more than four fingers above the horizon, a cry of 'Sail!' came from Nick Polwhele in the maintop, and when Matthew went aloft and stood on the fore topsail yard he saw a sight he would never forget – a sight that sent a cold shiver down his spine.

Ten miles to the west, spread out to seaward from Deadman Point, what looked like a great floating city of castles, parapets and towers was silhouetted against the yellowing horizon.

He turned and shouted down to the upturned faces of the men on deck.

'Armada!' he shouted. 'Armada in sight!' – and suddenly the men were cheering, he was cheering with them, and the hairs were standing up on the back of his neck.

The Fight

OFF PLYMOUTH, SUNDAY 31 JULY

By dawn, when the Duke of Medina Sidonia appeared on the poop of his flagship the *San Martin*, the wind had freshened and veered west-north-westerly.

He stood for a moment at the top of the ladder and looked out at the long lines of dark sails that stretched out on either side. Today was the day – the day he had been dreading since the moment he first received the royal commission to take command of the Armada.

'Good morning, your Grace!'

He turned, and Don Diego Flores de Valdes bowed stiffly.

'How are we this morning, sir? Your cold better?'

Don Diego (who was first cousin and sworn enemy of Don Pedro de Valdes, Dorothea's uncle) had moved on board to become the Duke's Chief of Staff, and the Duke was aware that however much he detested the man's condescending manner and overweening self-satisfaction, he would be castigated later if he refused to listen to his advice. So although a headache was sending shooting pains through his left temple, he replied that he was quite well, and enquired whether the tactical situation had developed at all overnight.

'Indeed it has, sir.' Don Diego pointed to the south-west. 'There they are!'

The Duke's eyesight wasn't what it had been, and he could only just make out the ships on the starboard quarter. But he had learnt enough about naval tactics by now to know that if those ships were indeed the English battle fleet, then the enemy had already scored the first victory without even firing a shot.

'But . . . I don't understand – are they not to windward? And didn't we agree last night that our most important single aim was to prevent them gaining that advantage?'

Don Diego looked a little pained. 'Yes, I'm afraid we have to admit that they are, sir.'

15 The Fight

'But how – '

'I will explain, sir, let me explain. The trouble is . . . the trouble is, the urcas, sir. You see – they can't sail as close to the wind as our galleons, and we couldn't risk leaving them unprotected. If you recall, the whole council was agreed upon that last night.' Don Diego spread his hands. 'So – I'm afraid – we have been obliged to choose between the lesser of two evils. But may I impress on you, sir, that it is only a *small* advantage? They can't attack us without approaching us, and when they approach us we shall force them to close quarters, where our superiority is overwhelming.'

The Duke sighed and hoped that Don Diego was right.

'I *know* I'm right, sir! Besides – consider – we have a fair wind to take us up the Sleeve, and except for a very few absentees our fleet is as strong as the day we left the Tagus. No – I think today will prove interesting, very interesting, and by the end of it your misgivings will be at an end.'

As the rising sun disappeared behind a bank of cloud, the fleet came to life. Trumpets called soldiers to quarters; the stern-lanterns on senior officers' ships were extinguished and the nobles, adventurers and gentlemen volunteers heard morning Mass before breakfasting and putting on their armour.

The Duke of Medina Sidonia and Don Diego were joined by others of the staff: the King's bastard and personal representative, Prince Ascoli; Maestro de Campo Don Francisco de Bobadilla; the sea captain of the *San Martin*, Marolin de Juan, and the flag lieutenant, Baltasar de Zuniga, who was keeping the narrative of events.

The Duke decided that it was time to assert his authority. 'Baltasar – let's have a look at that battle plan. What do you think, Don Diego – isn't it time we assumed our formation?'

They spread out the formation chart on a table and studied the plan in which the position of every ship had been designated three months before. The flagship, *San Martin*, was in the centre, astern of Hugo de Moncada's three remaining galleasses, and the six squadrons were ranged on either side in long lines that were originally intended to curve forward 'like the horns of an Andalusian bull' as Don Pedro de Valdes had put it.

Matters had been arranged so that each general in command had reason to believe himself to be in a position of the highest importance. On the larboard and northernmost 'horn' sailed the Levantine vanguard under Alonso de Leyva, the brilliant young officer who was secretly designated as understudy to the Captain General; on the starboard and southerly horn sailed Juan Martinez de Recalde, general of the rearguard Biscayan squadron and one of the most courageous seamen of the day; closer in sailed the galleons of Castille under Don Diego, and the Duke's élite Portuguese squadron; and forming the central main battle line came the Guipuscoans and Andalusians under Miguel de Oquendo and Don Pedro de Valdes, whose ships boxed in the convoy of unwieldy hulks and auxiliaries, which carried arms, mules and soldiers for the invasion.

'Modified battle formation,' Don Diego announced. 'That is what we need.'

'Modified?' queried the Duke.

'Yes. We cannot have our horns pointing ahead now, sir.' Don Diego demonstrated with thumb and forefinger outstretched. 'That would leave the main body unprotected. No, what we must do is curve the horns back towards the enemy, so that when he closes with our van and rear we can catch him thus, as between the pincers of a crab.'

A few minutes later a signal gun was fired from the flagship to order the formation. At the same time the banner of the Blessed Virgin was hoisted from the foremast. At first it fouled the standing rigging, and flailed about like a huge bird in a trap; then the tack lines were eased, and as the wind caught it and it bellied out ahead, the Duke of Medina Sidonia looked up and crossed himself.

'A crab,' he muttered to himself, standing alone by the stern-rail. 'Not a bull, but a crab. . . .'

The operation of opening out to battle formation took over two hours, and while it went ahead the activities of the English fleet were largely ignored. But towards nine o'clock, when over fifty enemy ships had formed up in a group to the west and a dozen or so were working their way to windward inshore, a flyboat was seen to break away from the main body of the English fleet and head for the northern horn of the Spanish formation.

It was Jonas Bradbury's pinnace, the aptly named *Disdain*. Running before the wind, she bore swiftly down on the Levantine squadron and – when she was no more than a cable off the wing ship – discharged a long-range four-pounder harmlessly into the towering stern of *La Regazona*, the biggest ship in the Armada; and while the staff officers aboard the *capitana* were still open-mouthed at this example of English impudence, the *Disdain* gave a demonstration of just how handy English ships could be: the helm went down, the bowlines were sweated, and the little ship dashed off to windward, sailing on a closer luff than many of her Spanish spectators had believed possible.

The first engagement started soon afterwards. Mistaking *La Regazona* for the flagship, the Lord Admiral closed with her and the *Ark Royal*'s long-range culverins thundered for the first time. In reply Don Alonso de Leyva attempted to force the English to close quarters, but in the attempt was himself forced to stand out across the concave rear of the crescent, so that the two leviathans began a private duel in which the *Ark Royal*'s superior sailing qualities and longer-range guns enabled her to dictate the range and score a few hits while remaining unharmed by the several discharges of ship-smashers and basilicos from the Levantine.

Meanwhile the other horn had come under heavier attack from the *Revenge*, the *Victory* and the *Triumph*, which had taken up positions to windward of Recalde's *San Juan de Portugal* and were filing past her in line ahead in the manner first developed at Smerwick eight years before.

On hearing these first broadsides João immediately went below to put on his corselet, and half an hour later he joined the group of gentlemen volunteers on the after deck of the *Duquesa Santa Ana*.

He was feeling rather cold and apprehensive, and he looked a lot thinner than he had when he had bade Sara farewell.

'Now my dear Count,' said João's friend Fernando, who considered himself something of an expert on naval warfare, 'let me explain the position to you. The way to understand a sea engagement, as I'm sure you will already appreciate, is to view it as if the battle were taking place on land, and to regard each vessel as a company of infantry. As you saw this morning, the English Admiral followed the best traditions of warfare by first sending us his defiance, following which he and his Vice-Admiral have chosen to engage our *capitana* – or at least, the vessel they think is our *capitana* – and our *almiranta general*. That their Lord Admiral has engaged the wrong ship is of course quite ludicrous – not to say dishonourable – though I doubt if it will affect the outcome. What is more important to understand is that these gun engagements that we are now witnessing are no more than mere preliminaries, in which each participant chooses his opponent, and tries to weaken him before grappling and fighting at close quarters.'

'Just as artillery is sometimes used to weaken an enemy's resolve before the charge, I suppose,' João remarked.

'Just so – precisely that!'

'So really, the proper battle hasn't begun?'

They were joined by the other supernumeraries: Alonso Valiente, Christoual de Funes and Padre Jorge, whose bald head appeared above the hatch coaming as he came up the ladder in habit and sandals. As the forenoon proceeded, more of the Spanish fleet was drawn into the conflict, ships brailing topsails and turning to the wind to fall back and join the *Regazona* and Recalde's *San Juan*. The crab formation had been somewhat broken now: each claw had been bent inwards from the tip, and the *Regazona* had been forced to run for safety into the main body.

'But what is that Biscayan up to?' João asked of all in general. 'Why has he broken away like that?' He turned to Fernando. 'Can you make anything of what's going on, dear boy? I do wish we could get on with it and have the real battle. All this puffing and banging strikes me as a diabolical waste of good roundshot!'

'The English have hauled clear, sir!' reported the flag lieutenant on board the *San Martin*. 'The *Gran Grin* and the *San Juan* have spread topsails and are resuming station!'

'Thank you, Baltasar – keep a record of it, won't you? Can you see if they're damaged?'

Baltasar gazed astern at the two galleons of the Biscayan squadron which together had borne the severest brunt of the English attack that morning. 'I can't say sir. But they have all their masts and sails.'

The Duke turned to Don Diego. 'The wind – we must regain the wind, don't you agree?'

' "Must" sir? That's a strong word – '

'Then shouldn't we at least try?'

Don Diego bunched his lips impatiently. Any fool could see that the *Regazona*, *San Juan* and *Gran Grin* had been quite outmanoeuvred by the English galleons. The only way to beat them – he'd said so a hundred times – was to lure them into close quarters.

'Sir – I explained this morning – the urcas must not be left unprotected – '

'What are the zabras for? Can't we throw a screen of small ships round the urcas and bring the galleons back upwind? It's only just afternoon – we have several hours of daylight left, and now the English have drawn off we may catch them unawares. Nothing venture nothing gain, General, don't you agree?'

In fact, there was little else they could do bar sailing on down-wind, so

Don Diego agreed on condition that the fleet manoeuvre as one, and a few minutes later the signal gun was fired and every ship began following the Captain General's movements as the *San Martin* altered to the wind.

For nearly four hours, the attempt to recover the wind went on, and in that time many of the urcas went down to leeward of the galleons, so that the whole formation virtually turned itself inside out; but however determinedly the Spanish set their bows to the wind, the English were always able to sail closer, and by four o'clock every ship captain in the Armada knew that the attempt was futile.

'Very well – resume battle formation,' the Duke eventually conceded. 'But at least we did try. No one can say that we didn't try.'

He went to the stern rail and gazed down at the swirling water forty feet below. He had not lost the day, no, but he had certainly not won it either, and if the English continued to keep their distance, their longer-range guns might eventually be able to do some damage.

And what of Parma? He still had no word of confirmation that the invasion was ready to cross from Dunkirk. Eddystone Rock was astern too, so the possibility of an assault on Plymouth discussed at the council of war the previous night was now out of the question.

A servant brought him some biscuit and cheese, which he munched thoughtfully, watching as seagulls swooped for the crumbs.

If he didn't have word from the low countries by the time he reached the Isle of Wight, he must anchor the fleet there – that was what had been agreed the previous night. And if he anchored the fleet off the English coast, what new risks might he run? Wasn't Giambelli, the Italian who had invented a devastating weapon called a 'hellburner', now in the employ of the English? He shivered. The amazing manoeuvrability of the enemy ships and the range of their guns had already cast a shadow on the Enterprise: he had received reports that the English had remained virtually untouched by any of the broadsides fired at them.

How long would the powder and shot last? How long would the will to fight last? How long, indeed, would the water last?

There was a discreet cough behind him, and when he turned his flag lieutenant bowed.

'Sir,' he said. 'There has been a collision. General de Valdes's ship – the *Nuestra Señora del Rosário* – has lost her bowsprit.'

He turned back, shocked and angry.

'How?' he demanded. 'How can such a thing have happened?'

It had happened very easily – in fact Tristram, who was on board the *Nuestra Señora del Rosário* and had witnessed the collision, thought it was a miracle it hadn't happened before, because the process of getting back into station had been a coxswain's nightmare, with thousand-ton urcas and galleons manoeuvring at perilously close quarters in a freshening wind, so that mighty aftercastles and forecastles passed within yards of each other and shipmasters and bosuns held their breath as disaster after disaster was narrowly averted.

The *Rosário*'s was the simplest of all collisions: the ship had come up astern of the *Santa Catalina*, another Andalusian galleon, and in doing so had completely taken her wind, with the result that the *Rosário* had overhauled her so quickly that not even the emergency striking of forecourse and topsails could prevent the sickening crunch of wood on wood and the twang and thud of parting stays and braces.

Standing on the aftercastle with Joaquim and Thomas Bitus, one of the Irishmen on board, Tristram watched as the mariners fought with axes and tackles to clear the tangle of ropes and broken spars and to rig a temporary stay to support the foremast. Oddly, he felt little satisfaction at this setback. Since sailing from Lisbon he had become increasingly involved as a staff lieutenant and tactical adviser, and had been thrown much more into the company of Ensign Rodrigo and the General himself. He had come to like both. Don Pedro's ardent patriotism concealed a very genuine desire to acquit himself with honour and to make a success of this Enterprise, and Rodrigo reminded him of Matthew: as eager for glory and approval as his brother had been eight years before when he had come home with his father from their service in Ireland.

Now, Don Pedro was standing on the for'd end of the aftercastle staring bleakly at the shambles, and Tristram could only feel sorry for him.

'Still and all,' Bitus remarked at his side, 'praise be that it wasn't worse. We can run before this wind and make repairs overnight. And with God's help . . . glory be to the Holy Ghost, what was that?'

Half a mile on the larboard beam, one of the ships in the Guipuscoan squadron had suffered a massive explosion.

The pinnace came up fast on the *San Martin*'s starboard side, and her coxswain cupped his hands to make his report direct to the Duke, who stood as mournful as ever by the stern rail.

15 The Fight

'Galleon *San Salvador*, your Grace! Her powder barrels have gone up! Aftercastle and maindeck quite destroyed and the stern in flames! Many burnt, wounded and drowned, your Grace! I have advised her master to prepare for a tow stern-first so that the wind will take the flames clear!'

For once, the Duke of Medina Sidonia needed no advice from Don Diego. The *San Salvador* had on board the Paymaster General and a large part of the King's treasure. 'Signal gun!' he ordered. 'All ships turn together!'

On board the *Rosário* Tristram's reaction was instinctive. 'General – we must not do it!'

Don Pedro turned and glared at him. His sea-captain had already been given his orders to come to the wind, and the whipstaff had been put over. Along with every other galleon in the line the *Nuestra Señora del Rosário* was slowly beginning to turn.

'What d'you mean, Inglés?'

Normally, Don Pedro addressed him as 'Teniente'. 'Inglés' was the title he invariably used when he was displeased.

Tristram forced himself to be calm. 'I mean, General, that we must not cast about. The foremast is but weakly stayed, and without headsails we shall be unable to keep off the wind! We shall turn like a weathercock, sir!'

'And what if we do? We obey orders in the Armada, Inglés. I'll thank you not to forget that.'

The General turned abruptly away. Tristram knew him well enough not to try to press the point: standing there in the gathering dusk with the wind freshening and the ship beginning to plunge as she turned across the swell, he reflected that it really didn't matter at all if Don Pedro chose to hazard his ship. Earlier it had been difficult to feel pleased about the evening's two disasters; now Don Pedro's obstinacy made it easy for him to stand back and say nothing.

For some time it seemed that he was to be proved wrong. Though the men on the whipstaff had considerable difficulty in preventing the ship's head coming to the wind, they managed it, and the *Rosário* kept her station in the main body at the end of the line of urcas. But as the wind continued to freshen the efforts of the steersmen became the more frantic, until the whipstaff was hard over and the ship was still not answering, but luffing up into wind.

Suddenly a jerk was felt throughout the ship as the forecourse took the wind on its other side. There were shouts of 'Aback! Forecourse aback!'

from for'd, and almost immediately the makeshift foremast broke off at deck level and crashed down against the main yard.

While the ensuing chaos reigned, Tristram Pascoe went right aft out of the way. If the General needed advice now, he would have to find it elsewhere.

It had turned into a squally evening. The sunset was a forbidding yellow, and the sea was becoming black and choppy. The Duke had sent two galleasses to the *San Salvador*'s assistance, and an efficient operation to extinguish the fires, pass a tow and take off the casualties had prevented the English fleet from closing in and taking advantage of the Armada's misfortune.

Now, minutes after ordering the fleet to resume its easterly course, when the two galleasses were making headway and the *San Salvador* was being brought back into the main body, this new disaster was reported to him.

'Signal gun!' he ordered. 'Captain Marolin – prepare to take the *Rosário* in tow. Baltasar! Take the longboat away and inform General de Valdes of my intention.'

Once again the fleet came about; once again the huge hulls plunged and rolled as they crossed the swell. Working by lamplight, the flagship went herself to the rescue of Don Pedro. Boats under oars plied back and forth with lines; voices bellowed in the darkness, and after half an hour or more, a hawser was passed from the disabled ship's bows to the stern of the *San Martin*.

The Duke watched from his poop as the tow was secured, and when all was ready approved the order for the main and forecourse to be set. Slowly the *San Martin* gathered way before the wind; the hawser rose dripping out of the black water and tautened until every last drop of moisture was wrung from it in a fine spray – and then it parted and the frayed end came whining back like a flying snake, slamming against the stern and shattering the glass in the quarter lantern.

'Your Grace – this is madness!'

He turned. Don Diego was standing before him in livid fury.

'I am taking your cousin in tow, General. Is that madness?'

Don Diego approached closer so that other staff officers would not overhear the conversation. 'Sir,' he said. 'You are putting the entire fleet at risk. We are at this moment losing our formation, and if we do not resume it *at once*, we shall be strung out right across the Sleeve by morning. Is that what you want?'

'I cannot desert one of my generals,' the Duke muttered. 'Before ever I sailed from Lisbon, I swore that whatever happened, I would never desert my ships in their hour of need.'

On the other side of the poop deck the staff officers glanced across at the Captain General and the Chief of Staff, aware of the tussle of wills that was going on and the personal reasons of enmity between the Valdes cousins which lay behind it. Another of the Duke's closest advisers, Maestro de Campo Bobadilla, crossed the deck to add weight to Don Diego's arguments and after a further few minutes of heated exchange, the Duke gave way. A galleass, four pataches and the Andalusian half-leader, the *San Francisco*, were ordered to remain with the disabled ship while the fleet re-formed; and having ensured that all his orders had been passed and acknowledged the Duke of Medina Sidonia returned to his stern-rail to stare at the wake and wrestle with his conscience.

Ensign Rodrigo was close to tears.

'Teniente! The General wishes your presence immediately in the waist! Sir – they are leaving us in the lurch! We have been abandoned to Drake! The General wishes us to go in the patache but I have told him that we should rather die than leave his side – but he is insisting!'

Tristram went up on deck with Joaquim. They found the General supervising the transfer of soldiers into a pinnace that was leaping up and down on the leeward side.

'Ah – there you are, Teniente. Quickly now – there's no time to lose.' He nodded to windward, and through the darkness Tristram could just make out the shape of an English galleon. 'Listen: these are the last orders you'll have from me. Take charge of this boat and head for the Biscayans – Recalde's *San Juan de Portugal* was furthest in the rear when we were separated. And you are to go too, Rodrigo – no I insist on it. It is your duty, boy, your duty.' He gripped each by the hand and embraced them quickly. 'And – thank you, Teniente – thank you from the bottom of my heart for your loyal service. Now may God go with you, and may we meet again one day, whether in this world or the next.'

Picking their moment, Tristram, Joaquim and Ensign Rodrigo jumped down into the heaving boat. Minutes later, as the oarsmen pulled clear of the ship's side, the first English guns roared out, and a plume of water shot up alongside.

MONDAY 1 AUGUST

Drake had been given the honour of leading the overnight pursuit, but soon after midnight Lord Admiral Howard was shaken with a report from his officer of the watch that the lookouts had lost sight of the *Revenge*'s stern-lantern.

Arriving on deck he found that the squally weather had given way to a light westerly wind with mist patches through which a quarter moon glimmered from time to time. Yawning in spite of himself and gathering a cloak about his shoulders against the night chill, he questioned Lieutenant Preston on the last bearing of Drake's stern-lantern.

'It was dead ahead, my Lord,' Preston reported, still peering forward into the darkness. 'I expected to see it again immediately on setting the bonnets.'

'What of the rest of the fleet?'

They turned and gazed aft and were able to make out a couple of dim shapes. 'I would have expected to see more than two,' Howard muttered. 'Are we burning a quarter lantern?'

'No, sir. I thought it unwise, in case we had perhaps overtaken the *Revenge* – '

Howard nodded his approval. 'But the question is – do we press on or fall back?'

'I'm for pressing on, sir,' Preston said quickly, and Howard smiled at his enthusiasm.

He was still weighing up the situation when the lookout on the foretop sang out: 'White light, fine on the starboard bow, far, sir!' and a few minutes later, with the ship rolling and yawing in the following sea, Preston climbed the mizzen shrouds and confirmed the sighting.

Howard stayed on deck until he could see what looked increasingly like a stern-lantern, and when the ship had closed to long culverin shot, sail was reduced and the Admiral went below to snatch some more sleep.

It seemed as though he had only just dropped off when he was woken again, this time with an urgent request that he come up on deck immediately.

He was out of his bunk straight away and went barefoot up the ladder and onto the sloping poop.

A grey dawn was coming up, and a glance ahead told him at once the reason for the urgency of his call.

Preston was already issuing orders to call the hands and prepare to come to the wind, and with good reason, for the lantern they had mistaken for the *Revenge*'s had been that of the *San Martin*, and for nearly six hours the *Ark Royal*, *White Bear* and *Mary Rose* had been keeping station on the flagship of the Spanish battle line.

'Permission to close haul sir?' Preston said on seeing the Admiral.

'Yes please. But have a care, Amyas. Be sure to see that the *Mary Rose* alters with us.'

The whipstaff went over and the men heaved on tacks and bowlines, and as the *Ark Royal* clawed her way to windward and out of danger the two other galleons which had stayed with her overnight followed suit.

The crisis over, Howard gave his lieutenant orders to remain well clear of the enemy until the remainder of the fleet (which was ten miles astern) had caught up; and when the Admiral had gone below for his breakfast, Preston was joined on the quarterdeck by Mr Clerke, the master gunner, and John Gidley, one of the gentlemen volunteers.

'Thought we were going to be busy for a minute,' Clerke remarked laconically.

'You and me both!' Gidley returned.

'What I don't understand is – why didn't they take the advantage we offered to 'em on a plate? Why didn't their galleasses row themselves to wind'd and encircle us?'

Gidley put his tongue in his cheek and lowered his voice so that the officer of the watch should not hear. 'I reckon if truth were told, Mr Clerke,' he said in his Dartmoor drawl, 'they were probably as fast asleep as we.'

The wind died light that day and the two fleets floated slowly on, making barely a knot through the water. It was a day for reorganization and debate: each side had had a taste of the other's tactics, and neither liked the look of what they had seen. On the one hand, the English had refused to be drawn into a close-quarters fight and the range and rate of fire of their guns had been impressive, and on the other, the Spanish fleet had proved itself to be better-disciplined and more willing to fight than their enemy had expected. The Lord Admiral feared that the Armada might make an assault on Torbay, Weymouth or the Isle of Wight, and the Duke of Medina Sidonia had been warned by intelligence agents to expect to meet Lord Henry Seymour's squadron sailing from the Narrows to meet him.

In the morning Drake took the *Nuestra Señora del Rosário* for a prize, and Don Pedro was entertained to dinner aboard the *Revenge* before being presented like a plum pulled out of a pudding to the Lord Admiral.

In the afternoon the *San Salvador* – stinking of burnt corpses – was abandoned by the Spanish and towed into Weymouth by Thomas Fleming's pinnace, the *Golden Hind*.

Meanwhile, as the two fleets went on eastwards, more and more ships came out from the south-coast ports to volunteer their services to the Lord Admiral, and on passing Berry Head they saw a great crowd of cheerful Devonians watching and waving from the cliffs.

OFF PORTLAND, TUESDAY 2 AUGUST

For the first time since leaving the Groyne, João had had a good night's sleep, and when he was awoken for early Mass he found himself feeling positively optimistic. The gales of the journey north were at last over; the previous evening had been clear and calm, and – miracle of miracles – he wasn't even feeling seasick.

Receiving the Holy Sacrament from Padre Jorge, he felt within him a renewal of hope and trust in the power of the Blessed Virgin to protect him from all ills.

On deck, after a breakfast of hot gruel and ship's biscuit, he found a similar atmosphere of cheerful confidence among the officers, and upon enquiry he discovered the reason: in the early hours of the morning a breeze had sprung up from the south-east so that for the first time since the two fleets had met off Plymouth, the Armada had the weather-gauge.

'Now we shall have some sport, my dear Count!' chortled Fernando when João joined the group of gentlemen on the poop. 'You see that headland over there? That's the Portland Bill, and the English have just put about, having failed to slip to windward between ourselves and the land.' He rubbed his hands. 'So it looks as if they're going to be forced to fight us on our terms after all, and I'm sure you know what *that* will mean!'

At that moment a signal gun was fired from the flagship for the fleet to wear, and the decks of the *Duquesa Santa Ana* were suddenly alive with men running hither and thither to take sheets and braces in hand and swing the yards over as the stern came through the wind. At the same time trumpets sounded in every ship to load broadsides and run out guns, and Captain Valiente – who like every other sea captain in the fleet faced the death penalty if he allowed his ship to leave her station in the formation – started bellowing at the men on the whipstaff to steady the ship on the new course.

João smiled uncertainly at this bustle of activity and turned to Fernando. 'Do you think we ought to put on our helmets, Fernandinho?' he whispered.

'Not *quite* yet,' Fernando replied, and when he pressed João's hand the Count had a sudden longing to be further comforted by his friend in a way that would have been quite inappropriate to the time and place.

The Armada had by now turned to the south before the strengthening breeze, and with the English line converging on the same tack only half a mile to leeward, it became clear to all that an engagement was imminent.

Major Barabona came clanking up in full armour to issue his instructions to the volunteers. 'Now gentlemen – Count – will those of you who are not involved in the preliminaries kindly keep well out of the way of the gunners and harquebusiers? If we can bring a suitable ship to a hand-stroke, Captain Valiente has my strict instructions to bring the ships bow to bow and poop to poop, so that you will not be obliged to fight with gentlemen of lesser rank than yourselves. So I wish you good luck and good fighting!' – and bowing quickly, he hurred off to bark orders at his ensign.

The enemy was closer now, and from the head of the line came a sudden cannonade as the first broadsides were exchanged.

João had a sudden feeling that he was going to be sick. He put on his helmet and started fiddling with the visor. 'Perhaps it might be better if we went downstairs – ' he began, but at the same time there was a thundering crash as the nearest English galleon opened fire.

It was as if he had been plunged into the fires of Hell. The English culverins were belching out flame and smoke; roundshot was buzzing overhead and great plumes of water were leaping up close to the ship.

João stood on the poop in the smoke and the noise, paralysed by fear. 'Oh dear God!' he said again and again. 'Oh dear God, dear God, dear God!'

The deck heaved and shook as the *Duquesa* fired her first ten-gun broadside. He staggered back, clutching at the rail to steady himself. A heavy harquebus, balanced on a tripod, went off with an ear-splitting crack at his side. Captain Valiente was screaming at the helmsman to bear away and the sailors to check away the tack lines; Major Barabona was bellowing orders at his soldiers, and the master gunner was standing lash in hand with men and boys scurrying round him to reload and run out the cannon. In the waist a massive spar with a vicious-looking grappling hook was being hoisted and swung outboard, and the soldiers were hurling abuse at their opponents and challenging them to come alongside and fight honourably.

But the English ship clearly had no intention of coming any closer, and was perfectly able to open the range when her master wished it. When she had discharged a second broadside she bore away to leeward and loosed off a couple more rounds from her stern ports before pulling quickly away and making room for the next galleon in line, which came purposefully down on the *Duquesa*, a lick of white froth under her bow, her captain standing nonchalantly on her quarterdeck with a feather in his hat and a sword at his side. But though this was a lighter-armed vessel than the first her sting was no less deadly: before the gunners on board the *Duquesa* had been able to reload, six demi-culverin had been discharged at shorter range, and one round had smashed into the forecastle.

In the pause that followed, João turned to find Fernando sitting on the deck with a surprised look on his face.

'Are you all right, dear boy?' he asked.

Fernando tried to make some reply, but was unable; and before João could get to him, he had collapsed face down, to reveal that a piece of roundshot had taken away the lower part of his spine.

But there was no time to mourn the heroic passing of his dear friend, for the Hell returned with increased fury. Surely this was Armageddon at last: every ship in every squadron was locked in the most violent combat. The smaller pieces were fired at will now, but the noise of muskets and harquebuses was nothing to the roar of the larger pieces. A pall of smoke enveloped the ship and the air became acrid and foul. Men were screaming in pain and terror. Ragged holes were appearing in the sails. The mizzen yard had been shattered, and a chip had been taken out of the foremast.

On and on it went: ship after English ship bore down, loosed off a broadside and went on her way. Each time one passed on, João implored the Blessed Virgin to make it the last, and each time another approached he experienced the same feeling of paralysing fear, until at last his poor insides gave up the unequal struggle and he fell victim to that shaming incontinence which terror sometimes causes.

The action lasted all day. On both sides and in every squadron there were accounts of the highest gallantry. Finding himself separated from the rest of the fleet, Frobisher, with the *Triumph, Centurion, Mary Rose*, and *Golden Lion*, fought off a determined attack from Hugo de Moncada's galleasses; General Bertendona of the Levantine squadron offered a close-quarters fight to the *Ark Royal* herself; the *San Marcos, San Luis, San Mateo*, the *Rata Encoronada, San Felipe* and *San Juan de Sicilia* all acquitted themselves in the highest traditions of Spanish honour and chivalry. William Coxe, captain of the pinnace *Delight*, handled his ship with heroic courage when surrounded, and when some of the Spanish fleet attempted to regain their lost weather-gauge at the end of the day's fighting, Mr Edward Bancks went after them in his two-hundred-ton bark *Mayflower* and fought them back.

Afterwards, veterans of Lepanto declared that the violence of the battle off Portland Bill had far exceeded that of the Spanish battle with the Turk seventeen years before.

'I'm shamed,' Matt Pascoe said that night when they supped together in the cabin. 'And you know why, Father.'

Harry swilled down the last of his ale and grimaced at the foul taste of it. 'Bloody stuff's gone off!' he muttered.

'Didn't you hear what I said, Father?'

'Aye, I heard.'

'Then will you at least have the courage to deny it?'

Harry spread himself more comfortably on the bench and looked at his son in mild amusement. 'What's the matter, lad – you complaining because you haven't had your balls shot off?'

'I'm complaining because I don't like seeing my own father playing a – a – '

'Well? Let's hear it then! What've I been playing?'

They faced each other across the table, Harry's eyes narrowed against the lamplight, the timbers creaking rhythmically as the *Russell* ran up on Channel before the south-westerly.

'All right – I'll say it. Playing the coward.'

'If you weren't my son I'd fight you for that.'

'If I weren't your son, Father, I wouldn't have said it.'

'So. Think I'm a coward, do you. Well – I can't say I set great store by what you think.'

'It's not what I *think*, Father, it's what I know.' Matthew shook his finger: 'The only damage we've sustained in this ship – mark this – the only damage done to us this day has been a parted mizzen brace, and that was more likely from an English piece than a Spanish. There's not a scratch on any one of our company, not a timber splintered nor a canvas holed. Fact – as far as I can make out, the only ill we've suffered on board this bark since sailing out of the Fowey is stomach ache. Stomach ache! Is that what we'll be telling our folks about when we get back to Polruan pool? "Oh wife, dear, the ale was off and the noise of the guns something terrible!" I tell you Father, I'm ashamed, and I'm not the only one. There was moments this day when I seen Davy and Nick and even that papist Roscarrock look at you with disgust writ clear on their faces. And the men aren't fools, neither. Do you think they can't see that you're holding off at twice the range of every other bark in the line?'

Harry snorted contemptuously. 'That's only because I've got a mite more sense than they, lad. No – truth is, there was a lot of sound and fury for nothing today. Have we sunk any of their ships? No, sir, we have not. Have we driven them back to Spain? No, sir. Have we stopped their passage east? No again, sir.' He leant back and passed a hand across his stomach. 'You're not the master of this ship yet, Matt, but when you are – and it won't be all that many years from now – you'll thank me for keeping her in one piece for 'ee. And if preserving my ship and crew from injury without disobeying the Lord Admiral's orders puts any man out of countenance, then he'll just have to bear it, for while I'm captain of the *Russell* I'll fight and sail my ship my way, Master Matthew, and you can save your breath to blow on your broth.'

Matthew Pascoe stood up and put his hand on the deckhead beam to steady himself. He looked down on his father's thinning white hair, and experienced a sudden whiplash of anger and frustration.

'All right, I'll tell you something, Father,' he said quietly, 'something I never told you afore now. It may come as a surprise to you to hear that – that I always looked up to you, right from my first years. I was proud of you because you were a sea captain and you weren't afraid of no one. I wanted to be like you, Father – to go to sea in my own ship, and fight for England like a good Christian. And when the time came a month or so back for us to stand up and be counted and I seen you counting pennies and cutting your nose off to spite your face, well, it sickened me, and I said so, as you will recall. But I paid out a bight of slack for you, and when you put about and allowed that we must refit the *Russell* and take her to war, well, I thought maybe I'd misjudged you. But today you proved me wrong. Fact of the matter is, you were scared, Father. You were scared of getting a lump of shot in your guts, and you thought if you stayed out of range no one'd notice. But they *did* notice, and if I ever see a chance to redeem the good name of Pascoe – and of the bark *Russell* and the village of Polruan – I'm going to make sure we take it, Father, whether you like 'un or not.'

That said, Matthew went quickly out of the cabin and onto the deck; and for a long time he remained abaft the mizzen, his heart full of anguish at offering such a rebuke to his father, whom he wished above all to respect and obey.

WEDNESDAY 3 AUGUST

The wind was light again, and by dawn the two fleets were drifting slowly on towards the Needles, whose sharp white rocks stand out from the westernmost tip of the Isle of Wight, guarding the western entrance to the Solent.

After the battle off Portland Bill the Lord Admiral had sent pinnaces ahead to Portsmouth with urgent requests for replenishments of munitions and beer, and now, with the early August sun blazing down on a calm sea, the whole wide stretch of the Solent was dotted with sails as hundreds of little ships came out to offer their services to Drake.

It was to Drake that they looked for leadership: though Lord Howard had been appointed in overall command of the Queen's Navy, it was Francis Drake's genius for tactical surprise and resolution in the cannon's mouth that inspired others to follow where he led. That the Spanish fleet was now in the Channel almost every person in Europe was aware, but while it was referred to by the collective title of 'the Armada', the English fleet became personified in the name of Drake. Drake had led the English out of Plymouth against the wind; Drake had won the weather-gauge; Drake had taken the first prize, and Drake had engaged the Armada off Portland Bill in the fiercest sea engagement of all history.

But while Drake and the Royal Navy seemed to be working miracles at sea, the army was not inspiring a quarter as much confidence. The men of Essex were taking an age to march down to Tilbury; the battalion of Londoners detailed off to reinforce the estuary defences had not assembled; a desperate shortage of funds, munitions, victuals and beer was inciting many to talk of mutiny, and the near-certainty of being on the losing side if the Spanish landed was hardly encouraging the men of

Sandwich, Canterbury, Faversham and Rochester to rush headlong to the flag.

In Kent especially, where invasion was most likely, a strange mixture of optimism and pessimism prevailed: provided Drake kept the Armada from our shores, people said, all would be well. If he failed, the consequences did not bear thinking about. Though the seaward defences had been improved and a vast system of warning beacons had been set up, the inland forts were largely ill-prepared, the defensive ditches were silted up and the officers in command – including the Earl of Leicester – were regarded by many as a crowd of fawning toadies, more concerned with winning the approval of their political superiors than with the defence of the realm.

Most thinking people knew these things, and their knowledge percolated right down to the humblest ostler and milkmaid. Similarly, everyone knew that once Parma reached London the Queen would be unthroned and some continental papist put in her place. Every person over forty could recall the bad old days of Mary Tudor, of torturings and burnings, of compulsory religion, foreign priests, Latin Masses and the unbending authority of Rome. Who wanted all that back? Who wanted their smells and their bells, their hobbledy-gobbledy, their inquisitions and their autos-da-fé?

Everything depended on the Navy. If the Navy lost, England was lost. It was as simple as that.

Drake had led an assault on some of the rearguard stragglers that morning, and for two hours a fierce exchange between the *Revenge* and the flagship of the urca squadron had taken place; but soon after midday the wind died right away, and the two fleets lay becalmed.

That afternoon Lord Howard, who had been impressed by the tight discipline of the Spanish fleet, decided that it was time to bring more order to his own, and accordingly the fleet was split into four squadrons headed by himself, Drake, Frobisher and John Hawkins.

When the council of war was over, pinnaces took the new order of battle to each English galleon and bark, and six merchant ships in each squadron were told off to set upon the Armada in the night to keep the Spaniards awake.

The *Russell* had been placed with Hawkins's squadron, and was one of the ships detailed. At the evening quarters muster Matthew Pascoe called the whole ship's company together and persuaded his father to talk to them and cheer them up before the battle; but as the flat calm persisted through the night, the plan had to be abandoned, and the *Russell* remained unblooded.

OFF THE ISLE OF WIGHT, THURSDAY 4 AUGUST

João was awakened by the sound of running feet and shouted orders on the deck above his cabin.

He listened to the now-familiar sounds of the ship's company being called to quarters. He heard the low rumble of eighteen-pound roundshot being rolled along the deck, the muffled commands from ensigns and corporals, and a few minutes later the boom of gunfire.

Padre Jorge had risen from his knees and crossed to where João lay curled up. 'Come João,' he said gently, and beckoned to the Count to get out of his cot.

João was bathed in sweat. 'I can't, Father! I can't go up there again with those guns going off. Say I am sick, say I've lost my mind – tell them anything, Father, but don't make me go up there again. Please don't make me go up there again. . . .'

Padre Jorge spoke to him as to a little boy. 'Listen child, what would your Maezinha say if she could see you now? Think – today may bring us victory at last. Don't you wish to share in that victory? Don't you wish to be a part of God's plan to win England back for our Blessed Lady?'

João turned away from him, sobbing. 'I shall be killed! I know I shall be killed! I've had a premonition that I shall never see Portugal again!'

'You are not alone in such thoughts,' Padre Jorge insisted. 'I have heard the confessions of every man aboard this ship, and there are few who have not had the same forebodings. It is every man's duty to overcome such fears, João. And it is your duty as a nobleman to set an example of courage – to go fearlessly into battle just as Our Lord set his face fearlessly towards Jerusalem. And besides,' he added a little less sympathetically, 'the horrors of battle will be as nothing to the fires of Hell which await those who give in to cowardice.' He took João by the hand. 'Come,' he said.

João sat up in his cot and made an effort to compose himself. He pulled on his hose and his undershirt, crossed himself and stood while his servants helped him with his armour. Then, gripping his hands together to stop them shaking, he went up to the quarterdeck – quite unaware that in overcoming his fear in this way he was at last learning the meaning of courage.

The *Duquesa Santa Ana* and the *San Luis de Portugal* had been caught straggling, and a skirmish had broken out. But this was a different sort of fighting: there was not a breath of wind, and in order to get to within range, ships of the Hawkins squadron, led by the *Victory*, were being towed by their longboats in order to isolate the two lame ducks from the main body.

The galleasses came into their own now: the *Patrona* had taken the great *Rata Encoronada* in tow in order to bring her added firepower in support of the endangered ships, and the *San Lorenzo* and *Girona*, in line abreast, were racing to the rescue, their great banks of oars rising and falling like the wings of monstrous birds, their sharp bows carving two neat wakes, whose smooth waves spread out in a widening W as they cut along over the glassy sea.

The skirmish developed into a battle. As the two fleets floated slowly eastwards past Dunnose on the Isle of Wight, the *Ark* and the *Golden Lion* came up, towed by half a dozen boats each, and the cannonades clapped and boomed against the cliffs a mile or so to the north. The *Girona* and the *San Lorenzo* took the *Duquesa* and the *San Luis* in tow, and the six Armada ships withdrew into the protective main body of the fleet.

At the same time a light breeze sprang up from the south-west, and a more general action developed. Frobisher's squadron, which was again close inshore, had been swept eastward by the stronger tides, and seeing an opportunity to cut him off, the Duke of Medina Sidonia took the *San Martin* and a few ships of his vanguard to engage him, while the remainder of the Armada kept Drake, Hawkins and Howard busy further out to sea.

For the second time in four days it looked as though the *Triumph* was cornered, and desperate measures were taken to save her. All boats were lowered and lines passed to tow her upwind; and seeing her predicament, the Lord Admiral sent more launches under oars to assist, and a couple of galleons to attack the Spanish flagship on the flank and draw him off.

Watching this complicated engagement develop from the poop of the *San Martin*, the Duke prayed fervently that the English might at last be lured into close quarters. They were east of the Isle of Wight now: he could see, under the bulge of the mainsail, the entrance to Portsmouth harbour and the stretch of water known as Spithead, which was dotted with sails as what looked like a regatta of small craft came out to watch the battle or offer assistance.

The *San Martin* was now in hot pursuit of the *Triumph*, and barely a cable's splice on the starboard beam Recalde in the *San Juan* had joined in the chase, in company with one of his zabras. Standing with the Duke on the poop deck, Don Diego, Francisco de Bobadilla and Baltasar de Zuniga watched with growing satisfaction as the *San Martin* gained on the *Triumph* and the chance of a decisive encounter with the English flagship became more of a certainty.

The grappling spars were ready; the cannon fully charged; the men at immediate readiness to board. At last, at last, the English were going to be forced to fight in the way they should always have fought: in the honourable Spanish way at a hand-stroke rather than at the cowardly long distance so far dictated by their culverins.

The Duke turned to Don Diego. 'I believe we have him, General. I do believe we have him!'

The other nodded his agreement, and the Duke was suddenly aware that his own optimism had made itself felt throughout the ship – that for the first time every man on board saw victory within his grasp.

A sharp report made him turn: Recalde's zabra had fired a light piece to attract the attention of the flagship, and was coming close under the stern. As he watched, a figure in the sternsheets cupped his hands and shouted urgently up: 'My Lord! Cast about! We're in shoal water! We shall all be aground!'

He turned quickly to his navigator and saw horror in the man's eyes. In the excitement of the chase and the noise and smoke of battle, all thoughts of natural hazards had been forgotten, and one glance at the wide stretch of discoloured water ahead seemed to confirm the warning.

'Signal gun!' he ordered without even bothering to consult his staff. 'Fleet cast about! Come to south-south-east!'

Three men pushed the staff hard over, and the yards were braced to larboard as the *San Martin*'s head came round onto the new course; and at the same time, every other ship in the fleet followed the senior officer's motions, and the engagement was broken off.

Medina Sidonia beckoned to his flag lieutenant.

'Baltasar. Take dictation. To General Juan Martinez de Recalde: I wish to convey my thanks to you for your warning of danger.' The Duke paused, combing his beard with his fingers, the strain and fatigue showing in his expression. 'There can be no doubt,' he continued, 'but that your prompt and timely warning averted the grounding of many ships, and the person responsible for calling attention to the hazard is to be commended for his alertness.'

Soon afterwards the Duke's pinnace bore up alongside the *San Juan de Portugal* and Baltasar went aboard.

Martinez de Recalde received him on the poop. Baltasar bowed and handed over the commendation. 'The Captain General has asked me to discover the name of the pilot concerned,' he told Recalde.

Recalde – a tall, weatherbeaten veteran, thought by many to be the finest seafarer alive – glanced at the letter, his eyes narrowed under bushy brows, his legs braced against the gentle pitch and roll of his ship; and when he had read it, he sent for one of his pilots. A minute later a dark-haired lieutenant in his late twenties came up from the chartroom.

'There you are, Pilot!' he said, handing the commendation over. 'A pat on the back from the Captain General!'

Tristram read the letter with a dead-pan expression that concealed inner delight: although the *San Martin* had been approaching the Owers bank and the water had been shallower, the tide was flooding, and the Armada could have stood on for another three miles without any hazard of grounding.

'It was nothing more than my duty, sir,' he replied solemnly, and handing the letter back with a bow, he returned to his chartroom.

Recalde shook his head and turned to Baltasar with a shrug and a smile. '*Inglés típico!*' he remarked.

FRIDAY 5 AUGUST

The *Little Hare*, one of Lord Henry Seymour's flyboats, dropped anchor off Greenwich soon after seven, and within minutes of the arrival a skiff was crabbing across the tide to William Wray's landing stage.

'I take it you haven't breakfasted?' Wray asked when he had welcomed his guest.

Marlowe had eaten little and slept less on the Channel crossing and was ravenously hungry. He glanced at the set table and savoured the smells that were wafting in from the back kitchen. 'I know nothing more certain to sharpen a man's appetite than a fast sea crossing and the prospect of Mrs Tripp's cooking!' he replied cheerfully, and his timing was impeccable, for a moment later Wray's buxom housekeeper entered bearing a tray loaded with all the essentials of a good English breakfast.

'So,' Wray said when they were seated and Marlowe was tucking in. 'Will they be ready to come out?'

Marlowe laughed with his mouth full – not a pretty sight – but Wray was too interested in the Duke of Parma's invasion force to take much notice of his agent's table manners.

'Ready?' Marlowe said indistinctly. 'Sir – they are as unready as a fleet can be. As unready and as unwilling also. Their barges are barely fit for the canals let alone the open sea, and their flyboats are so slow in the building that I doubt if they will have more than a half-dozen prepared. Even then, they can be picked off one by one by Justin of Nassau's nimble ships as they come out of Dunkirk. Their soldiers know very well that they will have to be packed like puddings in a basket, and consequently have little will for a fight. Parma himself seems to have lost all interest: he has been sitting in Bruges and twiddling his thumbs this past month. My own opinion is that he knows already that the Enterprise cannot succeed. Certainly he won't consider venturing forth until the Armada has full control of the Narrows.'

'And the Dutch?'

The tankard paused halfway from the table to Marlowe's lips. 'The Dutch, sir, would like nothing better than to see the whole of Parma's rotten fleet essay out of Dunkirk. I think it would take the Sea Beggars an hour, or perhaps a little less, to sink the lot of them. Indeed, Admiral Seymour's patrol off Dunkirk is a thorn in their flesh. As long as his squadron remains, they know that Parma will not come out, and until he comes out they'll be denied the chance to rid themselves of their oppressor.' Marlowe took a gulp of ale and returned to his gammon. 'And it's my opinion that Parma knows it, too. It's my opinion – not intelligence sir, only my opinion – that he's dragging his feet deliberately, preferring the probability of keeping his hold on the low countries and losing the Enterprise to the certainty of losing both.'

From under the table came a mournful groan, followed by a few gentle thumps. Barty had overheard many such private conversations before over the past ten days, and would much rather have been out with his master on Black Heath.

'What of the Navy, sir?' Marlowe ventured. 'They were saying in Nieuport that Drake has done little more than snap at their heels to date.'

'Indeed?' murmured Wray, but as it was not his policy to give his agents information they had no need to know, he made no further comment, and instead invited Marlowe – who had aspirations as a playwright – to turn his hand to drafting a speech for her Majesty to make to the Army on her proposed visit to Tilbury in a few days' time.

SATURDAY 6 AUGUST

The wind had remained fair. Bloodied but quite unbeaten, the Armada continued eastwards in tight crescent formation, pursued by the four squadrons of Lord Howard, Drake, and the newly-created knights Sir Martin Frobisher and Sir John Hawkins.

Slipping gently along between Kent and Picardy, with brightly coloured standards and pennants flying from every masthead, the Armada entered the Narrows, and on board the *San Juan*, Ensign Rodrigo entertained Tristram and Father Joaquim to his vision of the future.

'Imagine, Teniente, Padre, what an invincible force will be formed when all these ships sail under one flag! When England, France and the low countries come under our single rule and the curse of Lutheranism is ended for ever! What power will be ours! Why – with Europe united under our leadership, our strength will be greater even than that of the Roman Empire at its height! No nation will dare assail us: our rule will extend to the Americas and the Indies and every corner of the globe, so that a new era of peace will dawn for all mankind!'

A signal gun from the *capitana* interrupted him: the flagship was striking her topsails and altering a point to starboard to head towards the land, and as the *San Juan de Portugal* followed suit and the sailors ran out along the yards to reduce sail, Tristram caught his first glimpse of Calais, whose fortifications were bright in the afternoon sun.

Assisted by wind and tide, the Armada bore quickly down on Calais Cliffs, anchoring in good order on a further signal from the flagship.

One minute the great fleet was under sail and the next it was stopped, the sailors furling sails and coiling ropes and the ships swinging slowly to stem the wind and tide; while to windward the English had reacted swiftly and were also anchoring, so that the closest ships in the two fleets were separated by no more than the range of a culverin shot, and the people of Calais were presented with a front-seat view of the greatest gathering of warships since the beginning of time.

That evening, at the council of war held aboard the *San Martin*, the Duke reviewed the state of his fleet. Munitions had fallen to less than five rounds per gun; there were nearly three hundred men dead or wounded, and much of the victuals and water were going bad; but provided the Duke of Parma came out of Dunkirk promptly with his invasion barges and the wind didn't veer north-westerly, there still seemed to him to be every chance of success.

But would Parma be ready? That was the question that had nagged him for weeks, and although he had sent messengers ahead almost daily to seek confirmation from Parma that he would keep their rendezvous off the Cape of Margate, he had still received no word from him.

Soon after the council of war he had cause for further concern: Admiral Seymour's squadron of thirty-six ships – five of them large galleons – came down on the ebb tide as the sun was setting and anchored to seaward of the main English fleet. These, he knew, were fresh ships with crack seamen and gunners on board and a full quota of powder and shot.

Pacing his deck he wondered and prayed and hoped and worried, and ended up leaning with his hands on the stern-rail and staring down at the water as he had done so often before.

He shivered. In one of the nearest enemy ships, a solitary voice had started singing, and although he did not catch all the words that floated across the water, he knew enough English to understand the message they contained:

> You Spaniards all that do devise
> To hurt our Queen in treacherous wise
> And in your hearts do still surmise
>   Which way to hurt our England,
> Consider what the end will be
> Of Spaniards and of Popery:
> Hanging is still their destiny
>   That trouble the peace of England

That jeering Kentish voice seemed to personify all that was evil about the English national character. He crossed himself and bent the knee.

'Lord,' he prayed fervently, quoting Christ's words on the Cross. 'Forgive them, for they know not what they do.'

OFF CALAIS, SUNDAY 7 AUGUST

Soon after hearing Mass at dawn, the Captain General received some good news and some bad news. The good news was that Rodrigo Tello, one of the couriers he had sent ahead of the Armada, had returned from a meeting with Parma in Bruges and had managed to slip out of Dunkirk in a flyboat without being attacked by the Dutch.

'That's excellent,' he said, when Tello had been shown into the stateroom on board the *San Martin*. He turned to Don Diego. 'Don't you agree, General? It means that those Sea Beggars or whatever they call themselves don't have quite such a hold on Dunkirk as some would have us believe.'

Don Diego inclined his head cautiously. 'Let's hear the full report before we make up our minds,' he suggested.

Tello cleared his throat, loth to be the bearer of bad tidings. 'Sir,' he said, 'although the Duke asked me to convey to you his pleasure on hearing of your success in bringing the Armada thus far, I should be failing in my duty to you if I did not also tell you that – from my own observation – the army seems ill prepared for the invasion of England. I have seen the state of affairs at both Nieuport and Dunkirk, and I can only describe it as a sorry one, and as you will see in his letter, the Duke of Parma does not expect his fleet to be ready until the thirteenth of this month.'

Medina Sidonia stroked his beard and turned to Don Diego. 'The thirteenth . . . that's six days from now. Can we wait that long?'

Don Diego paced across the stateroom and back. 'We should be very foolish to try it, Captain General. The mayor here has already warned us of the dangers of this exposed anchorage, and with the wind in this quarter our fleet presents an easy target for fireships.' He stopped pacing. 'But if the army is not ready, the army is not ready, and there is little we can do about it.'

Tello was clearing his throat and blinking very fast. 'Your Grace – I feel it my duty to mention this – '

'Well?'

'The fact of the matter is, sir, that I regard the Duke of Parma's estimate as optimistic. He has not lately visited Nieuport or Dunkirk as have I, and he has not seen the true state of the barges and flyboats.'

'And what is their true state?' Don Diego snapped.

The miserable Tello shook his head. 'It is not good, sir, not good at all.'

The Duke dabbed at his nose with a handkerchief. 'So when do *you* think he will be ready?'

Here Tello's courage failed him, for although it was his judgement that the invasion fleet would not be ready in two months let alone two weeks, he suffered from a desire common among staff officers to tell his superiors what they wanted to hear.

'A fortnight, sir,' he said quickly. 'I would say a fortnight.'

After Tello had been dismissed, the Captain General and his Chief Staff Officer looked at each other.

'If the weather holds that long and we are not attacked by fireships, it will be a miracle,' Don Diego muttered.

'Then we shall protect ourselves against fireships and we shall pray for a miracle,' the Duke replied. 'Unless, General, you have an alternative proposal?'

Ship's company prayers were held on board the *Russell* that Sunday morning and soon afterwards, when Matt had read out the seafarer's psalm and the men of Polruan had joined together in the saying of the Lord's Prayer, a pinnace hailed and asked to come alongside. A few minutes later Richard Hawkins, captain of the *Swallow* and son of Sir John, was piped aboard in the bosun's chair and led aft by Davy Treffry to speak with the owner.

'Mr Pascoe?' he asked as he ducked his head on entering the cramped space of the master's cabin.

'Aye, that's me,' Pascoe answered defensively, already wondering why Hawkins had invited himself aboard.

Hawkins turned to Matthew.

'My lieutenant,' Harry said. 'And also my son.'

Matthew held out his hand. 'Pleased to have you aboard, sir.'

'I'd offer you ale,' Harry said, 'but I wouldn't recommend it if you value an easy stomach.'

'We have a tot or so of Malmsey left,' Matthew suggested, but Hawkins declined.

'I've not come to drink your wine, Mr Pascoe. I've come to make you a proposition.'

'Oh aye? And what's that?'

Hawkins glanced round at the simple wooden furnishings of the cabin. 'How old would this ship of yours be, Mr Pascoe? Thirty years?'

Pascoe sprawled down on the bench and indicated Hawkins to do likewise. 'Getting on that way, aye.'

'So you'll be thinking of rebuilding. Or buying anew.'

Harry looked at him quickly. 'Maybe. If ever we see the colour of the Queen's money after this little outing. I spent upward of a hundred pound of my own money refitting this bark, Mr Hawkins – '

'And that's why I've come to speak with you, Mr Pascoe.'

'Oh?'

There was a brief silence. Hawkins glanced at Matthew, who had remained standing at the door.

'I've come to make you an offer, Mr Pascoe. We want to buy your ship.'

Harry sat up quickly. 'You want what?'

'I'm acting for the Lord Admiral, Mr Pascoe, and he acts for the Queen. We want eight fireships to send down on the Armada, and we want them today. We've got spring tides and a fair breeze – '

'Fireships! You want to make this ship into a fireship!'

'It'll be to your advantage, Mr Pascoe. This ship of yours won't see many more seasons of service without rebuilding, and that'll cost you as much as a new ship. What is she - ninety ton?'

'Hundred and twenty,' Harry lied. 'But if you think – '

'Hundred and twenty ton at three pounds a ton comes out at three hundred and sixty pounds for the whole ship including masts, sails and furniture. Say four-fifty by the time you've added in your anchors and cables and your pieces. You'll get a neat ship for that price, Mr Pascoe – especially down in Fowey.'

'Polruan,' Harry corrected.

'Polruan, then. And what's more, you'll have the satisfaction of knowing that your ship has served in a way few others can. We need two from each squadron. And not pinnaces, either. Mr Meldrum's volunteered his ship the *Elizabeth*, my own father's giving the bark *Bond* and Sir Francis himself is giving the *Thomas*.'

'It's my life, this ship,' Harry muttered. 'That's what you're asking, Mr Hawkins. Not my ship. My life.'

'We'll build another,' Matthew said quietly.

'We?' muttered Harry, and laughed bitterly. 'We?'

'I will, then.'

Pascoe shook his head in bewilderment and Hawkins, seeing the agony

358

this Cornish shipmaster was undergoing, could not help feeling sorry for him.

'I can't do it,' Harry muttered eventually. 'I can't see my ship burned, not for anyone.'

'No one denies it's a hard choice – ' Hawkins began, but Pascoe interrupted him.

'I've told you, Hawkins – I won't do it. That's my last word.'

The other's manner became suddenly less sympathetic. 'I hope for your sake it isn't, Mr Pascoe. Your ship hasn't been much noticed in the fight so far, and if you refuse to make her available now when she's needed, I doubt if the Queen's treasurers are like to look with favour on any claims you may make for reimbursement. You say you've spent a hundred already on her, and there's your crew to pay on top of that. Think on this, Mr Pascoe: if you refuse to put your ship at the Lord Admiral's disposal, do you suppose you'll ever see another penny of the Queen's money? I think not. In which case, you might as well cut your losses – up anchor this minute and slip off home to Polruan, for as I see it, your services will be no longer required.'

This announcement brought about a long silence from Harry, during which he glanced from his son to Hawkins and back to his son, biting his lip with teeth blackened from tobacco, and absently worrying at the strands of a rope's end with salt-hardened fingers.

The silence ended with a long sigh. 'All right – tell you what I'll do.' He turned to his son. 'I'll make you a present of her, Matt. This ship's yours – I give her to you, and Mr Hawkins here's my witness. She's yours to do with as you please – '

'Father – '

'No, Matt. I haven't struggled these past thirty years to make a bonfire of my life's work. You're the owner and master of the *Russell* now, and if any man asks what happened to my ship, let 'un be told that I gave her to my son.'

Again, there was a long silence, and now it was Matthew who struggled to decide. For some time he had known that his father was thinking of handing over command of the *Russell* to him, and the prospect of skippering his own ship had long been the brightest light on his horizon. He had spent many an hour in the night watches thinking of how he would run a taut ship and mould a company of men into a loyal and willing crew.

But what Hawkins had said was true: the ship would have to be rebuilt within a few years, and without compensation for the expense of this adventure he would be unable to afford the work. The *Russell* would be careened for the last time; the repairs would be beyond him, and she would be left to rot and split open like a sheep's carcass on Polruan Strand.

'What about the ship's company?' he asked Hawkins at last. 'Will they be paid and given a passage home?'

Hawkins immediately resumed his congenial manner. 'Of course. We can ship you and every last soul on board to the Medway ports today, if that's your wish, Mr Pascoe.'

'No,' Matt said quietly. 'I want to see this business out. If our ship's to be burned, we'll burn her ourselves. Isn't that right, Father?'

But Harry's head was down in his hands and he was unable to make any reply.

'There's a lot to be done, Davy, and little time to do it,' Matthew told his bosun as soon as Hawkins had departed and Treffry had learnt what had passed in the after cabin. 'I want half a dozen hands to remain on board and turn this vessel into a hellburner. The rest must be transferred to the other west-country barks, to take passage home when this business is over. And if any man hasn't the stomach for the fight, he can be landed in the Medway – there's plenty of ships plying back and forth. In the meantime, we've to double-shot all guns, tar all masts and standing rigging, fix firefenders at bow and stern to give the grapplers a hard time, and re-stow the powder barrels in the forepeak.'

Treffrey nodded. 'What about victuals? Can we save them?'

'As much as we can, aye, but don't make too much noise about that, for I'll be claiming every last biscuit and candle off the Queen in due course, as you can imagine.'

'When do we sail?'

'Midnight or soon after. When tide's at full flood.'

'What – we put all sails in slipping ties and ride from a stern anchor, I suppose – '

'Aye, and lash the whipstaff before we take to the longboat. Old John Young, skipper of the *Bear*, will put us right on the way of it.' He met Treffry's eye. 'Are you with me, Davy?'

Treffry glanced up at the mainmast. 'Aye, I'm with you, Matt.' He chuckled sadly. 'She's been a right old heretic in her time has the *Russell*, so I reckon she'll burn hot.'

Now it was nearly midnight: the flood tide was gurgling past the ship's side, and the old bark was swinging gently to a stern anchor, her bows pointing at the Spanish fleet less than a mile to leeward.

For Matthew the day had passed quicker than any he had known. While the preparations had gone ahead aboard the *Russell* and those with scurvy or ship-fever had been transferred to vessels due to sail back to Chatham that evening, the majority of the crew had been put aboard the *Frances of Fowey* and the *William of Plymouth*, and Harry Pascoe had been invited aboard the *Victory*, as a mark of gratitude from Admiral Hawkins for giving his ship to be burned.

Matthew, Davy Treffry, Nick Polwhele and three other Polruan men had stayed on board the *Russell*, and now all that remained was to wait for the signal from the *Revenge*.

Matthew had manned the whipstaff. Davy and the others stood by the fore and main masts with the tails of the slipping ties in hand. One man stood right aft, ready to slip the cable. The wind, freshening now, was whistling softly in the shrouds and rattling the halyards against the masts.

'All ready for'd?' Matt called.

'Ready,' Treffry called back, and Nick, who was up by the foremast, echoed, 'Aye – ready!'

More minutes passed, and the *Russell*, as if growing suspicious of what was to be done to her, rolled and yawed uneasily in the spring flood.

'There she goes!' Treffry called.

Matthew looked in the direction of the *Revenge* and saw the two red lanterns.

'Slip the ties!'

Down in the waist the men yanked hard on the slipping ties, and the sails clapped out and filled immediately, tugging the ship forward against the stern anchor.

'Stand by aft!'

'Standing by!'

'Slip!'

'All gone aft! All clear aft!'

The ship was instantly alive: the sails were straining out ahead and the water was swishing under the forefoot, and Matthew – in command of his own ship for the first time in his life – was gripped by a sudden anguish at the sacrifice he and his father had been forced to make and the cause in which they made it.

But there was no time for such reflections now: the seven other fireships were coming out from the fleet and forming up in line abreast, and minutes later he saw the first flames flickering aboard the *Thomas*.

'Right lads! Light the matches!'

The trails of gunpowder flared to the bonfires between decks. Treffry came aft: together, he and Matthew lashed the whipstaff to keep the *Russell* steady on her last course. Flames were already breaking out of the forehatch and making an eerie glow upon the sails.

Matthew was last into the longboat. Every man took an oar: they rowed in silence, staring back at the line of burning ships. The boat jerked forward and the sweeps groaned against the thole pins. They were into wind and tide. It was a long way back to the *Victory*.

OFF GRAVELINES, MONDAY 8 AUGUST

'Hellburners!' The word that had been whispered all day was suddenly spoken aloud. Those floating torches coming down on wind and tide were full-sized barks, not twenty-ton pinnaces, and a terrible value of gunpowder could be contained in such ships – enough to equal the damage done by Giambelli's famous device in Antwerp, which had killed eight hundred men with a single explosion only three years before.

But the ships of the Armada were not caught unprepared. While rumours had spread through France that England was already subdued and Elizabeth overthrown, and while the merchants of Calais sold eggs to the Spanish provisioners at twenty-five times the normal price, the Duke of Medina Sidonia had taken his precautions. A screen of eight pataches had been placed at immediate readiness with orders to grapple and tow fireships, and instructions had been issued to every ship in the fleet on actions to be taken in the event of attack.

Above all, it had been impressed upon commanding officers that they must not panic. The patrolling screen under Captain Serrano would likely deal with every last fireship. If one slipped through, ships' boats should be used to ward it off. And if all else failed – but only in the last resort – ship captains were authorized to buoy and slip cables and hold off, returning to the anchorage as soon as the danger was past.

But these were hellburners, not mere fireships, and although the pataches had managed to grapple the two wing ships, the remaining six continued on course for the Armada, and as the fires reached the powder stores and double-shotted guns, a series of explosions sent gouts of flame and showers of sparks high into the sky, illuminating the dark lines of ships in both fleets and sending a thrill of terror through every spectator, whether afloat or ashore.

On board the *San Martin* the Duke of Medina Sidonia stood among his staff officers and hesitated. All through Sunday he had been careful to play down the threat of fireships and play up the prospect of an early victory. Ordered by the King of Spain to command the Armada, bring it to the Narrows and make rendezvous with the Duke of Parma, he had already achieved an astounding success. Were eight fireships to wreck all that?

'There is no cause for alarm,' he declared to the nobles and generals who hedged him about. 'All ships must hold their position unless directly endangered – '

Another magnificent explosion (it was the *Russell's* powder store) illuminated the sky. At the Duke's elbow Don Diego spoke urgently. 'Your Grace, I must advise you – this may be the first squadron of many. You saw their ships arriving today. If we allow them among us, we shall be powerless to protect ourselves when they send down the true hellburners!'

The Duke looked about him at the white faces of his advisers, marvelling that these war veterans should be so much more afraid than he, the country bumpkin.

'Are you saying we must haul clear?'

'It's imperative, sir. In good order, while we have time.'

The Duke sighed inwardly. He really could not afford to ignore his Chief of Staff's counsel. 'Make the signal then. Fleet to make sail in good order. All ships are to buoy their cables and return to this anchorage as soon as the fireships are clear.'

The signal gun barked, and at once the Armada was alive with shouted commands, trumpet calls and the thunder and crack of canvas as topsails were set and galleons, galleasses and urcas slipped – or cut – their cables and got under way.

Mercifully there was a fresh wind, and within the hour the *San Martin* was able to make up against the east-going tide and return to the anchorage. She was accompanied by her most faithful companions: Recalde's *San Juan*, the *San Mateo* and the *San Marcos*; but as the sheet anchors went down and these and a few other ships obeyed the original instructions issued by the Captain General it was already becoming grimly apparent that although no single fireship had found a target, the terror they had caused had wrecked the tight discipline of the Armada.

Within the space of a few hours it had been turned from an invincible fleet united under the Christian banner into a rabble dispersed over a wide area, each ship acting for herself in the belief that the Devil – Drake – would take the hindmost.

The English fleet got under way at first light, and those ships of the Spanish Armada which had re-anchored weighed soon after. The fight began when the *Revenge* closed the Duke of Medina Sidonia's flagship, the *San Martin*, which was thereafter kept under almost continual attack for nine hours. The *San Felipe* was surrounded by seventeen English ships which pummelled her with heavy fire from all sides, smashing her rudder, bringing the foremast down and killing hundreds. With heavy rain squalls sweeping in from the west, the *San Mateo* went to the *San Felipe*'s assistance, and was severely punished by the English guns as a result. Inshore, Hugo de Moncada's galleass the *San Lorenzo*, having lost her rudder in a collision during the night, had driven aground on the sandbanks below the Calais fortifications and was the victim of repeated attacks from the *Ark Royal*'s pinnaces under the command of Amyas Preston, who was badly wounded. The auxiliary urca *San Salvador* was engaged by two English flagships and her poop exposed to enemy fire for four hours until, holed at the waterline and leaking badly, she was rescued by the *Rata Encoronada*.

Dozens of other galleons were pummelled by the English guns and sent limping away downwind towards the Zeeland Banks.

Alonso de Leyva, Miguel de Oquendo and Juan Martinez de Recalde fought with outstanding gallantry, as did the major galleons of the Castillian and Portuguese squadrons, all of which paid for their bravery with huge losses of men and appalling damage to their ships.

They fought until the shot ran out, and then they went on fighting. They fought with harquebus and musket and longbow. They fought no longer for Spain or Christendom, but for their lives. They fought for the hope of seeing loved ones again, for the spring flowers of Castille, for the orange groves of Andalusia. They fought for shady courtyards, blue-tiled arches, the scent of herbs, the promise of kisses. They fought for bread and wine on the table, the laughter of children, the love of wives, the honour of families.

The wind shrieked and whistled in the stays. The ships heeled sharply over, spray whipping back in white sheets over decks that ran with blood.

It was the hardest battle of them all, and the one that later caused the most bitter recrimination among the English admirals. Howard was later accused of wasting his time and his men in the futile attempt to take the stranded *San Lorenzo*; Frobisher of allowing himself to be delayed by the *San Martin* and her companions instead of going after the bulk of the fleet downwind, and Drake – as ever – of thinking only of Drake and prizes and chasing after treasure ships.

As the day wore on and ship after ship ran out of roundshot, the reality dawned: the Invincible Armada was invincible no longer, but no more than a scattered fleet of wrecks, their hulls holed and leaking, their generals and camp-masters, nobles and hidalgos grey-faced and hollow-eyed with physical exhaustion and the stark knowledge of defeat.

And right at the end of that terrible day, when Recalde had ordered his last broadside and the English culverins were falling silent for want of shot, one more English galleon bore down upon Recalde's *San Juan de Portugal*.

Every man on board who was still able to lift a sword or hold a musket had been pressed into service now. Corpses hung from the shrouds and rolled about the deck. The bonaventure mizzen was down; the starboard bulwarks were stove in, several guns were dismounted and the exhausted mariners at the pumps were barely able to keep the flooding in check.

On came the English galleon, her sails hardly holed, her guns run out of their ports, her striped English standards stiff as boards in the north-westerly; and as she came, Recalde, who had not once moved from his place on the poop that day, issued his orders to his company commanders.

'Hold fire! Hold fire until at point blank!'

Suddenly the two ships were at close quarters, the galleon luffing and brailing her topsails, a west-countryman bellowing up to the *San Juan*'s poop which towered over the English quarterdeck.

'Well fought, Admiral!' he shouted. 'We salute you as good soldiers! Strike your colours and we'll offer you safe passage and fair terms!'

'What does he say Inglés?' barked Recalde, and Tristram, whose hand was on the trigger of a cocked harquebus, shouted that the Englishman was offering terms.

The translation brought forth a strong reaction from all on board the *San Juan*, and the leader of the chorus was the Irishman Thomas Bitus, who was standing in the maintop with a musket, and who gave forth a stream of the vilest abuse.

'Bloody Protestant cowards! Bloody dung-eating English heretics! Bloody Lutheran hens, the lot of ye!'

It was the last insult that tried the English patience too far, and a single musket shot brought the Irishman tumbling out of the top, to fall headfirst to the deck with a terrible smack of bone and brains.

Recalde's order to fire was lost in the cannonade of minions, falconets, muskets and harquebuses; and Tristram, who had become acquainted with Bitus and had liked him for his roguish humour and vast repertoire of Irish songs, fired with the rest, at random on the English quarterdeck.

Immediately the English cannon roared at point-blank range, and a dozen greatshot smashed into the ship's side and whizzed between the masts.

Seconds later, as the galleon bore away close under the stern of the *San Juan*, Tristram was able to look directly down on her aftercastle.

Writhing in agony on the deck was a giant of a man, white-haired and red-faced, whom he recognized instantly. Nor could there be any doubting that man's identity, for all the unexplained circumstances that had led to his being there; and though Tristram could not be sure that it had been his ball that had felled him, he knew that he shared the responsibility for bringing him down.

He sank to his knees at the splintered stern-rail, and as the *Victory* opened out on the quarter, Admiral Hawkins and his officers heard a single, terrible cry of 'Father. . .!' borne down to them on the wind.

PART IV

CONSUMMATIONS

Let Tyrants Fear

Harry Pascoe was shouting as loudly as any when Matt, Davy and Nick brought him down the ladder. Under the surgeon's direction they strapped him down to the table and gave him a tot of aquavitae to numb his senses before cutting away his lower garments, which were soaked in blood.

Matthew forced himself to look upon the wound. Close to the groin, his father's white and ginger hairs were matted with blood, and a terrible hole was oozing fluid.

The surgeon – Mr Edgecombe – was a small, neat man in a large, bloody apron. He had been setting bones, sewing wounds and amputating limbs all day, and seemed quite unmoved by the groans and cries of the men who lay all about him, humming to himself as he went about his work as if he were potting seedlings rather than mending bodies.

He rummaged about among a jumble of saws, trepans, scalpels and forceps, eventually choosing a pair of long, flat-nosed pliers, which he snapped open and shut a few times. 'Was not the good King Solomon,' he sang under his breath, 'ravished in sundry wise. . .' and without further ado he plunged the instrument confidently into Harry's thigh.

Pascoe bucked against the straps and let out a roar of agony. Nick Polwhele turned away and was sick.

The surgeon probed remorselessly deeper. 'With every lively paragon,' he intoned, 'That glistered 'fore his eyes. . . Ha! Here we are!' He drew out a bloody ball the size of a small chestnut and tossed it across to Matthew. 'A keepsake for you,' he said, and bent to rinse his forceps in a bucket of sea water under the table. Then, having poured a mixture of wine and oil into the wound – which brought forth another pitiful cry from his patient – he rummaged again among his instruments, humming to himself as he threaded catgut into a curved needle.

'Hold still, old man,' he murmured, putting in the first stitch and drawing the skin across the hole; and while Harry grunted and writhed against the straps he continued with snatches of a popular song while he sewed up the wound.

'There you are, good as new!' he declared after a few minutes' work, and while his assistant gave the patient a good sluice down with seawater, Surgeon Edgecombe flexed his shoulders and looked about him at the crowd of torn and broken bodies that awaited his attention. 'Who's next, then? Come along, Bosun, don't be shy!'

The north-westerly gale had freshened further overnight, and by dawn the Armada was close hauled on the port tack with the Zeeland Banks to leeward under the starboard bow and the English little more than half a league to windward on the port beam.

Strung out across a cold, grey horizon, the tattered fleet was in a desperate state. Masts were broken; banners were blown to shreds, and tangles of spars and rigging trailed in the water. Sails, shot through and torn, thundered and flapped like birds dying in traps.

As in most other ships, the *Duquesa Santa Ana* had a leadsman taking soundings now, and every man aboard who was not delirious or dying could hear his mournful cries and knew that the ship was running into shoal water.

'And a half, seven. . .! And a half, seven. . .!'

On the poop Padre Jorge made the sign of the Cross over the kneeling members of the afterguard, who had come to receive a last blessing before the ship foundered.

'*In nomine Patris et Filii et Spiritus Sancti.* . . .'

'And a quarter, seven. . .! And a quarter, seven. . .!'

'*Confiteor Deo omnipotenti,*' began Padre Jorge, and immediately the nobles and gentlemen joined in, their voices being snatched away on the wind: '*beatae Mariae semper Virgini, beato Michaeli Archangelo.* . . .'

The *Duquesa* plunged slowly on, foam hissing and surging at her sides, the forecourse thundering and flapping from its broken yard.

Kneeling in his nightshirt, João spoke the words of the public confession with a desperate fervour, for the death he had always feared was now staring him in the face. Soon the ship would shudder to a stop on the sandbanks and they would be at the mercy of the white-crested breakers.

'. . .*omnibus Sanctis, et tibi Pater: quia peccavi nimis cogitatione, verbo et opere: mea culpa, mea culpa, mea maxima culpa.* . . .'

My fault, my fault, my most grievous fault. . . . Those words which he had spoken a thousand times before took on a new meaning now. Looking out over the unending procession of green-grey waves, João began to see how much time he had wasted, how many opportunities had been missed, what chances of happiness had been thrown away into the ever-running tide of time.

'By the mark, seven. . .! By the mark, seven. . .!'

'Therefore I beseech the Blessed Mary, ever a Virgin, blessed Michael the Archangel, blessed John the Baptist, the holy Apostles Peter and Paul, all the Saints, and you, Father, to pray to the Lord our God for me. . . .'

'A quarter less, seven! A quarter less, seven. . .!'

João bowed his head and began to weep – for himself, for poor Fernando, for his sweet Maezinha, for his dear sisters and even for his estranged Irish wife, the wife whose graceful serenity had placed him under a shadow of unease from the very moment of her first arrival.

He took the Madonna she had given him and signed himself with it. Not for the first time he remembered the strange circumstances in which it had been found and saw again the face of the starving vagabond he and Fernando had stumbled upon in the dunes above the shore.

That vagabond . . . he could see him now. Why was it that the very memory of his face was in some strange way familiar? For a brief instant, he recalled the dark blue eyes staring defiantly back at him, and the way Sara had intervened at his flogging.

'Deep . . . six!' chanted the leadsman. Six fathoms. They must strike bottom at any moment.

'Holy Mother,' João prayed, holding the effigy up before him. 'You saved me from going to Morocco with Sebastian, now save me, I beseech you, from drowning!'

'*Misereatur vestri omnipotens Deus*. . .' Padre Jorge continued. 'May Almighty God be merciful to you, and forgiving you your sins bring you to everlasting life. . . .'

The absolution complete, Padre Jorge prepared to distribute the Holy Sacrament from a silver goblet, and the noblemen stood in line to kneel before him in turn and receive the Body of Christ. But just as he was about to place a wafer in the mouth of the first communicant, the man at the whipstaff gave an excited shout.

'Wind's backing, sir! Wind's backing!'

The effect upon all who heard that shout was the same. Everyone – from the noblemen on the poop to the swabbers on the forecastle – stopped, and stared, and wondered.

In the space of a few seconds the wind had backed a full point to west-south-west, and every ship in the Armada was altering to the north. The Zeeland sandbanks were no longer on the bow but on the quarter.

'And a half, seven! Deep, eight. . .!'

Pressing the Santarém Madonna to his lips, João fell to his knees, and all on the aftercastle of the *Duquesa* followed suit.

'By the mark, *ten!*' cried the leadsman, his voice breaking in relief.

It was a miracle, there was no other word for it. Suddenly – in every ship of the Armada – the men were weeping and cheering and giving thanks to God for staying His hand against them.

The westerly wind held, and the Armada continued north all day. That evening a council of war was convened aboard the *San Martin*, and when his admirals and generals had assembled in the great cabin the Duke reviewed the state of the fleet.

In the previous forty-eight hours four major ships had been sunk and dozens of smaller ships were missing. There was no single galleon without major damage. All but a few rounds of shot were expended. The water supply was running short, and much of it was foul. Many of the hulls were all but waterlogged. Hugo de Moncada was dead, and Recalde had collapsed from exhaustion. Most ships had left their bower anchors on the seabed off Calais.

'But the most pressing question with which we are faced,' the Duke told his listeners, 'is whether or not we should attempt a return to the Narrows to keep our rendezvous with the Duke of Parma.'

Don Diego gave his opinion in his usual forthright way. 'Sir,' he began, 'we have already been granted the clearest possible sign from Almighty God that our ships are to be preserved, for without the miraculous change in the wind this morning we should all have been wrecked by now upon the Zeeland Banks. It is equally clear that for the present it is not His will that we should attempt to turn about in order to re-enter the Narrows, for to do so would mean standing back towards the sandbanks from which we were so providentially delivered. Equally, with the wind in the present quarter, it is impossible for us to close the coast of England and attempt a landing. We are therefore bound to continue northwards until the wind permits a more useful course.'

The Duke looked to the others, most of whom were nodding their agreement. 'And . . . if the wind should alter to the north again? Are you saying that we should alter with it and turn to fight our enemy once more?'

'Exactly that, sir,' agreed Francisco de Bobadilla, who had become one of the Duke's closest advisers since the first engagement off Plymouth. 'Although it may not be possible to rendezvous with the Duke of Parma, there are some excellent havens on this coast, and it is well known that the English of the north-east are well-disposed to our cause.'

'Nevertheless our ships are in dire need of repair and replenishment,' de Leyva put in, 'and I think we should consider the possibility of wintering in Norway in order to make a further attempt in the spring.'

This suggestion brought forth several long faces, and the Duke voiced the opinions of the majority when he overruled it.

'To set course for Norway would mean to run before the wind, and I fear that if we do so the English will be able to claim with justification that they have put us to flight. Let us rather do as Don Diego suggests, and hold to the north while this wind lasts, returning southward if and when it changes.'

'And if it does not change?' asked de Leyva.

Martin de Bertendona, who had a shrewd idea of the way the Captain General's mind worked, spoke for the first time. 'If the wind does not alter, I suggest that we accept the will of God and continue our passage northward, rounding Scotland and sailing west of Ireland and Cape Clear, and so back to Spain.'

Until that moment a return to Spain had not been mentioned, but now that the possibility had been voiced there was a curious little silence in which each member of the council experienced a mixture of hope and guilt.

The Duke of Medina Sidonia looked to the others for their opinion, but few seemed anxious to give it.

'Then shall we agree upon that, gentlemen?' he asked tiredly. 'Shall we agree that we return to the Narrows if the wind permits it, and that if it does not we shall – er – return by the Northern Seas to Spain?'

There was a murmur of assent. The Duke turned to his secretary. 'Make a note of that decision will you, Baltasar? And . . . let us also make a contingency plan for a return via the Northern Seas. Let us muster the best pilots in the fleet. Let them work out a safe route for all ships, so that if we must return to Spain without a victory, we shall at least return in safety and good order.'

The meeting broke up, and the Duke went on deck to see his generals into their boats.

Afterwards he stood alone in his customary place by the taffrail, staring at the English fleet which was keeping station a mile or two astern; and although he knew that duty dictated that he should pray for the wind to go round to the north so that they could re-enter the Narrows and attempt the invasion of England, his most sincere wish now was simply to have done with this sorry enterprise and return home to his slow, contemplative life among the orangeries of San Lucar.

'Nevertheless not my will, O Lord, but Thine be done,' he muttered, and sighed deeply.

On board the *San Juan de Portugal* the work of repairing damage continued almost non-stop for two days, and Tristram played a large part in organizing the operations and persuading the men not to give up hope. Divers went down to patch holes on the waterline; the blacksmith was busy at his anvil making clamps and angle-irons; a heavy spar was lashed to the mainmast to strengthen it. Under the direction of the bosun, the men passed two cinching hawsers round the hull and tightened them with capstan bars so that they acted like belts, preventing the ship from splitting open at her seams.

On Tuesday night the wind increased and backed further to the south-west, so that Wednesday found the Armada in loose crescent formation still heading north up the east coast of England, with the enemy fleet at their heels a mile or two astern.

Towards evening, when the wind dropped, the English put on more sail and closed with the rearguard; but when the *San Martin* shot off three pieces and struck topsails as a signal for the Armada to lie-to and prepare for action, only sixteen ships obeyed.

It was not a mutiny so much as a demonstration that the majority of ships had no fight left in them, and although the English were unable to press the attack for want of roundshot, this last brief confrontation confirmed for them that the Spanish will for battle had been broken and that their only thoughts now were of survival.

Tristram was sent for on Thursday morning and transferred by flyboat from the *San Juan* to the flagship. He was met by Baltasar de Zuniga and taken aft to the Captain General's quarters, where charts of Britain and the Northern Seas were spread out upon the table.

'This is the English pilot, sir,' Baltasar informed the Duke, who held a handkerchief to his nose and regarded Tristram with sad, gentle eyes. 'Teniente Pascua Inglés.'

'Yes,' said the Duke. 'We have met before, have we not, Lieutenant? At your wedding, I believe?'

'It was indeed, sir.'

'Well, I expect you know already what we require of you. It may be that our Blessed Armada will be obliged to return to Spain by way of the Northern Seas. We shall therefore need a safe and simple route for our ships to follow. You were the man who sounded a warning to the fleet off Portsmouth, and I believe you are the man to devise our route back to the Groyne.'

Tristram bowed from the neck and made a movement that suggested a clicking of the heels. 'It will be an honour to perform such a duty, your Grace,' he replied.

The Duke nodded and made a sweeping gesture with his hand. 'You have the finest charts and instruments available. I wish to have a route on the chart and in writing, a route that will take us clear of all danger, a route so simple that no captain will be able to claim that he did not understand it.'

Tristram set to work, but while he appeared to concentrate entirely upon his task, his thoughts returned repeatedly to the moment three days before when he had seen his father in agony on the quarterdeck of the *Victory*.

He looked at the chart. It might be within his power now to devise a route back for the Armada that would take it through the most hazardous waters. He could argue that the shortest way must be the best way, and invite the Captain General to lead his stricken fleet between Scotland and Orkney through the Pentland Firth, where tides were strong and the dangers many.

Was that the way? Should he remorselessly pursue his aim of destroying as many Spanish ships as possible? Having murdered his own father – whether in spirit or in deed was immaterial – could he now deliberately engineer the deaths of so many more sons and fathers?

No, he could not. The Armada was already beaten, there had been enough slaughter. His duty now lay in saving life, not taking it. He must obey the Captain General's directive: the route back to Spain must be safe and simple.

And do I want to return to Spain? he wondered. What is left for me there? Dorothea? I never want to see her again.

Sara. . .?

The thought of her caused him to stop work, and he stood with the dividers in his hand, swallowing and blinking to fight back his tears. No, he told himself angrily, I shall never see her again. João is aboard the *Duquesa*, and the *Duquesa* is no doubt the least damaged ship in the whole Armada. The Count will get home, the Count will pay to get home. He will return to Sara and imprison her once more, and I shall remain condemned to wander this earth as Joaquim said, appearing to be what I am not, and forever trying to convince myself that I have done my duty.

Very well then – let us go north of the Shetlands. What does it matter if we freeze to death in the Arctic Ocean? What does it matter if we are wrecked on the coast of Norway? But it does matter, it does matter. These men are not devils. They fought as bravely as any Englishman might hope to do. They have dear ones at home. Children, wives, mothers, fathers. . . .

Dear God, have I killed him? Have I killed him?

To return . . . or not to return. To go back, to try – at least try – to go back to Cornwall. . . . Is that the nobler course? To make peace with my family, to give myself up to the Justices, to explain. . . .

And from here we must sail west-south-west, taking us clear of Ireland. Safe, and simple . . . Down here then, until Polaris is at fifty-eight degrees.

From here southward . . . three hundred long miles – say five days' run – and thence south-south-east for the Groyne. And if – yes, if ever the opportunity offers, I shall escape. That must be my duty: to make the best provision I can for the safe return of this Armada, and to return to Cornwall to make peace with my family. And if I am to die in the meantime –

'Finished?' Baltasar said at his elbow, and Tristram looked quickly round to find that his work was being observed by the Duke and his secretary.

'Yes – yes, just this moment – '

'Describe it to me then,' the Duke ordered, 'so that my secretary may put it into writing.'

Feeling as nervous as in the early days when Mr Bryant had quizzed him aboard the *Russell*, Tristram took up the dividers and used them to trace out the proposed route.

'Your Grace – the course that I recommend to be held first is to the north-north-east, until we be found under sixty-one degrees and a half; and then we must take heed lest we fall upon the Island of Ireland for fear of the harm that may happen to us upon that coast.

'So, parting from these Islands, and doubling the Cape in sixty-one degrees and a half, we should run west-south-west until we be found under fifty-eight degrees; and from thence to the south-west to the height of fifty-three degrees; and then to the south-south-east, making to the Cape Finisterre, and so procure our entrance into the Groyne or to Ferol, or to any other port of the coast of Galicia.'

The Duke nodded in silence for some while, bending to examine the chart for himself. He had already consulted two other pilots on the possible routes back, and this proposition appeared to him to be the most straightforward.

'Yes,' he said eventually. 'That seems to me to be both safe and simple, Pilot.' He turned to Baltasar. 'See to it that this route is copied without error and sent to each ship captain; and let every such captain be warned that those who disobey it shall pay for their disobedience with their lives.' He turned back to Tristram. 'You have rendered good service, Inglés. Now go back to your ship, and may God bless your endeavours, and bring us all to a safe haven.'

Harry awoke to a cacophony of groans and babblings. As in most other ships of the English fleet, scurvy and typhus were now taking a serious hold aboard the *Victory*, and in this area between decks which had been set aside for the sick and wounded there were more casualties of poor rations and foul beer than of Spanish ordnance.

'Father? It's me. Matt.'

He opened his eyes and found his son looking down at him.

'What day is it?'

'Friday. We're off the Firth. Are you thirsty?'

He nodded, and Matthew gave him a few sips of fresh rainwater from a scoop.

But Matthew had not come to his father's cot to give him a drink of water, and when Harry had taken enough Matthew laid the scoop to one side and crouched to speak with him on the same level. 'The wind's changed, Father. Veered north-west two hours past. But the Armada's not altered. They're standing on to the nor'-nor'-east.'

'So. . . .'

'So, we reckon they'll not make an attempt at a landing. Sir John says we'll never see 'em off English shores again.'

'Are we still at their heels?'

'Aye, but not for long. Sir John sent to the Lord Admiral this morning to recommend that the fleet put into the Firth for provisions and water. And – ' Matthew broke off a moment, wondering how to broach a special request. 'And he's asking for a volunteer cox'n for the flyboat *Speedwell* to take his despatches back to London.'

He looked keenly down into his father's face, but Harry, whose perception was blurred by pain and fever, failed to see the implication.

'I want to volunteer for the duty, Father,' Matt said quietly. 'It's a real chance. If they take me on, I'll be in the Queen's pay.'

Harry gazed up at him. The wound in his groin throbbed abominably, but through those waves of pain he understood that his son was asking to be released from the duty of playing nursemaid and seeing him safe back to Polruan.

If any other member of his family had made a similar request he would have reacted with outrage and hurt; but with Matthew it was different. Matthew was his favourite, the son who was going to make up for all the shame and agony he had suffered in his life, the son who would win wealth and fame for the name of Pascoe.

'Can I have your permission?' he was asking. 'There'll be Davy and Nick still aboard to look after 'ee, and as soon as the *Victory*'s been replenished she'll turn south for the Downs and thence to Plymouth. I reckon – I reckon you'll be back at Hill House by the month's end.'

Harry's eyes turned to look up into his son's face, and the hint of a smile came to his lips.

'You go and volunteer, lad,' he whispered. 'Don't worry about your father, he'll make out one way or t'other.'

Matthew took his father's hands between his own and knelt to whisper his thanks and make his farewell; and a few moments later he was gone, and Harry was left in his cot with the oak timbers groaning as the ship rolled and the feverish babblings of the sick and dying going on around him.

That evening, when the Duke was munching biscuits on the poop of the *San Martin*, the English fleet was seen to cast about onto the starboard tack and stand in towards the Firth of Forth.

Suddenly the familiar sails that had remained within a few miles of the Armada for the past twelve days were dropping astern.

The sun appeared for a short while, then disappeared again behind louring clouds. Pacing up and down his deck, the Duke went over in his mind all the many events of the past fortnight, trying once again to fathom out where he had gone wrong.

Should he have attempted an assault on Plymouth? Should he have disregarded Don Diego's advice about going to the rescue of Don Pedro? Could he have placed his ship in any greater danger at any time during any of the battles?

No, he had little upon which he could rightly accuse himself. He had listened to his generals and taken their advice. The fleet had been disciplined, armed and ready for the fight. There had been no shortage of courage or honour among his generals – indeed in some cases there had almost been too much.

But could he have prevented that fatal moment off Calais when the fleet had cut and run? Ah, that was indeed the turning point, the moment when their fortunes had started to decline.

And how was he to face his Majesty? What explanation could he give for so abject a failure? That they were all mistaken? That they should not have believed that their mission was a holy one or that God was on their side?

The water swirled and eddied beneath the high stern. Gulls cried out mournfully overhead, gliding down close to the waves, mounting rapidly upwards, balancing on white-frayed wings.

Gradually he became aware of another sound, one that was vaguely familiar, one that reminded him of summer evenings on his estate in Andalusia. It was a donkey braying.

He thought at first that he was losing his mind, that the weeks of fatigue and anxiety were taking their toll; but there it was again, quite unmistakable and louder too, and a moment later he saw the cause of it.

Earlier that day he had approved a request from Juan Lopez de Medina, the General in command of the urcas, that livestock carried for use by the invasion forces might be cast overboard in order to save water and fodder. Now, spread out over a wide area, horses, mules and donkeys were swimming in the sea.

The donkey he had heard came close by the *San Martin.* It was swimming vigorously, braying all the time, its head turned upward at the ship as if it could not believe that its human masters were leaving it to drown. Seeing its pale, accusing eye, the Duke of Medina Sidonia turned quickly away, and buried his head in his hands.

Six days after turning south before the north-westerly wind, on

Thursday 18 August, Mr Harding's flyboat came briskly up the Thames on the last of the flood, bound for Greenwich Reach with personal despatches for the Queen's Secretary. But as the tented army encampment at Tilbury drew abeam on the east bank a barge under oars flying the colours of the Yeomen of the Guard came down towards them and they were hailed by an irate-looking officer who stood in the sternsheets.

'Bark *Speedwell!*'

'At your service!' Mr Harding shouted back cheerfully. (He looked like a pirate, and his crew of fourteen west countrymen – including Matthew Pascoe – took pride in emulating his fierce bearing and outlandish dress.)

'Turn about, *Speedwell!*' the yeoman shouted grumpily. 'Don't you realize we've got her Majesty arriving any minute?'

'And don't *you* realize that we're carrying urgent despatches from the fleet?' Harding replied, and some of his crew nudged and winked among themselves, proud of the fast time they had made from the Firth and pleased that their skipper wasn't going to take any nonsense from this fancy-dress soldier.

'Turn about, I say!' bellowed the yeoman. 'The river's closed for her Majesty's visit!'

There was clearly no point in arguing further, but having got so far upriver Harding wasn't prepared to sail away again, especially as the Queen's Secretary was likely to be with the royal party and able to receive the mails while at Tilbury. With this in mind, and disregarding further orders from the yeoman, he took one of his quick decisions.

'Up helm, Mr Pascoe!' he ordered. 'Stand by starboard anchor! Brails in hand! Look alive, look alive! Strike the foresail! Brail up! Let go! Take her round to starboard, Matt, that's it – lovely job!'

It was all done in the space of two minutes: the sails were brailed, the anchor down, and the *Speedwell* turning slowly to stem the tide as she came to her cable.

'You can't stay here!' the yeoman roared, looking as if he were about to have a fit. 'See that slipway, that's the royal landing stage!'

'So much the better!' Harding replied. 'I'll be needing to step ashore to deliver the Admiral's despatches!' He turned. 'Mr Pascoe! I want the boat bailed and manned in five minutes. Mr Atkins! We'll have the neatest harbour furl you've ever made, or I'll know the reason why!'

'Are you going to move or are you not?' bellowed the yeoman, whose barge was now lying off the starboard side.

'No, sir, I am not!'

This took the Queen's man, who was not used to such cheerful disobedience, by surprise. But while he was considering the threat of dire punishments, the sound of a fanfare came to their ears, and the royal barges hove into sight coming downriver from Greenwich.

The yeoman appeared to lose his nerve. 'Right, that's it!' he shouted, looking suddenly white with apprehension. 'Get all your men out of sight! Out of sight, the lot of them! We can't have vagabonds in the view of her Majesty!'

Harding put back his head and shouted with laughter, and told this obedient servant where to get off, saying that it would do her Majesty no harm at all to clap her royal eyes on half a dozen true British sailormen. But for all that, when the royal barge came by and the silver trumpets blared and the soldiers paraded and cheered on the shore, the crew of the *Speedwell* were quite overawed by the bejewelled lady who was lifted onto the back of a large white horse, and later, when the Men of Essex were cheering and word came from shore that Queen Bess had gone among the common ranks of her army and made a fine, bold speech to the soldiers, Mr Harding ordered that every man aboard drink her health in spirit wine; and in the evening, when Harding had put Sir John's despatches into the hand of Mr Walsingham himself, all hands had a dance and skylark on the deck, and the bosun said that if the Spaniards tried to land in old England after this he'd eat his leather seaboots, or his name wasn't Thomas Atkins.

Elsewhere people were not so confident of an English victory. On the way south from the Firth of Forth the fleet had been dispersed by severe gales, and many observers were inclined to believe that the handful of ships arriving in any one port was all that remained of the Royal Fleet.

In Paris rumours were spreading that in the battle off the Isle of Wight the *Revenge* and fifteen English galleons had been sunk and several others captured. Independent reports from his agents convinced Bernadino de Mendoza, the Spanish Ambassador, that the English fleet had been routed, and on the strength of these reports he sent word to Madrid and Rome confirming that by the time the report was received, Spanish soldiers would have landed on English soil.

At last the tide of affairs appeared to be turning in Spain's favour. His Holiness would be honour-bound to pay up the promised million ducats;

France would be obliged to submit to the Catholic League; the Dutch thorn would be removed from the Spanish side.

Even in the home ports of the Medway and the Downs it seemed that the English had been badly beaten. With her Majesty's Treasurers keeping their customary tight hold on the purse strings, the chase northward had been carried out in the face of severe shortages of provisions, and an epidemic of typhus and ship-fever was killing a hundred Englishmen a day. Every ship returning from the fight was landing dozens of sick and injured men, and in Margate, Chatham and Rochester the sailors who had saved England were dying penniless and naked in the gutters.

For Harry, time had lost all meaning. Slumped in a cot, his wound suppurating and throbbing, his face flushed with a high fever, he was assailed by voices and visions of the past. As the *Victory* came south down the east coast of England he sailed through another sea, a private nightmare-sea of doom and delirium.

He wrestled with Mr Drew on the greensward above St Saviour's Point, and Mr Drew turned into a black snake. He visited brothels in Plymouth, but the women he bedded turned into sirens that ripped at his privates with long, claw-like nails. He discovered a boat off Gribbin Head and plunged a dagger into the heart of a dying priest, and when he tossed the silver Madonna to Sam Gristy, a woman in blue rose up out of the sea: her face came closer and closer and she had a pale, white eye that enveloped him and saw deep into his soul so that he awoke drenched in sweat and screaming for mercy.

And then one day Davy Treffry and Nick Polwhele came down to him and lifted him onto a stretcher and he was carried up on deck. The ship had arrived off Margate: it was raining, he was being taken ashore. They put him down in the market-place and Treffry told him that Nick would stay by him while he went off to search for rooms. A fine drizzle fell, and the crowds surged and jostled. He was shivering and sweating by turns. The crier rang a handbell and read out a broadside and Harry thought it was another dream, for the people were cheering and the crier was proclaiming in ringing tones a speech that seemed to have no remote bearing upon the disaster that had befallen him. It was a speech full of grand phrases, a speech that might have been made with the deliberate intention of arousing his contempt and the contempt of every other sailor who had sailed and suffered for his Queen and his country.

'My loving people . . . let tyrants fear . . . under God . . . my chiefest strength . . . loyal hearts and good will . . . not for my recreation . . . but . . . for my God and for my kingdom, for my people, my honour and my blood . . . the body of a weak and feeble woman . . . the heart and stomach of a king . . . any prince of Europe . . . invade the borders of my realm . . . I myself . . . your general, judge . . . rewarder of your virtues . . . I know already . . . you deserve rewards and crowns; and we do assure you . . . they shall be duly paid. . . .'

A few hours later Treffry arrived back having found a barn some way out of town where the farmer said they could have shelter for the night.

Harry was one of the lucky ones: the following morning he was carried aboard the *Diamond* of Dartmouth which, after four days' hard sailing into westerly gales, arrived in Plymouth Sound. Then, after another sea passage, he dreamt he heard seabirds calling and breakers on cliffs and that he was being carried ashore on Polruan Strand; he was going up the long, steep hill with the grey stone cottages on either side; women were weeping and praying as he went by; the bells of St Saviour's were ringing; they reached the top of the hill; he heard voices he had never expected to hear again.

The voices, the voices . . . they crowded in on him, swept over him like breaking waves: Martha's voice, Gristy's, Ann's, Aunt Bridget's, Nathan's – even Tristram's. . . .

And then there was a sudden silence and the only voice left was a woman's. She was kneeling by his bed and gripping his hand. 'Harry! Harry!' she whispered. 'You're safe home! It's me! It's Jennifer!'

He opened his eyes and turned his head towards her. Tears ran freely down his cheeks. For the first time in his life, Harry Pascoe understood the meaning of love.

The Winds and Waters Rise

As the Armada continued north-north-east, the weather grew colder and mistier. Many of the men – especially the black slaves and moorish Andalusians – suffered terribly from the cold. Many had bartered or gambled with their clothing, and were now naked or in rags – soaked to the skin day and night, shivering continually, staggering exhaustedly as they went about their duties. Many lay huddled on the decks and waited for death.

Every day, in every ship, men were dying of exhaustion, ship-fever or injury. Those who could afford it secured extra rations by bribing the provisioners, and a number of noblemen paid large sums to have themselves transferred to ships which they believed had a better chance of making a safe return to Spain. For the rest there were eight ounces of mouldy biscuit, one pint of slimy water and half a pint of wine per man per day.

The ships were dying, too. Every morning when the muster was taken a few more were reported missing. Some, like the Levantine carracks, were seen to turn away eastward for Norway and were never seen again. After a squall on 17 August the *Gran Grifon* and several other urcas were no longer in the formation. It was as if they had separated themselves from the rest in order to die with dignity.

When the Armada had rounded the north cape of Scotland and had completed the westerly leg to the fifty-eighth parallel the autumn gales began, and for two weeks a succession of south-westerly storms shrieked in from the Atlantic. With the wind in this quarter, each ship captain was faced with a terrible decision: whether to put Spain astern again and stand to the north-west into the Atlantic on the larboard tack, or risk closing the perilous Irish coast and head south-east on the starboard.

Holding to Tristram's original directions the Duke of Medina Sidonia kept well out to sea, and sixty or more ships stayed with him; but now, desperate for food and shelter, two groups parted company with the main body, one heading for northern Ireland under de Leyva and the other for the south under Recalde.

If the map of Ireland is likened to the profile of a dog begging, its head turned to one side, its hindlegs in Cork and Kerry, its ears in Donegal and Down, then the western parts of Mayo and Galway become its forepaws held one above the other.

It was between these forepaws that many of the Armada ships sought shelter. But that barren, windswept coast is not an hospitable one even in summer, and now it was to prove fatal for dozens of ships and thousands of men. The great *Rata Encoronada* went ashore in Tullaghan Bay. The *Duquesa Santa Ana* was beached in Loughros More May. Under de Leyva, a few hundred survivors struggled overland to Killybegs and crowded aboard the galleass *Girona*; but within twenty-four hours of their setting out for Scotland, the *Girona*'s rudder had carried away, and on a night of shrieking winds and towering waves she was driven down on the coast and smashed on the Giant's Causeway.

Meanwhile, under the painstaking dead reckoning of the English pilot, Tristram Pascoe, Recalde's *San Juan de Portugal* had made a landfall off the Dingle Peninsula.

Recalde was dozing in his cabin when Pascoe came down to speak with him. It was 15 September: since separating from the main body a fortnight before, the *San Juan* and a dozen or so other ships had battled southward into a succession of gales, and during that time Recalde, who had collapsed from exhaustion after the last battle, had never stirred from his bed.

Now he lay weak and wasted in a canvas cot and received his navigator's report.

'Land in sight, sir,' Tristram told him. 'We believe it to be Mount Brandon. If it is, we may be able to weather Sybil Point and find shelter in Smerwick Harbour.'

'Where's the wind?'

'North-west, sir. It veered in the night and appears steady. We're keeping a close luff, but the tide's on the turn and will be ebbing until four this afternoon.' Tristram hesitated, aware that Recalde had visited Smerwick eight years before. 'I believe you have knowledge of this coast sir, and such knowledge is much needed now. We shall have to decide quickly whether to try for Smerwick or cast about and stand out to clear the Blaskets.'

Recalde nodded. 'I shall be on deck as soon as possible,' he said. 'In the meantime, hold up to windward.'

Tristram bowed to acknowledge this order and went on deck. The land was already much clearer now. Consulting the chart, he began to identify the landmarks he had heard Sara speak of so often: Mount Brandon, its peak capped by cloud; Sybil Point and the Three Sisters, cliffs that faced northwards and guarded the entrance to Smerwick, and Mount Eagle, whose slopes ran down to the sheer cliffs of Slea Head to the south.

He was joined by Joaquim who, like every other man and boy in the Armada, was suffering from exhaustion and starvation. He looked at Tristram with gaunt, hollow eyes.

'Is there a safe harbour here, Tristão?'

Tristram nodded. 'Smerwick, Father.' He pointed south-east at the Three Sisters. 'Beyond that headland. But whether we can round it against the ebb is another question.'

They had assumed their roles so completely now that there were times when Tristram believed that he really was a lieutenant in the service of Spain and Joaquim his confessor.

'So this is Corcaguiney,' Joaquim muttered.

'Yes, this is Corcaguiney.'

Recalde came up at that moment, supported by two of his servants. His beard was ill-kempt and his skin yellow and stretched taut over his cheekbones. He took one look at the coastline under the starboad bow and turned to Tristram. 'The ebb's running, you say?'

'Starting within the hour, sir.'

'Then we'll not weather the Sisters. We must put about.'

'Sir – if we don't obtain fresh water and food soon – ' He stopped himself. The consequences were too obvious to state.

Recalde considered for a few moments, looking out over the long grey waves as if they were his personal enemies.

'What about the Blaskets?'

'They lie to the south, sir, and are treacherous. There are rocks and tide-rips – '

'Yes, but there's a haven at the eastern end of Great Blasket where a ship may lie in safety when the wind's in the westerly quadrant.'

'That may be, sir, but the passage into Blasket Sound demands local knowledge and fair weather – '

Recalde staggered against his two servants as the ship rolled heavily.

'What else can we do? If we keep on this tack we shall founder on the Sisters, and if we try to stand out to sea we shall go upon the Blaskets. There's no alternative, Pilot. We can't make an offing against this wind, so we must take shelter where we can find it. We must cast about and head south-south-west – ' Recalde's finger traced a track on the chart ' – until we can double this island – Inishtooskert. Then we'll turn east and thread the needle into the Sound.'

Recalde was not a man to argue with: having announced his decision, he had a stool brought up on deck and lashed to the mizzen, and from there he set about conning the ship through some of the most dangerous waters to be found on the coasts of Ireland.

With the wind on her starboard quarter and the ebb tide gathering strength, the *San Juan* made good speed towards the Blaskets. As the ship closed the islands the razor-sharp rocks of Carrigfudda and Beginish rose up on either side, and no man could look upon them – or the 'Fatal Cliffs' of Blasket Island – without a shudder of fear.

The Atlantic rollers curling and crashing about her, the *San Juan* turned south-east and entered the narrow channel between the Beginish and Great Blasket, and following in her wake came her tender and the *Bautista*, vice-flagship of the Castillian squadron. These ships dropped anchor south of Beginish Island, a few cables off the White Strand of Great Blasket, which faces east across the Sound.

When all three ships were safely at anchor and Recalde had been helped below, Joaquim and Tristram were joined by Ensign Rodrigo, who still retained a remnant of youth and vitality in spite of the rigours of the past weeks. 'Teniente!' he exclaimed. 'What a deliverance, what a miracle! If I had not seen with my own eyes what that man has done today, I would not have believed it possible!'

But Tristram hardly heard him. He was staring eastward across the Sound to Slea Head, aware that beyond it – only a tantalizing five miles distant – lay the homestead and castle of Ballingolin, of which Sara had spoken so often and so fondly.

Recalde sent a landing party ashore to the mainland that afternoon but eight of the men were captured by English soldiers and only the boat's crew returned. The following day fifty harquebusiers attempted to get ashore on Coomenoole Beach but they were prevented by a heavy swell and the arrival of English reinforcements. At the same time, it was necessary to make the anchorage more secure, as a swift ebb tide ripped through the Sound, and the ships were short of anchors after the débâcle off Calais, and in danger of dragging.

On the third day the wind dropped and a covert landing was made at Dunquin to obtain provisions and water, but after that, as armed English soldiers were now patrolling the coast by the dozen, it was decided to restrict landings to Great Blasket Island, where there were a few stone dwellings, a fresh-water spring, and a meagre supply of food.

Since the battles in the Sleeve, Joaquim had become very weak. Now, in the secrecy of the confessional, he repeatedly urged Tristram to attempt an escape on his own.

'Go while you have the chance,' he told him. 'If you are caught by the English, tell them the truth. And if you manage to evade them, you can seek refuge with Dona Sara's family.'

Tristram was torn by conflicting aims and loyalties. Since seeing his own father in agony on the *Victory*'s deck, he had felt it his duty to return to Polruan and make peace with his family, even if that meant paying the price for the crime he believed he had committed; at the same time, while longing to be reunited with Sara, he hated the thought of leaving Joaquim to his fate on board the *San Juan*, and even felt a certain obligation to complete his task as pilot and bring the *San Juan* safely back to Spain.

Early one morning, nearly a week after the ship's arrival in the Sound, he went ashore with the landing party and took a solitary walk up Croaghmore to think things out. Stretched out on the heather with the guillemots balancing in the wind above his head, he went over all the possibilities.

He recalled his last conversation with Sara under the fig tree. Although they had agreed to meet in Ireland if at all possible after the war, they had been unable to plan anything definite. All he had been able to promise was that he would do everything he could to find her. Somehow, somewhere (they had been so sure of this!) they would be reunited.

But that had been before the cataclysm of the past weeks, and although he was sure that his own feelings towards Sara were unchanged, the battles and the long voyage had knocked something out of him, so that he no longer felt worthy of her love or had the confidence to seek her out.

But there were yet more complicated reasons for not attempting an escape, for the sense of guilt he now felt over his father was like a self-inflicted injury which had destroyed his sense of direction and purpose in life. Suddenly, he had no clear idea of what he should be doing. All he was aware of was a deep sense of longing. But for what? To go home and make peace with his family and Jennifer? No, it was more than that. With the wind blowing away his tears, he saw that his greatest wish now was to be released from wars and treachery and the vile hatred between Christian and Christian. It was a weariness of the soul, a yearning for peace, perhaps even a wish for death.

He stared bleakly across the bay to the grey Kerry Mountains and felt the hope drain out of him. 'I can never face Sara again,' he said aloud, and was just reflecting that death was not a thing to be so greatly feared after all, when the sound of a trumpet from the *San Juan* attracted his attention.

He stood up. The wind had increased and backed, and with the ebb tide flowing, the two galleons in the Sound had swung dangerously close together.

He began running fast down the path to the landing place on White Strand. All thoughts of escape were forgotten. His ship was dragging her anchors, and there was work to be done.

He found Rodrigo trying to take charge on the forecastle, and every spare man with an ounce of strength left in him was being employed hoisting one of the cannons out of its carriage in order to use it as a jury anchor. But the *San Juan*'s aftercastle was already only a matter of yards from the *Bautista*, and although Tristram saw that the best way to avert collision was to use the longboats to tow the ships apart, it was already too late, and within minutes of his getting aboard the two anchored galleons had collided and were crashing and banging against each other.

For nearly an hour, amid shouts and curses and bellowed commands, ropes and hawsers were passed, sheet anchors were dropped and yards and rigging braced this way and that to disentangle the two ships, and this chaos was still continuing when the roar of gunfire attracted attention to two more ships that were entering the Sound from the north.

The first, the one-thousand-ton *Santa Maria de la Rosa*, was low in the water and firing her guns to signal that she required assistance. The second was the urca *San Pedro Mayor*, which had lost her mainmast.

With the wind and tide behind them, they came quickly into the Sound. The *San Pedro* put down a couple of good anchors, but the *Santa Maria* had only light ground tackle, and within minutes of dropping a single kedge she was dragging down-tide towards the reefs off Dunmore Head.

There was nothing that anyone could do to assist her. The seamen on board the *San Juan* and the *Bautista* were still engaged in anchor-work, and the *San Pedro Mayor*, having found good holding ground, was now a long way up-tide.

Away she went: yawing back and forth as her anchor caught the bottom, her guns firing, the men on deck shouting and panicking – until she came to a sudden, ominous halt. Very soon afterwards she began to settle in the water.

On board the *San Juan de Portugal* work stopped as the men watched the awful sight of a ship sinking. On the aftercastle Tristram, Joaquim, Rodrigo and several others of the afterguard gazed in silence at the spectacle.

She went down with dignity, on an even keel, her masts upright, her flags flying. And then – quite suddenly – the sea closed over her, and she was gone. Only a swirl of bubbles, a few pieces of flotsam and a handful of men struggling vainly in the water remained to mark her grave.

'Pilot!'

Tristram turned to find that Recalde had come up on deck. He still looked very ill, and leaned heavily on his servant.

'Sir?'

'Take the gig and pay a call on the *San Pedro*. Find out the extent of her damage, inform her captain of the dangers of this anchorage, and offer him any assistance he may require.'

Tristram sprang to obey the order.

'And – Pilot! You'd better take your confessor with you. I think they will need the services of an extra priest.'

The *San Pedro* was a vessel of about five hundred tons, and had been converted for use as a hospital ship. Though she had been bruised in the last fight off Gravelines, most of her damage – including the loss of her mainmast – had been sustained in the storms endured in the past month. Between decks, hundreds of injured and sick men lay groaning for water, and those of the original crew who were still on their feet were hollow-eyed and lethargic.

Tristram and Joaquim were met by a swarthy officer who spoke with a Castillian accent. They discovered from him that although some salt bacon and oats were still available, the men were dying of thirst.

They sent the boat straight back to the *San Juan* for water, and when the first barrel arrived went between decks to distribute it among the skeletal figures who lay in filth and excrement.

These poor creatures looked upon the lieutenant and his Jesuit confessor as if they were angels of deliverance: they blessed them and reached out to touch them; and while Tristram held the dipper to cracked lips, Joaquim answered questions about where the ship was and how far from Spain, whispering encouragement and kindness to those on the point of death.

When they had been at work for over an hour there was a shout from above for them to come back on deck.

With a downward sweep of the hand the Castillian beckoned them to follow him, and led the way up the ladder to the aftercastle and into the great cabin. Here a dozen or more hidalgos and noblemen lay in cots, some babbling and laughing in delirium, a few praying aloud, but the majority quite silent, as if resigned to death.

Tristram was about to distribute what water was left to those who could still swallow, when he heard a voice speak his own name in the Portuguese way. 'Páscoa!' the voice croaked. 'Páscoa! *Venha-cá!*'

It was João. He lay on his back in a nightgown, one hand grasping his genitals, the other gripping the Santarém Madonna to his breast, his little mouth working and his dark brown eyes staring imploringly up in the dim light of the cabin.

Tristram's reaction was to back away, but he felt Joaquim's hand grip his arm and push him forward.

'Excellency!' he whispered, and bent over the cot. He filled the dipper and offered it to João. But the Count was already too close to death to be able to take it.

'Would your Excellency like the last rites?' Joaquim whispered, and the movement of João's head seemed to indicate an affirmative.

Joaquim knelt and made the sign of the Cross. 'Have you any last confession, my child?'

João's mouth opened and shut, but no sound came from it. All he could do, it seemed, was stare at Tristram.

Speaking rapidly in Latin, Joaquim began the rite of Extreme Unction. Producing a little bottle of holy chrism, he prepared to anoint him.

'Is this really necessary?' Tristram muttered.

'He's a human being like any other,' Joaquim whispered back. 'And we must forgive in order to be forgiven. Now hold this for me, boy, he hasn't got long.'

Lying in his cot with these two ragged men peering down at him, João knew that his time had come at last and that all his fears and premonitions of death had been well founded. Maezinha was dead, and so were Fernando and Padre Jorge. He had spent his last escudo on having himself transferred to the *San Pedro*, and though he had signed promissory notes to secure himself this cot and obtain extra food and water, it had been to no avail.

For the past week he had lain here in delirium, had dreamed dreams, met faces from the past and given way to temptation, seeking some last comfort in the sin of self-abuse. But who was this man? Why was it that his staring eyes and ragged beard were so hauntingly familiar?

Suddenly, as the oil was applied to his forehead, chest and feet and the last words of absolution were spoken, he knew positively where he had first seen that wild English face. It was that bodyguard of Sara's – the very creature he had found in the dunes wearing the Santarém Madonna.

He was filled with a sudden last surge of strength. Releasing the medallion on his wasted chest, he managed to point a finger at Tristram, and a long, guttural snarl rose in his throat. '*Vagabundo!*' he managed. '*Traidor! Espião!*'

Vagabond, traitor, spy. . . .

Joaquim's reaction was immediate and instinctive. His hand went to João's throat and pinned him down on the mattress so that he could utter no further sound; and Tristram watched in horror as the ex-priest strangled the last thread of life out of him.

Joaquim released his hold and straightened. 'Say nothing of this,' he whispered. 'Have him buried as soon as possible, and take Dona Sara's Madonna off him before you do so.' Then, with a brief shake of his head, he turned and went quickly out of the great cabin and up to the deck.

They returned aboard the *San Juan* that evening when João's body, along with several others, had been sewn up in canvas, weighted and committed to the waters of Blasket Sound.

On arrival Tristram was sent for by Recalde, who wanted to hear full details of the *San Pedro*'s seaworthiness. The report was not a cheerful one. Though the hull below the waterline was still fairly sound, the topsides were damaged and leaky and hardly fit to withstand more rough weather, and fever had spread so extensively among the men that there were scarcely any seamen fit enough to sail her.

'So what do you recommend, Pilot?' Recalde asked. 'That we leave them here to die?'

'Not at all, sir,' Tristram replied quickly, 'but if she is to have any hope of making a safe return to Spain she will need someone able to captain her and organize repairs, for her master and bosun are dead and her pilot is gravely ill.'

Recalde remained silent for some time. 'Very well,' he said at length. 'I can think of no person better suited to that duty than yourself, Pilot, for our departure from this Sound is not a difficult one, and I shall hardly need your services to find my way back to the Groyne. So . . . I shall commission you here and now to take over command of the *San Pedro Mayor*, and to do whatever is necessary to bring her safely back to Spain.'

Tristram received this order with no inward pleasure. Accepting such a duty, aboard a ship where ship-fever was so rife, was as good as signing his own death warrant.

Pacing the afterdeck with Joaquim, he told him the news.

'I'm not a superstitious man,' he said, 'and I'm not afraid to die. But that ship is doomed, I know it. I have only been given the command so that Recalde cannot be accused of deserting the *San Pedro* at the time of her need. So I think we shall have to say goodbye, Joaquim. It would be quite wrong for you to come with me this time. The *San Juan* has a good chance of making a safe passage back to Spain, and – if you're careful – you should be able to start a new life again in Portugal.'

It was dark now, and the wind had dropped a little. Across the Sound, on the lower slopes of Mount Eagle, lamps were glowing in the stone cottages of Dunquin.

Joaquim chuckled. 'Provided I give Colares and Braga, Coimbra, Lisbon and a few other places a wide berth, eh?'

'Yes. You may find it safer to remain in Northern Spain for the time being.'

'Or even go and live in France?' Joaquim suggested, serious faced.

'That's always a possibility – '

Joaquim stopped pacing. 'My good friend,' he said quietly. 'Do you really think that I would allow you to take over command of that death-ship without me at your side?'

'But Joaquim . . . you were the one who suggested that I should attempt to escape on my own – '

'And you refused to countenance the idea. So. I'm saying just the same thing to you. Where you go, I go. We agreed to that a long time ago, didn't we? So there's no need to discuss it again.'

That night Tristram sat up late, trying to write a last letter to Dorothea. In it he made the hopelessness of his task clear, and reassured her that he was resigned to death. 'If I fail to return to you, my dear, you must be brave: you will have been widowed in the most honourable of all causes, and are free to find a new husband and a new life.' But having written those words, the full extent of their deceit came home to him, and he destroyed the letter, thinking it better to write nothing at all than to perpetuate a lie.

So the following morning, after bidding Rodrigo an emotional farewell, the lieutenant and his confessor – or the spy and his accomplice – were transferred by boat to the *San Pedro*.

There was a great deal of work to be done, and few hands to do it. The first priority was to restore as many of the men as possible to some semblance of health. For that the most urgent requirement was fresh water, and the *San Pedro*'s boat went back and forth filling and refilling the barricos at the spring on the hillside above White Strand.

The other ships sailed a few days later, and the *San Pedro* was left alone in the Sound while she completed her repairs and preparations. On Joaquim's advice Tristram had the decks washed down with seawater and the befouled bedding taken ashore and burnt. He set lines out for fish every night and caught whiting and plaice which were grilled over charcoal and given to those still able to eat. Most important of all he fostered among the men a will to survive, and in this way, within a few days, many of those who had given up hope were on their feet again and able to assist in the repairs and preparations for the voyage that lay ahead.

Then, early one morning, the capstan was manned and the anchors weighed; the forecourse and mizzen were hoisted, and with a fresh north-westerly wind to take them out, the *San Pedro* slipped out of Blasket Sound, staying close to the island to avoid the reefs off Dunmore Head before heading south-west between Inishvickillane and Barrack Rock.

For a day and a half, it seemed that the fair wind and moderate seas would hold; but on the second night another gale came in from the west, and by morning the ship was plunging and shaking into high seas, the mizzen had blown away to shreds, and the men were exhausting themselves once more at the pumps.

For four days they battled southward, and by the end of that time even Tristram's slenderest hopes of reaching Spain were gone.

Soon after sunset that evening he was able to snatch his first sight of Polaris, and its altitude of a little under fifty degrees – indicating that they were somewhere due west of Land's End – forced him to acknowledge the dismal truth that they had been making barely forty miles a day since leaving Blasket Sound.

He took some biscuits and water down to Joaquim in the great cabin. 'At this rate we shall be another fortnight before we sight the coast of Cantabria,' he said tiredly. 'But we're making so much leeway that we shall founder on the Gascon coast long before that.' He faced Joaquim. 'As I said, this ship is no more than a floating coffin.'

Joaquim had grown very weak in the last few days, and had the unmistakable look of one who knows that he is going to die.

'We knew that before we set out,' he said. 'We must all go some time, Tristão, and when that time comes it's as well to accept it with dignity.'

'But – I'm not ready to die!' Tristram muttered. 'I want to bring this ship to a safe harbour, and I want to see you back to full health. And – and there's another reason – '

'Sara,' Joaquim murmured.

'No, not Sara. My father. I saw him, Joaquim – with my own eyes! Would you be willing to die with such a deed on your conscience?'

'There is no reason to blame yourself – '

'But there is! There must be! I know it may not have been my ball which struck him, but I fired with the rest, I assisted in the deed.'

Joaquim was silent for some time. At length he asked: 'Did you know it was he before you fired?'

'No. . . .'

'Then your action was not deliberate, and you bear no more guilt than any other.'

'And yet – I know that I am guilty. Though my father wronged me often, the wrong was not altogether on his side. I was a disobedient and wayward son, Joaquim. I took pleasure in rivalling and scorning him. I never honoured him as a son should honour a father. And if . . . if he is dead, then I shall have made a widow of the woman I once loved and an orphan of my own son.' He looked into Joaquim's eyes, begging for guidance. 'Can you see now why I'm not ready to die? Could you end life with such blood and betrayals on your hands as I have on mine?'

The ship shuddered and creaked as she rolled. Joaquim looked kindly upon Tristram, whose head was buried in his hands. 'You have already done much to save life as well as take it, Tristão, and you must count it a blessing that you are able to acknowledge the shared guilt of war, for it is not given to many to do so.'

'Nevertheless, I still feel a great need to return to Polruan – '

'Then do so! You've been given a ship and a fair wind! Haven't you already told me that we shall never reach Spain? So why not turn for England?'

Tristram was no longer able to think logically. 'But . . . you always said that would mean imprisonment!'

A gleam of the old humour appeared in Joaquim's eye. 'My dear, good friend,' he whispered. 'Are we not in a prison already?'

In the event, Tristram had the decision taken from him, for the following evening the wind backed south-south-westerly and as the men were too weak to sweat the luffs it was impossible to come to the wind and the only safe course to follow was one that took them up the Sleeve with the wind astern.

The ship's motion was easier the moment she turned away from the sea, and Tristram cheered the men by telling them that they were heading for France. But he was hardly cheered himself, for he had nothing but dead reckoning to go by and had little idea how far west of Land's End they had passed.

For three days they ran on before the wind with never a sight of ship or land and only the seabirds and the foam-streaked waves for company. Rummaging in the great cabin, Tristram found a small cache of meal, biscuit and raisins that had evidently been put aside by his predecessor, which he shared equally among those on board who could still eat.

On the fourth evening after turning north-east, he went below to tell Joaquim that they were close to land. 'We passed a rock a little while back, and I believe it was the Eddystone. I want to get you up on deck, Joaquim. In this weather we shall have very little time to alter course once we sight land, and we may drive upon the shore.'

'I suppose if we're going to die we may as well do so together,' Joaquim replied, and his words reminded Tristram of a similar exchange with Sara months before.

They went slowly up to the poop, where Joaquim sat propped up against the mizzenmast, and with rain squalls sweeping down over them and the ship rolling and plunging, they continued eastward before the gale.

The night seemed to last an eternity. Wave after wave came curling up astern, lifting the ship upward on its breaking crest and crashing down under the bows in a maelstrom of froth and spray. The men on the pumps were too weak to work for more than a few minutes at a time now, and as the bilges filled and the ship settled in the water her movement became more sluggish. By dawn it was only a matter of time before the ship went down, and all on board were aware of it. Those who could do so had come up on deck: they lurked in rags wherever there was shelter and gazed for'd into the rain and blown spray for the first glimpse of land; and when it came it came suddenly – not as a low hump on the horizon but as a sudden towering cliff over to starboard, with thundering rollers exploding into spray and monstrous whirlpools of white water all around.

Where were they – the Lizard? Start Point? The Gribbin? Bolt Head?

There was no time to speculate, no time to bear away, strike sail or put out the anchors. Seizing the whipstaff, Tristram did what he could to bring the ship's bows away from the headland, and perhaps he managed to alter her course by a few degrees.

But it was not enough: there was a rending jolt as a rock tore into the hull; then, for a minute longer, the *San Pedro* was free again and being carried along beside the headland towards a cove upon whose sands she fetched up with such a sudden impact that the foremast came down with a crash.

It was every man for himself after that. The seas were breaking over the ship and pouring down between the decks. Some men had already committed themselves to the water; others hung back, screaming in terror or saying their last prayers.

'Come, Joaquim!' Tristram bawled, bending to help him up. 'We're going to swim for it!'

But Joaquim had already gone to land upon another shore.

Tristram rode in on a wave and struggled out of the surf, and with dawn coming up picked his way up over the clifftop and across fields, putting as much distance as possible between himself and the *San Pedro Mayor*.

That this was England he had no doubt, and the steep hills and red earth soon convinced him that he was in Devon. For an hour he scrambled on over hedges and along ditches, avoiding farmhouses, skirting a village and crouching out of sight when an early cart went by along a muddy track; and when he came to a stream he lay full length and drank deep from its waters before hurrying on inland.

As a watery sun rose above the rolling farmland he stumbled into a field of milch-cows that were standing by a gate, evidently awaiting the arrival of the milkmaid to relieve their swollen wells.

'Steady my lovelies, steady!' he whispered in the way his own mother had done so many years before, and kneeling in the mud, began milking the nearest. At first he tried to catch the spurting milk in his mouth. Later – sobbing from exhaustion – he fastened his lips upon the udder and sucked the warm cream like an infant at the breast.

No Place for Ladies

Sara was sitting on the low stone wall at the bottom of the Quinta de Santo António and looking out over the empty harbour. It was the beginning of October: the last wagon-loads of grapes had been trampled in the stone *lagares*; the last barrels had been filled and stopped and stored; the last muted celebrations and feasts were over. Now the autumn sun was shining and Sara had come down to her special place to savour the peace of the afternoon and escape the unceasing noise and chatter of the household.

It was over four months since the Armada had sailed, but it seemed far longer, and there were times now when she could hardly believe that she was the same person who had stood waving on the shore as the fleet sailed out of the Tagus.

She remembered the many changes of mood in the city. It had been impossible not to share those moods, for Lisbon was a place whose very squares and palaces, walls and alleyways seemed to vibrate with the latest rumour, the latest surge of optimism or plunge into bleak despair.

At first, after the ships sailed, there had been pride and patriotism, and confidence that with the Portuguese squadron at its vanguard, the Armada could not fail to win a great and glorious victory. Then there had come news of the gales and delays, and the churches had been full of flickering candles lit by the womenfolk for the safety of their men. Later still had come that terrible time of silence, when people went about reassuring each other that no news was good news and that with God on their side 'our boys' would win through.

Later there had come that wonderful day when trumpets had sounded in the city and broadsheets had been printed announcing that half the English fleet was sunk, that the Spanish Army was marching on London and that the Enterprise was as good as won. But that wave of euphoria had lasted no more than a few days, for very quickly after it came other reports – of fierce battles in the Sleeve, of a disaster off Calais, and of Parma's soldiers stuck in Dunkirk.

Throughout this time Sara had had no news of Tristram or of João. The latest rumour to reach Lisbon was that the Spanish fleet had sailed north to make a landing in Northumberland or Scotland, but the rumours had become so many and varied now that she had learnt to discount them.

She watched a cat walking sedately along the top of the boundary wall and thought about her secret meetings with Tristram, wondering if she would ever see him again and wishing that the fig tree might tremble and his head appear once more under the umbrella of leaves.

It had been difficult living under the same roof as Dorothea, and there had been times when she had found it almost impossible, for Thea seldom spoke of Tristram with any affection and for some time now had made no secret of the fact that she was more concerned for Rodrigo's safety than her husband's. There had been times when Sara had needed all the self-control she could muster to prevent herself rising in Tristram's defence and giving herself away.

Miguel (he had been named after his uncle, Miguel de Cervantes Saavedra) had been born at the end of June. Before the birth Sara had often wondered whether Tristram had been right in saying that the baby was his, but one glance at the child told her that he was, for he had the same intense, dark blue eyes, and an unmistakable Englishness about him that could only come from Tristram Pascoe.

Dorothea had entered a period of deep depression after the birth, rejecting her baby completely and refusing to nurse him or have anything to do with him, so that Sara had felt obliged (and only too happy) to act the part of mother and give Miguel the love and tenderness that every baby needs. And because of Dorothea's open resentment at the 'burden of motherhood' she claimed Tristram had imposed on her, any last feelings of guilt on Sara's part were finally dispelled.

Nevertheless the present arrangement could not continue indefinitely: Dorothea's depression was easing, and she was beginning to look forward to a settled life in Andalusia. All that prevented her removing at once was a shortage of funds, and she was confident that the deficiency would be made good as soon as her Uncle Pedro returned from the wars.

Ironically, Sara now dreaded Thea's departure. She had become devoted to Miguel in the past weeks, and he to her. To see him taken away by a mother who openly admitted that she felt nothing for him would be like losing a child of her own. Worse, she would lose her last link with Tristram.

The years should by now have taught her that it was better not to dwell too much either on the past or the future and to live each day for itself; but instead of allowing the memory of him to fade, the passing months had only intensified her longing for him, her concern for his safety, her hopes of seeing him again, so that she was now hardly capable of thinking about anything else and spent hours here in her garden, looking out over the old city, alone with Tristram in her thoughts.

She didn't hope, or pray or even give thanks; but if she concentrated entirely upon Tristram she was sometimes able to achieve a small separation of spirit and flesh, so that for a few moments she could leave herself sitting there on the wall and fly away to be with him, wherever he was, whatever he was doing.

A shrill voice came from the house. 'Sara! Sara!'

She turned. Dorothea, wearing a flouncy dress and quantities of pearl necklaces came pattering down the path looking flushed and excited.

'News from the fleet!' she announced breathlessly. 'Admiral Moitinho awaits you in the library!'

With Dorothea speculating anxiously at her side, Sara returned up the path to the house, where she found her elderly brother-in-law looking solemn under the tile-blue stare of St Anthony.

He bowed formally and consulted a paper that bore a heavy seal. 'Countess,' he said, 'I am directed to inform you that the first ships of the fleet are reported to have arrived in the ports of Cantabria.'

Dorothea gave a shriek and put her hands to her face, peeking out between her fingers when Moitinho did not immediately continue. 'Well?' she sobbed. 'Which ships? Which ships have returned? What news of Uncle Pedro and his ensign? What news of the Count and – and the Teniente?'

Moitinho gave a little bow: as well as naming the first ships to return to Santander and Corunna, the letter he had received from Madrid had confirmed that the Enterprise had failed, and had charged him with the task of preparing the families of the high-born for bad news.

He turned to Sara. 'The Captain General has returned to Santander in the *San Martin*, Countess, but the fleet has been somewhat dispersed by headwinds and storms, and it may be some time before all are accounted for.' He cleared his throat, glancing about the library with eyes set deep beneath bushy brows. 'It is – it is a matter of time, ladies. It is the wish of his Majesty King Philip that all of Spain and Portugal offer up prayers for the safety of our glorious soldiers and – and we must wait patiently and submit ourselves to the will of Almighty God.'

Sara glanced at the letter in Moitinho's hand, and noted that it ran to a considerable length. 'But is that all the information you can give us, *cunhado?*'

'It is all the information I can divulge at this stage,' Moitinho replied carefully, and the formality of his manner and the way his eyes failed to meet hers told Sara that he must be withholding a mountain of uncomfortable truth.

During the succeeding days further reports arrived in Lisbon, and few were even remotely encouraging. Rumours began to circulate that many ships had been wrecked on the voyage home. Word arrived of the fate of several of the Armada generals: Hugo de Moncada had been killed heroically off Calais; Miguel de Oquendo was ill with vexation, and the Captain General himself had abandoned his ship at Santander and was being carried in a litter to Andalusia, too weak – or too ashamed – to present his humble duty to the King on the way.

Slowly the rumours hardened into probability. With every day that passed, more stories of sinkings, deaths, drownings and wreckings came in, and a numb acceptance spread through Portugal and Spain that the Invincible Armada had not been invincible after all but had suffered a terrible defeat.

The strain and worry affected Sara and Dorothea in quite opposite ways. Desperate for news of Tristram and yet forced to disguise her feelings, Sara became ever more withdrawn and remote while Dorothea – concerned principally about Rodrigo and the security of her inheritance – hopped ceaselessly from possibility to possibility, voicing aloud all her thoughts, fears and speculations.

After a week of wondering and worrying, Sara's patience ran out. 'I can wait no longer,' she told Thea one morning as they came out of the family chapel after morning Mass. 'I have made up my mind to travel north to Cantabria.'

Dorothea removed her mantilla and handed it to a servant. 'But – Sara – it's a fortnight's journey and winter is almost upon us – '

'The journey will be nothing in comparison to what my husband will already have suffered,' Sara replied. 'If what they say is true, there are men dying of starvation and disease. I can't sleep at night for thinking of it, my dear. I must go. I've already decided.'

She turned away to hide her face, afraid that Dorothea might somehow divine the true reason for her concern. But she needn't have worried: Dorothea was laying a hand on her arm and lisping, 'Sara! You are the noblest, the finest person I know! Only you would risk so much for your husband!'

'There is nothing noble about it, my dear,' Sara said in all honesty. 'It's simply that I can't go on waiting here for news that never arrives.'

Dorothea had a sudden, glorious vision of herself arriving in Cantabria and being cheered by battalions of heroes as she descended to the harbour to receive the tragic news of her husband's death from Rodrigo's lips. 'Then I shall accompany you!' she announced, her face suddenly radiant. 'I shall be your travelling companion. I shall offer the journey to Our Lady in the hope of a plenary indulgence, and count it an honour to share with you the hazards and hardships of the road – and, if God wills it, the joy of finding our loved ones when we reach our destination.'

'But what about the baby? You surely can't bring little Miguel on such a journey?'

'Oh – let him stay with his wet-nurse! What's a wet-nurse for, after all?'

'My dear,' Sara said gently. 'If anything happened to him in your absence you would never forgive yourself, would you? And though Laurinda has plenty of milk for him, she is quite unable to care for him alone. I shudder to think what might happen if neither of us were here to look after him.'

Thea pouted. 'But I want to go with *you*, Sara! Uncle Pedro has estates in Gijon, so if we have to winter in Cantabria we can stay with him. It will be lovely there in the spring! Oh – what a pest that baby is! Why did I have to have him! Why did I ever have to get married to his stupid father in the first place?' – and she burst into tears and ran upstairs.

Sara gave her time to calm down and then went up and found her lying face down on the bed.

'Listen,' she said. 'If we take the journey slowly, I don't see why we shouldn't take Miguel and his nurse with us. I don't mind seeing to them – I would enjoy doing so. You won't have to do a thing for either if you don't want to. But I can't let you leave him behind, Thea. If you insist upon that, I shall feel constrained to remain here with him and you will have to travel alone.'

Dorothea lifted her head and regarded Sara with dark, sullen eyes.

'Oh – all right,' she said crossly. 'But I bet he wrecks everything.'

They entered Santander just under three weeks later, after an arduous journey from Lisbon escorted by a small bodyguard and a few servants. Covering about twenty miles a day, they had travelled across the Alentejo to Badajoz before striking north-east over the sierras to the plains of Salamanca and Valladolid. From Burgos they had crossed mountain passes and plunged down through ravines. They had encountered hail, lightning, cloudburst and landslide; and on the last day of their journey they had come to the gentler country near the coast, where the green, undulating hills reminded Sara of her beloved Ireland.

Santander itself was not so appealing. As they entered the city the curious looks of the local women in their tall head-dresses and the insolent stares of the fishermen mending nets at their doorsteps told the travellers quite clearly that visitors were not welcome. There was evidence of defeat wherever they looked: the walls were lined with castaways; the inns, boarding houses and monasteries were full of the sick and wounded, and a dreadful slouching mood of death and despair pervaded every street and alley.

The town itself was walled, and consisted of sixty or more houses with the castle and principal church at the east end, the fishing port at the west, and two breakwaters (one with a crane) embracing the inner harbour. Cut into the town centre under a large, arched bridge, the tidal canal carried all the filth that the people of Santander cared to drop into it, and when Sara and Dorothea arrived at the St Nicholas gate, the whole place was throwing up a mighty stench.

In the harbour thirty or more ships of the Armada lay at anchor off the mole, and it didn't take an expert eye to tell that they had been badly beaten by war and weather. When Dorothea first caught sight of them she gave a little cry of anguish.

'Oh my God!' she gasped. 'Look at them! Look at what has become of our fine ships! Holy Mother, what those men must have endured!'

The officer of the guard who received them in the castle square was a small, self-important infantry captain, and he did nothing to lift their hopes. He had no news of the *Duquesa Santa Ana*, and was amazed that they hadn't already heard the news about the *Rosário*, Don Pedro's flagship.

'What news?' Sara asked.

'That she was captured by Drake, of course! And on the very first day of the battle, so I understand.'

'Captured?' shrieked Dorothea, and went into hysterics. 'I can't believe it! I won't believe it!'

'This is no place for ladies,' the officer told Sara when Dorothea had calmed down a little. 'The ships are full of fever – they've even stopped the men disembarking now, for fear of spreading the disease – and we're very hard pressed for victuals.'

'He's right, Sara,' Dorothea put in, still weeping. 'We can't stay here. The whole place stinks.' She turned to the officer. 'Where can we go? We need somewhere clean – somewhere quiet – '

'Try the convent at Santillana,' the captain suggested, anxious to get the visitors off his hands. 'You'll like it there, and the Abbess should be able to find room for you for a few nights.'

Sara looked out at the floating wrecks in the harbour, and the thought went through her mind that Tristram might at that very moment be on board one of them – might be dying perhaps, alone, without comfort. 'No,' she said abruptly. 'I came here to seek my husband, and I don't intend to leave until I hear news of him.' She looked down at the officer. 'I'm sure you can find a room somewhere if you try, Captain – however humble it may be. As you can hear, we have a baby with us. We must sleep somewhere. I insist on it.'

The officer drew himself up and stuck out his chest, but his Roman nose still only came up to Sara's chin. 'Señora – it is quite out of the question. It is impossible. For your own good, I have to tell you – '

' "Countess" if you please, Captain. I addressed you by your proper title, so I shall be obliged if you will address me by mine. And I will not accept that it is impossible. All things are possible. We require accommodation. Kindly arrange it.'

The captain looked extremely cross, but Sara's commanding presence and insistence won through. 'Very well, *Countess*,' he said pointedly. 'But don't expect luxury, because you won't get it.'

They were given a draughty chamber with a stone floor and a small barred window. When Dorothea saw it she exclaimed that she couldn't possibly sleep in such a place, but as there was no other to be had in the whole of Santander and Sara was determined to stay she had to give in.

Laurinda brought Miguel up and stopped his crying by putting him to the breast while the other servants swept the room and put covers on the mattresses.

'What a pigsty!' Dorothea muttered. 'What a stinking pigsty!'

Sara was helping the servants with the beds. 'It's better than nothing,

Thea. And I'm sure the men must have had to endure far worse conditions these past weeks. I think we've been lucky.'

Thea paced up and down with her arms folded, her small, white face looking pinched and tired. 'Well all I can say is, you've got a funny idea of luck, Sara. Look at this bed! How can I be expected to sleep a wink in a bed like that!'

'I slept in a bed like that for the first fourteen years of my life!'

Thea sniffed. 'Yes, but then you're Irish, aren't you?'

'And proud of it,' Sara said quietly.

There was a knock on the door, and an emaciated man with a slight beard and hollow, staring eyes was admitted. He stood on the threshold staring in at them, his eyes drawn first to Dorothea and then to the baby sucking at Laurinda's breast.

Thea gasped and crossed herself. 'Mother of God!' she whispered. 'It's Rodrigo!'

It was a very changed Rodrigo – a Rodrigo whose face was no longer aglow with the bloom and innocence of youth but stamped indelibly by disease and starvation.

Dorothea ran to him and fell sobbing on his neck, and for several moments he supported her in his arms. Facing him, Sara experienced a sudden dread, a fear of the unknown: it seemed to her that Rodrigo's gaunt, unblinking stare held within it a reflection of the horror and hopelessness of war, and foreshadowed unspeakable revelations.

'Come, Thea,' she murmured, and took her arm. 'We must be brave, we must all be brave. Let's sit down, and Rodrigo can tell us everything he knows.'

He had difficulty in beginning, and Thea had to prompt him with questions. 'Where is my uncle? Is it true that his ship was taken? And where are all the other ships?'

Rodrigo bowed his head as if he bore sole responsibility for the whole débâcle. 'Yes, it's true – the *Rosário* was taken. But the ship was not won fairly in battle – she was disabled by a collision and fell astern of the fleet after the first day. Your uncle heroically chose to remain on board. You must prepare yourselves for bad news, ladies. He was taken prisoner by El Draque and is said to be held for ransom in England.'

Thea gave a little gasp and put her hands to her mouth. She gazed upon Rodrigo with tears streaming down her cheeks.

'And the others?' Sara asked. 'Surely you know more than that, Rodrigo?'

Rodrigo glanced at the wet-nurse, who had put Miguel over her shoulder and was patting his back to bring up his wind. It was all very well for the Countess to say that he could tell them all he knew, but in matters of war there were many things that could not be told: things that no member of the fair sex should hear or be expected to understand.

'As far as your husband the Count is concerned, I know that his ship was always in the forefront of the battle and fought bravely and honourably, Countess. But after the battles – '

'What battles? Where? When?' Thea asked.

'In the Sleeve. We fought with them – the English – several times, each time more severely. And off Calais they put fireships amongst us and we were forced to withdraw or have our whole fleet burnt or blown sky-high. Then afterwards, Our Lord and His Blessed Mother worked a great miracle by changing the wind. But after that – on the way north – many of the ships were separated. It's difficult to explain. The *Duquesa* was one of the ships that went with de Leyva – '

'So the Count – is he alive?' Sara asked.

For a moment Rodrigo looked from one to the other, unable to find words to break the news; then suddenly all the horror and strain of the past weeks, together with the sight of a baby being suckled and these gentle ladies hanging on his words were too much for him, and he broke down and wept unashamedly.

'Oh Countess, please be brave! He died of ship-fever aboard the hospital ship! There were so many who died in the same way, so many so many!' – but it was all too much for Rodrigo, who accepted the invitation of Thea's open arms and sobbed like a child upon her bosom.

Sara made the sign of the Cross and put her hands to her face; but she was shocked at her inner relief at the news, and when she lowered her hands some while later, her eyes were still dry, and Rodrigo was still being comforted by Dorothea.

She could bear it no longer. 'And . . . the Inglès?' she managed. 'Have you any news of the Inglès?'

Rodrigo released himself from Thea's embrace and made an effort to look like a soldier.

'The Teniente conducted himself at all times with honour and bravery,' he said. 'When the *Rosário* was abandoned at the General's insistence, I accompanied him to Recalde's *almiranta*, the *San Juan de*

Portugal, where he served as a pilot and was commended by the Captain General for saving the fleet from grounding. Also, it was he who planned the return passage for the fleet.' Rodrigo shook his head sadly. 'And I think that if more ships had followed the route he devised, they would be safe back in Spanish ports today.'

There was another long silence during which Sara tried to will Dorothea to take up the questions. When she didn't, and Sara asked again about Tristram, she saw Thea glance at her quickly.

'But – if he was with you aboard the *San Juan*, Rodrigo, why is he not with you now?'

'After we left the *Rosário* he remained on board the *San Juan* until we took shelter at Dingle – '

'At Dingle! You went to Dingle!'

'Not exactly Dingle, Countess. It was an island, I forget the name.' Rodrigo gave a great sigh. 'Then, we were joined by other ships, one of them the *San Pedro*, the hospital urca I mentioned. All on board were dying, and Recalde put the Inglés in command of her, with orders to try to bring her back to Spain.' He turned deliberately to Thea. 'You too must be brave, Señora. The *San Pedro* has not returned to this coast. The ship was in no state to make an ocean voyage and her crew was sick and weak. They had only a little water. There is little hope.'

While Thea gave a stifled cry and took this further opportunity of falling into Rodrigo's arms, Sara stood up and turned quickly away. They must not see her face at this moment: they must not suspect so much as a tenth part of her feelings.

She closed her eyes and tried to speak to Tristram in her thoughts as she had done so often before. She called out to him silently, despairingly: Tristão, Tristão! Where am I to go now? What am I to do? Are you really dead? How am I to know? How can I live without knowing, without the hope of seeing you again? What's left for me, Tristão? I'm frightened: I'm frightened of death and of life and of not knowing. I'm frightened of what you've suffered – you and Joaquim together. I want you beside me Tristão, I want you to walk in through that door *now*. I want to hear your voice and have your arms about me. Why couldn't I have gone with you? Why couldn't I have suffered what you have suffered? Why didn't we fling caution to the wind and go away across the ocean to live together in peace and love. . .?

A gust shrieked suddenly in the eaves, and rain pattered on the window. When Laurinda had finished feeding the baby, Sara took him from her and held him close, with his head soft and warm against her cheek.

Sara spent all the following day making enquiries about the *San Pedro*, but when she returned to the garret room under the tiles she knew no more than Rodrigo had told them the previous afternoon.

'There's little point in staying here at Santander except to wait for more ships to return,' she told Thea, 'and everyone I've spoken to says that few more will return before the spring. So I think the best thing we can do now is to travel west along the coast calling in at the harbours and ports on the way to Corunna. Do you agree?'

Thea glanced at Rodrigo, who looked the better for spending a day in her company, 'Would you accompany us, Teniente?' she asked, promoting him there and then. 'My uncle's family seat is at Gijon, so I shall wish to call upon my relatives there. If Uncle Pedro is being held by the English his ransom will have to be attended to, and I'm sure you, who were the last person to speak with him before the capture, can be of great assistance in such matters.'

Rodrigo bowed and said it would be an honour, and Sara recognized in their mutual glances the sure signals of love in full bloom.

They set out the following morning, and because Rodrigo was so weak, he travelled with the ladies in the carriage, sitting next to Thea, who unashamedly took his hand in hers when he placed it casually at his side.

Winter was setting in now, and the state of the road was appalling. Each day, as they bumped along in the carriage, Thea and Rodrigo allowed each other a little more liberty, until their passion became an open secret among the company of travellers. Sometimes Thea would sleep against Rodrigo's shoulder, and sometimes Rodrigo would rest his cheek against Thea's breast. When the carriage stopped to change horses and the passengers alighted, the lovers would stroll off together arm in arm. Once, Sara came upon them unexpectedly when they were embracing.

'What will you think of me?' Thea whispered that evening when they were preparing to spend the night side by side in a fourposter bed. 'But I can't help myself, Sara dear – I love him. I love him more than I have ever loved any man, and I no longer care who knows it! I would even die for him – can you understand that?'

They stayed the first night at Santillana and the second at San Vincente; on the third they were delayed by a broken wheel, and it wasn't until the fifth day that they entered Lanes, having covered barely fifty miles since leaving Santander.

They stayed at an inn that night, and Sara and Thea had rooms separated by a thin board thrown up by the innkeeper to cater for more guests. Through this partition it was impossible for Sara not to hear, soon after midnight, someone enter Thea's room; and the creakings and rustlings and the muffled sighs that followed the anonymous arrival told their own unmistakable story.

In the morning Sara's servant greeted her mistress with the news that Señora Dorothea was not well.

Sara went to her immediately and found Thea shivering under a heap of blankets. Her colour was high and her skin hot; her teeth were chattering, she said she was aching all over and had no stomach for food.

'I think she must have caught a chill, Rodrigo,' Sara told him when he joined her for breakfast. 'So I think we shall have to stay here while she recovers from it.'

Rodrigo blushed. 'May I be allowed to visit her?'

'Yes of course,' Sara said lightly. 'I'll show you up to her room, Rodrigo. I don't expect you know where it is, do you?'

The fever rose rapidly, in spite of Sara's attempts to prevent it. Within a few days Thea was slipping in and out of delirium, eating nothing, shivering and sweating by turns, her cheekbones pushing closer to the skin every day, as if she were turning into a skeleton before their eyes. Rodrigo was desolate: he told Sara that Thea's symptoms were those of ship-fever, and was convinced that she must have caught it from him.

'If she dies, Countess, I shall never be able to forgive myself!'

Sara was sorry for him – she was sorry for them both. 'Hush, Rodrigo. Thea is not going to die, so there is no need for you to accuse yourself.'

But in spite of Sara's optimism Thea's condition worsened and within a week of their arrival at Lanes, her skin had become dark and mottled with angry red spots, so that all her good looks were gone. Soon after, she began to have convulsions and entered a coma. When she regained consciousness in the night, she asked for Rodrigo.

He sat with her for a further day and a night, sometimes pressing a cool cloth to her cheek, sometimes adjusting her pillow, sometimes holding a cup of water to her lips. What he said to her during that long vigil Sara never discovered, but she was moved by his devotion, and his attentions undoubtedly prepared Dorothea for the end.

Eight days after the onset of the fever a priest was sent for and Thea was given the last rites. When the ceremony was over she asked to speak privately with Sara.

'Will you look after Miguel for me?' she whispered.

'It's the least I can do, my dear. I shall look after him as if he were my own.'

Thea tried to smile. 'Yes . . . you . . . you are a much better mother than I, Sara . . . and you've been such a good friend. . . .' For a few moments her mouth moved but no sound came. Then she managed to continue: 'I have not been such a bad friend, either. Did you . . . know that?'

'Of course!' Sara whispered. 'Ours has been a true – a deep friendship.'

'We're all . . . we're all the same, really. Aren't we?'

Sara held her hand. She was obviously slipping away now.

'I kept your secret, Sara. I never said . . . anything – '

'Thea – my dear – '

Those eyes which had once been so alluring now seemed to stare into eternity. 'Will we go to Hell, Sara? You and me? For not – for not confessing – you know – adultery.'

Sara went cold.

'I've known for a long time, Sara. It was . . . I saw you. It was like . . . in the gospel. . . . Under the fig tree, Sara, under the fig – '

Her body shook momentarily and she gave a pathetic little cry. Then she slumped back on the pillow and lay still.

A Face at the Window

Now it was winter again and .the year of 1588 was nearly over. The pilchard boats were upturned on Polruan Strand until the spring; the north wind brought sleet and snow, and every evening at Hill House Jennifer Pascoe sat with her family before the big log fire and told them stories she had learnt at her mother's knee.

Sometimes it was 'The Wrestlers of Kenid Jack', sometimes 'Elowen and Prince Pascow', sometimes 'Peter Prynn and the Piskies'.

'Once 'pon a time, a very long time ago. . .' she would start, and Jessica – who was the very image of the little girl her mother had once been – would shiver with excitement and snuggle up against her side, gazing intently up at her face as the story began and the magic was worked once more.

And when Davy and Kevern had seen Satan and decided never to go near the Hooting Carn again after dark, or Elowen had been brought back to life with a potion of blackberry juice and had married Prince Pascow, or little Peter Prynn had tasted the Piskies' magic food and his mother had exclaimed: 'My sweet life and soul, where've 'ee been all this time, my little lovebird?' Jennifer would put her work-rough hands together and say, 'And that's the end of the story my dears,' and pack the little ones off to bed.

But life in the Pascoe household was not always as satisfactory as the ending of a winter's tale. Harry's convalescence was slow: his days were passed in a chair in the front room and his nights in the fourposter upstairs with Jennifer lying at his side. Since his arrival home in October she had insisted on doing everything for him herself. She had fetched and carried for him, washed him, dressed his wound, applied poultices to draw out the poison and had been kept awake almost nightly by his restlessness and recurring nightmares. Once she had woken up to find him weeping like a child in her arms, unable to explain why; on another night he had started up and bellowed to the whole house to back the fore-topsail and put the helm a-lee.

In the daytime he would sit in the front room smoking tobacco, muttering under his breath, going back over every decision he had taken during that week of battles with the Spanish, wondering what Matt was up to (he talked more of Matt than anyone else) and pestering Jennifer to ask Justice Mayhew again about his compensation for the loss of the *Russell*.

'Four hundred and fifty pound, that's what the Queen owes me, Jennifer!' he would say, conveniently forgetting that he had made over his ship to his son. 'It's a small price to pay for sending the Spanish Armada packing, and you can tell 'un that from me!'

Harry was not the only member of the family who made demands on her. Arthur was growing up fast and had to be got off to school every morning; the three girls were all still under seven and not yet old enough to be of much help in the household, and poor Nathan was just the same as ever: still getting under everyone's feet, still booming with laughter at the slightest thing, and now forever asking when Matt would be coming home.

Not that they had had no word of Matt. He had managed a short letter to his father while his ship was in Plymouth a month before, in which he gave him the amazing news that he was now serving under Edward Fenner as second coxswain of the *Swiftsure*, with good prospects of being made a lieutenant and commanding one of the Queen's own ships one day.

Perhaps it was that single item of news that had done most to cheer Harry and convince him that his decision to hand over the old *Russell* had not been in vain, and the knowledge that his son was making a success of life restored his self-esteem and did much to speed his recovery.

So the Christmas season came round again. Arthur was sent out to collect holly and ivy from Pont Pill woods and the house was decorated and candlelit for the vigil of the Nativity. Davy and Jill, who had recently moved to Pont village, brought their family over for Christmas Day, and that evening the two families sat down to a feast of goose and pigeon. Harry reminisced about old times with Davy; Jill talked to Arthur about his schoolwork, and the younger ones chattered and giggled and clapped when the plum pudding, ablaze with aquavitae, was borne proudly in by the mistress of the house.

After the meal Harry made a speech. He had put on his best clothes for the first time since his return from the battles, and sat at the head of the table with his bad leg outstretched on a stool. Watching him, Jennifer could not help remembering a night years before when she had sat at his table for the first time and there had been a family row about whether Ann should have more help in the house.

While her husband enlarged upon the great debt owed to those who had given their lives so that English families could celebrate Christmas in the way they chose rather than be dictated to by Spain, Jennifer reflected that there was another debt – just as great – owed to the womenfolk who had remained behind, who had borne the strain of worry and waiting, who had slaved daily to raise their children and who had received back their menfolk and nursed them to health.

Perhaps their service had been the greater, for theirs had been an obligation rather than a choice. Few women enjoyed the drudgery of keeping house or the pangs of childbirth, yet thousands of men and boys had rushed to answer the call to arms and seek the glory of the battle.

Looking at the serious faces of her children (who knew better than to misbehave when their father was speaking) – and especially at Jessica, with whom she felt the closest bond of kinship – she thought about her own childhood and remembered with pride and sadness how her mother had struggled to feed and clothe her, and how she had taught her to keep loyal to the Old Faith.

The Old Faith . . . was all that gone? She remembered evenings when she had walked with her mother up to Roscarrock Hall and had knelt in the family chapel while a priest said the Latin Mass. She remembered her mother's devotion to the saints and the rosary and – later – Jill's suspicious questions about whether she prayed to the silver Madonna that had once hung on a chain about her neck.

But even the memory of that Madonna was now tarnished, for since returning from the wars, Harry had told her the secret of how her own father had come by it: how it had been taken from a dying Spanish priest and how, he believed, it carried a curse with it, a curse that had fallen upon the priest, Sam, her own mother and finally Tristram.

Yes, all that was past. Sir Gregory Roscarrock – her own grandfather – was dead, and the Roscarrock property was to be split up and sold off to the highest bidders. And since the fight with the Armada, Amyas Roscarrock had started attending Matins every Sunday at St Saviour's.

How strange life was! Why – all the Spanish enterprise had succeeded in doing was to unite the people of England and identify the cause of Protestantism with loyalty to Queen and country. And yet . . . somewhere deep inside her there still flickered a flame of affection for

Mary, Joseph and the family of saints and martyrs, and she couldn't help thinking that a similar flame of loyalty burnt in the country at large. How did that old prayer go? 'Hail, holy Queen, Mother of mercy. Hail, our life, our sweetness and our hope. To thee do we cry, poor banished children of Eve. . . .'

' – so I give ye a toast, one and all,' Harry was saying. 'To the Queen and Merry England, and God bless us every one!'

'God bless us every one!' piped the children, and drank the toast in skimmed milk while their elders enjoyed a more powerful draught of Gascon wine.

The Treffry family stayed overnight, and the following morning Jennifer was up before dawn. While Susan and Faith stoked the fires and set the table for breakfast she put a wicker basket over her arm and went out into the barn to collect the new-laid eggs. Poking about in the corners and collecting the speckled brown offerings, she was just thinking about the previous evening and the happiness they had shared, when she was startled by a voice whispering her name.

She froze. 'Where are you?' she asked.

'Up here!' came back the whisper, and when she looked up to the hayloft she found herself face to face with Tristram Pascoe.

Tristram could hardly believe that he was face to face with Jennifer, however: motherhood and maturity had turned her from a slim, sloe-eyed girl into a plump matron with a basket of eggs on her arm and the cares of the household on her mind.

He was lying on the loft floor with his head out over the opening of the trap door. When she looked up he was for a moment speechless: since landing at Hope Cove two months before, his single purpose had been to avoid arrest, make his way back to Polruan and speak with Jennifer, but now that he had achieved it and she was standing open-mouthed below him with terror in her eyes and the chickens clucking round her skirts he wondered if the difficulties and risks of the past weeks had been worthwhile.

She backed away as if he were about to pounce on her.

'Don't be afraid, Jennifer. I'm not come to harm you.'

'Oh God!' she murmured. 'Oh – dear God!'

'Listen,' he whispered. 'Is my father alive?'

Her eyes widened. 'Yes – '

He felt a flood of relief. 'Thank God!' he breathed. 'Oh – thank the dear God that made me!'

'Tristram – you can't stay here!'

'But is he hurt? Is he wounded?'

'Yes, but I can't speak with you, Tristram. If they find out you're here . . . oh, dear Lord and Saviour! Why did you have to come back? Don't you realize the danger?'

'Aye, but I must talk to you, Jennifer. I must explain. Tell me – is my father badly hurt? Will he live?'

She was so terrified that she seemed unable to speak. She kept staring at him and shaking her head.

'I must know, Jen. I must know if – if he bears me any malice still. And Arthur – is he well?'

'I can't speak with you, Tristram! If they found out – '

'*I must know!* When was my father injured? Was it in the battles with the Spanish?'

'I can't speak now! Not here!'

'When then? Where? I'll meet you anywhere you say. Please.'

She appeared to think rapidly, shaking her head in bewilderment, staring down at the eggs she had collected in the basket. Eventually she said: 'I'll be walking back from Pont village tomorrow afternoon.'

'Alone?'

'Well . . . yes. But – '

'I'll meet you. I'll wait for you.' He reached down to her, and at the same time saw the fear in her eyes change to what might be pity or even love.

She reached up and their fingertips touched. 'You must go, Trist,' she whispered. 'It's not safe for any of us.'

'Till tomorrow then?'

'If I can.'

They heard the clatter of a milk pail outside, and the terror came back into her face.

'Get out of sight! I must go back in. Here – ' She took two eggs out of the basket and put them in one of the nests.

'Thank you!' he whispered, but the barn door was already closing behind her, and he was left in the darkness wondering if he dare risk another night in Polruan in order to meet her again and discover from her all that he needed to know.

She went back into the house with her mind in a turmoil, and for the whole of that day all she could think of was Tristram.

There had for a long time been a rumour in the village that he had escaped from captivity and was working for Spain, and over the past eight years Jennifer had deliberately put him from her mind. He had become as good as dead to her, nothing more than a wraith in the past, the knowledge and memory of which were better suppressed. She had forbidden Arthur to ask questions about him, had struck him off the list of her prayers, had shown anger when Nathan dared mention his name. Tristram had been put away into the attic of her mind: her daughters were not even aware of his existence. He had been a young man who had gone wrong, who had turned against his religion and his country and who had deceived them all. He had, as Reverend Drew liked to put it, 'embraced the evil of Rome'.

And yet. . . .

She stood at the window and stared out at the grey sky.

And yet, he was the same Tristram. The same Tristram, for although he was older, though his beard was thicker and his look wilder, he had caused all the same feelings in her: the same fast beating of the heart, the same deep stirrings, the same ache of – what? Love? Kinship?

She pressed her hands against her eyes and immediately saw the family as it had been the previous night, at peace and in happiness round the festive table. While they had eaten and drunk, laughed and talked and made a toast to one and all, *he* had been out there somewhere, perhaps in the hayloft, perhaps even peering in through the night-black window. Wasn't that what he had been doing all these years, in a way? Though she had put him from her mind and forbidden the mention of his name in her family, had he not remained in spirit outside the dark windows of her life, creeping furtively about out of sight and peering in at her?

Somehow she survived the day. The cows were milked and the pigs fed; the Treffrys departed to walk back to Pont village; Arthur went off to school; Harry was helped downstairs and put in his chair in the front room by the fire, and Nathan was set to work splitting firewood. But wherever she went, whatever she did, Jennifer could not erase the memory of Tristram's face looking down at her from the hayloft, nor forget the rumble of his voice and the dark blue of his eyes that had sent a shiver up her spine.

In the evening she could not bring herself to tell the children the story they demanded.

'Why not, Mother?' Bridget asked, stroking her hand lovingly back and forth. 'You *always* tell us a story afore we go to bed!'

'Yes you always do!' Nathan boomed. 'You always tell a story!'

Even Harry seemed disappointed. 'Are you ailing, Jennifer?'

'No, I – I just don't feel like telling stories tonight,' she said. She turned to Arthur, who at twelve was getting more like Tristram every day. 'Why don't you tell 'em a story tonight, love?' she said. 'You must know them all by heart, near enough.'

'Off you go, Art,' Pascoe put in. 'And you, Nat. Leave your mother and me in peace for a change. You can take 'em up to their beds and hear their prayers like good lads.'

His authority was still absolute. Bridget, Ann and Jessica kissed their parents and went up obediently, and Nathan – who was already beginning to see Arthur as an older brother – went willingly enough too, so that Harry and Jennifer were left to themselves before the fire.

She stood by his chair and took his hand in hers. His hair was quite white now, and his injury and the fever that had followed it had aged him considerably. She looked down into his watery eyes and saw that she was now the wife of an old man.

'What's troubling 'ee, my lovely?' he asked quietly.

She smiled. Harry could be very gentle and loving when he chose. 'Just a woman's frailty,' she murmured, but knew that she was deceiving him and felt guilty already.

'It's more'n that,' he said softly. 'Isn't it?'

'Perhaps. . . .'

'What then?'

She couldn't tell him the whole truth: it would have been too much for him to bear. And yet she needed to speak of it, needed to share it with him. 'I had a dream,' she said. 'Last night.' She looked at him. 'About Tristram.'

His eyes dropped away from hers. 'That,' he said and lapsed into silence.

'If . . . if he ever were to come back, Harry – '

'He won't.'

'But *if* he did – '

'Then it'd be any man's duty to have him arrested and sent to Launceston gaol where he belongs.'

A glowing log rolled onto the hearth. She retrieved it quickly and put it back into the fire and then crouched, tongs in hand, gazing into the flames. 'Well in this dream, he *did* come back.' She turned to face him. 'He come to me and asked if you were alive, and when I told him yes he thanked the God who made him. And he said – he said he wanted your forgiveness.'

'It was a dream,' Harry said.

'I know that, but it – it was more, too. As if God was speaking. And I been thinking about it all day, and whether 'twere a dream or a vision the message of it's still the same, Harry. Tristram's your son and he wants your forgiveness, I feel it – I feel it very strong – '

She knelt before him, her hands in his. 'It's not a question whether he's done right or wrong, Harry. It's whether we forgive him that matters. Whether we forgive him, and whether he forgives us.'

He looked down at her in silence for several moments. 'Do you still feel aught for him, Jen? Is that it?'

'No! No! But seeing him – in that dream, so real – it made me think. We never speak of him, but he's always there, isn't he? Like a skeleton in the wall. Always there, never quite forgotten. And he always will be, Harry – he always will be until we forgive him, because until we do that the good Lord won't forgive us our trespasses, as the great prayer says. We'll not be forgiven, and our minds won't be at peace.'

Harry stared into the fire for a long time. Much had changed in the past few months, there was no doubt of that. Never before had he been so dependent on a woman. Never before had he seen all that went on in a household, day after day, just to keep a few children clean and fed and their clothes mended and their woes listened to. And there might not be many more years for him on this earth. He was fifty-four now, and no longer a fit man. Yes, his wound was healing well and he'd be able to get about a bit soon, but only with a stick, and he'd never stand on a deck again and experience the magic of taking his own ship to sea. That was for Matthew to do now, and it looked as though he'd make a better fist of things than his father if he carried on in the way he had begun.

But Tristram. . . .

His thoughts wandered back over the years. He remembered Ann, mousey little Ann who had been second best after Martha. And Martha . . . what would she have said to hear that he'd married her daughter and made children with her? Glancing back into Jennifer's face he remembered those first days when she had come to stay at Hill House. He'd fallen for her then and there, no doubt of it. There had been so much of her mother in her – still was, come to that. And yet she had loved

Tristram once, and that love had set father and son at even greater
enmity. What had been the lesson old Drew had read out in church some
weeks back? Something about the father being divided against his son
and the mother against her daughter and the mother-in-law against her
daughter-in-law. How did it go? Something like: 'Think ye that I come to
bring peace into the world? I tell you nay. . . .'

Well, he thought, me and Tristram were divided right enough. And
we haven't had much peace this last twelvemonth. Wars and rumours of
wars, more like. The good Lord was right there, and no error.

He wondered if Tristram were still alive. They'd heard, years back,
that he'd escaped from justice and become an outlaw, and Mayhew had
put it about the village that he was believed to have crossed to the
Continent to work for the Catholic League. And Jennifer talked of
forgiveness! How could he forgive a son who had turned against his
family, his upbringing, his religion and his country? How could he do
that?

'Will you?' she whispered. 'Will you forgive him?' And then her hands
tightened suddenly on his and her eyes filled with tears and she added,
'For my sake?'

'You're a good woman, Jen,' he muttered.

'No I'm not! God knows that even if you don't. But if you love me at
all, Harry, you'll tell me that you forgive Tristram in your heart and bear
him no more malice. Will you do that?'

And then – he didn't understand exactly how it happened – it was as if
a little wheel of reason made a quarter turn in his mind and he saw the
whole thing in a different way. What harm could there be in forgiving his
own son if it put Jennifer's mind at ease and scrubbed out the memory of
a dream? Wasn't what she was saying close to the sort of sermons that his
old Uncle Will had preached from the hedgerows forty years before when
Bloody Mary was still burning heretics for saying that sinners could be
saved by grace alone? And wasn't the very resentment and malice he had
borne against others at the root of so many of the frustrations he had
suffered? He sighed deeply. Why had it taken him so long to learn such
an easy lesson?

'Aye, I'll forgive him,' he said quietly, and as soon as the words were
out of his mouth it was as if a burden had been lifted from his shoulders.

Was that enough? She wished that it could be. She wished that Tristram had not asked her to risk so much by meeting him again, and could almost convince herself that there was no need to do so.

But there was a need, and she knew the reason why. If Harry had been guilty of misusing his son and Tristram felt the need for forgiveness, she shared their sense of guilt in equal proportion. For though it may have appeared to an outsider that Tristram had made every advance, Jennifer knew that his advances would never have been made had she not invited them. It had been she who had led him on that hay-making day when they were children, she who had caught his eye every Sunday at St Saviour's, she who had watched from the clifftop when he risked life and limb for a few gulls' eggs. And though he had beckoned to her from the wall of Roscarrock's estate, she had run willingly to meet him, and it had been she who had drawn his hand through the wall and pressed it to her bosom.

'Tristram Pascoe, Tristram Pascoe, never never let your lass go,' she had whispered in his ear during those honeymoon nights near the beehives when Arthur had been conceived, and hers had been the Madonna that he wore about his neck that day he sailed out on his first and last voyage in the *Russell*.

So now, however much easier it would have been to let Friday slip by without going to meet him, she knew that she owed it to herself as much as to Tristram to do so, and having done her visiting in Pont Village and taken a bite to eat with Jill, she set out an hour or so before sunset to walk back to Polruan.

After following the course of the creek for a hundred yards or so, the track diverged and climbed up through the woods emerging between small green fields bordered by walls of slate and granite, and as she neared the crest of the hill at Essa Spring, she met the full force of a south-westerly gale that was funnelling down between the high banks, so that she had to battle directly into it in order to make headway. Head down against the stinging rain, she was just wondering if Tristram might have had second thoughts about their meeting when her wrist was suddenly grasped and she found herself face to face with him.

He gave her no time even for a greeting, but pulled her quickly – and a little roughly – through an open gate and into the field above the woods; and having shut the gate he hurried her along under the hedge and then down into Pont Pill wood. 'In here,' he said. 'In where?' she gasped, but he was already making her duck her head and pushing her into a lean-to shelter of laths and turf so well disguised she had not seen it until they were within a yard of its entrance.

Crouching under the damp roof of turf and bracken, she found herself looking into the eyes of a man gone wild, and was suddenly terrified of what he might do to her.

She looked wet and frightened: he wanted to hold her and reassure her. But when he reached out to her she shrank away from him, holding both hands before her to ward him off. So he drew back and gazed at her crouching out of breath before him, the rain dripping off her cape, her face reddened by the wind.

'Thank you,' he said in a low voice. 'Thank you for meeting with me, Jen.'

'I must be mad!' she said under her breath. She glanced at his bed of leaves, the remains of a rabbit, a few egg shells. 'How long've you been living like this?'

'A month or two.'

'What – here?'

He shook his head. 'I was wrecked in an Armada ship two months ago. In Devon. I've been travelling rough ever since.'

She nodded. 'I did hear there were a ship come ashore. They took some prisoners as well, so I believe.' She looked at him again. 'They'll hang you if they catch you, d'you know that?'

He nodded, and the way he looked at her made her feel suddenly weak.

'You look like a wild animal,' she whispered.

He smiled. 'I left my best clothes behind.'

'You speak different, too. Like – like a gentleman.'

'A lot's happened to me, Jen.'

'Looks like it, an' all!'

Outside, the trees swayed and creaked, sending a sudden heavy patter of raindrops down on the shelter.

'What did they say about me? After we were taken off?'

She looked down, as if ashamed. 'That you were papists. That you'd be tried and hung for treason.'

'And did you believe them?'

She nodded. 'What else could I do?'

He said nothing for a while, then: 'I'm . . . not what people think, Jen. I'm not a papist.'

'What are you then?'

He remembered the lengthy theological discussions he had had with Marlowe at Cambridge. This was neither the time nor the place to rehearse those, even if Jennifer could have taken them in. He said: 'I'm nothing.'

She smiled timidly. 'You've changed so much, Trist!'

'We've both changed.' He reached out and took her hand, and this time she did not resist. 'Are you . . . happy?'

She nodded, but avoided his glance. 'Happy enough. Contented.'

Yes, he thought, that is what she looked – contented. Aloud, he asked: 'And – my father?'

'He's changed, too.' She sighed, and struggled for words. 'He bears you no malice now, Trist. All that's in the past.'

He had been surviving on his wits since the day he had crawled out of the surf on the beach at Hope Cove. He had slept in barns, caves and improvised shelters. Making his way westward from Salcombe, he had lived rough, stealing milk and eggs from farms, trapping birds and rabbits for meat, always on guard, always tired or cold or wet or all three. Now, receiving what amounted to his father's absolution from Jennifer, he was suddenly moved.

'Was he badly hurt?'

'Aye, but he was either lucky or blessed by a miracle. Davy said plenty others died of far slighter wounds.'

'Davy . . . Treffry?'

'He was your father's bosun aboard the *Russell*.' She relaxed for the first time, and he saw tears in her eyes. 'I just come from seeing Jill.'

'Jill. . . .'

'They've four lovely children.'

'And Matt?'

'He's been away since before the war. He's doing very well, Trist. He'll be a gentleman one day. He's sailing with the Royal Navy now.'

'And Nathan?'

'Just the same.'

He held both her hands in his. They sat face to face under a roof of wattle and ferns.

'Arthur?'

'He's a fine boy. Quiet. Like . . . like you were.'

'Is he all right with my father?'

'Aye. He's all right.'

423

He looked down at their hands: his own scratched and torn, hers small, capable, work-hardened. 'And you Jen?'

'I'm a wife and a mother, Trist. I've three little girls as well as Arthur. I shouldn't be here by rights, I only come because – ' She grasped his hands tightly. '*I* need *your* forgiveness,' she whispered. 'So does Harry, come to that. We've both wronged you.'

'Jennifer! There's nothing to forgive! Nothing at all!'

She leant against him and wept. 'Why must Christian folk be so divided?' she whispered. 'Why must we hurt one another so?'

He remembered what Joaquim had said about the futility of attempting a return to England, and knew that in spite of what he had said, he had still fostered one last shred of hope that he might be able to make some sort of life for himself with Jennifer. Believing his father dead, he had imagined himself returning to Polruan in order to take over the role of husband and father and fulfil his responsibilities towards Jennifer and Arthur. He had imagined himself taking them away to live in another hundred under another name. But with his father alive and Jennifer the mother of three other children, that last possibility – so carefully preserved, so often derided by Joaquim – was gone.

'God knows – God knows,' he muttered.

'Will you tell me something, Trist?'

'What?'

'You did - you did truly love me, didn't you? It wasn't just pretend, was it?'

'No. It wasn't pretend. I did love you. I still do, come to that. But . . . as a cousin. You understand?'

'Yes. I understand, Trist.'

He opened his shirt. 'Look. I got it back for you.'

She stared at the Madonna on its chain round his neck. But when he began to remove it, she said: 'No – I don't want it back, Trist. Please – I don't want it back!'

'But it's yours by right, Jennifer – '

She was shaking her head. 'No! It's not mine, it was never mine nor my mother's nor my father's! It was stolen, Trist, stolen – ' She put her hands to her face. 'It's got a curse on it!'

'Only when it's stolen,' he murmured, and put it back out of sight.

She looked up. 'So – do you know more of it's history?'

'A little. It's saved my life more than once and – ' He stopped short. They said nothing for a long time.

'Can I ask you something else, Trist? Once – after you'd come back from Portugal, you told me you'd worked in a garden. For a lady.' She looked up. 'You loved her, didn't you?'

Caught off his guard, he stared back at her, unable to speak because of the great wave of despair that was breaking over him. 'Yes,' he sobbed. 'Yes.'

She smiled through tears. 'I knew it straight away, Trist. And the knowledge of it helped me, in a way. It helped me over Harry. I'm glad – glad you found someone.'

She sniffed hard. They were both weeping openly now.

'What'll you do? Will you go to her?'

He shook his head miserably. 'I can't.'

'Why not?'

'There's nowhere for me now, Jen. Nowhere, except some stretch of barren shore in Africa, or an isle in the Indies. I'm as much an outlaw in Spain or Portugal as I am in England.' He made an effort to be calm. 'But – I've made my peace with you. I couldn't have gone on living had I not spoken with you as we've spoken today.'

She seized his hands suddenly. 'Go to her Trist! Go to the one you love!'

He stared at her.

'I told you – years back – I told you that I was the only one that could make you happy. I knew it all along, but I never realized the true meaning of it till this minute – '

'It isn't as easy as that, Jen. After what I've done, I don't know if I could look her in the eye – '

'But you must *try*, Trist. You can't give up. If you love her and she loves you, then you must go to her, whatever the risk. I'm right, aren't I? I know I'm right.'

'Love is not love. . .' he whispered half to himself, and then, to her: 'Kiss me, Jennifer. Kiss me, and then go quickly, and may God bless you and – ' his voice broke. 'And my father, and Arthur – and one and all at Hill House.'

He caught her in his arms and held her for the last time. For a few moments longer they stood at the entrance of the lean-to.

'Shall I come with you to the road, Jen?'

'Better not. I'll be all right on my own. Goodbye Trist. God bless you, and keep you safe always. And – and remember what I said, won't you?'

And then she turned quickly and started climbing up the hill to the field above the wood: back to her home, her husband, her children and her stories by the fire; and when she was out of sight he collected together the few oddments that were his worldly possessions and set out at a run like the hunted animal he had become – away from Polruan, away from Jennifer and away from the life that might have been once, but could never be again.

Again Ballingolin

Sara never gave up hope of finding Tristram. After Dorothea's death, she and Rodrigo travelled with Laurinda and the baby along the coast to Corunna where they made further, unfruitful enquiries. By December the state of the roads was such that a return to Lisbon was out of the question, so they travelled back to Gijon where they spent the rest of the winter as guests of Dorothea's relations, the de Valdes family.

By the time spring came they had still heard nothing of Tristram or the *San Pedro Mayor*. Sara was running short of funds, and could not presume upon the hospitality of her hosts indefinitely; and having signed a paper to legalize her adoption of Miguel, she felt it her duty to return home and look after him properly.

But where was home? If she could have found a ship bound for Ireland, she would have gladly taken Laurinda and her son – she loved being able to call him that – back to Ballingolin. But now that the last Armada ships had limped back into port, all Europe acknowledged the supremacy of Queen Elizabeth's Royal Navy and there were very few Spanish captains willing to risk a meeting on the high seas with Drake or any of his brothers-at-arms.

In the end it was Rodrigo who helped her to make the decision. He was anxious to return to his family in Andalusia and offered to escort her to Lisbon. So as soon as they had received one last report from Santander that nothing had been heard of the *San Pedro*, they took their leave of their hosts and set out on the road south.

They travelled in easy stages, first along the north coast of Galicia to Corunna, then southward, stopping at Santiago de Compostela to make a pilgrimage to the shrine of St James before continuing through Vigo, Braga and Porto. Partly out of preference and partly to lighten the carriage in which Laurinda travelled with Miguel, Sara insisted upon riding a horse, something she had seldom done since leaving Ireland; and although she suffered from stiffness of the muscles at first, she found that the effort of riding helped to take her mind off her worry and grief.

427

She thought about Tristram almost constantly now. Plodding slowly on, hour after hour, she would go over in her mind every wildest theory of what might have happened to him. At night she would lie awake and think of him, sending messages to him and trying to listen for messages back. Sometimes she was sure that she received a reply; sometimes there was a dead silence that filled her with bleak despair. By the end of May, when the little caravan of travellers finally arrived in the courtyard of the Quinta de Santo António, she knew that her mind would never be at rest until either she had proof positive of what had happened to Tristram or – and she still held onto a faint hope – they were reunited.

Her sisters-in-law had heard of João's death some months before, and were well over the shock. They were not greatly upset to hear of Dorothea's passing, either.

'Haven't you heard the news?' Teresa exclaimed. 'We've had Drake himself sailing up and down off the Tagus again, and English soldiers landing at Peniche. Corunna was invaded only a month ago, and they say that the English are planning an attack on the Azores. And the King has ordered the building of a brand new Armada, did you know that? My husband says that this time we must offer them a clear alternative: either to abandon their piracy or face guaranteed, assured retribution. So if you thought the war was over, Sara, think again!'

The three sisters had come round to the Quinta de Santo António on the morning following Sara's arrival, and the ladies were now up in Sara's room with the balcony doors open to admit a cooling breeze.

'So what are your plans?' Graça asked. 'How long will you stay on at Santo António?'

Sara was surprised by the question. 'How long? I've no idea. I suppose indefinitely.' She saw Iñes glance at Graça. 'Is there any reason why I shouldn't?'

'Yes, there is a difficulty, as a matter of fact,' Teresa said. 'You see – Santo António is not legally yours, Sara. It belongs to the Santarém family, and must be shared by João's surviving next of kin until his eldest nephew reaches maturity.' She smiled. 'It's a very ancient estate, you understand, and we couldn't possibly allow it to be split up or pass out of the family.'

'But I was married to João! Am I not a part of the Santarém family?'

'Well yes and no,' Teresa said. 'You never provided poor João with an heir, did you? And after your – your trouble at Colares, Maezinha decided that you would not be a proper person to inherit the estate.'

'It was quite clearly laid down in her will,' Iñes added. 'There would be no point at all in contesting it.'

Sara looked round at them. 'So . . . I am no more than a guest here, is that it?'

'But a very welcome guest, dear,' Teresa said, and Graça added, 'For the time being.'

Iñes looked at Teresa. 'Of course I suppose she could go back to live at Colares,' she suggested. 'Would you prefer that, *cunhada?*'

Sara felt suddenly tired and dispirited. Far from mourning their brother, the three sisters seemed excited at the prospect of taking over his property, and were already vying with each other to play the part of matriarch in Dona Marguerita's place.

And what if she did go to Colares? It could never be the same without Joaquim and Tristram, just as Ireland would never be the same without her father and brothers. Perhaps that, really, was the secret of contentment and inner peace she had sought for so long: perhaps it was not the mountains and bays of Corcaguiney that drew her back but the knowledge that she would be where she belonged and would be loved as one of the family.

When she looked up at her sisters-in-law, there were tears standing in her eyes. 'What I should prefer above all,' she said quietly, 'is to be allowed to take my adopted son with me, and go back to my home in Ireland.'

'Well,' Graça said with obvious satisfaction, 'I'm sure *that* can be arranged!'

But it was more difficult than Graça had supposed. For two months longer Sara stayed on in Lisbon with Laurinda and Miguel, who at one year was turning into a cheerful, adventurous child with a gurgling laugh and an insatiable curiosity that sent him crawling at high speed up and down the passages of the old house, with Laurinda – who adored him no less than her mistress – in hot pursuit.

Sara had hoped to find a ship going direct to Dingle, but when she heard that a Dutchman bound for Cork had put into Lisbon, she decided that this was the best opportunity she was likely to get for some time, and applied through Admiral Moitinho for a passage.

So, on a blazing day in July, she paid off her servants, said her last goodbyes to her sisters-in-law and, after a tearful embrace with Candida, took Laurinda and Miguel down to the harbour and went aboard the *Bonanza*, where they were made welcome by a fair-haired giant called Arie van de Eifel, who laughed a great deal, spoke Spanish with a diabolical accent, and ran a very taut ship.

They sailed on the afternoon ebb. As they went out past the old Tower of Belem, Sara remembered the day of her first arrival, and all the vain hopes and expectations of happiness with which she had stepped ashore. Staring back at the old city, she couldn't help reflecting on all that had happened during the years she had spent at Lisbon and Colares; but at the same time, like a chink of light that finds its way into a dungeon, there was at the back of her mind the slender hope that Tristram might still be alive after all, and that he would be waiting for her when she arrived at Ballingolin.

The sea voyage was fast and uneventful, and though they were sighted by English warships, their Dutch colours allowed them to go un-challenged, so that within ten days of departing from Lisbon the *Bonanza* was at anchor in the wide, sheltered reaches of Cork harbour.

The following day Sara, Laurinda and Miguel – who was now being called Michael – were rowed up the Lee river to the city landing stage.

Setting foot on Irish soil again, hearing Irish spoken, seeing the dear faces of her countrymen – it was too much. She stood on the quayside and wept for joy.

They set out by wagon after resting for two days in the city. Though Sara had been certain she had forgotten nothing about Ireland, she was nevertheless overcome, as they travelled on through the country, at the sudden changes of light, the sunbursts and cloudbursts, the green fields, the white clouds and the mountains fading away into blue distance.

They went west from Cork, following the Lee River and climbing steadily into the Derrynasaggart Mountains. They rose early, ate simply, travelled lengthily and slept soundly. Descending to Killarney, they left Macgillycuddy's Reeks and the flat, black waters of Lough Leane behind them and travelled over easier country, coming at last to the very doorstep of Corcaguiney: Tralee.

They rose before dawn the following morning and saw the sun come up over the Slieve Mish Mountains as they made their way along the coast road to Castlegregory. By midday they were climbing up into the Connor Pass with Brandon Mountain rising up to the west and the Owenmore valley with its loughs and silted estuary far below them.

Then, after a long, slow ascent, the carriage at last topped the pass, and there, spread out below, were Dingle Harbour, Ballymacadoyle Hill, and Ballingolin Castle itself.

She cried out at the sight: it was a shout of happiness and hope, a shout that came from deep within her; and having told the driver to stop, she took Michael in her arms and walked a little way off with him to look down upon this dear corner of the earth for which she had pined and wept and prayed so often.

Could there ever have been a more beautiful day upon which to make her return? It seemed impossible. Cloud shadows were racing over the sea and climbing rapidly up the slopes of Ballysitteragh; there were fishing boats out by Crow Rock and Beenbeg Point. To the west beyond Mount Eagle, Great Blasket Island lay like a wallowing monster, with the Atlantic stretching away to a far, far horizon.

The southerly wind blew her tears backward off her cheeks. Shaking her head almost in disbelief of her own eyes, she touched Michael's down-soft head with her lips, and whispered what her father had said to her on this very spot, so long ago: 'Ireland is the fairest country in the whole world; and there is no place in all Ireland more beautiful than Corcaguiney.'

She smiled through her tears and looked down at the child in her arms. 'So don't you be forgetting it, will you, Michael?'

They continued on down the hill to Dingle. This was the same road she had travelled with her father that evening when the news had been broken to her that she was to marry and go to Portugal, the day a silver Madonna on a chain had been put about her neck.

Taking the road above the town, they skirted Dingle and went round the harbour and along the last track to the castle. It was the same, and yet different. The trees were bigger, the castle smaller.

They heard a shouted order to halt, and a horseman barred their way. A face peered into the carriage where she rode with Laurinda at her side and Michael in her arms. It was a face with a bristly red beard, a button nose and blue eyes. And then the owner of the beard crossed himself and spoke. It was her brother Roger.

'My soul from the Devil!' he whispered. 'If it isn't my own lovely sister!'

He clattered ahead and called for the door to be opened. The wagon jolted in over the sill and entered the castle yard. A man washing his arms at the water butt turned, saw her and gave a cry that was first disbelief and then joy. She fell into Roger's arms and then Shane's. She was weeping and laughing at the same time and so were they, grown men that they were. And while this tearful reunion took place and the geese performed a march-past in her honour, another figure emerged from the house: a white-headed figure that was shrunk by age but still upright and hale; and when Sara saw him, her own father, her brothers fell back to allow her to go to him; and she took his hands and knelt before him, thanking God in the presence of them all for allowing her to return to them in safety.

'But whose child is this, Sara?' Gerald asked when he saw Laurinda approach with Michael.

Sara lifted Michael and held him proudly. 'He is mine by adoption, Father. His mother was my close and trusted companion, who died last autumn when Michael was barely five months old.'

Gerald offered a finger to Michael, who grasped it tightly in his fist. 'And his father?'

'He was an Englishman, Father. A pilot in the Armada. He was a good, courageous man, but – but he was lost at sea.'

They sat in the great hall far into the night: her father, Shane, Rhett, Roger and Sara. Leonora Hussey had died seven months before. Brendan was away in the north with O'Neill. The tide of events that had swept through Ireland had been like a flood going past their very doorstep. Dingle had been sacked; English soldiers were marching about the peninsula; Armada ships had been wrecked on every part of the west coast from Bloody Foreland to Cape Clear. At Tralee, twenty-four Spaniards had been hung without trial on the orders of Lady Denny.

But she was home, home – that was all that mattered now, and frequently during the evening she stopped in mid-sentence, gazing upon the faces of her father and her brothers and thanking God again and again for bringing her back to Corcaguiney.

That night she lay awake hour after hour, listening to the distant screech of an owl, her mind bombarded with thoughts: of the events of the day, her conversations with her father and brothers, all the news she had heard and the million memories of childhood which this stone-flagged room evoked. Eventually, abandoning any hope of sleep, she got out of her bed and stole barefoot up the spiral staircase to the battlements.

In the starlight, with a gentle breeze whispering in the beeches behind the castle and the low note of a cow bell in the stockade, she was overtaken suddenly by a new onrush of longing for Tristram.

She knew that having at last returned in safety to Ireland she should now accept that he was gone, and put him from her mind. She knew that she had a great deal to be thankful for, and that she should be content now to live in peace with her family. But though she might pretend contentment to others, she would never be able to deceive herself, would never be able to stop thinking about him or hoping that he would one day come to her. Even if she lived to be a hundred, he would still be alive to her, still a person to talk to in her thoughts, still the same Tristram the Cheerful who had run naked across a palace square, who had called himself John Kelly from Cork, who had made love to her among the rushes by the river at Colares.

For hadn't Tristram been the real reason for coming home to Ireland? Hadn't she been secretly convinced all along that he would be waiting for her here? Wasn't that, really, why she refused the offer of the house at Colares and had risked a sea voyage? How strangely she had deceived herself into believing that she was coming back just for her family, just for Ireland!

But it had not been just for her family, she saw that now. Much as she loved her father and brothers, and beautiful though this peninsula was, neither could take the place of Tristram's love.

'Where are you, Tristram, where are you?' she whispered softly, and felt a sudden panic that he might even now have made his way secretly back to Colares.

But they had agreed that that was out of the question. They had said that if they met anywhere it must be in Ireland. He had said – what had he said? What had he been able to say? That his love was for ever and would never change; that he would be with her in his thoughts whatever happened, wherever he went; that he was sure that someday, somehow, they would be reunited.

But he was not here and they had not been reunited, and that tiny chink of hope in her dungeon of despair was no more than a figment of her imagination, a cruel trick played on her by Fate. Already she was beginning to see what it would mean, living here in Ireland without Tristram. She saw the years stretching out ahead of her: years in this castle, being a mother to Michael and housekeeper to her brothers, looking after her father in his old age, holding on, living in the past, waiting for death.

She turned and went silently down to her room, and when dawn crept in through the slit window, she was still awake, and even more convinced that by coming so hastily back to Ireland she had lost her last chance of finding happiness.

Later that morning she and her father walked together along the shore of Dingle Harbour. The previous evening she had made no mention of the unhappiness of the past years, but now Gerald asked her about Dom João and the life she had led at the Quinta de Santo António, and his questions showed an insight that amazed her.

'But there were happy times as well, Father,' she said. 'Colares – now that was a fine and beautiful place indeed.'

Gerald Hussey glanced at his daughter. 'Is it a piece of your heart you have left behind you, Sara?' he asked gently.

'Perhaps,' she replied lightly, and was grateful to him when he did not press her further on the question.

They turned and began making their way back. In the field behind the castle a mower was cutting the sedge, working bent-backed with a sickle. Overhead, the sea crows flapped and gulls wheeled lazily. Woodsmoke was rising from a fire above Dingle and spreading out over the slopes of Ballysitteragh.

'So what will you do now?' Gerald asked.

She tried to sound happier than she felt. 'I shall stay here where I belong, Father. I shall live in peace while I may.'

He was silent for a while. ' I think you will need more than an ancient father and wild brothers for company before long, Sara. You're still young. There's no reason on God's earth why you should not find yourself another husband.'

'I don't think that's likely, Father.'

He chuckled and changed the subject. 'Shall we go over the field and say hullo to the horses, then?' he suggested, but they had gone only a few more yards when he stopped. 'No. You go on ahead, Sara. I'll join you later.'

He was leaning slightly on his stick. 'Is anything wrong, Father?'

'Nothing at all. Now will ye do what I say like a good girl and go on ahead?'

She obeyed, feeling puzzled at his manner. But he was much aged, and she decided that she must learn to humour him.

She walked on up the hill from the shore. The ringing sound of a hammer on a hot shoe came across the harbour from the smithy in Dingle. As she approached the solitary mower, he straightened and flexed bare shoulders that were criss-crossed with scars.

The clouds whirled suddenly overhead. He was dropping the sickle and coming towards her, reaching out to her, speaking her name. She stumbled towards him, unable to believe that she was not dreaming. Then she fell into his arms and she knew that he was real: that he was not a dream, that he was Tristram.

He stood with her there in the field of sedge, still hardly able to believe that it was really Sara, drawing back to gaze at her, hugging her, thanking God, promising that he would never allow them to be parted again.

'I always knew you'd come,' she whispered. 'I always knew it.'

He took her face in his hands and kissed her, reverently, on the forehead. Gazing into his face, she laughed and wept at the same time, and he smiled back at her in that gentle, apologetic way of his, the way she remembered, the way she loved so much.

She took his arm, and they began walking down to the beach where Gerald stood waiting.

'How much does my father know about you?' she asked.

'That I'm English, that I was your servant, and that my only wish is to serve you again.'

'But I don't want you to be my servant, Tristão.'

He looked suddenly troubled. 'All I want is to live near you, Sara. When I decided to come to Ireland I knew that all I could hope for was to be – to be your gardener, like Joaquim.' He shook his head. 'I – I don't deserve more than that.'

She saw her father watching them from the shore. 'You shall be my husband or nothing at all,' she said quietly.

'But Sara – have you forgotten? I'm married!'

She seemed not to have heard him, but was gazing down at the shore, where her father had been joined by a maidservant with a child. 'Look,' she said. 'That's your son.' She stopped, and turned to him. 'And he's mine, too, Tristram. You see – I adopted him. When Thea died. Last winter.'

He shook his head, hardly able to take it all in.

'Thea . . . how – '

'Of a fever. I was with her. We became friends at the end, Tristão. She begged me on her deathbed to look after your child.'

'So – '

'Wait. There's something else you must know. João is dead also. I don't know how exactly but they said he was wrecked on the coast of Ireland – '

He looked away. 'Yes. I know about João.'

'So we're free to marry, Tristão. If that's what you'd like.'

She was smiling through tears. He reached up and touched her face gently, as if to make sure she was real. Then, quite simply, he bent the knee to her and pledged his love and loyalty.

As they continued down the hill to the shore, she gave a sudden laugh, clenching her fists in delight. 'Oh – look, Tristão, look! Michael's taking his first steps!'

Tristram felt a great tide of love rising up inside him and brimming over. At last, all the years of hatred and horror were behind him; at last he had found the love and permanence which he had craved for so long. And seeing his own son struggling for the first time to walk upright, he made a promise to himself: that he would from then on give his whole life to the cause of peace and be to Michael all that he might have wished his own father to be to him; that where he had known bitterness and resentment, Michael would know tenderness and love. And like Michael, he too would have to learn to walk upright: he would have to put away the habit of war and try to regain some of the innocence he had lost since first setting sail from Polruan in the *Russell*.

They were just a few paces from the others now. He stopped and crouched down, holding out his hands to Michael; and the little boy, encouraged by Sara, let go of his nurse's hand and managed a few tottering steps before being caught up into his father's arms.

EPILOGUE

Footprints on the Sands

They rode side by side along the curving beach of Ventry Bay, with the waves crashing upon the sands as the two horses thundered along.

Snatching a glance at Sara, Tristram saw her as he had never seen her before: a Sara set free at last, a Sara dressed in the simple way, her long hair flying backward, her body moving in unison with the plunging neck of her mount, her whole being animated by the freedom of wind and sea and sky.

The breakers thundered and the seabirds wheeled; the hooves splashed down over a wave as it spent itself on the sloping sand; they went on round the curve of the bay, and climbing up over the dunes, came to a halt on the western headland.

Sara sat back in her saddle laughing, out of breath. 'Now do you understand why I talked so much of Corcaguiney?'

'I'm beginning to!' he replied, and leaned across to her. For a minute they made conversation without words.

The Madonna had slipped out of his shirt and hung on its chain. Sara lifted it and held it in her palm.

'Would you like to wear it?' he asked.

'No. If it belongs to anyone, it belongs to you.'

He took it off. 'I don't want it any more, Sara. It has too many memories for me.'

She nodded. 'And me. Let's just throw it back into the sea, Tristão.'

He held it out. 'Would you like to do it?'

'You do it for both of us.'

She watched him wrap the chain round and round the silver image; then, leaning back in the saddle, he flung it with all his strength, sending it in a high arc over the breakers and into the foam-streaked waves.

'There,' he said. 'I think that's where it belongs.'

'Maybe it is,' she agreed, and turning their horses they set off back along the beach at a trot, with the horses' hooves leaving deep, firm imprints in the sand.

437